BLOOD VOW

BLOOD VOW

KARIN TABKE

HEAT
NEW YORK

THE BERKLEY PUBLISHING GROUP
Published by the Penguin Group
Penguin Group (USA) Inc.
375 Hudson Street, New York, New York 10014, USA

Penguin Group (Canada), 90 Eglinton Avenue East, Suite 700, Toronto, Ontario M4P 2Y3, Canada (a division of Pearson Penguin Canada Inc.) • Penguin Books Ltd., 80 Strand, London WC2R 0RL, England • Penguin Group Ireland, 25 St. Stephen's Green, Dublin 2, Ireland (a division of Penguin Books Ltd.) • Penguin Group (Australia), 250 Camberwell Road, Camberwell, Victoria 3124, Australia (a division of Pearson Australia Group Pty. Ltd.) • Penguin Books India Pvt. Ltd., 11 Community Centre, Panchsheel Park, New Delhi—110 017, India • Penguin Group (NZ), 67 Apollo Drive, Rosedale, Auckland 0632, New Zealand (a division of Pearson New Zealand Ltd.) • Penguin Books (South Africa) (Pty.) Ltd., 24 Sturdee Avenue, Rosebank, Johannesburg 2196, South Africa

Penguin Books Ltd., Registered Offices: 80 Strand, London WC2R 0RL, England

This book is an original publication of The Berkley Publishing Group.

PUBLISHING HISTORY
Heat trade paperback edition / December 2012

Library of Congress Cataloging-in-Publication Data

Tabke, Karin.
Blood vow / Karin Tabke. — Heat trade paperback ed.
p. cm.
ISBN 978-0-425-24752-5
1. Werewolves—Fiction. I. Title.
PS3620.A255B57 2012
813'.6—dc23
2012026296

PRINTED IN THE UNITED STATES OF AMERICA

10 9 8 7 6 5 4 3 2 1

PEARSON

To my readers, thank you for hanging in there with me
on this wild and wonderful ride!

And to those hearts who love two . . .
thank you for inspiring me.

One

STUNNED, LUCIEN AND Rafael watched helplessly as the traitorous immortal wolf Fenrir vanished in midair, taking Falon with him. No amount of horrified staring made them reappear, and long minutes later Rafe forced himself to look at his brother. Just behind Lucien stood their equally stunned packs, Vulkasin and Mondragon. With them stood Anja, Rafe's chosen one. Or rather, the female Rafe had chosen to mark in order to save Falon's life. The pale Siberian beauty stood tall and regal, a glorious smile splitting her face.

Rafe looked past her gloating and back to his brother. Deathly pale, Lucien's wide eyes stared into the night sky as if he still hoped Falon would magically materialize before them. Rafe shivered hard then, remarkably, even feeling a twinge of compassion for his brother.

Which was beyond comprehension considering what Lucien had done. Taking Falon as his own, marking her when he knew how Rafael loved her. It didn't matter that the Blood Law was on his brother's side at the time. Now, it meant shit. Falon was his! As she always had been and would always be.

Because even after giving her up, even after marking Anja, Rafe had never stopped loving Falon. And now, his beloved was gone! *Vanished.* Bone-numbing fear settled deep within him.

Lucien's long mournful howl shivered through Rafe. Instinctively, Rafe answered his brother's desperate cry, calling to Falon who, if she were to survive, would be living a nightmare as the captive of the traitorous Fenrir. The wolf who, because he had been rejected by his parents and his pack nearly one thousand years ago, turned to witches and black magic and teamed up with the Slayers to kill his own kind. Now, with the Blood Moon rising imminent, that accursed wolf wanted Falon as his chosen one to set the foundation for his dynasty.

It would not happen!

As Rafe's howl dwindled to nothing more than a deep rumble in his chest, he struggled for control. For insight. For a way to rescue Falon. For a way to bring her back to him, where she belonged.

Falon! Rafe called to her with his mind, at the same time as Lucien.

Help me! she cried.

Where are you? Lucien desperately asked.

I don't know. Her strangled voice faded into the night.

I will find you! Rafael vowed.

"Gather the swords!" Lucien commanded as he strapped his own weapon to his back. "We're going hunting!"

Rafe growled, not in disagreement, but furious desperation. "Your lie caused this." Rafe sneered in his brother's face. "Because you refused to believe that your chosen one was Slayer, Falon is gone."

Lucien shook his head. "Regardless of the past, Brother, this was destined to happen."

"I would not have marked Anja," Rafe hissed. He moved in toe to toe with his brother. "You would not have had any right to, Falon!" Rafe lowered his voice to a deadly whisper. "I swear to every god that exists, if Falon dies because of this, I will skin you alive."

Lucien shoved his brother away. "We can argue whose fault it is when she's safe. But one thing we won't be arguing about is that she's mine. Remember, I gave her the choice to stay with me or return to you. She chose *me*."

He strode past Rafe to the open container, housing the crates of poison swords they had come to retrieve to transport north to the final battleground.

Six weeks from now, the Blood Moon would rise, and beneath it the entire Lycan nation would arm themselves with these swords against their mortal enemy, Slayers. Only one faction would survive. The swords would stack the odds in the Lycan's favor. One nick from the poison metal would render a Slayer helpless in less than a minute, making the delivery of the true death, decapitation, a breeze.

"I'm not waiting on these swords," Rafael said as he strapped his double scabbards on and sheathed his own swords. They thrummed with vitality, eager to kill. Like Rafe, his swords craved Slayer blood. "Not while Falon's scent is fresh."

Lucien stopped in his tracks and lowered the end of one of the heavy crates. "We go together."

"I'm going with you!" Anja said quietly but firmly from behind Rafe.

He turned, irritated that she would insert herself in this matter but could he blame her? He was going after the woman he loved. Anja knew there was no threat or amount of begging she could do that would keep him from going after Falon. She had no choice but to go along with him, no doubt hoping that some harm would come to Falon and with her gone, Rafe would finally learn to love Anja. But as he'd told her from the beginning, it would never happen. Rafe would love only Falon. No woman could replace the space she occupied in his heart. Dead or alive, Falon was the only woman who would ever hold his heart and soul in her hands.

Roughly, Rafe ran his fingers through his hair and begrudgingly nodded. He had no choice. While he had no love for Anja, she was, for the moment, still his chosen one. For Falon's life, Rafe had promised his brother he would mark another before the next full moon. Honor bound, he had. He regretted every moment since. Except that Falon's life had been spared.

He nodded again and turned to the packs Vulkasin and Mondragon. Once a united powerful pack, so powerful nothing but Slayer black magic could harm them, and now? For the past sixteen years they were split straight down the middle because Lucien had never believed that Rafe slew Lucien's chosen one because she was a Slayer. He believed Rafe had slain her for personal gain, to control the pack, not co-alpha as they had done. Their mother's people, Mondragon, had followed Lucien, while his father's people, Vulkasin, stayed with Rafe. No one had benefited from the split. They were stronger as one united pack.

Now that the truth was out that Mara was a Slayer and not a mere human as Lucien was so sure she was, it should heal the aching wound of the blood feud.

Rafael shook his head. If anything, the packs would fight over Falon. When Mara had returned from the dead, and shown herself as the Slayer she was, Lucien did what Rafe had thought he had done sixteen years ago. He killed her. She died a true death. So the proof of what Rafael claimed all those years ago voided the Council's verdict, giving Falon, his chosen one, to Lucien as replacement for the one Rafael took.

He should not have been shocked when Lucien admitted Mara was a Slayer. Shock aside, Rafe had been infused with so many emotions, predominantly fury at his brother for refusing to see what he knew to be the truth about Mara. But the Blood Law prevailed: an eye for an eye, and Rafe had been forced to give his chosen one to his brother in exchange for the one he took from Lucien. It had been a lie! And because of it, Falon had not only laid with his brother, but allowed his mark and returned it. Damn it all. They were as separated now as the day Lucien rode off with her barely alive in his arms. Rafe swiped his hand across his face. To save Falon's life, Rafe swore to Lucien he would mark another before the full moon. And so he had just this day. Had he waited—*Fuck!* Had he just waited . . .

Unease shifted through Rafe. With the proof that Mara was a Slayer, and a Clan Corbet Slayer—the worst of the worst—Lucien had violated a cardinal Blood Law. He'd lain with a Slayer, the act punishable by death. It would not matter that the bitch had used her black magic to trick him. Lucien was about to mark her when Rafe killed her. Lucien would have brought her into the pack. She would have bred half-breeds and destroyed them all from the inside out.

Rafe shook his head not wanting to think of the consequences of Lucien's foolhardy choices. He thought of Falon, of her in his arms again. His blood warmed.

As Rafe saw it, by the Blood Law Falon was his again. But convincing Lucien of that would not be easy. It would be impossible. Would he kill his brother to possess the one thing they both loved above their own lives?

Rafe's heart tightened again when he thought of the part of the family that had been lost to him all these years. He would give his right arm for the two families to reunite. But there could be only one alpha. Neither he nor his brother would step aside. But could he, despite all that had passed between them for so long allow the council to take his brother's life? Mentally, Rafe set that reality aside. He had only one focus at the moment.

He raised his nose to the wind and said to his brother, "He takes her north."

Lucien's jaw tightened as he nodded and said what they both feared. "To the battleground."

Despite Fenrir's release from the ring he had been held captive in for the last three hundred years, it warmed on Rafe's hand as if the wolf still resided within it. Skeptically Rafe raised it and regarded it with confusion.

"Why does it glow?" Lucien asked, stepping closer to eye the rich luminescence of the ruby. "The wolf is gone."

It recognizes its own kind.

Lucien and Rafael started at the old crackling voice.

Gleeful laughter reverberated around them. Even the others heard it. Wide-eyed the men looked wildly about for the source of the noise. Anja grabbed Rafe's arm, moving closer for protection.

"Gilda!" Rafael called, recognizing the druid witch's voice. When Rafe commanded the wolf from the ring to save Falon from the fatal wounds Master Slayer Balor Corbet had inflicted on her, Fenrir had destroyed the witch rather than honor their centuries-old bargain. Twin souls each century in return for the immortality and power Gilda had bestowed upon Fenrir. Immortality he used to partner with the Slayers to kill wolves. He was a traitor among his own kind.

Had she returned for their twin souls? She had the power to take them. Her tiny hunched-back form manifested itself before them in wisps of scarlet fog. "He destroyed my physical body, but not my magic!" she shrilled triumphantly.

"Will Falon live?" Lucien demanded.

The old witch cackled but did not answer.

Rafe looked at Lucien who stepped closer to the specter. Thrusting his right fist toward her, he showed her the ring.

"What power does it hold?" Rafe demanded, staying on high alert. He didn't trust the old bat any more than he trusted Fenrir.

Watch out for her, Rafe. She wanted our souls ten minutes ago, Lucien warned.

Rafe mentally nodded. *Let's see what she wants now.*

Gilda's energy sparked and crackled around them. "The Eye of Fenrir holds the same power it has always held."

Rafe shook his head, confused. "Fenrir was the power in the ring."

"Nay! 'Twas his prison. He is gone but the power remains."

"What power? How do I call upon it? How do I use it?"

"Foolish Lycan, the power your Great Spirit Mother instilled to restrain that traitorous wolf all these years. The power she used to create man from wolves! The wolf has flown but the power remains!" Gilda cackled. Her fluctuating form dropped lower so that she faced Lucien and Rafe. "It is the key to unlocking the power of the three," she mewled.

Frustrated, Rafe swiped his hand across his face. "Define the power of the three, Witch!"

"Three hearts of the two bloods must beat as one to defeat the black heart of Fenrir."

"You speak in riddles," Lucien snarled, stepping closer. "What must we do?"

"Destroy that accursed abomination!" Her voice turned cagey, bitter. Furious.

The hair on Rafael's neck stood strait up. "How?"

"Take that girl from him. He understands the untapped power within her. He will exploit it for his own gain."

"What if he kills her before we can save her?" Lucien asked, the pain of the question carved on his distraught face.

She cackled. "She is his *only* weakness. Your chosen one's heart he must win to attain the greatness he covets." Gilda cackled as her eyes settled on Rafe, then Lucien. "That wolf will not harm her."

"Why is Falon the *only* one?"

"She is of the two bloods."

Rafael knew that. Vulkasin and Mondragon blood were as much a part of Falon as of him and Lucien.

"What happens when Falon tells that piece of shit to go to hell? What will he do to her then?" Lucien asked.

"He will not harm her! It has been foretold by the gods that *she* is the one of the two bloods and the one pure of heart he searches for. His deformity is so severe and his heart so black only one such as she can balance it. To harm her would be to harm himself. He is greedy but not stupid."

"How do I call upon the power of the ring?" Rafael quietly demanded.

"Simply call upon it." She coughed roughly, fighting for breath. "But it is not enough to destroy that miscreant of a wolf."

"By gods, Witch, spit it out!" Lucien growled, raising his fists to the specter. "What must we do to destroy Fenrir?"

"There is only one true death for Fenrir. The girl must cut his black heart out with the Cross of Caus."

"What the hell is that?" Lucien demanded.

"'Tis the sword that drew first blood," the old witch wheezed.

Rafe looked at Lucien. *I will not leave Falon at the hands of that beast. We go for her, then the sword.*

"You must retrieve the girl. It will take the power of the three to unearth the Cross. Go now, before the door forever closes!" Gilda's maniacal laughter rang through them with the force of a dozen church bells. "Then bring me Fenrir's heart, and I will strip the Slayers of their magic forever!"

"How do I know you won't destroy us when you have what you want?"

"Bring me that wolf's black heart, and your debt will be paid. I give you my word."

"Where is the sword?" Lucien shouted.

Gilda's voice lowered to just above a whisper. "Where it all began."

"Where *what* began?"

"The persecution."

The red mist that was Gilda tightened into a funnel cloud rising above them, furiously rotating, the sparks of her anger raining down upon them.

"Fail and the Lycan nation fails with you!" she foretold.

The specter whirled around them before shooting skyward, then disappeared into the cloudless night.

Dumbfounded, Rafael stared into the black sky.

"The persecution began in the thirteenth century," Lucien said.

Rafe looked at the quiet ring, then to his brother. "Longshanks gave this ring to Peter Corbet for his services."

"Did he gift him with a sword as well?"

"I don't know."

"Where did Corbet come from?"

"He was a Marcher Lord," Anja said, stepping toward them.

"Marcher Lord?" Rafael asked. Why did that term sound familiar to him?

"The Marches border Wales and England," she explained.

Lucien nodded. "Those forests were heavily populated with wolves. It was there the killings began."

"Let's get the hell out of here," Rafe said.

"I'm going with you," Anja cried, digging her nails into Rafael's forearm. He growled a warning. She refused to release him. "Please,

Rafael. Don't abandon me." Her pleading crystal-colored eyes begged
him. "I am your chosen one."

He opened his mouth to tell her he was sorry that it was all a
mistake. That in light of Lucien's admission that Mara was a Slayer,
he'd been justified in killing Lucien's chosen one, and therefore was
not bound to their marks. He still belonged to Falon and she him.
But he didn't say it. Instead, Rafe nodded, doing what he always did,
the honorable thing. He allowed Anja to keep her dignity by going
with them and, for purely selfish reasons, Rafael wasn't going to turn
away the extra help.

"Thank you, Rafa," Anja said, leaning in to kiss him. Rafe subtly
pulled away, resenting her use of Falon's pet name for him.

"Maybe none of you will go anywhere," a deep vitriolic voice said
from above them.

T w o

THE HACKLES ON Rafe's neck rose as he looked up the stacks of containers surrounding them. Scores of silver-tipped arrows were aimed directly at them. Slayers, he silently cursed. They had approached with the stealth of coastal fog. His eyes narrowed as he caught sight of the insignia on their leather scabbards. These were not regular-issue Slayers.

The insignia was part raven, which delineated them as clan Corbet, the most powerful of all Slayer clans, but Rafe was not familiar with the additional griffon part of the insignia. His eyes narrowed to slits as he quickly assesed this new threat.

There was no mistaking them for anything but Corbet. The entire bloodline bore the same physical characteristics. Tall, blond, athletically built, and signature cobalt blue eyes. But unlike the Slayers he'd known, the ones that stank like shit, these had no odor. He glanced at Lucien.

Their black magic hides their stink, Rafe said to his brother.

Lucien nodded imperceptibly. *By their long hair and archaic garments, I would guess they're from the old country.*

That explained it. The new-world Corbets clung to the original Slayer credo—"Kill Wolves"—the new millennia making their job easier. These Slayers, however, were still stuck in the middle ages. Their hair was long, some of it braided, and they were dressed in traditional warrior garb of yore, from the intricate chain mail all the way down to their leather-strapped boots. And unlike the new-world Corbets, these Slayers did not carry automatic weapons but clung to their ancestral weapons of broadsword and bow.

"Someone forgot to take out the trash," Rafe sneered.

"Say a final prayer to your false gods, Lycan," the largest and evident leader said from where he stood in front of the dozens of men behind him.

In tandem, neither showing fear, Lucien and Rafe stepped forward. "Who are you?" Lucien demanded.

"Your ride to hell."

Shift! Lucien and Rafe mentally shouted at the same time. They did, both managing to grab their swords in the grip of their wolven jaws. As Rafe hurled his, Lucien leapt and swept his in a roundhouse move, cutting the leader down at the knees before he could pluck his bowstring. The packs shifted behind them and the fight was on. Arrows rained down upon them, but unless one caught a wolf directly through the heart, the wound wouldn't be fatal. A wounded wolf on adrenaline could do a lot of damage. Even to chain-mailed warriors.

Side by side, Rafe and Lucien, their vision blurred by their blood-lust to destory all things Corbet, tore a wide swath through the layers of their mortal enemy in a furious haze of violence, broken bones and torn flesh.

With a savagery born of the desperate will to survive, the wolves tore chunks out of the Slayers, littering the dock with blood and bodies. But for every Slayer torn apart, two more came at them. Like flies, they reproduced.

In the water! Lucien commanded his pack.

They snarled in protest not wanting to retreat.

"All of you, now!" Rafael shouted. It was the only way to preserve what was left of the packs.

As the packs disappeared into the cold dark bay, Lucien and Rafael held back, continuing to fight, too far from the edge of the dock to jump without being sliced to pieces. Back to back, as they always had until the blood feud turned them against each other, Rafael and Lucien snarled and fought as a circle of Slayers tightened around them like a noose.

Deep laugher reverberated around them. Lucien had wounded the leader, yet he had managed to rise, as did many of his wounded soldiers. Only the decapitated soldiers lay turning to dust on the dock.

Like the vultures they were, the Slayers circled them.

"Who are you?" Lucien demanded.

"I am John Corvus," the Slayer said, bowing from the waist.

Corvus? *Who the fuck is that?* Rafe cursed.

"From the maternal line of Peter Corbet," Corvus offered. "We've kept a low profile, but been busy across the pond."

The old-world Slayer stood straight and tall, his blue eyes glittering with malice and pointed his bloodstained sword at Rafe then Lucien. "Speaking of maternal lines, I had the recent pleasure of destroying what was left of yours." He threw his head back and laughed. "There will be no rising for the Basque pack of Mondragons, and no rising for either of you." He hopped down from the container as if Lucien's blade had never touched him and strode arrogantly toward them. "Your journey in this life ends right here. *Right now.*"

The noose tightened. *Over him, to the container, then into the bay,* Rafe said.

I'm right beside you.

As they leapt, the Slayers jumped high into their path, but they were thrust backward by a gale-force wind that slammed between the age-old enemies flattening each to their own side. Rafe cursed and stood up, and as he did, he was forced back again.

"They are mine, Corvus!" a booming voice exploded from beyond the darkness.

Rafael's skin skittered along his sinew and muscle. The last time he'd heard that voice he was ten years old. He would never forget it. It belonged to the one who'd slaughtered his parents. They had all thought him dead these last twenty-four years.

"Thomas Corbet." Lucien sneered, grabbing his sword. "I have waited twenty-four years for this day."

Rafe snarled beside his brother, grasping his double swords so tightly the bones in his hands cracked. He was not a scared ten-year-old this time but a seasoned warrior with long overdue revenge burning white-hot in his heart.

The eldest Corbet brother and only surviving one, landed beside Corvus, his blue eyes glittering in righteous hatred. He was as Rafe remembered him. Tall, powerfully built, and arrogant. His black aura radiated potent dark magic.

In response to Corbet's necromantic power, the ring on Rafe's hand warmed, startling him. The heat intensified.

Do you feel it, Lucien? Rafe asked his brother.

I feel it.

Not understanding the power of the ring any more than he did after Gilda's ambiguous explanation, but knowing it was his for the using, Rafe focused on the Slayers who stared mesmerized by the flaring stone on Rafe's left hand. Only Corbet and Corvus were unaffected and unafraid of its power.

Corbet extended his hand to Rafael. "The Eye of Fenrir belongs to me."

"You'll have to kill me to get it," Rafe threw back at him.

Corbet smiled, the gesture malevolent to its core. "That can easily be arranged."

Lucien raised his sword. "Try and take it then."

Corbet's smiled waned. "Unfortunately, I need both of you alive at the moment. But trust me when I say, once your usefulness has expired, I will have the ring, and both of your heads on each of my swords."

"I have come all this way for these two, Thomas, they are mine!" Corvus insisted, turning on his cousin.

As if he were schooling a child, the master Slayer looked dismissively down at Corvus. "I am the elder of the paternal line, the world leader of all clans. I decide what will be done with the twin alphas."

"Allow them to live so that they can slaughter more of our clan tomorrow?" Corvus spit.

Corbet's blue eyes morphed into deep shiny onyx, the ultimate Slayer tell, as he turned his full attention back to Rafe and Lucien. "So long as I live and they live, I have the power to resurrect every Slayer that has fallen beneath a Lycan bite since the first rising."

Foreboding riveted through Rafael. If Corbet was able to raise his dead, the nation was doomed.

Corbet threw his head back and laughed at his cousin's shocked expression. "Kill you today, Corvus? I will raise you from the dead on the eve of the Blood Moon rising!"

"Impossible!" Corvus challenged.

Corbet smiled tolerantly. "Cousin, you really must trust me on this." He speared Lucien and Rafe with a deadly glare. Raising his hand above his head, Corbet whirled his fist as if he held the end of a lasso. In the air a heavy silver chain materialized, lengthening with each rotation of his hand.

As he reared his hand back to cast it around Rafe and Lucien, Rafael leapt high into the air to the right. Lucien jumped high to the left.

The chain caught Lucien's ankle. Corbet laughed and yanked hard, pulling Lucien roughly from the air, sending him sprawling to the concrete deck.

"Come now, Lucien," Corbet purred, pulling Lucien toward him. "Let's see what you're made of."

Rafael dove into the frigid water of the bay below.

Three

FALON WAS FREE-FALLING. Her arms and legs spread, the heat of the air currents buoying her body from a dead drop. Loud whooshes of air tugged at her hair. Hundreds of deep whispers reverberated around her. She struggled to open her eyes. But each time she opened them, an intense burning blazed through her.

Luca! Rafa!

Falon! they shouted back to her, their voices desperate and far away.

It felt as if an eternity had come and gone. Where was she?

Her descent quickened, the air cooling. Her teeth chattered and her limbs trembled.

"Help me!" she cried.

Answering whispers swirled around her.

Familiar—the aimless gray souls that followed her in all of her conscious states.

Tell me what to do! Falon screamed as she continued to plummet.

"Return our lives," they cried.

How?

"Spill the two bloods."

What?

Did they mean she must kill Lucien and Rafael? It was an impossible request, for she would *never* sacrifice them.

"Spill the two bloods beneath the Blood Moon rising."

Where? she cried as hopelessness swept through her soul.

"Where it all began."

Where what began? What did they mean?

"The Lycan nation."

Falon screamed as her body was snatched out of the air by the jaws of the biggest, baddest wolf of them all.

Fenrir.

"RUMORS ABOUND, RAFAEL. And if they are true, I don't blame you for abandoning your brother," Corbet taunted from the dock above him. "With a lie, your brother stole your chosen one. He beguiled her, then marked her as his own." Corbet threw his head back and laughed uproariously.

Rafe swam to the piling beneath where Corbet stood. He inclined his head to his men, indicating they should all grab ahold of it. "Rumor has it she's pregnant with his child." Corbet laughed again. "Is it true?"

Rafe snarled, his beast jealously gnashed at his belly.

Go after Falon, Rafe, Lucien pleaded. *Hurry, before it's too late.*

Rafe hesitated. If he went after Falon, Lucien would surely die—and if he were dead . . . The ring flared—in protest or agreement, he wasn't sure.

"I'm going to skin your brother alive strip by strip, just like I did your mother." Corbet chuckled. "Do you remember, Rafe, how she begged me to stop? How your father, the proud arrogant Arnou begged and pleaded that I spare the beautiful Tamaska's life?" Corbet's voice tightened.

Rafe's beast snarled viciously.

"Let's see if the imperious Mondragon begs for his life."

Though Lucien had not uttered a sound, the copper scent of his brother's blood wafted down to Rafe. He steeled himself as he felt the intense burn of Lucien's agony. The ring flared painfully on his hand. In contrast, the beast within Rafe quieted. It was always its most quiet when it was most deadly.

Go, Rafe! Go while this bastard is preoccupied! Lucien called to him.

Rafael's vision blurred momentarily before clearing to precise clarity. There was no question in Rafe's heart what he would do. He had always looked out for his younger brother. Just as he would now.

"Argh!" Lucien roared in pain.

"Oh, that was a long one," Corbet chuckled. "Let's make it a set."

Lucien roared again in pain. And something in Rafael snapped.

Lucien watched with macabre satisfaction from where he laid crucified to the dock, impaled by half a dozen silver Slayer swords. Corbet held up a long strip of flesh from his belly, blood dripping from the raw strip of exposed flesh he just tore it from.

Falon! he called. *Rafe is coming for you!*

Corbet tore another strip of skin from him. Lucien bit back a groan, praying Rafe had left, praying— "Argh!" he screamed as Corbet slowly pulled yet another strip.

Tensing for another excruciating cut and tear, Lucien started. Like a lightning bolt, Rafe struck Corbet, sending the bastard tumbling backward against one of the wooden crates containing the poison Slayer swords, the impact cracking open the thick wooden slats.

Swords spewed onto the concert deck. Rafe grabbed the swords impaling Lucien's forearms and thighs and yanked them out. He turned, hurling them at the encroaching Slayers hitting his mark both times. Grabbing two poison swords, he tossed one to Lucien. Grabbing several more he distributed them to his men, then grabbed Lucien by the arm and leapt back into the bay with him. The cold water felt good on his wounds.

As they surfaced moments later, Anja's blood curdling scream tore through the night.

Fuck! Rafe cursed. Corbet had her. Why hadn't she jumped into the water with them?

"Would you like me to do you a favor Vulkasin?" Corbet taunted. "I understand you have marked one Lycan too many." He laughed. "If I eliminate the lovely Anja, then your archaic honor will not have to be tested and your precious Falon will indeed be yours." He laughed again. "What will poor Lucien do then?"

Anja screamed again.

"Makes you wish you hadn't rescued brother dear, now doesn't it?"

I'm going to tear that bastard apart one piece at a time, Lucien hissed.

"You have to the count of ten, Vulkasin, to offer up yourself or your brother in exchange for this lovely Lycan bitch."

Lucien looked at his brother. *You can't exchange yourself for her.*

"Ten."

I can't allow her to be tortured by Corbet, either.

"Nine."

The ring flared. *Corbet will not be able to kill me, not with the power of the ring.*

"Eight."

What if he takes it from you?

"Seven."

I would have to give it to him; he cannot take it.

"Six."

Damn it, Rafa!

I'll make the exchange. I owe it to her. You take the packs and go after Falon. I'll catch up.

"Five."

I'm not leaving you here. He'll kill you.

"Four."

Go damn it!

"Three."

Rafe!

"Two."

Tell Falon I loved her!

"One!"

"I'll make the exchange, Corbet!" Rafael said, leaping onto the deck.

Damn you, Rafe!

Go, Lucien. Now, before it's too late!

Ignoring his brother's command, Lucien swam deeper beneath the dock. The packs followed.

"Rafael Vulkasin, the mighty alpha whose honor has kept him from true greatness!" Corbet bellowed, his voice reverberating beneath the pilings. "Do you know why you will lose the battle of evermore?"

Silence.

Lucien moved farther away from the dock, giving the impression they were leaving.

"You will lose because you allow your honor to get in the way of what needs to be done." He laughed. "Take this little Lycan here. Did you really think I would release her?"

"You *have* no honor, Corbet," Rafe snarled.

"Precisely. It is why I have the power and you and your chosen one are bound in silver chains like hogs going to market."

Lucien crawled up a piling fifty yards down from where the Slayers held Rafe and Anja hostage. As the packs gathered around him, he gave them instructions, and they quickly got to work.

Shifting to wolves, with their jaws, they picked up the poisoned swords they had brought with them by the hilts. And like shadows, Lucien followed by the two sergeants at arms went one way, and the poison-sword-bearing packs back to where they had just came from.

Stealthily, Lucien made his way to the dockmaster's shack, rendered the guard unconscious, and snatched the keys for the giant crane midway down the pier and the two semis parked beneath the guard shack.

Before he slipped from the guard shack, Lucien shifted to human, disarmed the alarms, and tossed keys to Joachim and Anton.

"Drive the semis full throttle down the pier straight into those bastards," he whispered.

As the diesels roared to life, Lucien leapt the entire thirty-yard distance to the large crane operator's deck. In seconds it roared to life.

That ring had better have enough power to save your ass, brother, because I'm going to level that deck and everything on it, Lucien warned.

Manuvering the controls, he unlocked the heavy chain with a one-ton metal hook hanging from the end. In a deadly swath he whipped the heavy hook around, and as it swung dangerously across the deck, crashing into and toppling several containers, the semis barreled directly at the Slayers.

The bastards scattered as the Mack trucks headed straight toward Rafe and Anja, who were tied together and hanging like a smoked ham from the smaller crane near the metal sword container. As the heavy chain and hook came lumbering around toward them, Lucien roared and leapt from the operator's seat to the lumberous hook as it wobbled wildly out of control. Grasping the chain for balance, he hunched down as it swung directly toward his brother who struggled to get out of the silver lasso cocooning him and Anja. Just as Lucien reached down to grab him, Rafael burst out of the chains. Grabbing Anja, Rafe leapt high into the air and grabbed the chain above Lucien as it swung backward, then slid down onto the hook beside him.

Once Rafe was safely out of harm's way, the remaining pack rose from the darkness and hurled the poison swords at the Slayers as they reestablished their dominance on deck. Within minutes dozens dropped to the concrete, immobile. The packs swarmed on Corvus and his remaining men.

In a tidal wave of furnace-grade wind, the Slayers rose up into the night and disappeared.

Dumbfounded, Lucien and Rafael stood silent on the swaying hook, staring at each other.

"Holy fuck," Anton, Rafe's sergeant, whispered.

"I can't believe they just disappeared like that," Rafe said. He jumped down from the hook where it hung several feet above the concrete dock. Extending a hand to Anja, he helped her down.

"Are you okay?" Rafe asked her.

"I'm fine," she answered obviously more than a little shaken.

Lucien hopped off the hook landing beside his brother.

"What just happened?" Anja asked, shaking the cobwebs from her head.

"Thomas Corbet rose from the dead and is talking about raising more dead," Lucien said. "He must be stopped."

"Ghost walkers," Rafe whispered. "There are hundreds if not a thousand slain Slayers."

Fuck.

"Falon! She has seen them in her dreams!" Lucien exclaimed.

"What are you talking about?" Rafe asked skeptically.

"Not Slayer souls but Lycan souls slain by Slayers. They speak to her. I know it sounds crazy, but she told me they come to her, begging her for something. It's *resurrection* they want."

Lucien paced excitedly back and forth. "It makes sense that if there are Slayer ghost walkers there are Lycan."

Rafe's heart thudded violently in his throat. In that instant he knew if Falon were capable of resurrecting the ghost walkers, those souls that had been slain by a Corbet, that meant . . .

"Mother and father," Lucien whispered, stopping in his tracks staring at Rafe.

Afraid to believe, Rafe closed his eyes and heard his mother's voice begging for her life as Thomas Corbet skinned her alive. It had been the most disastrous day for Vulkasin, the imprint of the horror forever seared into his soul. His vengeance against all things Corbet exploded that day, mushrooming out of control. Like Lucien, Rafael would not rest until the entire bloodline was exterminated.

His heart softened as he dared to think of what the future may hold. His parents rejoining them in this life? His heart hurt it was so full of emotion. He dared not hope. Dared not—

"Falon is key—to everything." Including Rafael's heart. His gut rolled nervously as he remembered the night he first set eyes on her. She had been terrified, bloodied, broken, and at master Slayer Viktor Salene's mercy. She lay at death's door. He had given her his own breath. Taken her home as the beast within drove him to mark her. But his human wanted her, too. And that night, Rafael's entire world had shifted. It had yet to right, and as long as Falon lived, his world would always be off balance. She did that to a man. It was what he wanted more than his own life.

But Lucien had messed it all up! If only he had just left well enough alone!

As if reading his thoughts, Lucien's golden eyes burned furiously as he turned to face Rafe. They were equals in everything, including their unshakable love for the enigmatic woman who stood between them.

"We can stand here and beat the shit out of each other or we can track Fenrir down and get Falon back," Lucien said.

Rafael leashed his anger. His brother was right. All that mattered now was Falon's safety. Turning toward his pack, singling out Anton, Rafe said, "Take the swords to the rendezvous point in Lodi, then prepare the pack."

Lucien nodded and said to his own second, "Joachim, gather Mondragon, prepare for the rising as we have planned, then head to the battleground." He clasped Joachim's good hand. "Gods willing, I will see you in the north with Falon by my side."

Lucien grabbed a leather satchel, his cell phone, and iPad from the semi they had driven in to load the crates into. He stripped and shoved his electronics, clothes, and boots into the satchel, then handed it to Rafe, who did the same before turning to Anja.

"I cannot promise you that I can protect you from Fenrir," Rafe said, wanting her to stay behind. As much as he wanted the extra help, he didn't want Anja's. And selfishly, if she were not there, he would feel free to do so when he took Falon protectively into his arms.

Touching his cheek with her fingertips Anja smiled sadly. "Perhaps *I* will protect you from that terrible wolf."

Rafe grabbed Anja's hand and slowly lowered it to her side. "You deserve to be loved completely, Anja. I'm not that man."

"In the eyes of the Blood Law you are, and that is enough for me."

Rafe let out a long breath not wanting to waste time arguing. He handed her the leather bag, then looked to his brother as they both strapped on their swords and leather scabbards. "Let's go."

Four

SOMETHING IN THE universe had profoundly changed. Falon felt it down to the marrow of her bones. Her body vibrated with energy. Her senses were on fire, the scents swirling around her so clear, so strong, so defined, it hurt. As the breeze swept across her skin she shivered painfully as if every nerve was exposed.

The strong cadence of her heartbeat thudded around her, the percussion pounding in her ears.

Yet there was another heartbeat. It was louder and strong, but not stronger than hers.

She opened her eyes and stared into two intense red ones.

"Fenrir." She breathed in awe. Unmoving, she stared boldly as he shifted from the deformed hunchback wolf into the human version of it.

"You do not fear me?" he demanded quietly.

If she said she was not afraid she would be a liar. He was hideous to look upon. His face long, his jaws thick, his yellow teeth jagged and sharp. Mostly rough bumpy skin was smooth in patches with tuffs of wiry black hair sprouting like weeds along his arms, chest, and neck. He was easily twice her size.

She gasped as her memory came crashing back with the velocity of a meteor entering the atmosphere. Balor's brutal attack on them in the container full of the poison swords. He had killed Anja and slit Falon's throat!

Dear God, what happened to Lucien and Rafael? Her temples suddenly began to throb. Rubbing them, she closed her eyes. She had been dying, bleeding out. It had been so peaceful, no pain, except the desperate pleas from Rafa and Luca for her life . . .

Falon gasped, her eyes flying open. In his desperation to save her life, Rafael released Fenrir, and he slew Balor and that witch!

"Where is Lucien? And Rafael?" she demanded, pushing up from where she lay on the ground. It was cold, dark, and barren. Raising her nose, Falon inhaled the crisp coolness of the air. The sky directly above was a sparkling blanket of sapphire and diamonds. A star exploded and shot higher into the deep blue canvas, its radiant gold vapor trail winding behind it.

Great Spirit Mother, give me the strength to thwart this wolf!

"They are dead to you," Fenrir growled viciously. "I forbid you to say their names in my presence." He leaned into her, his hot putrid breath laving her cheeks. "And if you call for either one of them, I will destroy them both."

Falon blanched at the deadly threat. But it was not enough for her to roll over and play submissive. "They will come for me. You cannot stop them."

"I stopped them once, I will stop them again."

"By Blood Law you have no right to me. I belong to both alphas!" Falon blinked as she said the words. Because Rafe had been vindicated by the truth that Mara was a Slayer, she still belonged to him.

Didn't she? But she had traded marks with Lucien as well. Was their union null and void? Desperately, she didn't want her union with Lucien to be dissolved. But because Rafe exchanged marks with Anja would the Blood Law take the Siberian wolf's side?

Falon's heart thundered in her chest. Gods help her, but she would fight to have them both.

Fenrir threw his hideous head back and roared with laughter. "Do you think I care about the Blood Law?"

Blood drained from her cheeks. "What *do* you care about, Wolf?"

He smiled, the gesture grotesque. "Siring the most powerful pack on earth."

"For that you're going to have to find yourself a willing partner." Because it wasn't going to be her!

"Willing or not, I have found my true mate."

Foreboding swept through her at his implication, but Falon kept her composure. "You'll have to introduce me to her one of these days."

His grotesque smile widened. "It would be my pleasure."

Slowly, Falon inhaled a deep breath centering her anxiety. If this wolf thought for one minute she was going to—she shivered, unable to comprehend such a thing. Slowly she exhaled, and deeply inhaled again. As the air entered her body and was absorbed into her bloodstream, her cells sparked with energy. Fenrir was powerful, but he was not omnipotent.

Mentally she checked herself for pain or injury. Not a scratch. Far from it. She felt amplified. Electrified. Stronger than ever. The blood of the two alphas had infused her power significantly, but there was something more. Different. Mystical. Dark. Her urge to kill heightened. Her lust for the hunt unnerving, the yearning for blood unquenchable. But not for Slayer blood . . . Lycan.

Falon gasped.

Her desire to hunt her own kind, to crucify them then infuse her body with their blood was so overwhelming she felt faint. Dear God! What had happened to her? Had Fenrir forced his hatred for Lycan into her?

In a hideous revelation, her memory provided the answer. Balor Corbet's blood now ran through her veins. It had restored her life! Did she now possess his hatred for those she loved? And his dark magic? Shivering violently, Falon fought back the nausea that rolled through her. Corbet blood had destroyed so much of what Mondragon and Vulkasin held dear and yet that same villainous blood not only saved her life but had enhanced her senses to such a dizzying height she could barely control it.

Her beast snarled defensively at the evilness that prevailed within her. It would not be! She would never hurt a Lycan intentionally. She loved her people. Would die for them. For their cause.

It took all of her strength and concentration to center herself, to regain her composure. To tell herself that her Lycan blood was stronger than any Slayer blood that ran through her veins. Her love for Lucien and Rafael would trump any hate forced into her. Whether forced or accepted with open arms, the power of the three united was omnipotent. It could not be defeated. Not by Fenrir and certainly not by the Corbet blood that coursed through her veins. She was Lycan born and Lycan she would stay regardless of whose blood saved her life!

Ignoring Fenrir's menacing growls, Falon cautiously stood and wiped the dirt and brush from her clothing. The deformed wolf man moved closer posturing as if he meant to keep her captive. Falon flung her hands at him and to both their shock, his four-hundred-pound body moved back ten feet. Deep furrows etched in the early autumn earth, disrupting the pungent dirt.

"Do not crowd me, Wolf."

He snarled and snapped at the air, his unsightly human face elongating to that of a wolf before reverting back to human. It looked as if the wolf lacked self-control. She'd tread lightly but bravely and use that against him. What had both Rafa and Luca told her with regard to sizing up a threat? Show no fear and you open no door for attack.

"Why am I here?" she demanded, knowing the answer. When the deformed wolf did not immediately answer, Falon calmed herself and gauged her location, looking around the wooded glen that shielded them from the thicker surrounding forest.

Moonlight struggled through the thick copse of trees surrounding them. The scents were different though not unpleasant. Falon knew she was hundreds of miles north of home.

"Where are you taking me?"

"Where it will end," Fenrir said smoothly. His eyes glittered, and Falon knew by their glow there was more to his answer. "And"—he breathed, stepping closer to her—"where the new dawn of the Lycan nation will begin."

Her heart kicked against her rib cage. Did he mean—? "You will fight with us and not against us?"

A deep rumble began in his belly, echoing throughout his body before surfacing as laughter.

"The only *us* surviving the rising will be you and me, Falon."

For the second time since she came to, Falon's blood frosted. Life without Rafa and Luca was not an option. Life without her mother, Talia, and all the others she had come to love and respect was not an option. Life with Fenrir on any level was out of the question.

She needed to get the hell out of there and find Rafa and Luca. Together they stood a chance. Divided they would surely die.

"We're going north to the battleground?" Falon asked with a nonchalance she didn't feel. From beneath hooded lashes she judged the distance from where she stood to the thickest part of the forest just ahead of her and behind Fenrir. In such a restrictive environment, she'd have the advantage of being smaller and nimbler over his larger and slower. Yawning, she stretched her arms over her head and flexed her legs. The tightness in her heavy muscles loosened as electrical pulses sparked throughout her. She felt lighter than air but stronger than a superhero. She jumped and to her amazement soared higher than the tallest tree.

Fenrir snarled beneath her. And as easily as if she were a bubble floating by, he caught her with his huge hand and brought her carefully back to the ground. So much for him being slow on the uptake.

"You're strong, but I am stronger," he rumbled staring hotly at her.

"Why am I here?"

For a minute that stretched out like an hour, Falon watched the terrible wolf struggle for words. If she didn't know of his savagery, and his hatred for his own kind, she might almost find it endearing that he seemed to actually look as if he were shuffling his feet and about to ask her out on a date.

When his eyes fixated on her and the spark in their red depths flamed, she knew a bloodcurdling fear she had never experienced before.

"I have chosen you as my life mate."

Exhaling a long breath she hadn't realized she was holding, Falon bit her bottom lip as she fought back laughter. He looked like a lovesick puppy. If she spoke now she'd laugh and if she laughed . . .

"You mock me with your eyes," he snarled.

Teetering on hysteria, Falon struggled for composure. He was so imposing. Terrifying in his fury, but the human part of him was as vulnerable as any man's heart. And it was that human vulnerability she would exploit.

"So, all of this is about you wanting me?"

He nodded.

"Why me?"

"You are of both bloods and pure of heart."

It was true that both alphas' blood coursed through her veins. Pure and powerful, it would pass to her children. Her hand slid down her belly to the babe she knew with gathering certainty grew within her. Pure of heart? Maybe in the sense that the hatred between Lycan and Slayer had not been bred into her. She had learned it, though. She despised Slayers with a vengeance equal to Rafael and Lucien's. A vengeance so pure it contradicted the dark Corbet blood that infused her power.

"I cannot bond with you, Fenrir. I carry the heir to Mondragon."

"A lie!" he roared, moving so swiftly to her, she blanched in fear. No longer gentle, he grabbed her by the neck and pinned her to the cold forest floor.

"I don't lie," Falon rasped, knowing it was the truth. Grasping his huge hand as it tightened around her throat, Falon struggled for air.

"Destroy it!" he commanded.

Fighting for consciousness she shook her head. "Never," she said hoarsely. Darkness descended around her. Allowing her body to go lax, Falon closed her eyes and found a place deep within herself where she could go to center and balance. The place she could draw the most power from. Love and hate were separated by the thinnest of lines. She drew on both emotions, and her desperate will to live and save the life of her unborn child.

With each beat of her heart, typhoon strength power gathered in Falon's belly. As it crested, reaching a terrifying crescendo, she opened her eyes. Fenrir's narrowed menacingly. But behind the menace, fear flickered unsteadily. Not fear of her, but fear of losing her.

One by one she peeled his fingers from around her neck. With each finger, blessed air filled her lungs. It was when she was finally free of him, her breath restored, that Falon understood: he would not kill her. His desire for her was too great. And that would keep her alive. For now.

Slowly she rubbed her neck as she regarded him.

"You belong to me now," he said roughly.

Unthinking, Falon smiled. How many times had her proud Lucien said those exact words? And how true had they proved to be? So true that there was nothing left of her for any other except Rafa to claim.

Shoving Fenrir away from her, Falon stood. Her power simmered impatiently beneath the surface, her beast on the prowl, cautioning the Corbet blood to keep a low profile.

"I belong to Vulkasin and Mondragon. Not only will they never release me, I would never accept you."

"Not even for the lives of your lovers?" the wolf threatened.

A chill so deep it froze her blood momentarily paralyzed Falon before she could speak. "Not even for their lives," she lied.

"For your mother's life?"

"Leave her out of this."

Fenrir smiled, the gesture turning uglier. "Come here, lovely, come see what I can do."

Not wanting to witness his power but knowing she must understand its boundaries if she was going to defeat him, Falon stepped closer to where he stood.

He cast a circle of stones on the dewy earth. Extending his arms over it, he opened his hands palms down and slowly began to rotate them over and under each other. The earth began to steam and take the shape of—Layla, crying in the woods.

"Mother!" Falon lunged toward the circle.

"She can't hear you but—" Fenrir made a quick stabbing movement, and her mother cried out as she doubled over.

Falon snarled and slapped his hands down. The mist evaporated and the stones sizzled as if they reclaimed the magic.

Fenrir hissed in surprise.

"I have power, too, Fenrir. Don't forget that when you threaten someone I love." Moving closer to him she stood so close to him she could see the pulse of the yellow striations in his red eyes. "And understand I would do *everything* in my power to save them from you." She moved within inches of his face. "And understand this even more: if you hurt one hair on any one of their heads, any chance you have of winning my heart would die with them." She looked hard at him. He was a pitiful creature to be sure. For nearly millennia shunned not only by his own people but scorned by humankind. He had no place in either world.

"You admit there is a chance for me?" he asked with the excitement of an adolescent boy. By his hand alone, thousands of Lycan had died. By his hand alone he had perpetuated deep-seated hatred that should have died centuries ago. He alone was responsible for the continued persecution of Lycan. But she would give him a sliver of hope, buying time to escape.

"I admit nothing. My heart belongs to Lucien Mondragon and Rafael Vulkasin. It will as long as the three of us live."

"If you can love two alphas, you can love three," he pompously declared. He pulled her into his arms. "Accept me and I will give you the world."

Not in your lifetime, Wolf.

"Release me, Fenrir, and I will accept you into my packs."

His arms tightened around her. "I don't want them. I will begin my own pack. With you," he growled.

Tipping her head back Falon calmly threatened, "Find another to found your line because I will kill you if you force my hand."

"I am immortal."

Maybe, but even immortals had weaknesses.

"You have the power to set right nearly a thousand years of wrongs, Fenrir! Strip the power from the Slayers and return to your own kind."

"My own father and mother cast me from my pack! My siblings laughed at me. No pack would accept me."

"And for their faults all Lycan should pay?"

"Yes, and once I am alpha of the nation, I will have the respect I am due."

Falon scowled. "That is not respect that is fear-driven bidding. Terrorism. A true alpha leads by example." Falon nudged the angry beast. "Why not turn your power to right? Use it to equalize this terrible wrong. Do you hate so deeply that you cannot love?"

"Love?" he snarled, moving into her. "*Love?* My own blood could not find it in their hearts to love me. How could I expect another to?"

"Your parents were not fit to parent. For that, I'm sorry. But for you to be loved, you have to give it. It cannot be forced or extracted."

"The Slayers love me."

"They use you."

"It doesn't matter!" he roared. "I do not need love! I don't want it! There is only one thing I need."

"And what is that?"

"Your acceptance."

"Why do you *really* want me?" She didn't buy the "two bloods" thing. Why would he want two other alphas' blood?

"You represent all that is beautiful and strong in a Lycan. With your acceptance, the others would also accept me."

"They would think you forced me."

"Does the sight of me so disgust you?" he snarled.

"Your hateful heart disgusts me."

He laughed low, the sound sending shivers along her spine. "My hatred has kept me warm at night." He moved around her, his fangs flashing beneath the stars. "But it's not enough now. My body craves another kind of warmth."

"Find it somewhere else, Fenrir."

"I know a secret, Falon. A secret that if your beloved alphas learned of it, would turn them against you for all time."

"What secret?" she whispered, dreading the answer.

"Thomas Corbet lives."

She gasped in horror just as euphoria sang in her blood. *What was that?* Why would she feel joy at the news that such a vile human lived? Her beast snarled. She would kill him. But why would Lucien and Rafe turn against her if they learned that Thomas Corbet lived. She looked up to Fenrir for the answer.

"He's your father, Falon."

F i v e

DRIVEN BY THEIR love for Falon, Lucien and Rafael covered an
enormous amount of ground in a short period of time. Falon's blood
ran hot and potent in both of them. Combined with the Eye of Fenrir, their power surged. It wasn't until the setting of the sun the next
day that exhaustion overcame them.

They hunted as wolves, ate as wolves, and slept fitfully as wolves.
Fitfully was being generous. Lucien had not slept more than a few
hours over the last several days; fatigue wore on him. He saw Falon
everywhere. Smelled her, heard her—

"Lucaaaa—" Falon called from the forest.

Lucien's heartbeat spiked. He was up in an instant.

"Luca," she called again.

*He squinted against the sunshine, focusing. There, just mere feet
from him, Falon's laughing eyes and smiling lips beckoned him, teas-
ing and taunting with promise.*

"Falon!" he called as she skipped away from him, the lilt of her

laughter an invisible string pulling his heart after her. He could deny her nothing. She was the sunshine to his darkness. The calm to his storm. The very air that he breathed. It terrified him to love her so deeply. Life without Falon would be no life at all.

He stood still as he thought of Rafael, and understood more at that moment than at any time before what losing this precious woman could do to a powerful honorable man. Bring him to his knees. Snuff the life from him. Drive him mad with sorrow. As it had when he had taken her from Rafe.

"Lucien," she called pulling him from his deep thoughts. "Come, I have a surprise for you."

He smiled. She never ceased to amaze him. His passion for her was equaled only by hers for him. Falon Mondragon was a prize among prizes.

She disappeared behind a thick clump of shrubs. Hot blood thundered through his veins. He was rock hard. The need to lose himself inside of her was never more urgent. He slowed his pace and stalked her as his wolf would a rabbit. Hands out he leapt around the tree and grabbed her squirming body. She screamed with delight, wrapping her arms around his neck, pressing her warm suppleness against him.

Their gazes caught and held. Overwhelming joy filled him. She was in his arms again, where she belonged. Her cheeks pinked as she lowered her lashes coyly. When she slowly opened them and looked up at him, Lucien grinned.

"Hi," he whispered.

"Hi, yourself."

"I missed you."

Fisting his hair, Falon pulled his lips to hers.

When they met, Lucien tightened his arms around her waist, pulling her into him, until he felt every curve and valley of her body. She was so soft, so succulent, so—his. Not his brother's. His. Mondragon!

"I hope you have another dress," he growled. "Because I'm going to reduce this one to threads when I tear it off you."

She squealed and broke free from his embrace. "It's all I have!" she teased over her shoulder.

He stood rooted to the forest floor. She'd look sexy in a burlap sack, but the dress she was wearing defined a man's wildest fantasy. A simple black sheath that hugged her curves like a second skin begging for removal. It offered her luscious breasts up like an appetizer. It laced up the front giving a subtle glimpse of her deep cleavage and down her back to the gentle rise of her ass. He couldn't wait to unwrap her.

"Lucien, Lucien! I love you!" she cried happily as she stopped on a small knoll and faced him. She extended her arms to him. "I need you. Now, Luca." Her naturally husky voice dropped several octaves. Her bright blue eyes shone brightly, her nostrils flared and her chest rose and fell with each excited breath she took.

Ah, and how he loved her! He ran to her and scooped her up into his arms, twirling her around and around and around. He never felt so free, so light, so happy. He kissed her sweet lips. She was so soft, so fragrant, so female to his male. "Angel face," he breathed against her parted lips. "You never cease to thrill me." He pulled her harder against him. "Promise me you will never leave me."

Taking his face into her hands, she gazed at him with those big blue eyes he always lost himself in. She nipped playfully at his bottom lip drawing blood. Her eyes darkened as his heated. "Lucien, you are mine as I am yours. We are blood bound."

"And we are heart bound," Rafael's deep voice interrupted from behind them.

Lucien's arms tightened around Falon as rage unleashed within him. His beast, ever protective of what was his, reared its head. Though he acknowledged the heartbreak his brother had suffered at losing this *amazing woman, it changed nothing for Lucien. He would* never *release Falon.*

Falon smiled over his shoulder at his brother who approached. When Rafe stopped beside her, she placed her hand on his chest.

Lucien's jaw clenched so tight his teeth ground.

"My first love," she purred, smiling up at Rafe.

Jealousy ripped through Lucien. His beast snarled, snapping its jaws, rising dangerously close to the surface. Bewildered by Falon's words and her actions, Lucien dropped to a knee and reached for her. "You belong to me," he beseeched.

With her hand still on Rafe's chest, Falon turned to Lucien and smiled extending her hand. Fervently, he grasped it.

"I belong to you both."

Lucien's heart plummeted to his knees. She had said as much before Balor slit her throat. He thought it was her desperate attempt not to hurt his brother, but—

"You chose me!" he roughly reminded her.

Her gossamer smile widened. "I choose you both."

"It can be only one of us," Lucien ground out, having none of this nonsense. She was his, by gods, and she would stay his!

Rafe turned her away from Lucien, taking her fully into his arms. "My love, by the Blood Law, you belonged to me first. Lucien has no claim to you."

Lucien grasped her forearm and pulled her back into his arms. "You are mine, Falon. Mine."

Unperturbed by their tug-of-war, Falon continued to smile. "I choose you both."

Taking each of them by the hand she led them to a velvety green knoll. Sunshine shone warmly on the idyllic spot. She stepped back from them both and slowly unlaced the bodice of her dress. Lucien's groin tightened as his breath shortened. As she slipped off the black sheath, revealing more of her creamy smooth skin, his heart pounded with the force of a wrecking ball against his rib cage.

Her full breasts swelled, the pink tips hard and pebbled. He groaned, wanting to drag his tongue across each one. Her belly was taut and concave, her hips smoothly rounded. He swallowed. The apex of her thighs was smooth and bare of hair. The dress slid noiselessly to her feet. Smoothly she stepped out of it and knelt on the cool grass then back against it. The plump pinkness of her lips glistened with moistness.

Holy mother—

She lay back, spreading her long velvety hair around her like an ebony halo.

"Make love to me," she softly commanded them both. "Like the night in the pond."

Lucien looked at Rafe, his hunger for Falon ravenous. That same hunger was reflected in his brother's eyes. Neither one of them took a step toward her, though it was what they both wanted more than their lives.

Gritting his jaw, Lucien dragged his fingers through his hair. Rafael struggled with the same demon beside him.

Lucien took a step toward her at the same time Rafael did.

Lucien growled a warning. Rafael mirrored it.

Lucien shifted. Rafael shifted.

They lunged viciously at each other.

Lucien woke with a start. Sweat-soaked, his breathing labored, his heart pounded violently against his chest. Rafe stared at him from across the space they slept with the same agonized stare. Had he dreamt the same dream? Or had it really happened?

"I will not share her with you, Lucien," Rafael said slowly.

"Nor will I share her with you, Brother," Lucien said, standing up.

This was not a battle they would fight at the moment. It would take their combined stealth and strength to get Falon back, and right now, her life was the most precious thing to him.

"She carries my child, Rafe. I will never give him or his mother up."

"Nor will I release you, Rafael," Anja said, striding into the glen they had just awoke in. Surprisingly, she looked no worse for the long journey. Lucien eyed her suspiciously.

"We both know I was not free to exchange marks with you, Anja," Rafael said. "They are null and void. I release you."

"You cannot just cancel me out! We exchanged marks. They are binding!" she cried, her cool exterior cracking. Lucien could smell her desperation.

"I was not free to exchange them, Anja," Rafe explained. "My mark on Falon stands over mine on you because had the council known the truth as we know it now, I would have been vindicated for killing a Slayer and Falon would have remained with me."

Lucien stiffened, unable to argue the truth of Rafe's words. But they didn't matter. Falon loved him and he her. She had chosen him over Rafe.

"I would do anything to rectify this situation for you, Anja, except renounce Falon as my chosen one."

Her crystal-colored eyes flashed angrily at Rafe, then at Lucien before she honed furiously in on Rafe. "You vowed to be mine. I don't accept your release!"

Rafael growled softly. "I gave my vow to Falon first, it cannot be undone even if I wished it so."

"What of your honor, Rafe? Have you none where she is concerned?" Anja accused.

Cautiously, he stepped toward her and spoke very carefully. "It was because of my honor I lost her the first time! My honor be damned this time. I won't lose her again."

"So you condemn your brother to death?"

Lucien stiffened. It was hard enough listening to his bother tell his chosen one he was dumping her for Lucien's chosen one. Hard enough to keep his mouth shut out of respect while his brother handled his personal business. But when the topic turned to his condemnation, he caught his brother's hard gaze.

"That is a matter for the council to decide," Rafe said.

"I can't wait to see how your bitch reacts when they cut off his head," Anja sneered.

Lucien snarled, whirling toward Anja. "Be careful who you call bitch."

"In light of the circumstances, the council will not sentence Lucien to death. And certainly not now with the impending rising." Rafe nodded to Lucien. "If they do, then they'll have more than one pissed off alpha to deal with."

"So now you are both above the Blood Law?" Anja sneered.

"No, Anja," Rafe patiently explained. "But these are extraordinary circumstances in extraordinary times. As a nation we must stand together to survive."

"In that case, Rafael, I will await the council's decision on whether or not our exchanged mark stands or not."

"I don't need the council's blessing to terminate our union. It's over because it never was. Accept it."

Smugly Anja held out the leather bag to them. "Whether you like it or not, I am still your chosen one, not your precious Falon."

"Keep it," Lucien said, indicating the bag Anja held. "Falon is close. Her scent stronger." Even though Fenrir tried to mask it. He looked to Rafe. "Are you ready?"

"Yes."

They shifted, it being understood that Anja would continue to follow in a beta position.

As they ate up the miles, worry gnawed at Lucien. Not for fear of his life at the hands of the council. It was for Falon he worried. He felt her turmoil, her desperation to be free of the demonic wolf. Her yearning for the safety of his arms

Falon, he called, *I'm coming for you!*

Hurry, Lucien!

Six

FALON STOOD SPEECHLESS. Horrified, yes, but more than that, terrified. She was a *Corbet*. Not just any Corbet, but the daughter of Thomas Corbet, the worst Corbet of all.

Her recent conversation with Lucien came back to haunt her.

"What if I was a blood Corbet?" she had asked.

"Though it would kill me to do so, I would kill you," he answered.

And of course, she'd understood. Killing a Corbet was what every Lycan lived for. But for Lucien and Rafael, it was more than killing a natural predator. For them it was a personal vendetta.

And she *was* a blood Corbet.

And her mother knew! Why had she kept such a terrible secret from her?

But of course . . .

Her knees wobbled. Falon sank to the cold ground.

Layla had kept the secret buried deep because of the Blood Law. Lying with a Slayer was strictly forbidden, the penalty immediate death. Her mother would have been executed. And Falon? At the very least, she would have been shunned. But more likely, knowing Lucien's and Rafael's bloodlust for anything Corbet, she would have been killed. And they'd kill her now if they knew the truth.

Dear God! It couldn't be true! Not Thomas Corbet! Not the evilest of them all, the one who initiated the slaying of Lucien and Rafael's parents. Her *father*?

She dropped her head into her hands, violently shaking her head denying Fenrir's claim.

"No!" she choked.

But it all made sense to her now. The night Viktor Salene had tried to take her, he'd told her who she was. She'd refused to listen, writing him off as some random crazy guy who liked to dress up like Conan the Barbarian. Instead, she'd ended up in Rafael's bed. Accepted his mark.

The signs of her parentage had always been there, but she'd refused to see them. Her innate power, her visions, remembering the ring on her father's hand. Even her eye color and her build screamed Corbet.

"He fell in love with her," Fenrir sneered as he moved closer. He settled his large body beside her. "When they came to resurrect the ring, I heard it in their voices." He threw his head back and laughed. "I helped nature take its course. How could I not? I knew between them they would breathe life into my legacy."

Falon glared at Fenrir. "What legacy?"

"My nation will be born when I find the one of two bloods, a female of equal power and pure of heart. I knew Layla would bear Thomas a daughter. I knew she would be beautiful, strong, and intelligent. I knew all I had to do was bide my time and she would be mine." He smiled malevolently. "And so she is."

The two bloods? Not Vulkasin and Mondragon as she thought, but Slayer and Lycan! Oh, no, *please*, make it a lie!

Falon's heart crumbled into thousands of tiny pieces. How could she tell Rafa and Luca? How could she bear their contempt? They would be horrified, never want to touch her again. How could she ever look in the mirror again and like what she saw?

Fenrir moved closer to her, his musky scent cloying. Heat rose in Falon's cheek. Not embarrassment, but anger. It continued to rise until she was so furious, her limbs shook. She turned on Fenrir, shoving him away from her. Standing as he gathered himself from the tree he had slammed into, Falon walked purposely toward him, her hands out, her hatred bubbling furiously to the surface. Her beast snarled and snapped for release.

"I will deny it!" she shrieked. "You cannot prove it. And you will not use it against me! I swear by all that is holy and unholy, you wretched excuse for a wolf, if you reveal this to *anyone*, I will rip your black heart out of your chest and feed it to the crows!"

"You cannot kill me."

"I will call upon every soul you destroyed, Fenrir. I will lead an army of ghost walkers against you!"

His red eyes narrowed. "How do you know of them?"

"I have my own secrets, Fenrir."

"If you knew the secret to resurrect them you would have by now."

Was that fear in the mighty wolf's voice? Falon laughed caustically. "I will call upon them when I need them most." She moved closer to him. "Has that time come?"

"Bring me Corbet's heart, and your secret will die with him."

"He lives?" she gasped. Did her mother know?

Fenrir smiled the gesture obscene. "He is very much alive."

Falon looked around as if Corbet were standing in the shadows. "Where is he?"

"His magic is strong and he hides himself from me."

"Why?"

Fenrir shrugged his large deformed shoulders. "You would have to ask him that."

"He is the last person on earth besides you, I would want to converse with."

His red eyes flared. "Tread lightly, lovely, my patience only stretches so far."

"Mine has already snapped." Falon shifted as the beast took control of her for the first time in her life. Fenrir had met his match.

RUNNING SIDE BY side, Lucien called to Rafe, *Her scent is stronger!*

The cloying musky scent of the deformed wolf thickened the air around them. *So is Fenrir's,* Rafael answered.

As they crashed into the western edge of the Northern Cascades, Lucien caught the scent of blood. Falon's blood.

Shit! Rafael cursed. *She's down.*

Falon! Rafe called to her.

Hurry, she called back.

They looked at each other. Her voice was anxious but strong. She sounded angry and upset. Who the fuck wouldn't?

They stretched out, the swords rattling along their backs, their mouths agape, their long powerful bodies racing furiously for Falon.

They ate up the miles. As they came to a thickly forested peak, they abruptly stopped. Panting heavily from a jutting gray rock formation, they looked down into a shallow valley, sheltering a small clearing surrounded by towering western hemlock, Douglas fir, and red cedar. A light dusting of snow covered the rugged edges of the ghostly gray rock formations. And there, pacing along the edge of the glen was one fucking ugly beast of a wolf and standing defiantly in the center was the beautiful princess.

Lucien growled and shook his head as relief filled him. Falon never ceased to amaze him. She was safe and just as difficult as usual.

He shifted to human at the same time Rafe did.

"Poor Fenrir, if he only knew what he was getting himself into," Rafe said, shaking his head.

"If we leave her with him long enough, he'll beg us to take her back." Lucien couldn't wait to get her back into his arms.

Falon, Rafe called. *Don't look up, but we're here, on the jutting rock to your seven o' clock.*

Stand back! He's as strong as a Titan, she warned.

Why are you bleeding? Lucien demanded.

I attacked him and when he shook me off, I sliced my back on a rock. I'm fine.

Falon, we're downwind of you, I need you to turn around and face us, then get him to move around and face you so his back is to us, Rafe instructed.

I can't.

Of course you can! Just start talking to him and moving, he will follow, he said, frustrated.

I told him as long as he held me captive I wasn't going to talk to him unless hell froze over.

Well it just froze over damn it! Lucien cursed.

Fine!

"She's going to be the death of me," Rafe muttered.

Whatever you do, angel face, don't look up when we come in, Lucien cautioned.

I won't. But be careful. He's mean and royally pissed off at the moment.

So are we, Lucien said.

As humans they watched Falon maneuver Fenrir around. She

stood up and got in his face, screaming and yelling at him, her hands flying in angry gestures. Fenrir stood silent, and took it.

Good girl, keep him focused completely on you.

Rafe looked to Lucien. "Let's hope the poison metal works on immortal wolves, at least enough to slow him down."

"If it doesn't then it's on to Plan B," Lucien said.

Rafe looked at Fenrir's deformed human back. Both blades deep between the shoulder blades should stop him long enough for them to hack off a few body parts, grab Falon, and then get the hell out of there.

"There is no Plan B," Rafe said.

Grimly, Lucien smiled. "Then I guess we make Plan A work."

Pulling at her hair like a banshee, Falon railed at Fenrir. "And if you think I'm going to spend my time running after your kids, you can forget it! I'm not doing it. I'm not cooking for you, either, *or* hunting for you! Why did ya have to pick me? Why not some nice sweet little she-wolf? I'm only half Lycan. And I hate shifting. It hurts and I'm always ruining clothes!"

She stopped and put her hands on her hips, fighting to hold her fear at bay. "Hey! Are you even listening to me? Is this how it's going to be? I tell you how I feel and you ignore me? I swear you are so typical. You—"

It took everything Falon had not to watch in wonder as Rafael and Lucien, in their glorious wolf forms, their swords gripped in their powerful jaws, leapt from the jutting rock formation three hundred feet up and behind her. They shifted to human form in perfect symmetry just before they hurled those nasty poison swords into Fenrir's back.

As the blades struck home, Fenrir screamed in agonizing pain. Lucien landed on Fenrir's shoulders and shoved the blades so deep into his back the pointed tips erupted from his chest, blood spraying in a high arch across the trampled ground. Fenrir flung Lucien back so viciously he slammed into a tall evergreen, cracking the trunk in half. As Rafael came around to grab Falon, Fenrir backhanded him, sending him careening across the glen into another tree.

Fenrir's red eyes blazed furiously. He looked down at his bleeding chest and roared as he pulled the blades through with a sickening sluicing sound, and flung them at Falon's feet. He snarled and shifted, then bounded after Lucien. Lucien leapt from the tree with another sword in his hand. As Fenrir approached, Lucien flipped backward in a *Matrix* move, landing on Fenrir's back as the beast overran his target. Lucien plunged the sword deep into the wolf's shoulder. Fenrir roared, and shook him off, pulling the sword from the wound.

Falon grabbed the two swords at her feet. Fenrir howled triumphantly, flinging the sword back at Lucien. Lightning quick, Falon hurled the sword in her right hand intercepting Fenrir's sword slicing it in half before it impaled Lucien. Bellowing his rage, Fenrir shifted then turned on her and like Godzilla crashing through Tokyo, he thundered toward her.

Rafe! she called.

Behind you.

As Falon turned, Rafael launched a hundred-foot evergreen spear at Fenrir. Falon ducked and watched as the timber impaled his belly, the velocity shoving the trunk branches halfway through Fenrir.

Falon tossed the other sword to her right hand, and calling upon all of her power, she leapt for Fenrir's throat. He flung an arm out and grabbed her by the waist. As he raised his arm to fling her away from him, she stabbed the sword into his neck. His red eyes flared, furious.

"Why, when I would have given you the world?" he asked, frothy blood bubbling down the blade.

Falon pulled the sword out and stabbed it deep into his throat again. "Because I despise what you have done."

Lucien grabbed the sword from Fenrir's neck and hacked off the arm holding Falon. The beast screamed dropping to his knees. Rafe hacked off his right foot.

The delimbed monster floundered in the dirt.

Let's get the hell out of here, Lucien shouted, pushing her away.

Finish it! she cried, grabbing the sword from him.

There is only one sword that can kill him and this isn't it.

What do you mean?

When we're safely away, I'll explain.

Fenrir snarled, raising his slowly regenerating arm.

Shit, the three said in unison, backing up.

Wait! We possess the power of the three! Falon threw down her sword and grasped Lucien's right hand and Rafael's left hand. Immediate power pulsed through them. Chin raised, staring Fenrir straight in the eye, Falon raised their clasped hands in the air toward him. Brilliant red and gold sparks illuminated their auras. Each of their hearts stuttered, stumbled, and then restarted, beating as one. United with their combined powers.

Holding Fenrir's glare, Falon dared him to come closer. "Accept defeat, Fenrir."

"I am immortal!"

The ring on Rafael's hand flared red hot, the heat thrummed through each of them fortifying their stance.

Fenrir snarled, shifting to his terrible wolf, his body intact.

Rafe raised his fist and pointed at Fenrir. "I command you to return to the ring!"

Falon gasped. Was it possible?

Oh, my God, she mouthed when Fenrir's flanks began to shake like he had a case of the rickets. He dug his front paws into the earth churning it to mud as his body was invisibly pulled toward them.

"Now!" Rafael shouted.

Throwing his head back, Fenrir snarled, his hot breath raging around them, deafening in its roar. The beast's eyes burned like fanned coals, his furious aura flared red and black. The cacophony of his rage singed Falon's hair and skin. His body twisted, resisting the command.

The power of the three stood united as the firestorm raged around them. The heat became unbearable. Falon's skin was burning. She could smell it.

Lucien wrapped his body around hers protectively, while at the same time shielding Rafe with his left arm and shoulder.

And then, the heat was gone.

When the air settled around them, Falon let out a long relived breath. They had survived the wrath of Fenrir.

"What just happened?" she asked.

"I'm going to guess we scared the shit out of that wolf," Lucien said, unwrapping himself from around Falon.

Looking up to Lucien to thank him for protecting her, the words caught in her throat. "Luca, you're burned!" The skin on his back and forearm was raw and bleeding.

Shaking off her concern, Lucien pointed after Fenrir who had run deep into the thick cover of forest.

"We may not have been able to force him back into the ring but we threatened him enough to make him run," Rafe said.

Falon looked at Rafa who was unscathed. "How are you without burns?"

"Lucien's arm, and what he didn't cover, the ring did." Rafe looked at Lucien. "You're burned up pretty bad."

"I'm okay. Let's get out of here."

"We're not going after Fenrir?"

"No. We're too evenly matched." Lucien looked past her to where the wolf had disappeared. "The next time we come face-to-face with him, we'll have the advantage."

"The sword you spoke of?"

"Yes. And we have no time to waste. Let's go."

"Luca," Falon said, reaching out to his raw shoulder. "Allow me to heal you before we go."

He looked past her to his brother. "I'm fine."

Falon smiled softly and said to Rafe, "Rafa, would you give us a few moments alone. Please."

He opened his mouth to deny her, but instead he nodded and started for the bluff they had leapt from.

"Come over here," she said, drawing Lucien carefully by the hand to an undisturbed patch of earth along the timberline.

He eyed her warily.

"Why are you looking at me like that?" she asked.

Blinking like an owl, Lucien just stared at her.

"Lucien, what are you thinking?"

"That you're going to run back to Rafe."

Her heart pounded for this proud man. She touched his chin. "I love you."

"But you will return to him."

"I don't want to have this conversation right now, Luca. When you are stronger."

"I'm stronger now. Tell me."

She looked past his shoulder to see Rafael standing on the bluff, almost one hundred yards from where they stood. His intense gaze locked and held hers.

"I have some things to sort out, but, please, Lucien, believe me when I say I want to be with you. Just give me some space right now."

"You carry my child. I will not let you go."

She looked into his flaring golden eyes. "If I wasn't?"

"I still wouldn't."

She smiled. "Good."

He let out a long breath, and winced as she raised his arm. "These are bad, Lucien."

"I've lived through worse."

"I'm sure you have, but with burns, infection is what will do you in."

Facing him, she gently placed her hands on his forearms. Soothing warmth immediately radiated from her to his skin. He hissed. "I'm sorry, but the pain will ease soon."

She healed him inch by inch with her hands. His more severe wounds she gently licked. His body steeled beneath her lips.

Relax, Luca.

I can't.

"Yes you can."

He slid his arm around her waist and pulled her hard against him. "How can I relax when all I want is you in my arms and my brother hovers over us like a vulture over roadkill?"

Falon smiled softly and ran her fingertip along his bottom lip. He caught her finger in his mouth and sucked. Hard.

Oh, Lucien, how you tempt me.

His arm tightened around her waist until she was smashed against his chest.

"Tell Rafe to take a hike," he said against her lips.

Her blood warmed despite Rafael's audience. Maybe more because of it? Tipping her head back, Falon licked her dry lips. It was all the invitation Lucien needed. His lips crashed against hers in a breath-stealing kiss.

Oh, she wanted to move into him, taste him, touch him, be filled by him. But she could not do this, not now. Not here.

She pushed off his chest. "Luca, no, not here, not now."

His arms circled her waist. "Yes, now."

His eyes blazed possessively. She felt herself waver, but—

He growled low, pressing his forehead to hers. "You make me crazy, angel face."

Smiling softly she pressed her lips to the side of his neck where the skin was still raw from the fire. He hissed in another breath when she lightly laved it with her tongue. Feeling his swelling erection against her belly, she did her best to ignore it.

"Angel face," he breathed. "I need you."

She moved around to his back and admired her healing handiwork. His skin was almost as good as new. There was just one more spot, on the edge of his hip. Dropping to her knees, she gently grasped his thighs, and slowly licked the spot. Carnal fire flared in both their blood.

"Jesus," he moaned.

Her body was not immune to the call of his. Whenever she touched Lucien, especially as intimately as she did now, her muscles loosened and that wondrous spark of desire flashed inside her. But she resisted it. She had to. Because before there was going to be any lovemaking there had to be an understanding, and as she saw it, the survival of the nation required that the three of them remain inseparable. Their combined powers were formidable. Separated, even with two of them united, they would be defeated.

She'd made up her mind the night the three of them were in the pond. Come hell, high water, or Armageddon, she was going to have both of these stubborn alphas as hers and there wasn't going to be a damn thing they could do about it. Because she was prepared to play hardball to make them see things the way she saw them. That included seducing them singularly and together, until they understood what she had long known to be true: they were meant to be together as three, and three together they would be.

Convincing two proud brothers of that was going to be more of a battle than the one coming less than six weeks from now. She smiled as she licked one last time across Lucien's sensitive hip. She might lose a few battles but she would win the war, and to her the victor would go the spoils.

She nipped Lucien's hip and as she stood, gave him a hearty slap on the ass. "Let's go, Mondragon."

Shaking his head, Lucien looked at her with shock, but underlying that was the heat of his desire.

Seven

AS THEY APPROACHED a scowling Rafe, Falon curbed her impulse to run to him. For her plan to work, he would have to come to her. She could not tell him he could not live without her even as a threesome, he needed to come to that realization himself.

"Since we are so powerful as a trio, we must stay together," she announced. "I'm safer against Fenrir with the two of you than just one of you." She bit back a smile as she looked at the two scowling alphas. "Do you agree?"

"It will take the three of us to raise the Cross of Caus. So until then, we'll have to make the most of it," Rafe said, none too happy that his brother would be tagging along.

"Lucien?" Falon asked, looking up at him expectantly.

His fierce gaze told her his position if his words had not. "I'm not leaving your side."

She smiled. "Good, then it's agreed." Their scowls deepened.

"Oh," she added nonchalantly. "I want both of you to give me your word that no matter what, while we're together, there will be no fighting between you as you are now or as wolves."

"I can't promise that!" Lucien said.

"You ask too much, Falon," Rafe agreed.

She put her hands on her hips and threw a hardball. "Then I go it alone."

"The hell you will!" Lucien snarled, stepping toward her.

As exhausted as she suddenly felt, Falon raised her hands, pushing him away from her.

"Do not push me away," he whispered, his voice deadly.

Apprehension skittered through her. How far could she push without having it blow up in her face?

When Rafe made a move toward her, her resolve galvanized. The only way to get what she wanted was to stay her course. Falon raised her hands again. "Don't, Rafa. I'm not in the mood to deal with either one of your egos. Agree, or I go it alone."

They stood side by side, her two alphas. One her dark and decadent lover, the other her bright shining knight. Oh, how she loved them both. Falon fought back a smile. They were like two petulant boys at the moment, both wanting the same toy and refusing to share. But share they would.

She quirked an eyebrow.

"I will agree not to disable Rafael," Lucien said grudgingly.

Rafe looked at his brother and scoffed. "As if you could."

"I can and I have."

Rafe shook his head and looked hard at Falon. "I agree not to disable Lucien."

Her smile escaped. For now it would do.

Rafael's aqua-colored eyes flared. "I know what you're thinking, Falon. It will never happen."

"Never say never, Rafa."

He scowled and mouthed the word, *Never.*

Lucien gathered up their swords, and put them in the leather scabbards, then slid them across his shoulders. "Let's shift and head south. We need to hunt and find a place to regroup and borrow some clothes and provisions."

The sudden exhaustion that had settled in moments ago overcame Falon. She was so emotionally depleted; she could barely form another coherent thought. "I don't want to hunt," she mumbled, her legs shaking. "I just want to sleep for a week."

"We don't have a week."

Rafe looked at Falon. "Can you run?"

"I think so, but can we find something close?"

He nodded. "I'll find something."

As they shifted and ran south, Fenrir's mournful howl filled the air behind them. The hackles on the back of Falon's neck rose, and for one brief moment she stumbled, feeling a pang of pity for the wolf no pack would accept. But the reality of what he'd propagated over the last eight hundred years, drowned out every emotion except vengeance.

For hours they ran. Putting hundreds of miles between them and Fenrir. But finally, time and stress caught up with Falon. She dropped, unable to take another step. She had not eaten or drank since they left Vulkasin days ago. Rafael and Lucien moved toward her at the same time. Her eyelids felt like concrete.

"Please, don't fight over me. You promised . . ."

Rafael swooped her up into his strong arms. Immediately Falon's anxiety left her. She melted into the safe protective cocoon of his body. It was like coming home.

I've missed you so, she whispered, then fell asleep in his arms.

*   *   *

FALON WOKE TO the savory scent of roasting meat in a big soft warm bed. Stretching, she winced as her tight muscles bunched into knots before finally loosening. The cut on her back was tender. She would ask Lucien or Rafe to tend it—or not. It would set off a jealous jag of posturing and snarls. Geez—would they ever just get along?

But how could they, she asked herself. She was asking for two dominant males, each who had marked her and who she in turn had marked, to be cordial to each other when they both wanted to be the one she turned to for all of her needs.

She was being selfish. Even if there were no power of three, she wanted Lucien and Rafael for herself because *she* wanted them both. Swallowing hard as she thought of her father and the repercussions of it, she laid back against the headboard.

Dear God, if they knew about her parentage they would not only never be hers, but they would despise her for eternity if they didn't kill her first. It was not fair! She had no control over who created her. Why should she pay for their sins? As angry as she was over her parentage, guilt rode her harder. Rafa and Luca deserved the truth, but no matter how terrible the truth was, she could never reveal it. She deserved to live, but more than her life, she would not risk her child's life. And she could not bear to see the pain, hatred, and disgust in either one of their eyes when she told them.

She had no choice but to keep her secret. That resignation eased some of her tension.

Slipping out of bed, Falon got a whiff of herself. Ugh. She needed a bath but her stomach gurgled for food. She found a pale yellow, strappy housedress lying at the foot of the bed. She slipped it on and looked down. The thin linen material was sheer, her nipples clearly outlined. Great. She brought her hair around to the front, and looked down again. Covered. Not that hiding behind her hair and a thin piece of fabric would curb either one of her alpha's sexual appetites. They were insatiable and voracious. She was counting on that hunger to wrangle them to her way of seeing things. A different hunger had her attention at the moment. Her mouth watered as she headed down the hall toward the kitchen sounds and the delicious scent of food.

For long moments, Falon watched the brothers from where she stood at the end of the hallway. Rafael cooking, Lucien setting the table. A half a dozen empty beer bottles sat neatly lined up on the counter. It made for quite a hunky domestic scene. Her blood warmed. Was it remotely possible they could work this crazy idea she had out? Time would tell, but she didn't have a lot of that commodity. By the next full moon, just around the corner they needed to be united in every way possible to prepare for the rising the following month. The thought of all that they could accomplish boggled her mind. But she swallowed hard when she thought of her father. And what it meant to the two men she loved.

If they loved her as much as they professed, would it matter? Could love trump nearly a thousand years of persecution? The death of their parents? Her belly soured and suddenly she was no longer hungry. She would not survive being abandoned by either Lucien or Rafael for something over which she had no control. Nor could she survive being despised by them with every fiber of their being.

It mattered. Their hatred for Thomas Corbet was part of who they were, what they were, and what drove them each day. Falon forced herself to calm her nervous stomach. She needed to focus on how she was going to get herself out of this damn mess. Kill her father of course. And in doing so, destroy all doubt in Lucien's and Rafael's minds that she was a part of him.

Turning her attention back to what gave her pleasure, Falon stared at the brothers. It was good to see them so comfortable with each other. They had an unspoken easiness about them. It was uncanny how much alike they were yet how different—Rafael, controlled, methodical; Lucien, out of control but so passionate about what he did, it made up for his lack of self-control.

Falon smiled as her thoughts shifted to more primal things—like the night in the pond. It had been perfect. Her primordial soul craved it again. It had been the sexiest most amazing moment in her life. Could it be again in their real world? Here, in the huge bed she woke up in? Was it even possible to convince these two proud men that they both belonged to her? She wanted it so badly. She would find a way to make them want it, too.

She caught her breath, and in that instant Rafael and Lucien became aware of her. And the minute they sensed her presence their entire demeanor changed. They bristled possessively, and made straight for her.

She shook her head, raising her hands to stop them.

"Stop, both of you now." They did as she commanded. *Wow, would miracles never cease?* Letting out a long breath, she moved between them and as Lucien who was closest to her pulled out a chair, she sat down at the table.

"I haven't eaten in days. I'm still exhausted. So right now, I'd like to eat in peace, then get a bath and then, maybe talk."

"I cooked some venison," Rafe said.

"That I hunted," Lucien added.

Falon mentally snickered. "You're both amazing." She didn't dare look at either one of them for fear one would get jealous she didn't look at him first. So instead she looked around the spacious great room/kitchen, and asked, "Where are we?"

"A cabin just south of the Washington border," Lucien said.

"What about the owners?"

"When we were scoping out the area, we heard them talking about their plans to head out to Spokane last night," Rafe explained. "For a week. That should be time enough for you to—do what you need to do."

That was one anxiety she didn't have to deal with. Wondering if the owners were going to come home to the wolf version of the *The Three Bears*.

"I think I should be okay in a day or two. I just feel completely depleted."

Rafe served her up a huge plate of rare venison. "This should help."

She devoured it in minutes and when she licked her fork wanting more, she looked up to find both alphas' eyes on her. Lucien's lips quirked at the corner, and Rafael's eyes danced in amusement.

"Excuse me, but I was hungry," she said delicately.

Rafe slid his untouched plate across the table to her. "Have mine, Falon."

Shaking her head, she pushed it back toward him. "You need to eat, too."

"There's an entire deer left, Falon." He slid the plate back under her nose. The delicious scent wafted temptingly up to her. She dug in and ate, this time slower as she savored the seasoned meat.

Rafe and Lucien ate heartily and as she watched them under an appreciative eye, she smiled to herself. There were no vegetables or bread, just meat. Typical guy fare.

"So tell me about this sword," she said in between bites.

"Gilda said—" Lucien started.

"Whoa, slow down, cowboy. Who's Gilda?"

"She's the druid witch that originally gave Fenrir his power," Rafael explained.

"In exchange for twin souls every century," Lucien continued.

"I don't understand, how does she play in to this crazy scenario?" It was getting weirder and more complicated by the minute.

"I was desperate to save you, Falon," Rafael said, his voice cracking. "I would have done anything to that end. When the gods did not answer me, I called upon that maniacal wolf. I knew he could save you, and he did. For that I am eternally grateful but when he materialized, so did Gilda, and she wanted her souls."

"Fenrir was eyeing us," Lucien said. "As payment, but she didn't want just one century's worth of souls, she wanted three centuries worth. Fenrir was having none of that, he zapped her and she was gone."

"Then he restored your life and took off with you. While we were trying to reconcile the shock of it all—" Rafael held up his hand with the Eye on Fenrir. "The ring started to go hot on me again. When I asked myself why, she showed up in the form of a spirit and told me I still held the power. She was pissed Fenrir killed her, and she told us if we go to where the persecution began, which we think is in Wales or close to the Welsh border, we'll find the Cross of Caus, the only sword that can kill Fenrir. If we kill him, cut out his heart and hand it over to her, she'll give us a pass by not taking our souls."

"So all of that to get a witch off your back?"

"Not just any witch, a druid witch with power we cannot fathom. But more than that, by agreeing to her terms, she gave us what we needed most. The means to destroy Fenrir once and for all. He goes, the Slayers lose their magic, and finishing them off will be a cinch."

Falon saw the exchange between brothers as if asking if they should tell her everything. "What else happened?"

"Thomas Corbet is alive," Lucien said.

She gasped, nearly toppling her glass of water. It *was* true!

"He showed up at the dock, Falon. The bastard!" Lucien cursed.

Abruptly throwing his napkin on the table, he stood. "He's as arrogant today as the day he killed my parents. I cannot wait to get my hands on that bastard."

Rafe nodded. "I will not sleep peacefully until his entire bloodline is dead."

If she had been mule-kicked in the chest it would have hurt less. Struggling to remain calm was proving impossible.

Lucien stopped his pacing and pulled out the chair he had been sitting in. Turning it around, he straddled it facing Falon. Taking her cold trembling hands into his big warm ones, he said, "He spoke of raising the dead. Slayers, angel face, like our ghost walkers."

"How will he do that?" she asked, not liking how terrible she felt. She knew she should tell them about her relation to Corbet, but if she did that now, she would lose them both forever. She could not bear it

"I don't know," Lucien answered. "But it made me realize that they are real, not a legend."

Exhaling, Falon squeezed Lucien's reassuring hands, and let go. She rubbed her head, the sudden ache behind her eyes pounding like an anvil in her forehead. "They spoke to me again, when Fenrir was running with me. They said something about spilling the two bloods where Lycan were born."

"That would be the northern battleground," Rafe said.

"Which two bloods?" Lucien asked.

Falon swallowed. Was it her blood specifically? Or would any old Slayer and Lycan blood do?

"I'm not sure."

"Could it be you, Falon? You possess both bloods," Lucien speculated.

The heat blanched from her cheeks.

"Mondragon and Vulkasin," he elaborated.

She nearly passed out with relief. Under no circumstance could she find a way to tell these two men that she loved so desperately that the man who viciously killed their parents was her father. She wanted to deny it to herself. Knowing that Thomas Corbet and her mother had sex and *loved* each other? Dear God, how could Layla lay with him? *Love* him? After what he did? And Corbet? A man like him was not capable of love. Her mother had to hide her from him! He would have kidnapped her or killed her.

"Earth to Falon," Lucien said softly, lightly shaking her.

She blinked and mentally shook herself. "I—was just shocked to hear about Corbet. Oh, my God. What if he goes after my mother again?" The vision that Fenrir cast of her mother, alone, in the woods flared in her memory banks. Did she know that Falon knew? Is that why she was running away again?

And at that moment Falon hoped she never came back. How could she face her mother? How could she even look at herself in the mirror knowing what she knew now?

She exhaled loudly. And, dear Lord, how fair was it not to tell Lucien and Rafe?

Falon started as the front door slowly opened.

Anja.

"I'll get my bath now," Falon said as she slipped from the room grateful for the interruption.

Eight

"YOU COULD HAVE told me you were backtracking, Rafael," Anja complained sourly as she entered the kitchen. Immediately, her crystal-colored eyes scanned the room. Raising her nose, she sniffed. "She's here," she stated unhappily.

"You should be grateful we got her away from Fenrir. Without Falon, we stand no chance of surviving the rising," Rafael chastised.

Anja imperiously waved her hand as if shooing away a fly. "You give her too much credit, Rafael."

"You don't give her enough," Lucien said from behind her.

Anja turned and smiled at him. "Maybe."

Rafe took the leather pack with their belongings from her and tossed it onto the granite countertop. "I want you to return to your pack."

Anja whipped around to face Rafe. "Vulkasin is my pack, and as their alpha's chosen one I go where he goes."

Rafe swiped his hand across his face and looked past her to his brother, who stood staring at something that had captured his interest on the ceiling.

I could use a little help here, Lucien, Rafe said.

Lucien's gaze lazily dropped from the ceiling to his brother. *And make it easier for you to make a case for Falon? No, Brother, you can count me out on that one.*

Anja cannot travel with us!

Why not?

Aside from the fact I don't want her near Falon, she will slow us down.

Lucien nodded. *True.*

"You're talking about me aren't you?" Anja accused.

Rafe nodded, and explained, "Where we're going, you can't go, Anja. The three of us can travel much faster if we don't have to continually wait for you."

"Oh, bullshit, Rafe!" she exclaimed. "It has nothing to do with me and everything to do with *her*! You two want that selfish bitch just like you had her in the pond!"

When Rafael neither claimed nor denied her accusation, she insisted, "I saw it, Rafe! I saw how you and your brother made love to her at the same time! And, Rafael, I watched you watch your brother and her after."

Rafe ignored Anja and looked at Lucien. He'd had guilt about it then, but he didn't now. Not when he knew Falon had been and still was rightfully his. His brother's eyes sparked furiously.

"Lucien, I—"

"Shut up, Rafael. Shut up before I break my promise to Falon, and mop this floor with you."

Lucien stalked out of the house, slamming the door behind him.

Rafe turned back to Anja. He was done arguing with her. "There's plenty of food—eat, then I want you to meet up with your pack and go north with them."

Anja moved into him. Her essence was strong; she was fertile and if he took her now, his seed would bear fruit. "Please, Rafael, give me a chance. I'm strong. My line is strong." She grabbed his hand and pressed it to her belly. "My time is ripe. Make love to me, and tonight our dynasty will begin."

She was warm. Beautiful, and worthy of any alpha, but he didn't want her. He wanted the woman down the hall, his first love, his only love. His true mate.

"I'm sorry, Anja," he said, pulling his hand from hers. "I didn't mean for you to get caught up in my blood feud. I didn't mean for you to get hurt, but even if I could change the truth I wouldn't. I want Falon. I've always wanted Falon. I will always want her and only her." He stepped away. "I was just in killing Lucien's chosen one all those years ago, and so justified, Falon remains my rightful mate."

"*What about me?* I'm just supposed to say, 'Hey, no big deal, the council made a mistake,' and even though my world has been turned upside down and inside out, I'll just skulk off into the forest and lick my wounds while you fight over her like a bone?"

Frustrated, Rafe clasped his hands behind his head. "What do you want from me, Anja?"

"Your brother."

Stunned Rafe looked at her like she was mad.

"I come from a great line, Rafael. I deserve a great alpha. If I cannot have you because you insist on honoring your first mark on Falon, then I will take your brother."

Rafe shook his head unable to help himself from smiling at such a ridiculous request. Lucien would never accept Anja, though it would certainly solve Rafe's problem. But Lucien and Anja? He threw his head back and laughed.

She slapped him. "How dare you!"

Rafe grabbed her hand and pushed her away. "Lucien will not take another mate if he cannot have Falon."

His words sobered him. Lucien would howl at the moon for the rest of his life if Falon were not by his side. Coldness shimmied through him. Part of Rafe wanted to ease his brother's pain. They had both suffered so much for so long, but to ease Lucien's pain, Rafe would suffer. No, he'd found Falon, he'd marked her and she'd returned the mark. By first bloodrights she was his. He vowed to keep her at all costs. And in that, Rafe would not ease his brother's pain at the expense of giving up Falon.

Suddenly feeling just as weary as Falon, Rafe's shoulders slumped. "Eat, Anja, then go to your pack."

He walked away ignoring her soft sobs, feeling like a colossal dick. When had life become so damned complicated? Shit, when hadn't it been?

Rafael stopped outside the bathroom door at the end of the hall. Falon's magical scent mixed with aromatic soap teased his senses. His blood surged, the urge to lift her all silky wet from the tub and lay her down on the big bed and make love to her overwhelming. Since they rescued her from Fenrir, Lucien had had a private moment with her, but Rafe had not. He wanted it now.

Come in, Rafa.

He grinned and opened the door, quietly shutting it behind him.

He leaned back against the door and beheld the sultry vixen luxuriating in a steamy tub of white velvety bubbles.

"You look like you're enjoying yourself," he said softly.

She splashed bubbles at him and smiled shyly. "I am."

Rafe pushed off the door and strode across the slate floor. Bracing his hands on either side of her on the tile, he leaned down and smiled at her. Mesmerizing blue eyes held his captive.

His heart ached for her. His body hungered for her, and his soul cried out for her.

"Hi," she said, trailing a soapy finger across his bottom lip. Her cheeks blushed pink.

"Hi," he said, afraid he had died and gone to heaven. Maybe he had, and if that was the case, he died a happy man.

Sweeping her hair back from her cheeks, he slid his fingers into the thick softness. "Gods, I've missed you." Cupping the back of her head in his palm, he brought her lips to his. Lightning struck on contact. His body swelled. Overcome with emotion, he slid his arm around her waist and pulled her to him, pressing her full against him until each inch of her imprinted him.

"Oh, Rafa, I've missed you, too," she sighed against his lips.

The urge to cover her with his scent, mark her again as his was overwhelming. He could not believe she was here, in his arms.

"Stop thinking, Rafa," she murmured against his lips. "Just kiss me."

A slave to her touch, he lost himself in her lips. His tongue tasting her uniqueness, his fingers traced the curve of her cheek, her jaw. Down her slender neck to the high swell of her breasts. They plumped beneath his touch. He moaned, longing for more of her. "Falon," he gasped hoarsely. "I have missed your touch." He inhaled deeply. "The scent of your skin. The taste of your lips." He kissed her deeper, savoring the warm wetness of her. "I want you, all of you, here, now."

"I want what you want, Rafa."

"I want you as mine." Rafe looked into Falon's glowing sapphire eyes. They reflected the deep love he felt. "You belong to me."

Her eyes darkened, narrowing imperceptibly. "Not when you belong to Anja."

Alarm bells went off in his head.

He stiffened. "But you expect me to share you with my brother?"

Her body stilled beneath his. Her eyes focused, and a sad smile tugged at her lips. "It is the only way."

Shaking his head, Rafe settled her gently back into the tub and moved from her. His body and heart screamed for him to take her back into his arms, but his head prevailed. "I must share but you will not share me with Anja?"

Falon sat up, the water sloshing over the edge of the tub, and pulled her knees to her chest. "The difference is twofold, Rafa: You don't love, Anja, you love me. I love you *and* I love Lucien."

"By Blood Law, you belong to me, Falon," he said in a measured tone. "Everything that came after we exchanged marks is irrelevant. The break was forced upon us both because of a lie."

"It doesn't matter."

"How can you say it doesn't matter when it matters very much to me?"

"That was then, this is now. I cannot change how I feel."

"But you expect me to?"

She inhaled deeply. Something had changed. He detected a hardness about her that had never been there before. Had Lucien turned her or—his blood ground to a halt in his veins. Had Fenrir infected her somehow?

"Do you love me?" she softly asked.

"With every fiber of my being."

A smile flickered along her lips. "As I love you, Rafa."

"How can you love me with every fiber of your being when you love my brother, too?"

"I can't explain any of it, but please, never doubt my love for you."

"You make it hard not to when you so easily gave yourself to Lucien."

She stiffened. "Lucien was forced on me, Rafael. As I was forced on him! It was an impossible situation. I had no choice but to try.

And when I did—" Her eyes misted with tears. "I discovered a tormented man who had horded his love as miserly as you had. A man who despite your mark, took me into his pack and gave me what you had given me. A family."

She shook her head. "I don't expect you to understand. How can I, when I don't understand it myself. When I had no choice but to go with Lucien, I did. When I had no choice but to exchange marks with him I did. When I had no choice but to watch you take Anja by the hand to *our* room and mark her in the bed we made love in, I took it. Because, I had *no* choice! I did what I had to do. Because I loved you and because I love Lucien." She swiped tears from her eyes. "Now, I have a choice, and my choice is both of you."

"I have a choice, too, Falon, and I choose to have you for myself. The Blood Law will uphold that choice."

"And if I don't?"

He smiled thinly. "You will have no choice in the matter."

"You have said you would do anything for me. I'm asking you to allow me to love you and Lucien, in heart, body and soul. For me. For us. For the nation."

"The nation has nothing to do with this!"

"There is untold power in the three of us! You have felt it. You can't deny it."

"That doesn't mean I give my consent to let you fuck my brother when you are mine!"

She stood in the tub and reached out, touching his cheek. He flinched at the way his body instantly reacted to her sexy touch. Her sultry image evoked provocative thoughts. His head told him to pull away, his body craved more. "Rafa, do you remember that night, in the pond?"

"It was an illusion, a figment of our imaginations."

"Oh, no it wasn't. It was as real as the both of us standing here, and even if it were a physical illusion, the emotions were very real. You took me while Lucien held me. It was—amazing. It was unlike anything I have ever experienced. Unlike anything you or Lucien has experienced. There was nothing wrong with what happened. Everything about it was right. We are meant to be together. The power of three."

"I am an alpha, Falon! Alphas do not share."

"Alphas do what is best for the pack."

"How do you think my pack will look at me, their alpha, who shares his woman?" He jammed his fingers through his hair. "Weak. Pussy whipped, willing to take sloppy seconds."

She slapped him.

"Don't speak to me like that! I had no choice! And you! You—you walked away from me!" Tears flooded her eyes. "How do you think I felt when you wouldn't speak to me? I begged you to answer but you didn't." She dropped her head. "I did what I had to do, for myself, for you." She looked up at him with a tear-streaked face. "And for Lucien. He needed me, Rafa. And I needed him. We had no one but each other."

He grabbed her hand and kept it pressed to his cheek. "How do you think Lucien's pack will look at him? What you're asking is worse than asking us to cut off our balls."

He inhaled deeply and slowly lowered her hand, then released her. "You're killing me, Falon. I can accept that you love Lucien." He laughed sharply. "For the love of Singarti, I can even understand it. He has that way about him, he always has. Despite our blood feud, I never stopped loving him. But I will not share you with him."

"If he were willing, would you be?"

"No," he growled.

"You did once when no one was looking."

"It was a dream. Nothing more."

She grabbed his hands and brought them to her lips. "It was more than a dream! It happened. Make the dream a reality, Rafa. *Please.* We'll find a way to work it out. I promise."

The fight went out of him then. Not that he changed his mind but because he could not, despite her crazy request, stay angry with her. He loved her. Gods help him, but he loved her and, because he did, he would do almost anything for her, except—

"Pride has destroyed so much and wasted countless years and lives. There is no shame in loving me as your brother does."

"There is more than my pride involved."

"The packs would reunite."

"And what then? I step aside as alpha? Would it not be enough Lucien had you but now the pack?"

"The two of you co-alphaed before."

"We were sixteen and stupid."

"Now you're older and wiser." She looped her sultry arms around his neck. He stiffened not wanting to answer her siren's call. "The more I think about it, the more I realize the benefits of the three of us together aren't just mine." She stood up on her toes and pressed her lips to his. "The pack will benefit by us uniting on every level. The show of our love and power will instill hope and confidence in the entire nation. We know what we're up against now, and we will need everything we have. The power of the three will only strengthen the packs. Not weaken them as you think."

"It doesn't work that way."

"It will, if you *work* it, that way."

Rafe didn't want to talk about it anymore. The thought of watching Lucien take Falon from his bed to Lucien's made his stomach churn. He saw himself laying on the cold rumpled sheets that still smelled of her and their lovemaking, as he imagined Lucien's hands on her. He shook the image off. He had watched once, in the pond, when he went to Falon, and it had been—fuck! He would not consider it!

Falon smiled to herself, even as worry tugged at her heart. Her deadly secret cast a shadow over everything she did, everything she desired—over her entire future. If Rafael or Lucien discovered her parentage, they would—kill her.

"Rafa," she breathed, "promise me, no matter what, you will never stop loving me."

"I will always love you."

"Promise me you will never hurt me."

He pulled away from her. The tears in her voice were reflected in her misty eyes. "I would never raise a hand against you."

She swallowed hard.

"What is it?" He smoothed a damp tendril from her cheek. "I love you, you can tell me anything."

"I—I have Corbet blood in me now. If I could purge it from my body I would, but—what if it changes me?"

"You are too Lycan for the Corbet blood to affect you adversely."

"You don't hate me because of it?"

"It saved your life. How can I hate it?" He smiled and kissed her forehead. "It's not like you're a blood Corbet."

"But—" She wanted to say it, to hear him tell her it didn't matter, that his love transcended his hatred for all Corbets, Thomas in particular. But she couldn't bring herself to do it for fear she would lose Rafe and, in losing him with the truth, Lucien as well.

He cupped her chin in his hand, his loving eyes searching hers for what troubled her.

"But what?"

Exhaling, she closed her eyes and shook her head. Pressing her hand to his, she opened her eyes and smiled. "Nothing, my love. Nothing."

Rafael kissed her nose and left her, shaken and unsure.

Nine

AS FALON EXITED the bathroom she slammed into the hard wall of Lucien's chest. He steadied her. Electricity sparked between them. She swallowed hard and looked up into intense golden eyes. Like Rafe's, Lucien's touch would always stir her.

"Hey," he said softly, lowering his lips to hers.

"Hey," she said, leaning into him. His lips were soft, and oh so gentle. His hands slid up her arms, along her shoulders and up her neck. Tears stung her eyes. She was so torn. She didn't want to hurt either one of these proud men, but she could not choose one over the other.

"Luca," she whispered against his lips, "we need to talk."

"I don't want to talk," he whispered back, and captured her lips again in a soul-stealing kiss. He backed her into the bedroom, kicking the door shut with his heel. Lifting her up into his arms, their lips still connected, he carried her to the big bed and laid her down on it. His big body slid over hers as his kiss deepened.

Falon fought for composure. This could not happen. Not until they were one. Tearing her lips from his, she scooted out from beneath Lucien and up against the headboard. Pulling her knees up to her chest she blinked back tears.

Lucien stared at her, the fear in his gaze nearly doing her in. "Luca," she said, wanting to reach out to him and smooth away the fear. But she didn't. If she touched him, she would succumb to him and she was not going to do that to Rafa.

"I need you to listen to me."

He nodded.

"I love you, with all my heart, I love you." He opened his mouth to speak, but she shushed him with her fingers to his lips. "I love Rafa, too. I can't give you up to be with him any more than I can give him up to be with you."

Lucien's eyes narrowed.

"I want you both."

Moving her fingers from his lips he softly but firmly said, "You cannot have us both."

"Why can't I?"

He moved to the edge of the bed and shook his head, then dropped it in his hands and rubbed his eyes with the heels of his palms. Oh how she wanted to run her hands down his muscled back and soothe away his pain. "Because, I will not share the woman I love with another man, not even my brother. Because I am alpha and alphas do not share." He turned and looked at her over his shoulder. "Because I am selfish, and possessive, and territorial. It would kill me to know when you left my bed you were going to his."

Falon nodded as she tried to understand. All she had to do was put herself in either one of their places. Could she share Rafa with Anja? No. Or share Lucien with Mara if she were alive and not a Slayer? No again.

At that moment, it washed through her with crystal clarity that what she was asking of these two proud men was pure selfishness on her part. And cowardice. She didn't want to make a choice and be the one to hurt the other. Not that she *could* make a choice.

"Rafe has Anja, let him keep her."

Falon smiled. "It's not that easy, Luca. By the Blood Law that gave me to you, it gives me back to Rafael. He will insist, and I will rejoice, but I will be incomplete without you."

Lucien stared at her for long moments. This Lucien she had not seen before. Quiet, contemplative. Not when it had to do with her and the possibility of losing her.

"If you would hurt neither of our feelings with your choice, Falon, who would you pick?"

It wasn't a question she could answer. When she had no choice, she accepted her life with Lucien. Fell in love with him. He made her feel things Rafe didn't, but oh how she loved Rafael. He was every girl's dream. *Her* dream. Her first love.

Ah, but Lucien . . .

"If I picked you, my heart would be half empty. If I picked Rafa, my soul would bleed. Each of you completes me in your own way. I love you, Lucien. Madly. Soul deep. I love Rafael with all my heart, too."

Lucien stood, and she felt as if the air in the room was about to evaporate. "You're going to have to decide which one it will hurt less to live without. Your heart or your soul."

He walked out of the room, and quietly shut the door behind him.

Falon sank into the thick comforter and cried like a little girl who was lost at the mall. Afraid. Lonely. And heartbroken she would never see the two people she loved the most again.

"RAFE," LUCIEN SAID, striding into the kitchen, "a word with you."

Anja looked up from her plate to Rafael, who put down the sword he was cleaning.

Lucien continued through the great room to the front door. He moved down the long front porch. The thick loamy scents of the forest filled his nostrils. It was places like this where he felt most at home. No urban sounds, no threats, just him at one with nature. Grasping the railing, he stood back and gazed at the lush forest. Subtle animal scents punctuated the forest fragrance. The urge to shift and run was overwhelming. He could run for miles, hours, days but his problems would still be his constant companion.

He felt his brother's presence behind him. "I want to hate you, Rafa. I want to tear you apart, but I won't."

Rafe stepped beside Lucien and took up the same stance. Side by side, they looked into the forest with the same woman on their minds.

Rafael let out a long sigh. "I feel the same."

Lucien looked at his brother's profile. Proud, honorable, Rafael. The golden son. Lucien's stomach churned but his heart was full. "I'm sorry," he said, shocked that the words escaped his lips.

Rafael jerked back and, narrow-eyed, looked at Lucien. "For what?"

Lucien exhaled and looked back at the tempting forest. "For being an ass. For doubting you. For everything."

When Rafe didn't respond, Lucien looked at him to find a smile tugging his lips. "I'm glad you're amused."

"More like shocked."

Lucien shrugged. "No more than me."

Both of them turned back to the forest.

"She wants us both," Lucien said, and when the words came out of his mouth he realized that if that was the only way he could have the woman he loved, pride be damned, he would have her on her terms. The shock of all shocks.

"I know."

"I don't want to share her, not even with you, my brother."

"I feel the same."

Lucien looked at Rafe. "I called you out here to have it out with you, but all I feel is miserable. I don't want to go back sixteen years, Rafe. I don't want to lose Falon. I want to reunite the packs but I don't want to co-alpha any more than you do." He jammed his fingers through his hair and looked at his brother whose face reflected the same misery Lucien felt. "For the first time in my life, I don't know what to do."

"You two are pathetic." Anja sneered as she walked through the open door. "If your packs saw the way you're mooning over that woman they would turn on you faster than a Slayer! Have you no pride? Here you stand crying about who gets the girl when the entire Lycan nation stands on the edge of extinction! Neither of you are worthy to lead an army of ants into battle much less the great Lycan nation." She strode past them down the steps to the slate walkway that led to the driveway. "I'll be sure to tell the packs how you two are up here crawling on your bellies to her!" She shifted and leapt into the forest.

Lucien straightened and faced his brother. "She carries my child, Rafael."

Rafael stared steadily at his brother. "You forget I was there that night, too."

"Are you suggesting that the child is not mine?" Lucien growled.

"We won't know until the babe is born who the—"

The gods would not be so cruel! Or would they . . . ? Something in Lucien snapped. His fingers dug into the wooden railing splintering it. His beast howled furiously, demanding blood. His brother's blood.

Rafael's beast responded and in that split instant they shifted.

You gave me your word, Luca! Falon called.

Lucien snarled, and then leapt over the railing into the thick forest. He ran. For miles he ran trying to clear his head, to make sense of all this bullshit! When had his life become so complicated?

He knew the answer: the day he set eyes on Falon for the first time. Since that day, his world had been knocked so completely off its axis all he could do was hang on by his fingernails. And now what she wanted him to do, and Rafe! It was completely out of his comfort zone. Physically and emotionally. How the fuck did you share the woman you loved with another man?

Who did that?

He ran for miles but his head was no clearer than when he'd leapt from the porch hours before. As he knew it would, his journey brought him back to his destiny: The woman who tore him inside out. The same one he could not live without.

Shifting as he mounted the steps to the deck he breathed hard, his body sweaty, and no more at peace than when he left. Rafael's scent was close. Striding into the great room, Lucien found Rafe sitting in one of the overstuffed chairs by the cold fireplace. They both started when Falon literally glided into the room.

Lucien swallowed hard. Jesus, she was a vision in a transparent white gauzy spaghetti-strap ankle length dress—shit, her long tan legs played peekaboo with each step, the long slits of the skirt flowing like feathers around her. She looked like a beautiful angel. Blood shot straight to his cock, and he didn't care that he was standing naked and sweaty in the center of the room and making no qualms about what he wanted. Rafael growled from his corner and stood.

Barely perceptible, Lucien heard Falon's sharp intake of breath as her eyes swept his rigid body, then to Rafael's. Her nostrils flared in hyperawareness.

T e n

BLOOD SURGED THROUGH Falon, warming her bone deep. Lucien was so close she could see the drops of sweat trail haphazardly down his sculpted chest to his flat belly to his . . . She swallowed hard. His cock was thick and rigid, angrily demanding what she so wanted to give him. When she looked across the room to Rafe, she swallowed hard again.

Clad only in a pair of low-slung jeans, his long muscled arms and defined chest was hard with sexual tension. The thick ridge beneath his button fly swelled beneath her gaze. She tried to swallow again but her throat was so dry she couldn't. Slowly she raised her eyes to his and hissed in a sharp breath. The slow burn in Rafael's eyes accentuated by the flare in his nostrils drew her to him as if he were reeling her in. And God help her she wanted him. Right there on the floor, with Lucien . . .

Squeezing her eyes shut, Falon struggled for control. Her body wanted one thing, her heart and soul the same thing but her reason told her it was a futile dream. If she could not have them both, she would have neither, and as hard as that would be, she would not have to live with hurting one of the two men she loved enough to make that sacrifice. "I'm glad you're both here," she stammered, stumbling over her words.

"Falon—" Rafe began, stepping closer to her. His gaze swept her from head to toe, his beautiful aqua eyes pleading for succor she could not give him. Not on his terms.

Shaking her head she put her hand up to stop him. She had something to say and she was going to say it. But when Lucien grabbed her hand and brought it to his lips, then gently bit the fleshy part of her palm, she moaned. Heavy, hooded lids hung over her eyes as desire flared within her. He pulled her into his arms, and not wanting to upset Rafe who growled and strode toward them, Falon hung in Lucien's embrace. His hot sweaty body molded to hers, his thick erection digging into her belly.

"No," she whispered, feeling helpless to stop him. Not wanting to stop him. She wanted him to kiss her and stroke her in front of Rafe. She wanted Rafe to see how she craved Lucien's touch, what he did to her, then perhaps—

"Oh, God," she moaned when Lucien's hand slid down her back and cupped her bottom, pressing her harder into him.

He nipped her chin then looked past her to Rafe. "She wants me, Brother. I want her." He licked her throat, dragging his teeth along her jugular. "Tell him, Falon. Tell him how you crave me," he said roughly against her skin. "Tell him how it is between us. How it will always be."

"Yes," she breathed, unable to deny his words.

As if she were in a drugged state, Falon could not raise a hand to stop him even if she wanted to. Where was her will? Why couldn't she say no? Her heavy lids fluttered as she gazed at Rafael's handsome features hardened in sexual tension. Her heart slammed against her chest. He wanted her with the same insane need with which she wanted them both.

Rafa . . .

"We were meant to be together," Lucien crooned, nipping at her chin. His teeth drew blood, the scent of it stirring all three of them.

"Yes," Falon breathed, closing her eyes, praying that Rafa would see this was their destiny. "The power of three," she moaned.

Desire pounded like thunder through her when she felt Rafa's long strong fingers stroke her back. *Yesss*, this was what she wanted.

"Is this what you want, Falon?" Rafe whispered against her ear. "Me and Lucien fighting over you?"

"No . . ." She exhaled. "No fighting." Was she drugged? She felt heavy, sluggish, as if she were swimming while every inch of her was expectant and sensitive.

His big hands slid down her waist to her thighs. "Oh." That felt so good. When he pressed the thick seam of his fly into her back, Falon moaned and arched. Her nipples dug into Lucien's slick chest and her ass rubbed against Rafael's erection.

That neither one of them pulled her away from the other thrilled her. Was there hope? Her knees shook. If they were not on either side of her she would crumple to the floor. Lucien's arm tightened around her waist as Rafael's teeth sunk into the sensitive place where her neck and shoulder met.

Her lips parted as a deep sigh escaped and Lucien caught them in his. Surrendering to Lucien, Falon pressed her head into the crook of Rafa's neck while Lucien plundered her with his tongue.

Rafael growled, his patience pushed to its limit. Fear skittered along Falon's spine but the excitement of being in both men's arms at the same time overrode her caution. She was so hot for them, she was soaked and shaking.

She was playing with fire, and if she didn't back down now there was going to be a catastrophic explosion. If there were any hope that they would see her way, it would have to be in incremental steps. That they had progressed this far and the brothers were just now on the verge of tearing each other apart was progress.

Falon's fingers snaked into Lucien's wild hair and pulled him harder against her lips as her other hand fisted Rafael's hair.

Tearing her lips from Lucien's was probably one of the hardest things Falon had ever done in her life. Her body was on fire, every molecule flaring with white-hot need. Rafe snarled and grabbed Falon from Lucien's arms. Spinning her around, he shook her. "Is this what you want, Falon? Us fighting over you like dogs?"

"No—I—" Falon tried to shake the lust-induced fog from her head but she couldn't shake it all. "Please, Rafe," she said hoarsely. "Don't be mad at me."

His deep aqua eyes burned like green flames. "You don't make anything easy, Falon."

Though it nearly killed her to do so, somehow, Falon found the strength to maneuver out of Rafael's arms.

Shaking her head, she smoothed down the wrinkled fabric of the dress she had found in the closet. Nervously she stepped backward until her back hit a wall. Like the wolves they were, Lucien and his brother smelled her weakness for them and circled in front of her, waiting for their moment to exploit it. It made her nervous, and afraid of what these two men who she loved and trusted could do to her in the heat of passion when they both wanted her at the same time in the same place.

It would be a bloodbath.

"I don't want either of you," she blurt out.

Her words stopped them cold in their tracks.

Simultaneously their brows drew together and their eyes narrowed.

"You're a lousy liar, Falon," Rafael said.

"I don't want either one of you, if I can't have both of you," she stated, her words bolstering her resolve and at the same time cooling the heat in her body. Smoothing her damp hands down the skirt of the dress, Falon pushed off the wall, her will returning in slow drips. "So I will have neither of you." There, she said it. And she meant it.

She slid her hand down to her belly. "In less than nine months we'll know who fathered this babe, and he will be allowed to raise his child, but it will be the only child I ever bear." She drew in a deep breath and slowly exhaled. The identical shocked looks on their faces would have made a lesser woman laugh at the absurdity of these two mighty alphas left speechless. "Until then, we will travel together to find the sword. Because we are stronger together than separate, we must stay together through the rising." She smiled wanly, feeling no victory. "As long as we are together, Fenrir cannot harm us."

Falon inhaled again and exhaled. "I'm sorry for asking such a thing from either of you. It was selfish of me to even consider it." Intending to shift, she slid the dress from her shoulders and let it drop to the floor.

The heat in the room rose exponentially.

"Falon," Lucien said roughly, reaching out to her, "I cannot live without you."

Rafe stepped toward her. "I *will* not live without you," he said.

Oh, why did this have to be so hard? Her heart was torn in half, bleeding for these two men she loved above her own life. "Neither of you will have to. I'm here, I'm not going anywhere, I just will not be intimate with either of you." She raised her chin and looked at each of them. "I release you both." As she said the words she never imagined she would say to one of them, much less to both, her heart and soul imploded with the force of a wrecking ball. But there was no other way.

"I do not accept your release!" Lucien growled.

"There is no other way!" she cried angrily. "I know what I have asked of you two is selfish and humiliating to you as alphas. The last thing I want is to degrade you in front of your packs. I don't want you to suffer with jealousy or break your heart each time I lay with the other. Truly, I'm sorry for even asking. But please, understand, I cannot choose between you. And I won't." Moist heat stung her eyes. "Please, don't force me to."

"Falon!" Rafe yelled as she backed away from them. "You cannot do this!"

Tears blinded her vision. "I already have."

She shifted then, and leapt past them through the open door and ran to clear the heat in her blood and the ache in her broken heart.

Emotions stormed within. Frustration, longing, and anger. Why could they not see that the power of three meant unified on every level, heart, body, soul? Was it really so terrible what she asked? It was so clear to her, the rightness of it. With each long stride she took, her anger intensified. She was angry at Rafe and Lucien! Why did they have to be so stubborn and possessive? Her mood darkened. Was sex so important that they couldn't look past their own lust to the greater good of the nation? They loved one another; she could see it in everything they did. Why couldn't they allow her to love them, too?

The darkness in Falon sparked. Then caught fire as her frustration mounted. She was spitting mad. Furious at Rafael and Lucien. They were selfish, arrogant, and mean! How dare they tease her like they just did? Did they enjoy her pain? Did they care how she felt? That was a Lycan for you. No wonder the Slayers were bent on destroying them—she gasped at the turn of her thoughts, but more alarming was her rising bloodlust for revenge.

She growled as she picked up a familiar scent.

Anja.

That silver-haired bitch, she wasn't good enough for Rafa! How dare she even think she was? Falon lifted her nose and howled. Lust for a fight infused her. And she would have her fight.

Unaccustomed to such black rage, especially directed at a Lycan, Falon fought to control it. Its insidiousness terrified her, because while she knew what she was going to do was against the Blood Law, she could not redirect it.

Anja never saw what hit her. Falon caught sight of her and as the she-wolf ran north, Falon leapt over a wide wooded ravine and landed behind the Siberian wolf. She snapped at her hindquarters, severing the main tendon in her right hind leg. Anja howled in pain and turned to fight, but snarled defiantly when she realized her attacker was Falon.

"Jealous are you?" Anja sneered as she shifted to human, and faced Falon head-on. "You're a selfish bitch, Falon. Wanting them both. Mark my words, your selfishness will destroy the brothers and in so doing, destroy the nation."

Falon lowered her head and flattened her ears. Snarling, she moved around Anja, who had the good sense to shift back to wolf. As human, she would die; as wolf—she might survive. If Falon allowed her to. For all of Anja's bravado her quaking flanks and wobbly front legs belied her bravery. She was terrified.

Craving the she-wolf's blood, Falon snarled again, circling her, realizing she was out of control. Not of her Lycan beast but of her vengeful Corbet blood. But she couldn't help it. She wanted blood. Lycan blood. *Anja's* blood. Falon lunged, knocking Anja onto her back. Even when Anja submitted, Falon kept her pinned to the ground. She howled fighting the terrible battle of the two bloods within her, knowing she should accept Anja's surrender but unable to.

Consuming rage and the thirst for blood drove her. She attacked.

Falon, stop! Rafael commanded.

She ignored him. Lucien's big wolf body slammed into hers, knocking her off Anja's mutilated body.

Furious at the interruption, Falon lunged at Lucien. He snarled and sidestepped her attack, but nipped at her flank letting her know he had let her past.

Back down, Falon, Lucien snarled.

She lowered her head and looked to where Rafe had shifted over Anja's now human body. Jealousy tore through her.

Let her die! She is not worthy of an alpha!

Rafael speared Falon with a narrow-eyed glare. The black rage that consumed her tested her heart. Falon lowered her head and attacked Anja again. Lucien jumped in front of her, halting her assault while Rafe carried his chosen one to a safer distance.

Falon turned on Lucien, head low, ears pinned to her head. *I am stronger than you, Lucien, get out of my way.*

You think you are stronger.

You will fight me over her?

I will fight you over you.

Lucien lunged and just as he hit her, he shifted to human. Bear-hugging her, he took Falon to the ground. Shocked by his brazen move, Falon shifted and began her fight in earnest.

They rolled down a steep embankment into a cold mountain stream. Falon gasped, the frigid water shocking her system. Lucien took advantage and grabbed her in another bear hug and pushed her deeper into the water. The swift current carried them downriver.

The shock of the cold water yanked Falon out of her crazed frenzy. As the realization of what she had just done—not only to Lucien but to Anja—hit her, she screamed.

"Oh, my God, Lucien, I'm so sorry, I—"

"Hush, angel face, you're okay," Lucien soothed, holding her shivering body against his steady one.

"Oh, my God, what did I do to Anja?"

"She's alive; Rafe's taking care of her."

Falon began to shake uncontrollably. She had attacked a Lycan. Her own kind for no reason! What happened to cause her to do such an unthinkable act?

Clinging to Lucien like a baby, Lucien gathered her tighter into his arms and walked against the current, toward the bank. His strong stride defied the insistent current. As he emerged from the water, he gently laid her down on the loamy bank. Dropping down beside her, his worried eyes scanned her face for answers. "What the hell just happened?"

Rubbing the heels of her hands into her eyes, Falon shook her head. "I don't know. Something came over me—an uncontrollable rage. I couldn't stop it. When I caught Anja's scent—" She shivered and looked up at Lucien. "I just wanted to tear her apart."

He lay back on an elbow and eyed her carefully. "You just about did."

Falon put her hand across her eyes. Despite the chill of the water, the close proximity of Lucien's body comforted her. He leaned over her, brushing her hair from her face. "You're scaring me, angel face. This isn't like you."

She grabbed his hands and brought them to her chest. "I'm scared, too, Luca. I don't understand what's happening to me." She didn't dare tell him it was Lycan blood she had wanted.

He lowered his lips to hers, and said, "I vowed to always protect you, and that includes from yourself."

Her trembling body stilled beneath his kiss. One kiss, she told herself. It soothed her savage beast, and at least for now, it would not hurt.

Eleven

RAFAEL WATCHED ANJA slowly make her way into the thick foliage of the forest. He had healed her, but she was clearly still vulnerable. Her weakness would be evident when she reached her pack, and then there would be hell to pay . . .

Rage and confusion spiraled through him. Falon had known Anja was no match for her, yet she'd brutally attacked her. Her actions had been furious, ferocious. Violent in nature. Unprovoked and completely out of character.

Not an act of jealousy, as he'd first suspected, but something more. Something akin to unmitigated hate. And despite the severe stress they were all under, he just couldn't reconcile the idea of Falon hating the petulant and arrogant but ultimately harmless Anja. Not when Falon knew she, not Anja, held Rafe's heart in the palm of her hand.

He ran his fingers through his hair. Anja was damn lucky to be alive. As much as he wanted to be rid of her, he did not want her dead. She was an admirable Lycan and would serve an alpha well, just not him.

And if Falon had killed her? Jesus, her sentence would have been instant death! The Blood Law was unforgiving in these matters. He'd have lost her when he'd only just learned of his right to keep her.

Frustrated by what Falon had almost cost them all, Rafe clamped his hands behind his neck and looked up into the towering trees. When he had suggested Anja return to the cabin to regain her strength, she'd defiantly refused. He wasn't a complete prick. But he couldn't blame her, and he knew when he'd made the offer that it was a mistake. Falon might finish the job next time.

As maimed as Anja was, she swore she would inform the packs of what Falon had done to her, and while he'd never allow Falon to face death, she would nonetheless be severely reprimanded. He scoffed at that. Why did he even worry? As if they could force Falon. She had become a force to be reckoned with.

The hair on the back of his neck spiked. In the course of two months she had gone from a confused young woman to a formidable warrior. He'd never seen such natural power. Not from a Slayer or a Lycan. Maybe if you combined them both one could generate that kind of power, but all because a Slayer had bit her? It didn't make sense.

The ring flared on his hand, as if it knew something Rafe did not.

"What is her secret? Who is she really?" he murmured.

Nervous energy flickered along his spine. The moment he'd laid eyes on her he'd known she was special. With each passing day he was discovering just how special she was. A wry smile tugged at his lips. She was a full-time job—more than full-time. Hell, maybe he should just give in and share her with Lucien so they would both get some rest!

And if there was an alpha out there who could rein her in it was Luca. They had always been competitive when it came to women. Neither one of them had to do much more than look at a female and she would drop for either one of them. He grinned. He missed Lucien. Missed their camaraderie, their hijinks and their partying days. There had even been a few wild nights when they had shared a woman or two, but it was easy because they had no feelings other than momentary lust for her. Falon was 180 degrees different.

Even in jest the thought of sharing her rankled him beyond furious. *He* had marked Falon first. She'd returned the mark. She belonged to him. Period. Why should he share something, anything, with the brother that had caused him so much pain?

Argh! He punched the air.

Because he had never denied Luca anything, even when he knew it was not in his best interest. Because Rafe knew he would be there to pick up the pieces. And the one time he wasn't, Lucien brought a damn Slayer home! It was the price he paid for indulging his brother. The indulgence born of the guilt he felt for not doing something, anything to save their parents. Lucien had taken their deaths harder than anyone. Even, Rafe admitted, harder than he. And he had been devastated.

Was it any wonder he fathered and mothered his brother? Indulged him so that his pain was lessened? But then Rafe struck a disastrous blow, killing Luca's chosen one. It hit Rafe at that moment that it didn't matter that she was a Slayer. She was Lucien's. He loved her and Rafe took it away. The one person Luca trusted above all others, the one person he could always count on, killed his mate.

Self-loathing washed through him. He hated himself more at that moment than at any time in his life. He'd fucked up. Big-time. And now he had a choice to make. Break his brother's heart all over again, break Falon's in the process or find a way to make this fucking insane situation work.

Fuck!

Rafe lifted his nose and picked up Falon's and Lucien's scents.

His heart kicked against his rib cage when he thought of Falon and his stomach felt like a thousand swords hacked at it when he thought of her with Lucien. Due to the extreme circumstances in which they were thrown together, he knew her feelings for his brother were more than just a passing fancy. She loved Lucien, just as much as she loved Rafe. Hard to believe after the prick Lucien had been to her when she was Rafe's. But who could resist Luca? His brother was hard to resist on a normal day, impossible when he wanted something. And he'd wanted Falon more than anything in his life, except to save their parents. She hadn't stood a chance. Rafe knew exactly what would happen between them the minute the council announced their verdict. It was why he had reacted so violently.

The only good thing about the woman he loved falling in love with his brother and his brother loving her the same? Lucien had grown up. Falon had forced him to deal with his demons and move on from them. Much as she had Rafe.

He shoved his fingers through his hair. Decision time. He could force Falon, despite her attempt to release him from their marks, to accept him as her only mate but he would lose part of her if he did. Just as Lucien would if he forced Falon to choose him. And if either he or Lucien forced a choice? They would each lose a brother again. This time for eternity.

Fuck! He would not share her!

Would he?

Rafe shifted and followed the scents downstream. As he came to the edge of a narrow bluff he looked down to see Falon and Lucien lying naked on the bank, their limbs entwined, their lips locked. Falon's essence was strong. It permeated the forest, its seductive snare luring him down the steep incline. Rafe growled at her ardor for his brother. And yet, despite his anger, his blood warmed at the erotic sight of Falon writhing sensually beneath Lucien.

He shifted and moved closer.

Gods, she was sexy as hell. He could smell the warmth of her skin. Feel its sultry smoothness against his. The soft way it glided across him.

He wanted that. To cover her with his body. Take her into his arms. Feel her firm breasts scrape across his chest, and then feel the warm rush of her breath as she moaned in pleasure when she surrendered to him. Oh, yes, he wanted all of that and more. He would have it. On his terms.

Rafael stepped closer, preparing to take what was his, but then he stopped.

Even from the distance he was aware of Falon's bright blue eyes riveted on him. She bit her bottom lip as a long raspy moan slid from her throat.

Come with us, Rafa . . . her siren's call enticed.

He licked his dry lips and took a step closer.

Her knees rose as her long slender legs locked around Lucien's hips. Rafe's erection throbbed painfully against his hip.

He maneuvered farther down the steep embankment so that he was downwind of them. Falon's low moans of pleasure excited him, pulled him closer. As he approached the love-locked couple, his body tightened. The urge to tear his brother apart hovered in the shadows, taking second seat to his hunger for Falon. It drove him closer. So close that he stood just behind them.

She opened her eyes, and this time smiled a slow seductive smile that tugged at him balls deep. His cock thickened painfully. He didn't see Lucien; he saw only erotic pleasure on Falon's lips, in her eyes, in the deep sigh of her breath.

Her chest gleamed with a thin sheen of sweat.

Rafa, she moaned as she offered herself to Lucien.

Falon, Lucien growled, sliding into her.

Her back arched as her breath escaped her lungs.

Rafe wrapped his hand around his cock and with each thrust of Lucien's hips into Falon, he stroked himself. He held her sultry gaze as she accepted his brother. In perfect synchronization, Rafe stroked himself to Lucien's tempo, never once taking his eyes off Falon's.

When she bit her bottom lip this time, he knew she was going to come. And when she did, so did Rafe, and he was quickly followed by Lucien. Rafe's rough groans overrode Falon's primeval cries and Lucien's triumphant howl.

In a wild cacophony of primal cries, the three of them climaxed together. And with it, scissions of energy crackled around them. Jagged flashes of green, blue, and gold popped and snapped, first as singular streaks, then entwined with veracity and speed connecting the three of them. Falon's body thrummed with highly charged energy infusing both Rafe and Lucien with it.

Rafe did not resist the pull; he welcomed the power of the connection. Lucien stared in awe. Falon's eyes widened as she reached out to Rafe. He took her hand, the ring on his finger flared at the contact.

Power surged painfully between them. Hot air whooshed wildly around them, stoking the heat to unbearable. The velocity of the power shot through Rafe with the force of a tsunami. Unable to move, only to stare, he knew Falon and Lucien were experiencing the same thing. Just when it seemed as if he could not take the brunt of the force any longer, a nasty black lightning bolt struck Falon in the chest, separating them.

Their connection broken, Falon screamed in pain and—

"No!" Falon screamed, standing up and shaking her fists at the forest. "I will not succumb to your darkness!"

"Falon," Rafe said, pressing his hand to the raw mark between her breasts where the energy struck.

She grasped his hand, pressing it harder against her flesh. Her body steamed as his healing warmth infused her.

"What the hell just happened?" Lucien demanded.

Despite the traumatic events that had just passed, Falon stood tall and calm, smiling knowingly, as her dark blue eyes snapped with energy. "The power of three."

"What was that that separated us?" Lucien asked.

"Corbet magic."

"Corbet magic? How?" Rafe asked, not liking the sound of that at all. How could that happen when there wasn't a Corbet for miles?

"I don't know—I just know what it was," Falon said, stumbling over her words.

"Corbet knows what will happen if the three of us—unite," Lucien said seriously. "I guess that's his way of saying no fucking way."

But Rafe caught the twinkle in his brother's eyes. He knew exacly what generated it. *Son of a bitch.* Were they going to talk about what just happened before the disturbance? Rafe swiped his hand across his face. What *did* just happen? Damn it, he didn't want to dissect it and analyze it. It happened. Period.

"Let's just get the hell out of here," Rafe said, feeling uncomfortable for a lot of reasons.

As they turned back toward the cabin, Falon took Rafael's hand. His body immediately reacted. Heat, energy and I-want-to-fuck pheromones clashed.

He swallowed hard when he looked down into her bright eyes.

"Thank you," she said softly.

He scowled. *Thank you for not ripping his brother out of her?*

Rafael looked ahead to Lucien, who looked over his shoulder and graced Rafe with a shit-eating grin. *Bastard.* Rafe wanted to be pissed, he wanted to kick his brother's ass, but he didn't. Because what happened between the three of them just now, changed everything. Rafe wasn't exactly sure how, but they were beyond chest-beating pissing contests now.

The issue with Falon aside, Rafe had sixteen years to make up for and as he stood there looking at his brother, love swelled for him. He had missed Lucien. He was never going down that road again.

"For what?" he asked, knowing what she implied. Somehow, if he didn't actually talk about it, he wouldn't have to accept it.

"Trying."

He shook his head and brought her in under his shoulder as they continued to walk. "If anyone would have told me I would stand by while my brother fu—made love to you, and that I would get excited by it, I would have burned them alive for talking such trash." He looked down at her and smiled. His breath caught in his chest when she smiled happily up at him. "Just don't push it."

"Oh, I won't." She nipped his chest. "Unless I have to."

Rafe shook his head. "Why did you go after Anja like that?"

She stiffened but kept her pace.

Lucien slowed so that he fell in step with them. "You nearly killed her, angel face. Not cool."

The color drained from her cheeks. "I— Something dark and terrible came over me. I think it's the Corbet blood."

Rafe looked over Falon's head to Lucien, who looked as concerned as he felt.

"Maybe you need an infusion of our blood?"

Her body shivered again. "I don't think that's going to help."

"You were out of control, Falon. I didn't want to hurt you," Lucien said. "But you can't go around attacking your own people."

"I know that. It's just— Is Anja okay?"

"Yes, and on her way back to the packs," Rafe answered.

"She'll inform the council," Falon predicted.

"We'll deal with that after the rising. Right now we have to get out of here. We have a plane to catch."

Shockingly, for the first time in his life, Rafe didn't give a rat's ass what the council had to say on the matter. Everything had changed the night Falon stumbled bloody and bruised into his life. The game had changed and the rules were different. Who knew what tomorrow would bring? It was about surviving in the minute and to survive there could be no rules.

Twelve

FALON WOKE TO the pilot's voice announcing they would be landing in thirty minutes. She had fallen asleep with her head on Rafael's shoulder and her feet in Lucien's lap. She had never felt more safe or loved.

She had taken a huge chance back at the stream. Though she had made a vow that until they agreed to be as one with her, she would withhold herself from them both, that went out the window when Lucien had kissed her and she'd sensed Rafael nearby. She'd hoped at the very least he would watch and not become enraged but become aroused. And it had worked. Not only had Rafael become aroused he had joined in, and just as amazing was the energy they'd created as they climaxed together. It had been off-the-charts incredible. She still got breathless thinking about it.

But then Corbet had ruined it. And it had been Thomas, she was certain! How had he snuck up on them without them detecting his scent? Or was his magic so powerful he sensed what was happening and sent his magic from wherever he was? How terrifying if that was the case. It meant he could see and hear her. It meant he could disrupt her when she least expected it. It meant—

How dare he intrude on such an intimate moment! Oh, she couldn't wait to sink her teeth into that monster! The need to kill him flared hot. With his death she was certain the darkness in her would die, too.

"Hey," Rafe said, kissing the top of her head. "Relax, baby. We've got nothing but clear skies ahead."

She looked up into Rafael's sea green eyes and lost herself. His lips lowered to hers. Her body's natural response was to arch into him as her arms snaked around his neck. When their lips met, warmth swept through her. "Oh, Rafa," she whispered, molding herself into him. "I love you."

Lucien's fingers tightened around her feet.

I love you, too, Luca.

She smiled against Rafa's lips. Juggling these two alphas' egos was going to be a full-time job.

"Do I amuse you?" Rafa seriously asked against her lips.

Her smile widened and she giggled. "No," she said. He tickled her. She squealed and tried to move away from him, but Rafa was relentless.

"You think it's funny the way my brother and I growl at each other over you?"

"No!" she gasped when he tickled her again. "Rafa!" she cried and pounced on him, grasping his face and kissing him. His strong arms wrapped around her waist, pulling her onto his lap.

His erection poked her in the butt. But when he tickled her again, she squealed erupting into a fit of giggles and melted against him.

"Seat belts, children," Lucien said sourly.

Falon stuck her tongue out at him but did as he requested.

Fifty minutes later they had their luggage, which included their swords, clothing, and electronics. They rented a small van and headed west.

"I trust you two have a plan?" Falon asked as she enjoyed the landscape.

"We're headed to Westbury where we think Peter Corbet is buried. I'm going to guess he was buried with his sword."

"We're going to dig up a dead person?" she asked surprised.

Lucien glanced up at her from his iPad. "Really, Falon? You almost killed Rafe's chosen one twelve hours ago and you're worried about digging up the bastard that started it all?"

"It's—it just seems sacrilegious."

"The entire Corbet bloodline can go to hell as far as I'm concerned."

Falon swallowed hard and nodded. She was a Corbet, would he want her to go to hell, too?

The waxing moon showed them the way. She was sorry it grew dark. The English countryside was beautiful. But the closer they got to Westbury, the more uneasy Falon became. With each mile they drove west the stronger a new and foreboding scent became. She was plagued with the same feelings she'd had the morning Fenrir was released.

"I don't like this," she cautioned.

Lucien turned to face her. "What do you mean?"

"I can smell them everywhere."

"Who?"

"Corbets. And they know we're coming."

"I don't smell Slayers," Rafe said from the driver's seat.

"These aren't Slayers, they're witches."

Fuck.

It was the eve of the full moon. And as they rolled into what Falon would have guessed was normally a sleepy English village, now it was alight with torches, bonfires in the streets and—

"Oh, my God! Are those fresh wolf heads hanging on the village gates?"

It was as if they had gone back eight hundred years. The village people that mulled the cobblestone streets were dressed in medieval garb. Dark magic swirled eerily around them and punctuating each shopfront and building were bloody pentagrams.

"Wolves have been extinct here for hundreds of years. Where did those fresh kills come from?" Falon asked. While she was not technically a wolf, her heart went out to the animals that were slain simply because they represented an age-old hate.

"Could be something as simple as a spell or they could have been brought in to hunt," Rafe answered.

"Looks like some kind of Pagan gathering," Lucien whistled.

"Wiccan," Rafe said. "It's a damn witchfest."

As the van slowed to accommodate the throng of people in the streets, one by one they stopped and turned to stare. Pale faced and sullen, scores of intense eyes glared at them. Some from their sickly sweet scent she knew were Corbets, others smelled of sage and hemlock, a witch's scent.

"We're outted," Lucien hissed. As he said the words, the crowd began to chant.

Falon grasped Rafe's right hand in her left and Lucien's left hand in her right. Their combined auras flared red, blue, and gold, infusing the inside of the van with spectacular color.

The demonic chanting escalated.

Slowly the crowds backed away as Rafe kept his steady speed, refusing to back down.

"The Abby is three kilometers north of the village," Lucien said, looking at his iPad.

"Are you sure that's where he's buried?" Falon asked. Was it public knowledge?

"I'm not positive but there are some of his relatives buried there."

As they exited the witch-infested village, Falon's worry eased. Until they came upon the Chapel of Alberbury, or what was left of it.

"It's nothing but ruins," Falon said, disappointed, getting out of the van.

Malevolent scents assailed her as she walked toward the ruins. The howls of hunted wolves and the battle cries of their hunters filled the air. The pain of her ancestors cried out from the earth, the scent of their blood clogged her nostrils and the malicious triumph of her sire's forefathers rose up before her, demanding she forsake her Lycan heritage and join them in their worldwide extermination of the scourge. It was here in 1281 that her father's ancestor, Peter Corbet, was given the charter by Edward I to eradicate every wolf on the island. It was here they relentlessly called to her now, demanding she join with them on their never-ending quest to destroy the wolves.

No! Falon shouted. *I will not join you!*

But they would be heard, and more. The macabre specters of hundreds of dead Corbets rose from the earth around her, begging her for life, for the chance to avenge the deaths of all Slayers.

No!

Insistent they pressed upon her, raising their swords with the heads of dead wolves impaled on their tips.

"No!"

"*Resurrect us!*" they shrilled.

Falon clamped her hands over her ears, violently shaking her head. "No!"

They circled her, the blood of the wolves dripping from their swords to her hair, down her arms to her back and legs. She dropped to her knees shaking her head, refusing to answer the darkness.

Falon, Rafael called from far away. Yet his hand touched her shoulder. She shifted, snarled and snapped, sinking her fangs deep into his hand.

"Damn it, Falon!"

Panic choked her. Dear God what had she done? What was wrong with her? The same rage that possessed her when she attacked Anja exploded inside her now. But this time it was fueled by the blood of her ancestors.

She snarled again wanting more of Rafe's blood, and with that hunger, terror she had never experienced gripped her by the throat. She snarled again.

If she stayed—she would kill him.

"*Oh, Rafa*," she cried. "*Please*," she sobbed, "*stay away from me*." And then she leapt into the enveloping darkness where she could not harm either of the men she loved.

Blindly she ran from Rafe and Lucien. Any place they weren't would be safe. For them. She didn't care about her life. She cherished theirs above all others. Until she knew what was happening to her, and she could control it Luca and Rafa were in danger. First she had attacked Lucien, then Rafe, next? Would she kill one of them?

She could never live with herself. Moments later, gulping for breath, she found herself on the fringes of the village they had just passed through.

Falon! Lucien called.

Stay away from me! Please!

Tell me what's wrong.

Just find the sword! she cried. *Find the sword.*

The low drone of the chanting witches permeated the air around her. Did they know she was here? Were they waiting for her? Why? Feeling a pull she could not explain or resist, Falon walked solemnly toward the village square.

Like Daniel had centuries ago, Falon walked into the lion's den, but with no God, only her violent rage that linked her to these people and her untold power that could destroy any one of them or all of them if they provoked her.

Slowly she walked down the middle of the cobblestone main street. Completely focused on her, the witches kept a respectable distance between them. If any one of them had their sights on Rafe or Lucien they appeared to have lost it now. It was her shiny black pelt they salivated over now.

A wolf in hand was worth two in the ruins.

Oblivious to their taunting pitchforks and torches, Falon allowed them to cast a circle around her. Even as they cast spell after spell upon her, trying to force the wolf from her she ignored them.

With each incantation, her power withstood the ancient black arts. And with it, her rage escalated. Not for the taste of Slayer blood but for Lycan. Her Corbet blood was strong, and it wanted what it wanted.

For hours she paced the circumference of the widening circle. For hours, she howled her throat raw. For hours, the witches chanted, hummed, and droned their spells in their attempts to cleanse her of her wolf. For hours, she forced herself to stay within the circle while she continued to fight the black rage inside of her. It was the safest place for her alphas.

Into the wee hours of the next morning, Falon continued to force herself to stay within the confines of the magic circle, praying that Lucien and Rafa had unearthed the sword. For more hours after that she forced herself to focus her fury on her father and his people so that she didn't lose what tenuous grip she had on her sanity and go after the two men that she loved.

But the darkness in her was too strong. Unable to stand the confines of the circle any longer, Falon broke free of it and ran toward the ruins.

As she moved into the shadow of the thousand-year-old wall, the scent of fresh earth caught her nostrils. Moving around to the back of the tallest remaining wall she saw it. A freshly unearthed grave. Tentatively she stepped closer to it, afraid and excited. Had they found the sword? The sword that could kill Fenrir?

Falon shifted and slipped on her clothing she had torn off the night before. In human form, dark whispers of long dead warriors called to her. Promising victory and greatness.

"The blood doesn't lie," a deep, oddly familiar voice whispered.

She snarled shaking her head.

My blood is Lycan!

"You are Corbet!"

Falon snarled and approached the open grave. She had expected Rafa and Luca to have destroyed what was left of Peter Corbet. But what she saw when she looked down into the damp ground amazed and terrified her.

Thirteen

BLUE EYES SO much like her own stared back at Falon. Full sensuous lips parted into a genuine smile.

"Hello, daughter," Thomas Corbet said softly, as his body rose like a specter from the empty casket.

Rage, longing, and an unexpected elation slammed through her, momentarily confusing her loyalties. She grasped the protective amulet she never took off. Her father's, her mother had told her. *This was her father?* This was her enemy. The man who had killed Rafa and Luca's parents, kidnapped her mother and no doubt raped her, at least in the beginning. He was the most abominable man on earth and he was her father!

"I am not your daughter," she spat, stepping back from him. Looking expectantly behind him, Falon's gaze swept the quiet cemetery and beyond. Where were Luca and Rafa? A different panicked anxiety swept through her. Suddenly she didn't want them near.

What if side by side they saw her likeness to this man? What would they do? She didn't want to know. *Ever.*

Corbet landed lightly on his feet before her. Nervously Falon stood face to face with her father for the first time since she was a little girl. And for the first time she was glad there was no love lost between them.

He was imposingly tall, brilliantly blond with blazing blue eyes and if she didn't hate him so much, she'd think he was handsome. He was dressed in the old way, his broadsword sheathed in a gold and silver scabbard around his trim waist.

"The blood doesn't lie, Falon. My seed sprang you to life. My only regret is that I was not there to raise you."

She shoved out her hands, the force of her action pushing him back a dozen yards. "My only regret is that your seed gave me life! If I did not carry a child, I would slit my throat rather than acknowledge you as my father." She spat on the ground but continued to move toward him. "Why are you here, what do you want?"

He reached out a hand to her. "I am here because I love you. I want you to stand beside me during the rising, and fight for our cause."

She slapped his hand away but the contact burned her palm. She hissed, jerking her hand back. "How can you speak of love when you are so toxic?"

"You call the kettle black, Falon."

"My hatred for you knows no bounds, I agree, but it's because of what you have done."

"Are Vulkasin and Mondragon no less toxic?"

"They have been persecuted!"

"If they had the option to drop their swords today and walk away, they would not."

"And I would not blame them! After what you did to their parents you deserve to die the same way."

"What of your mother, Falon? She loves me. Has never stopped loving me. If you kill me, you would destroy her."

"Then she can die! I have no respect for her. How could she?"

"I see the rage inside you has not subsided."

Her head snapped back. "What do you know of it?"

"Your Slayer blood is rising, Falon. In a month it will control you."

"No," she breathed, terrified he told the truth. "It will not."

He laughed, not quite demonic more like gentle amusement, as a father would for a foolish daughter. "*Only* if the alphas accept you, but for full acceptance, they must know your true parentage." He moved closer and his voice lowered conspiratorially. "And we both know what will happen to you when they realize your father slew their mother and father." His aura snapped red and black around her, betraying his mood. "Come with me now and spare yourself the heartache. You can raise your child as a Corbet. I will protect you both."

Inadvertently, Falon's hand slid down to her flat belly as hot tears welled in her eyes. "They will accept that I had no hand in my parentage." She raised her blurry eyes to his. "They love me."

He pressed his hand on hers. It was big and warm, and oddly comforting. "But they hate Corbet more."

"No!" she cried, jerking away from him. "They will understand!"

He shook his head and stepped back. "If I could rewind time, I would change everything, Falon. I would not have allowed Layla to take you away from me even as I struggled with my destiny."

He strode past her to the stone wall behind her and leaned against it. "I didn't know if you were safe around me. I knew there was no way I could take your mother and you to my clan. I had no choice but to abandon you both at the time. It was the only way to save your lives."

"I wish you had let me die," she said harshly. "I wish my mother had resisted you. I wish—" She shook her head as hopelessness engulfed her. Everything, everyone she loved would be lost to her if her secret got out.

"You have the power of both bloods, Falon. If you swear fealty to Clan Corbet you will thrive amongst my kind. If you do not, you will die a Lycan."

"I *am* Lycan! If that is how I die, then so be it!"

"Then you will. Fenrir becomes more powerful each day. Do you think even with the Cross of Caus you can get close enough to destroy him?"

Falon knew that with the power of three, they had a chance, but she wasn't going to say it.

Thomas shook his head as if reading her thoughts. "The power of three will work *only* if your precious alphas accept your Corbet heritage. We both know that will never happen." He pushed off the wall and strode toward her. "Don't be so stubborn, daughter! You cannot beat Fenrir, and you cannot beat me."

"Why does there even have to be a battle? You've proven that a Slayer and Lycan can love. I'm proof of that!"

"This has been coming for three hundred years, Falon. I cannot stop it any more than you can. It's destiny. Only one survives."

"Don't show up!"

"Fenrir will show up and a thousand Slayers with him."

"Will you slay my mother?"

Her question startled him. And he refused to answer, and by his nonanswer, Falon knew what he would do. As angry as she was at her mother, Falon's heart broke a little for her. The man she loved could not see past his past to live a future that included the woman he loved. She inhaled sharply then exhaled. If they learned her truth, would Lucien and Rafe be able to look past their own pasts to share a future with her? Or would they be like Thomas, unable to love more then they hated? "Then you never really loved her did you?"

"I love her more than my life."

"Then yours holds no value."

Falon raised her nose to the morning breeze. Rafe and Lucien approached. Her stomach rose to her throat. They could not see her like this, with her father.

"Your lovers approach."

"Leave now before we destroy you, but leave knowing this: if you reveal yourself as my sire, to *anyone,* I will kill you."

"I'll give you two weeks, daughter. Two weeks to tell them the truth. If they do as you say, love you enough to look past your Corbet blood, then we will meet again at the rising. But if they cast you from them, the only way you and your child can survive is by returning to your clan."

"I will not tell them!" Dear God, how could she? It would destroy them. It would destroy her.

"Two weeks." He leapt over her into the ruins and was gone.

Fourteen

FALON SHIFTED AND raced toward her alphas. How she loved them both, separately and as one. In full wolf, they galloped toward her—one dark, one light—both with eyes bright and focused solely on her. She swallowed hard, wishing with all her heart Corbet blood did not run through her veins. But it did, and as much as she loved the two Lycan rushing toward her, she feared they would never be able to look at her without disgust if they knew her truth.

But how could she keep her terrible secret?

She nearly skidded to a stop when the answer hit her: destroy Thomas Corbet. And with him, her secret would die. She was Lycan and he her mortal enemy. Killing him would be as natural as the rise of the full moon every month. But could she, in cold blood, kill him before the rising?

Rafa and Luca nearly collided with her. Their happy growls followed by reassuring licks and gentle head butts would have made her cry if she were in human form. She closed her eyes and rubbed against each of them while making small sounds of contentment.

Why couldn't it be like this all of the time? No jealousy, just love and support.

We were worried sick about you! Lucien scolded.

We've been all over this damn countryside a dozen times! Rafa growled.

I'm sorry.

Why did you run away? Rafa asked roughly.

I— The darkness overcame me again, I didn't want to hurt you. She licked his face. *I'm so sorry.*

He nuzzled her face. *We're all under an incredible amount of stress. You have nothing to apologize for.*

They stopped in the middle of a wide-open heather field. Fully exposed to the warmth of the rising sun and crisp morning breeze. The clean scent of nature soothed. The physical toll of last night and this morning with no sleep and then the emotional drain of meeting her father face to face for the first time took its toll. Exhaustion overcame her and Falon collapsed on the soft underbrush.

Let me sleep, just for an hour . . .

SHE WOKE IN human form to warm fur in her face and soft snores in her ears. Blinking against the setting sun, Falon struggled to remember where she was.

Reality came back with terrible clarity. England. The witches. Her father. His ultimatum. Her answer to it. She closed her eyes, casting those unbearable thoughts from her brain. She had two weeks to tell the men she loved she was as much a Slayer as she was Lycan, and with that truth she'd lose them both. But without the truth the power of the three could not be set free. Was what they had now enough to see them past the rising?

In her mind, Falon had no choice. Unless she destroyed the source of her problem, her secret was not safe.

What she had to do was clear. And once the Lycan nation triumphed on the rising it would be a moot point. Falon would be the only survivor with Slayer blood left on the planet, and no one but her mother would know. And Layla would not share what was also her secret.

Right now, however, Falon was going to take quiet moments like this and greedily hold on to them. Smiling she rubbed her back against the big black wolf snoring behind her. Then she snuggled her nose against the soft golden fur her head rested on.

Rafa's rich earthy scent flirted with her nostrils. It was as unique to him as he was to the world. She smoothed the fur along his muzzle with her fingertips and smiled, remembering the first time she'd seen him like this. She had awakened beside him not knowing who he was or what he was. To say she had been terrified would be an understatement.

Two ocean green eyes opened and stared intently at her. Emotion for this Lycan swelled. She loved Rafa so much it hurt to breathe when he looked at her like this. Never had she wanted to hurt him. Never would she intentionally cause him pain. She was fiercely protective of his feelings. Yet—if he knew the truth about her, she would hurt him more deeply than she had when she accepted Lucien's mark. More deeply than when he learned she was pregnant, most likely with Lucien's child. She couldn't hurt him. She wouldn't. It galvanized what she must do.

She kissed his nose and whispered, "I love you."

He nuzzled under her chin and closed his eyes. The gentle, trusting action set her already tumultuous emotions close to unraveling.

Lucien stretched behind her, his big body tightening against her back. Luxurious heat radiated from his soft fur. When he snuggled up closer to her, her mood shifted. As only Lucien would, he laved his tongue in a long swath from between her shoulder blades, up the back of her neck, along her chin to her ear.

Erotic shocks of energy sizzled through her. Her body loosened. Closing her eyes, Falon moaned when he sniffed down her back, and then licked the dimples above her buttocks.

"Lucien . . ." she moaned. Her breasts scraped across Rafa's furry chest when she arched. Lucien growled again, but it was Rafa's human lips that caught hers when she gasped and arched deeper against Lucien.

Fisting Rafa's hair, Falon pulled him to her, wanting him to claim her as his. Like this, with his brother cradling her from behind. She needed him to mark her, to reestablish his claim on her. She needed him to show her by that action that he belonged to her, not Anja.

Oh, how she'd missed everything about him. His kiss, his touch, his scent. His love. Tears stung her eyes.

"No, no, Falon," he shushed against her lips. Running his thumbs along her cheekbones he smeared the tears away. "No tears, my love. Not now."

His lips slid across hers again. And like a child, she curled into him, knowing he would slay her dragons for her if she but asked. Honorable, golden Rafa. Her knight in shining armor.

Lucien's body stiffened behind hers and moved away.

Stay, Luca! she cried, grabbing a fistfull of fur pulling him back to her. *Please, for me, stay.*

His body stilled but did not reengage with hers. For now, it was enough that he stayed.

Rafael's fingertips traced the edges of her face, across her eyelids,

down her nose, to her cheekbones along her chin to her neck. Reac-
quainting himself with every inch of her. Tears welled again. How he
must have suffered when she was taken from him. How he must have
mourned. How he must have cursed her when she accepted Lucien.
She felt terrible for hurting him, but did not regret loving Luca.

How could she? Lucien and she, they had been lost, but in finding each other discovered their true selves. She could not have loved
Lucien if she had not loved Rafael first.

She could no more fight her feelings for both men than she could
keep the sun from rising each morning. They were equal parts to her
whole. How could she make them see that?

See that despite their pride, they belonged together? The three of
them as one.

Rafael's lips broke free of her. His gaze caught and held hers.

I vowed never to hurt you, Falon. I ask the same vow of you.

"I would never hurt you, Rafa. *Never.*" She kissed him deeply.
I give you my vow.

His hands dug deep into her hair, and the pressure of his lips
intensified. His body swelled as he covered her. Falon closed her eyes
and reveled in the power of his touch. Everything about Rafael
Vulkasin reverberated with bright golden power. The golden son.
The golden alpha. Her first love.

His scorching lips trailed down her neck, his big hands cupped
her swollen breasts. Moaning she arched into him, her head pressing
back against Lucien who had not moved. She sensed his anger but
his arousal as well.

When Rafa caught a sensitive nipple between his teeth and nibbled, she cried out and opened her eyes. From behind her head,
Lucien's wolf stared down at her. Her flesh flared with new heat. As
Rafael's lips taunted and teased her nipple, Falon could not drag her
gaze from Luca's smoldering eyes.

"Falon," Rafa whispered against a turgid nipple, "I have missed your body."

She moaned as his lips trailed down her belly. Biting her bottom lip, Falon whimpered when Lucien licked her throat. It was so sexy, one man, one wolf, both wanting her so much they were willing to pleasure her together. She moaned again. And, dear God, it was Nirvana. Not just physically, but in her head. An emotional aphrodisiac unlike anything she had experienced.

"The hot silkiness of your skin" He licked the cradle of her hip. "It tastes like candy."

She loved it when Rafa talked to her so low and sexy . . .

His lips swathed a trail from one hip to the other just above the rise of her mons. Her essence intensified, and when Rafa slid his tongue across and around her sensitive clitoris, she cried out. *God, that feels so good.*

She was so turned on, so on fire her thighs trembled. "Oh, baby, you are soaking wet for me," he murmured dipping his tongue between her swollen folds. Falon exhaled a long rush of breath . . . Dear Lord, that was amazing.

Lucien shifted to human and as he did, he gently took her hands and pulled her arms over her head until she was stretched taut.

Oh. My. *God.*

Rafael nudged her folds apart with his thick tongue and swept her clit with slow deliberate back-and-forth swaths. The sensation was devastatingly wicked. She was going to die of pleasure.

Rafa, she gasped. Lucien's lips covered hers.

Say my name, he growled low.

Lu-cah!

Rafa slid a thick finger into her. The sublimity of his touch took her breath away. Her hips rose a foot into the air. *Rafa . . .*

Falon's beast had long since stirred. Now she was on the prowl and would not rest until she had both alphas satiating her hungry body.

Lucien's tongue mimicked the same slow cadence as Rafa's finger. Rafa's lips clamped onto her hard clit and sucked as his tongue flickered feather soft across it. It was too much and not enough. Lucien's hands cupped her breasts, and in a spiraling explosion, she came. With Rafael between her thighs, her back came off the ground. Lucien's hands slid deep into her hair and cupped her head as his kiss deepened, catching her cries of passion in his kiss.

Her body jerked and trembled with emotion. Her eyes stung with unshed tears. Shaking her head, she sobbed in Lucien's kiss. Then gently, he licked away her tears.

"Did you like that, baby?" Rafa asked, his voice so gravelly she hardly recognized it.

"Yes," she breathed. "Thank you."

"I'm not done."

He spread her thighs and pulled her onto his thick erection. Her eyes flew open at the lush sensation of Rafa filling her. She gasped, and Lucien let go of her as her arms slid around Rafa's neck and her lips rose to his.

Rafa rolled with her away from Lucien and then pressed her back into the soft fragrant heather and slowly made love to her as if it were the first time. And in so many ways it was. They were two different people now. She was no longer innocent of who she was or where her destiny lay. She had come into her own and would settle for nothing less than everything.

Rafa had come into his own as well. He'd taken that final, momentous step facing the Blood Law, risking it all, and losing, but surviving. She had admired him when she'd fallen in love with him the first time, now she revered him. She would follow him to hell and back, as many times as he needed her to.

The powerful energy that thrummed through them with more voltage than a lightning strike, melded them. Tracing her fingertips across Rafa's lips, his eyes, his cheeks, Falon could not break her gaze from his soul-seeing eyes if she wanted to. Their connection was stronger now. Their separation having galvanized their bond. It was heaven being in Rafa's arms like this again.

Each time he moved deep inside of her, her muscles hugged him tightly, reluctant to let go. His cock was like a lightning rod infusing her with power. It was almost too much. Too much sensation. Too much love. Too much knowing Lucien watched, and too much knowing it hurt him. It was too much being loved and desired by these two powerful men, yet she could never settle for just one.

His stormy green eyes reverently held hers. They glittered with emotion and heat. "I love being inside you," Rafa said softly. Falon arched, digging her nails into his shoulders, the slickness of their bodies causing her to lose her grip. Their sweat mixed with Rafa's blood created a heady perfume.

Her beast raised its head, no longer content with slow. Falon rolled Rafa onto his back and in deep sensual waves she rode him. He pulled her hair around them like a shroud and raised his lips to her and worshipfully kissed her.

The tension in their bodies tightened. Their reverent treatment of the other shifted dramatically to primal mating. Their bodies slammed together, were torn apart only to slam together again. Their incessant need for the other accelerated, the long waves intensifying to churning whitecaps.

"Falon!" Rafa called hoarsely, as his body spiraled out of control. At that exact moment, Falon came undone. She screamed as the pressure in her body shattered.

Rafa rose up, sinking his teeth into her neck as he came with her in a wild torrential storm.

Falon's body crashed and rolled, the intensity of her orgasm nearly unseating her.

Off in the distance, Lucien's mournful howl shattered their intimacy.

Falon tensed, this moment she had so longed for lost to Lucien's vocal refusal to accept her union with his brother.

"I'm going to fucking kill my brother," Rafe snarled.

There was no time to gradually come down from the high they had just experienced. Falon was as angry as Rafa that Lucien would selfishly ruin such an important moment between them. How dare he? Rafael had not interrupted her and Luca back in the forest, why did he have to do this?

Lucien! she shouted as she and Rafe separated, and she stood on shaky knees. Her moment may have been disturbed but her body had yet to recover from the traumatic orgasm.

Like the alpha he was, Lucien's wolf sauntered slowly toward them, not chagrined but arrogant. As he approached, he shifted and glared at her.

"Why did you do that? Why did you try to ruin it?" she demanded. And as she asked the ridiculous question, she knew exactly what the answer was. And felt selfish and foolish for having the audacity to be even the slightest bit angry. This was not just about her. It was about *all* of them.

"Oh, I don't know," he shrugged. "Maybe because my brother marked you, *my* chosen one! And you couldn't fuck him hard enough."

"You have no claim!" Rafe said, stepping past her but keeping a possessive hand on her.

Shaking her head, Falon pushed Rafa's hand away and moved between the two brothers. Touching neither of them, she put her arms out halting them both as they made moves to go to fists. "We are three adults! Can we act like it?" she shrieked. She was at her breaking point. All of it: her father, Fenrir, her mother's lies, the eminent rising, and her broken heart for the two men she loved, was suddenly too much for her to bear. She needed them, *both* of them, if she were going to survive another minute.

When neither brother spoke, Falon sharply exhaled, focusing on releasing the tension inside of her. One of them had to remain calm. "We are past jealousy and chest beating. What we have is too precious to throw away. I'm not going to let that happen and I'm not going to keep refereeing." She looked at Lucien and had to bite back a smile. He looked like a petulant child whose favorite toy had been taken away. The urge to smile quieted. In reality, that is exactly what had happened. She felt for him, she really did, but now he would have to learn to share.

"Listen to me, both of you. I know this is hard, but I think you both are coming to the realization that this is how it has to be if none of us are going to be hurt more than if it doesn't work. With the three of us together as one, no one gets their heart broken. No one has to live without the other. No one will long for the other. And"—she looked pointedly at each of them—"neither one of you can deny that sharing me physically doesn't excite you on some primal level."

Unmoved by her impassioned words, they stared stonily at her. *Oh, my God!* They were stubborn.

"Do you love me?" she asked Lucien.

"You know the answer to that."

"Do you want me above all others?"

"You know I do."

"If you could not have me would you take another?"

His eyes narrowed dangerously. "No."

Falon tuned from Lucien to Rafael. "Have you released Anja?"

He nodded curtly.

It was tremendous, wonderful news. "Do you love me above all others, Rafa," she breathed.

"Yes," he answered huskily.

"Would you take another if you could not have me?"

"Not again, no."

She nodded and inhaled deeply then slowly exhaled. "I feel the same way about you both. If you both walked away from me this minute, I would not take another mate because I cannot happily live without one of you. It—it would be as if my heart or my soul was missing. I cannot exist unless I have both." Those pesky tears stung her eyes. "I know committing to this unusual relationship goes against everything male in each of you, yet, you are both confident and strong." She looked up into Lucien's glittering golden eyes. God he was beautiful. His dark hair hung wildly around his soulful face. The intensity in his stare would have unnerved most women. Lucien Mondragon would never be tamed, but Falon was more than woman enough for him, for the both of them.

"Earlier," she said to her angry alpha, "when you were kissing me, and it was—" Her cheeks heated. "During what Rafa was doing, I could barely control the emotion inside me. It was beautiful. And I know at the very least you were aroused." Her gaze swept his semi-erect penis, then swept back up to his stony stare. "Deny it all you want, Lucien Mondragon, but it gave you pleasure watching me receive pleasure."

He growled low but did not deny it. She moved into him and pressed her hand over his heart. It lurched against her palm. "You're selfish, Luca. Yesterday by the river, I knew Rafa watched, and it was the only reason I allowed you to make love to me." His eyes widened imperceptibly. The black striations around his pupils pulsed with each heartbeat. "It excited me. It made me come harder and faster, just like today while you watched." Her hand trailed down his taut belly to his thickening erection. She rubbed her thumb across the dewy head. "Even now the thought of me coming while you watch turns you on." She leaned into him and on her toes she kissed him. "It turns me on that it turns you on."

He grabbed her hand and forced it around his shaft. Hissing in a breath his eyes narrowed to slits. "What you are asking of me and Rafe is more than shared sex. You're asking that we live together as a unit of three. I don't know how to do that."

"Nor do I. But for you and for Rafa, I'm willing to learn."

He snarled and pulled her hard against his chest. "I love you with everything I possess Falon. *Everything*," he hissed. He looked past her to his brother. "I love Rafe almost as much as I love you but I don't know if I can do what you ask."

She smiled and ran her fingers through his long hair. "Oh, Luca, you are the most confident man I know. You have nothing to fear by loving me when your brother does, too."

She turned slightly to Rafe who stood, rigid and quiet.

"Talk to me, please," she asked softly.

He exhaled sharply and, as frustrated as his brother, he ran his fingers through his short hair.

When he didn't speak, Falon reached out to him, tracing her fingers along the rigid line of his jaw. "Rafa, please, talk to me. What are you feeling? I need to know."

He shook his head as if he didn't believe what he was about to say. "Yesterday, when I watched you and Lucien, it tore me up." He jammed his fingers through his hair again, his agitation plain to see. "Damn it, until I stopped and looked at your face. I saw it, the love you have for him, and the pleasure he gave you. It was fucking beautiful and as jealous as I was of that love, watching you, it— *Shit!*" He clamped his jaw shut, fighting the honesty. "And just now? While I was inside you, your love for me radiated through your pores. I felt how your body hit overdrive when Lucien kissed you when I was between your thighs. It made me harder, knowing you were so turned on."

Her heart slammed against her chest and she felt herself getting wet again. Lucien's nostrils flared, and his lips quirked.

Rafael moved closer. Reaching out, he trailed his fingertips along her shoulder and collarbone, softly stroking, his mind still not at ease with what she asked. Warmth shimmered like sparklers through her. Her heart skipped several beats, waiting for his next words.

"I won't be led around by the balls, Falon. And you can't play us against each other," he said.

Oh, my God. Was he—?

Afraid to speak—thinking it was a dream—Falon forced her words. "If anyone is going to be led, it will be me, Rafa." Holding his stare to prove her truth, she continued, "I will follow each of you wherever you choose to take me."

Lucien chuckled and kissed her just below her jaw where it met her jugular. Her body swelled against his lips, and she sighed. Would she ever get enough of these two? No. Never.

"Somehow, angel face," Luca said, turning her to him, "I can't see you rolling over on your back and playing submissive to either of us."

She smiled trying very hard not to jump up and down in glee. Though she had hoped and prayed for this moment, she never truly believed it would happen. That it did left her stunned and beyond excited.

When Luca swept his tongue along the pulsing ridge of her vein, she breathlessly exhaled. "You would be surprised how submissive I could be if I wanted to."

He nipped her skin and she melted.

"Where would you sleep each night?" Rafa asked from behind

her. He was so close his warm breath caressed her shoulder. Her knees trembled.

"With you both."

Rafa nipped her shoulder. "So greedy."

She closed her eyes and swallowed. Nervous anticipation spiraled out of control through her. "I could alternate or—*ah*." Lucien's lascivious tongue laved a scorching path between her breasts. It felt so good.

"If we united the packs, who would be alpha?" Lucien asked as his tongue teased a circle around her nipple.

"Like when you lived under the curse, one of you by day the other by night," she breathed, realizing that just might be the answer.

"An interesting concept," Lucien said, licking another circle around her nipple this time closer. *Oh*, please, *take it!*

"How do we raise our children?" Rafa whispered as his lips touched that sensitive place behind her right ear. She could barely stand her knees shook so hard.

"With love and dignity," she whispered. Her breasts swelled so painfully her nipples distended, begging Lucien for succor.

"You make a good case, Falon," Rafa whispered. "But you'll have to convince me how this can work." He slid his palms down her back to her buttocks, gliding his thumbs along the seam to her anus. She bit back a moan when he pressed her into Lucien's erection. "You can start now."

Fifteen

HOLY MOTHER OF God. It was really happening. Her two alphas coming together for her. No snarling, no chest beating, no dream. She was beyond thrilled. Beyond excited. Beyond grateful that these two proud men loved her enough to try.

Lucien dropped to his knees in front of her, as Rafael's hands slid around her waist then up to her breasts.

"I don't know what to do," she gasped, suddenly feeling shy and vulnerable. They were two, and so powerful.

"Just enjoy," Rafa breathed against her ear.

He pulled her gently back against him, holding her liquefying body steady, as Lucien spread her thighs and lifted one leg over his shoulder. Turbulent anticipation wracked through her.

"You're so pretty and pink, angel face," Lucien huskily admired, sliding a thick finger down her seam. "And so fucking wet." He leaned into her and kissed her smooth mons, then flicked her straining clitoris with his clever tongue.

Falon jerked against his mouth, inhaling a long, jagged breath, thankful Rafa steadied her from behind. His thick erection dug into her back demanding attention.

Their unabashed need for her combined with their willingness to share was headier than any drug-induced high. She was more than up for the challenge to please both of her men and eager to do so. Sinking her fingers into Lucien's thick hair, Falon snaked her right hand behind her back and cupped Rafa's heavy balls.

He moaned, moving into her as Lucien wantonly consumed her flesh. His tongue dragged across and around her hard nub, stimulating it harder. His full lips suckled her swollen folds. The succulent sound of her juices as he lapped her incited her desire to dizzying heights. She squeezed Rafa's balls then slid her hand to the base of his shaft and squeezed harder when Lucien's tongue dove deeply into her.

"Ahh," she gasped, losing her balance. Again, Rafa steadied her and, not missing a beat, Lucien lifted her other leg over his shoulder. Now she was completely in their power. She trembled violently, afraid she might disappoint them.

"Relax, sweetheart," Lucien whispered against her sultry opening. "We got this."

Falon liquefied, giving in to all of it when he caught her clitoris between his teeth and slid a thick finger deeply into her. Her head lolled back against Rafa's chest as her muscles clamped around Lucien's finger. Oh, that felt so— "Luca!" she cried when he sucked her clit into his mouth and spanked it with his tongue. Out of nowhere, the orgasm blindsided her, wracking her body with short, hard jolts of ecstasy. Her fist tightened around Rafe, and as she tried to control her spasming hips, she pumped him from root to head.

Lucien kissed her wet lips as she gasped for breath, anticipating the next wave of hedonistic pleasure even as she basked in the current sensual meltdown. When Luca inserted another finger into her, Falon's body dissolved. Greedily, she pressed her hips into his face wanting him deeper, harder— Air hissed from her lungs when Rafa rolled her sensitive nipples between his fingertips and nipped at the soft skin behind her ear.

It was sensory overload at its very, *very* finest. Her hips moved wantonly against Lucien's mouth and fingers. She was slippery wet. "Ohh . . ." she moaned, when he slipped a finger into her anus. She was so wet, so worked up, so ready for total invasion he had no trouble slipping in. The sensation pushed her hard to the edge of no return.

Waves of emotional awareness churned inside of her. This was amazing, and beautiful. It was— Her body shuddered fiercely as the tension in every molecule rushed skyward for relief then, in a cataclysmic eruption, spilled over. Desperately she turned her head and caught Rafa's lips, screaming just as the orgasm tore through her. Like a live wire, her body quivered and jerked, impaled by lips, fingers, and tongue.

As her overstimulated body tried to regulate the pleasure pulses rippling through her in waves, Lucien kissed a slow trail from her soaking wet pussy to her belly. Gently he lowered his shoulder and her liquid legs wobbled. "I can't stand," she whimpered.

"On your knees, Falon," he commanded her.

Only because she was greedy for more did she find the strength to obey. Lucien moved in behind her, and gently pushed her forward so that she was on all fours. Rafe stood in front of her, his glorious erection bobbing in front of her. Sticking out her tongue, reverently she lapped him from his thick root to the soft wide head.

Tilting her chin with one hand so that he could watch, Rafa caught and held her gaze. With his other hand he grasped his cock and moved into her begging mouth just as Lucien filled her from behind.

It was beyond anything she imagined, the sublimity of both of them willingly inside her. It was too perfect a moment. All three of them moaned in glorious pleasure. For long seconds they didn't move as their body parts familiarized themselves with this new erotic event.

Rafa swelled in her mouth as she continued to gaze at him. Lucien was buried balls deep into her pussy, his cock twitching in tempo to their matching heartbeats. Falon closed her eyes and allowed Rafa's to catch up and beat the same cadence.

Hot power thrummed through her to them and through them back to her. Awestruck by what they created, Falon opened her eyes.

"You okay, baby?" Rafe asked as he smoothed the hair from her face.

She closed her eyes briefly, then slowly opened them.

"Ready?" Lucien huskily asked from behind her.

She had been ready from "hello." Pressing her swollen pussy into Luca, her mouth tugged at Rafa's equally swollen cock. They moaned as one, the sound deep, sexy, and hungry.

Slowly, Luca slid back, his hot cock dragging against her sensitive tissue as Rafe, still holding his cock steady, slid his hand around the back of her head to steady her, and gently pushed past her lips, then deeper until his cock head hit the back of her throat. As Rafe withdrew, Lucien thrust deeply into her. Her charged body shook violently with emotional and stimulus overload.

Rafa's cock was velvety hard, molten hot candy in her mouth. She sucked him hard each time he thrust into her, and was grateful for his steadying hands. Lucien pounded against her sweet spot each time he thrust into her. His cock was thick with blood and the veins defined. When that wonderfully sexy piercing of his slid up and down her vaginal walls, it redefined erotic. Alone it could make her come. But Luca always gave more than the bare minimum. He always gave her his all. He made sure she enjoyed each sensuous inch of him.

"Angel face," he hoarsely whispered as he grasped her by the cradle of her hips sinking deeply into her. "You have no idea what you do to me." Then in a slow, deep, sensual cadence, he fucked her cunt in perfect symmetry to Rafa fucking her mouth.

No words could describe what she felt at that moment, so she didn't try to think of them. Instead, Falon let completely go, allowing the tumultuous waves of sensation to sweep her higher, battering her with relentless, intense pleasure. Sweat slickened her skin, and her lips were wet with saliva, affording Rafa's cock swift easy movement in and out of her mouth. Lucien's fingers dug into her skin, and Rafa's fingers dug into her scalp. They were twin wrecking balls on her body, and as she visualized what they were doing to her, she came in a wild crazy inferno of overflowing sensation. And as her body gyrated wildly around them, they drove into her, releasing their seed in both ends of her. The velocity of their orgasms spiraled from Lucien through Falon and into Rafa in a lightning-hot flash of energy that consumed them.

In a blinding finish their hypersensitive bodies halted as if suspended in time, then crashed into a heaving, sweaty mound of quivering flesh.

Long minutes passed before any one of them could move. Gently, Lucien and Rafa slipped out of her, and she collapsed onto the soft downy grass. Breathing so heavy she doubted she would ever catch her breath, Falon's body continued to tremble with aftershocks.

Lucien kissed the inside of her thigh and gently licked their combined moistness from her, careful not to touch her throbbing pussy. If he did, she might explode again. Rafa smoothed her hair back and kissed her eyelids, her nose, her chin, then nudged open her lips with his tongue and kissed her deeply.

Never had she felt so loved or so sexually content. Yet as those thoughts occurred to her, her shameless body thrummed.

Lucien growled softly between her thighs. "You are insatiable, Falon."

"I am," she said breathlessly. "But only with you two."

Rafael's tongue licked the seam of her lips before he withdrew and looked deeply into her eyes. "Tell us what you want."

She swallowed hard. She wanted everything.

"I want this to never end."

She gasped, raising her hips against Lucien's salacious lips when he suckled her clit.

Rafa's eyes flared. "You look so goddamn sexy when you cry out like that." She moaned in agreement and in pleasure. He nipped at her chin, then nipped again when she writhed beneath Lucien's mouth wreaking havoc on her. "You like this?" Rafa roughly asked. "Lucien going down on you while I watch?"

"Yes," she moaned as her skin flushed. She loved it.

"I want you to come, Falon, because you want to please me," he said possessively.

"Yes," she gasped, focusing solely on his blazing eyes.

When Lucien slid a finger across her clitoris she hissed in a long sharp breath and closed her eyes.

"Open your eyes," Rafe commanded.

She did so immediately.

"That's it, baby." He slid his hands up her arms and pulled them above her head so that she was pulled taut. "Now, I want you to tell me what you want Lucien to do to you and how good it feels."

Embarrassment flushed her skin hot.

"Don't be shy, baby."

Falon swallowed hard, wondering if she had ever been so aroused by mere words. When Lucien moved away from her, she cried out. "No! Luca, don't."

"Don't what?" Rafa prompted.

"Don't stop touching me."

"Tell him what to do, Falon."

She swallowed hard and kept her gaze locked on Rafa's. His nostrils flared and his skin glistened with sweat. He was as aroused as she.

"Luca," she whispered. "Touch me."

"He can't hear you," Rafa said.

"Luca," she said louder. "Touch me."

"Tell him where."

"Between my legs."

Lucien slid his fingers along the inside of her thigh. She moved to accommodate them, too embarrassed to give him specific instructions.

"Tell him where," Rafa commanded.

"Higher, yesss." Oh, that felt so good. "Now, inside." She bit her bottom lip when he slid a finger into her.

"How does it feel?" Rafa urged.

"Good. So good." She arched and said, "Now move in and out. Slowly."

Agonizingly slow, Lucien moved his finger in and out of her. "Oh, yes, that feels really good."

She felt rather than saw Rafael grab his cock. His eyes darkened as he slowly began to stroke himself. "I want to fuck you so bad right now, but that would be giving you what you want, and right now, I want you to know we're in control. Not you."

His lips nipped at hers. "Do you understand that, sweetheart?"

"Yes," she moaned. She understood perfectly.

Rafael lowered his lips to hers and whispered, "Stop moving."

"Wha—"

"Stop responding to Luca."

Falon swallowed hard but did as he commanded.

"Now tell him to lick your pussy." He brushed his lips across hers and added, "And don't move a muscle when he does." Her shallow breaths bounced back into her own mouth, Rafa was so close to her. His eyes held hers while his left hand still held her arms above her head by the wrists and his right hand slowly stroked his cock. She had never felt so erotically charged as she did at that moment.

"Luca," she said hoarsely, "lick me—my pussy. Hard."

She squeezed her eyes shut when he slid his finger from her.

"Open your eyes," Rafa commanded.

She obeyed and it took every bit of willpower she possessed not to move when Lucien's long, thick, and very talented tongue burrowed deep inside of her.

"How does that feel," Rafe asked against her lips.

She licked her dry lips, catching his bottom lip as she did. He moaned his pleasure, as his eyelids fluttered in a brief lapse of control.

"Good," she whispered, not trusting her voice.

"Only good?"

She swallowed hard as Lucien's wanton lips and tongue tantalized her beyond the pale. "Better," she gasped, resisting the urge to close her eyes and liquefy, "than good."

"Open your mouth, Falon," Rafa commanded.

She did and nearly creamed herself when he slid his forefinger into her mouth. "Now suck."

When she did, the pull from her pussy connected with the pull of her lips making it almost impossible not to move into it. "Eyes open, sweetheart," Rafe breathed. His thick erection moved up and down her hip as she sucked in the exact cadence of Lucien's treacherous mouth.

Her skin flushed with a fresh coat of sweat. Her body trembled despite her Herculean effort to keep perfectly still.

"Do you want my dick inside you?"

She nodded and sucked his finger deeper into her mouth. His body shuddered. "Tell Lucien to stop."

Oh, she didn't want to. "Stop," she said against Rafa's finger.

When Luca moved away from her she saw Rafe exchange a look with his brother and knew they had their own plans.

"Keep still, baby," Rafa said softly as he withdrew his finger from her mouth and released her hands.

And just like that she lay spread eagle on the ground, dripping wet, more aroused than she had been in her life and neither one of them touched her. Falon swallowed hard against her dry throat.

"If you move, Falon, we walk away."

Not breaking her gaze, she silently nodded. Her body thrummed with violent need. Even the cool evening breeze could not bring down her temperature. Rafael sat down beside her and traced his finger along her bottom lip. "I love this lip." He kissed it, and then sucked it into his mouth. "It's so full and pouty." He laid back into the grass and said, "Sit on me."

Falon hurried to accommodate him, and when she slowly impaled herself on his thick erection she could not help a long slow groan of pleasure. His hands slid along her thighs to her hips and held her immobile as he gained control of himself. Rafe was as close to the edge as she was. "Don't move," he breathed, "until I tell you to."

It was the hardest thing she had to do. Sit immobile and impaled by Rafa's luscious cock. Her interior liquid muscles though paid no attention to his command. Spasmodically, they contracted around him, hungry for what was being denied them.

"Lean forward," Rafa instructed. As she did her bottom lifted and

Lucien, who had moved behind her, knelt between Rafa's knees and slid his finger along her spine, down between her butt cheeks and, oh, she swallowed hard, along her sensitive anus.

Her muscles clenched around Rafa's rock hard cock.

"Don't move a muscle," Rafe said sharply.

"Easy, angel face," Luca whispered in her ear. "Easy." He slid his finger deep into her and she nearly snapped in half. Rafa stiffened beneath her and she knew he fought for control as desperately as she. When Lucien had her completely loosened he slid his finger from her and gently probed her with his cock head. Not taking her eyes off Rafa, Falon held her breath as he slowly filled her from behind.

Once she was completely and fully filled by them, Falon let out a long shaky breath. They were amazing and as insatiable as she. Rafael's brilliant eyes glittered. "I'm going to move now, and then Lucien, but you will stay completely still."

She made a small whimpering sound of dismay but quickly stifled it.

Rafa moved into her, and as he moved back, Lucien slid deeper into her. All she could do was remain frozen and absorb the onslaught of sensation. She forced her eyes to remain locked on Rafa's. His flickered as his nostrils flared. His features had sharpened to hard planes. Their tempo picked up rhythm.

She was the hull of two mighty pistons, as each one thrust the other retreated. Her thighs quivered and her juices saturated each thrusting cock, soaking all three of them.

The tension in her body was so intense, so tight, so bittersweetly painful she began to feel faint from sensory overload.

Lucien's breathing intensified; Rafa's body beneath her slickened with her juice and his own sweat.

"Now, baby, come for me now!" Rafa commanded hoarsely.

Her body obeyed and the floodgate slammed open and every cell in her body screamed with relief.

Energy swirled and snapped within her. The intensity pounded like thunder through her, reverberating in Rafe and Lucien and the three of them came together in a colossal three-way orgasm that obliterated any doubt that they were meant to be as one, the power of three.

Sixteen

IN A TANGLE of limbs and satisfied sighs they lay beneath the rising moon. The full globe shone golden, casting comforting warmth across the field. What they'd just done—it had been the most erotically intense sexual encounter Rafael had ever experienced. He wondered if it were just him or if Luca felt the same way.

"Is that what you wanted, Falon?" Rafael asked as he trailed his fingertips along the inside of her sultry thigh. But he already knew the answer. Her essence was as intoxicating as a drug, lulling him into a perpetual sexual trance that he doubted he would ever fall out of. His lust for this woman would never be slaked. And today it had hit a high he never imagined existed.

She moaned and flexed her legs while wiggling her toes. "Mmm, more than I imagined it could be."

"Be careful how you move, angel face," Lucien said drowsily from the other side of Falon. "Your sweet tits are tempting me every time you move."

Falon giggled and shook her chest, eliciting a groan from Lucien. He snatched a nipple between his lips, and Falon squealed and tried to push away. Giving no consideration to Rafe whose head was resting her hip, Lucien pushed Falon into the heather, and maneuvered himself between the thighs Rafe had just been stroking.

Rafe's cock swelled as Lucien slid into Falon's ever-wet pussy. God she was amazing. He had wondered how she would handle two oversexed alphas, and now he knew. She was handling them both quite effectively, and shock of all shocks, he felt no jealousy. Even more odd was he enjoyed the camaraderie of the three of them like this. No inhibitions, no secrets, just love and acceptance. Rafe sat back and ran his fingers through his hair. Jesus Christ, he was impatient for her again. He envied Lucien as Falon's knees came up and her legs slipped around his waist. Her skin was so soft and silky. Her pussy so sweet, and succulent.

Lucien nipped at her breast and said, "Did you like it when Rafe commanded you?"

She arched, and closed her eyes. "Yes."

He scraped his teeth down her jugular. Rafe's cock swelled harder, but he would not interfere. This was Lucien's time with Falon. They would both want one-on-one time with her. He'd give Lucien his, and then he'd enjoy his own. Just as he'd enjoy their not so private time with her now.

"Why did you like it?" Rafe asked, very interested why such a dominant female would give up her power in such a vulnerable way.

She opened her eyes, looked past Lucien at him, then looked back into Lucien's waiting gaze. "Because it was nice to be told what to do instead of being in control. I felt as if the weight of the world had been lifted from my shoulders for just that brief amount of time."

Lucien smiled and kissed her. He moved slow and deliberately, in and out of her, taking his time, which made Rafe antsier. He wanted

Falon again but when he looked up to the rising full moon he knew they were running out of time. At midnight they would be their most powerful, and it was then they would need to make their move to steal the Cross of Caus.

Giving them the privacy they deserved, Rafe grabbed his clothes and sword, and moved away from them toward the path behind the ruins that led to a small waterfall and pond. The air had cooled considerably and he needed to bathe. The last thing he wanted was for those damn witches and goblins in town to hone in on Falon's scent because it was smeared into his pores.

He surfaced in the frigid water, then moved back as Falon and Lucien came running hand in hand down the rolling bank. They jumped into the water together.

Rafe shook his head and laughed when Falon grabbed his leg under water. She surfaced behind him, and pinched his ass. He reached behind him and dragged her around to face him. She laughed louder and allowed the buoyancy of the water to lift her legs around his waist.

"Thank you, Rafa!" she cried, hugging him to her.

His heart sang with happiness because she was so happy. He'd never seen her so lighthearted and carefree. "For what?"

"For being brave enough to give the three of us a chance." She kissed him full on the lips, and dissolved into giggles. "I can't wait to see the look on the council's faces when we return all fuck-happy and united." She laughed, and looked back at Lucien who had a smile twisting his lips.

"They're going to have to make up a new Blood Law to define us."

Rafael scowled knowing it was not going to be easy to convince the council or the packs that what they were doing was best for the nation.

"Oh, stop thinking of what everyone is going to think!" Falon pooh-poohed him. "You are alpha, Lucien is alpha, and I am alpha. We have chosen each other as our chosen ones. We are true mates in heart, body, and soul. There is no human or Lycan that can take away what we have built between us."

"As the eldest, I will take on the council if there is an issue," Rafe said solemnly.

"No, Rafa," Lucien said, stepping closer. "Together the three of us will face anyone who has an issue—as one united front. I suspect Anja's sire, Sasha, is going to have a huge issue with this, but know that I will stand beside you. I'm certain word has reached the northern packs by now that Mara was a Slayer."

"Oh, no! Luca! Will they try to charge you?"

"No," he said arrogantly. Typical Luca.

"The council will insist on a trial," Rafe said, knowing he would fight for his brother's life to the very end.

"They can go fuck themselves for all I care. Their time is past. After the rising, we will establish a new covenant," Lucien said, shaking his wet head and stalking for the bank. He grabbed his clothes where he had dropped them, and began to dress.

With Falon still wrapped around him like a spider monkey, Rafe waded out of the pond to the bank where she slid off him. Lucien handed her the flimsy little dress she insisted on wearing.

"We can worry about that later. Right now"—Rafe lifted his nose in the air; Falon and Lucien did, too—"we have bigger problems."

They looked up and saw that they had been surrounded by dozens of black shrouded figures. Rafe jerked his jeans on and picked up his swords.

The Coven of Caus. Protector of the Cross of Caus, Lucien said.

How do you know that?

When you took off last night we met them when we went looking for the sword. Not an amicable group, but a determined one, Rafa answered tossing Lucien one of his swords.

Falon, move between us and take each of our hands. As one, we walk up that hill and through them. If they have a problem with that, then we respond, Luca instructed.

The coven began a low deep chant, a spell calling upon a greater force to rid them of the scourge of the wolf.

When Rafe, Falon, and Lucien stood united, connected, intractable, power surged between them. In step and focused they strode toward the tallest of the witches who was surrounded by torches, never once breaking stride.

The coven tightened as they approached. Their chanting rose in volume.

Keep walking, Rafe said. The ring on his right hand flared softly with awareness. Rafe knew it well enough to know that it had an all seeing eye and it knew when the shit was about to hit the fan. And from the glow of the demonic eyes staring from the dark hoods just ahead, the shit was royally going to hit the fan.

As the chanting reached a fevered pitch, Falon snarled, and raised her hands, clasping their hands high above her head. Putting her head down like a bull, she shouted, "Move or die!"

Abruptly the chanting stopped, but Rafe wasn't fooled. The air hummed with dark powerful magic.

The tallest of the coven stepped forward and before he slid the hood of his cloak back, Rafe knew who it was. For as long as he lived, he would never forget the stench of the man who killed his parents.

"Corbet," he hissed.

What the fuck is he doing here? Lucien cursed.

Falon gasped and stumbled. Her hand pulled free from Rafe's

even as he moved to catch her fall. It was that one millisecond before he had her hand again that Corbet struck.

A hot shot of laser energy sliced across Rafa's chest. The velocity of the hit sent him to his knees, but he did not break his contact with Falon.

She snarled, throwing her wild mane of hair over her shoulder, and yanked him up.

"Corbet, you're going to regret that!" she yelled, and with her own power she shoved her hands, palms open toward him. He went flying backward several feet, landing heavily on his back.

Like an engine, Falon barreled through the witches that stood in her way, dispelling their magic.

As she came upon Corbet, who had regained his composure and drawn his swords, Falon smacked one out of his hand and snatched it out of the air.

She turned it on him and pressed the point to his throat.

"Tonight you join your brothers in hell."

Corbet smiled, and shook his head, his blue eyes so much like hers, not blinking once.

"You will not kill me," he taunted.

Falon pressed the sword into his skin, puncturing it. Blood spurted in a small pop then leveled off spreading in a sputtering wave with each heartbeat.

His eyes glittered excitedly. "You cannot."

She pushed the blade deeper. Blood bubbled, thickening around the sword tip.

"How does it feel Corbet? To know you're going to die?" she taunted.

"I'm not dead yet."

Falon's hands shook but she pressed the blade deeper into his throat. Blood gurgled like an overflowing fountain.

"Say good night, Slayer," she whispered.

"You will need my blood to raise your ghost walkers," he said hoarsely, struggling to speak against the blade in his neck. Grimacing, he looked past her to Rafe and Lucien. Fury and hatred washed off them in hot intense waves. "I have the power to resurrect your parents," he said, coughing as blood filled this throat. "Kill me and that option goes with me."

Rafael snarled, and Lucien grabbed the Slayer by the scruff of his shroud. "You lie."

"To raise the ghost walkers the two bloods must unite," he wheezed. "The blood that slew them and the blood that binds them." Corbet tried to laugh but he coughed instead, gagging on the blade. "I am the last Corbet directly descended from the original Slayer." His eyes glittered as he looked at Falon and challenged her to reveal her secret. She swallowed hard, knowing the time was not right to tell Rafa and Luca. She kicked Corbet away, much to Rafe's and Lucien's fury.

Corbet grabbed his neck, blood seeping through his fingers and backed up the embankment.

As Rafe and Lucien turned to go after him, Falon grabbed each of them by the arm to stay them, and watched Corbet disappear into the field as his coven of thieves noiselessly followed him.

And just as they had been fifteen minutes before, there were now alone.

"Why did you let him go, Falon?" Rafe demanded.

She opened her mouth to answer but the truth lodged in her throat. And she could not lie to Rafael's face.

"What was the purpose of that?" Lucien said, looking across the silvery field. "In chains he will be at our beck and call to raise the ghost walkers."

Her father was testing her, to see if she would slay him or reveal her truth. She would have slain him, she was so close—but she hadn't, because if she had, Rafa and Luca would not have forgiven her for taking away what they believed to be the only opportunity to raise their dead parents. Of course they didn't know that in her alone she possessed the two bloods. Thomas Corbet be damned!

"He's messing with us," Falon said softly. "Making you yearn for something he would not give you even if he could."

Lucien grabbed her suddenly trembling arms. "But *you* have the power, too, Falon. Don't you?"

"If I do, I have no clue how to use it."

"That's a question for Sharia. That old woman knows more than she lets on. The sooner we find the Cross, the sooner she can shed light on the secret to the ghost walkers," Rafe said, moving past them and gathering up their clothes and swords.

"Rafa!" Falon called, running to him. "Wait." She suddenly felt shy when he turned those piercing aqua green eyes on her. He was so big and strong and golden, and though she did not fear him, his power could be intimidating sometimes, as it was now.

She swallowed hard as her blood pounded through her. He had a way of making her feel very much the female to his male. She reached up and touched the gaping wound on his chest. Anger was surpassed only by her concern for him. She didn't ask for his permission to heal him. She was his chosen one, and not only was it her duty but her pleasure.

Standing up on her tiptoes, she leaned into him. Placing her hands on his hard chest, starting between his muscular pectorals, she pressed her tongue to the deep cut and slowly and lovingly lapped his wound, inch by inch until there was nothing more than a faint pink scar. When she was done, she leaned harder into him and looked up into his blazing eyes. Love shown with the brightness of a thousand suns in them. He nudged her chin up with his fingers and lowered his lips to hers.

"Thank you," he whispered against her.

Falon steadied herself. Rafael Vulkasin was heady stuff and her blood had warmed with her happy chore.

Her lids fluttered open, and she looked deep into his soul. She loved this man as fiercely as she loved his brother and it would be her death if he ever stopped looking at her the way he looked at her now.

"You're welcome."

Lucien cleared his throat behind them. "The moon waits for no one."

As they finished dressing and strapping on their leather scabbards, Rafe led the way to the van.

"We discovered last night that the Cross is concealed in a labyrinth of tunnels beneath the village museum. It's in plain sight but protected by a powerful spell," Rafe started to explain. "The problem isn't going to be breaking the spell. I think if we unite, call upon the ring and focus all of our energy on it, we'll break it. It's getting to it that's the problem."

"Are the tunnels locked?"

"And guarded by spells," Lucien explained.

"Does Corbet know about the sword?" she asked, thinking he had to. How could he not? And why she wondered, didn't he use it?

"The location of the sword isn't a big secret," Rafe said. "It's listed as one of the village's relics. But what it can do is a secret. I don't think Corbet knows. If he did, he would have either hidden it a long time ago so no one could destroy Fenrir, or used it as his own."

"Why protect Fenrir now? Their magic is beyond him."

"So long as Fenrir lives, the original magic he gave them lives. Without that foundation everything that came after it will evaporate into thin air. As it has always been, without that monster, the Slayers are nothing but despicable humans with no power to fuel them except their hatred."

Falon understood now. And at midnight they would be their most powerful but for that power to be they had to be in wolf form. "We go in as wolves?"

"Yes, but with our swords."

"We stay together," Lucien said.

Several moments later, they pulled up just outside the village. It glowed like a golden orb beneath the glow of the full moon.

"It looks like a festival of sorcerers, pagan priests, and witches," Falon said, leaning forward to get a closer look. Even on the outskirts of the village where they were, people ran hither and yon dressed in elaborate medieval costumes, most of them masked in ghoulish animal masks.

"They've gathered here to pay tribute to the Marcher witches."

Shivering as if cold worms crawled along her neck, Falon asked, "Just exactly how do they pay tribute?"

"Back in the day, human sacrifice. But now they burn an effigy," Lucien answered.

"How do you two know all of this?"

Lucien smiled and handed her a pamphlet from the dashboard. "It's all there, except the location of the sword. That we sniffed out with the help of the Eye of Fenrir."

Falon shook her head and wished she could fast-forward through the next four weeks to the day after the rising when they rose triumphant from the ashes of battle so that she and the two men she loved and the child she carried could live happily ever after.

She glanced at the multicolored pamphlet but a slight commotion caught her attention. Looking past Lucien through the windshield to a group of masked people who were dragging a large duffel bag out of the trunk of a van parked about thirty feet from where they had parked, her hackles rose. Her night vision was as honed as a wolf's and— "There." She pointed to the group that surrounded the bag. "That's a person in there."

Rafa shook his head, and said, "That's none of our business, Falon. We have to get that sword tonight or we lose our window of opportunity."

"They're going to sacrifice that person!" she insisted. How she knew that she had no clue but she knew it was true.

Lucien began to undress to shift. "Not our business."

A familiar scent caught Falon's nose. It was similar to her own, but different. It came from the bag. "Well, I'm making it our business."

Seventeen

SHAKING HIS HEAD, Lucien looked to his brother for help. Rafe looked as exasperated as Lucien felt. For the first time since Falon had proposed they agree to their . . . unorthodox . . . relationship, he was actually glad for it. It was going to take both of them to manage her.

"Falon," Rafe said, "you're sidetracking what we have to do."

Lucien touched her arm and said softly, "I admire your compassion, angel face, but there is far more at stake here than what happens to one person."

"I just can't stand by and do nothing when I know their intention is to harm that person," she said firmly.

A little help here, Rafe, Lucien shot his brother.

Falon slipped out of her dress, stuffed it into the leather pouch attached to her scabbard, and slipped it over her shoulders like a backpack. "The three of us can prevent it."

"Fal—" Rafe started but she shifted, and took off after the retreating group.

"Fuck me!" Lucien cursed and did the same. Rafe was right behind him.

You owe me big-time for this, angel face, Lucien complained.

Falon swished her tail and nipped at his snout. *It will be my pleasure.*

Picking up the scent, they maneuvered into a tight gauntlet and followed the shrouded figures as they hugged the outbuildings of the main thoroughfare.

The muffled cries of the captive wafted back to them and the hair on Lucien's back rose. *It's a child.*

We have to save her!

Let's do it then, Rafe said as they picked up their pace.

As they approached, the group slowed as they came to a halt at the back door of an ancient stone building.

Falon, Lucien said, *Rafe and I will rush them, you grab the kid and head back to the van. We'll catch up when we've taken care of business.*

Be careful.

It was like shooting fish in a barrel. Too easy. Lucien and Rafe scattered the group with snarls. Falon swooped in and bit off the hand that held the bag. The owner of the hand screamed in outrageous agony as Falon dragged the squirming bag away. When they turned to pursue, Lucien and Rafe closed ranks, snarling their warnings.

The building door slammed open and the stench of Slayer assaulted them.

Lucien grabbed the hilt of his sword from behind him with his powerful jaws and in a wide sweeping motion hacked at the knees as the enemy barreled through the door.

The poison worked quickly, immobilizing each Slayer cut by the blade. But more came at them.

Lucien shifted to human and grabbed his other sword. Double fisted, he cut and hacked his way into the column of Slayers.

Their initial screams were silenced when Rafe severed their heads from their shoulders. It was over as soon as it began.

"That was almost too easy," Lucien said as he wiped the blood from his sword with the tunic of one of the dead Slayers. His head jerked up and the hair on the back of his neck rose. He looked over at Rafe who stood rigid, nostrils flaring.

Corbet scent permeated the area.

Falon! Lucien called. When she did not respond, he sheathed his swords, shifted, then ran with Rafe right beside him.

As they approached the dark still van, they slowed. Corbet's scent became stronger.

Falon? Lucien called.

Shhh, she said as she stepped from behind the back of the van cradling the child in her arms.

Corbet is close, Falon, Rafe warned.

Her chin snapped up and, even in the darkness, illuminated by the glow of the moon, Lucien could see an eerie dark glint in her eyes he had never seen before. She looked predatorily primordial. Deadly. The look gave him momentary pause. He had seen Falon in hunt mode, he'd witnessed her bloodlust for killing Slayers but he had never seen such a haunted hungry look on her face as he did now. Was it all becoming too much for her?

Corbet is not near, Falon said, looking down at the child in her arms and smiling softly.

He is, I smell Corbet blood! Rafe insisted as he shifted and approached Falon.

Lucien smelled it, too. Clan Corbet had a distinct scent, they were easy to discern because of it, that and their physical features. Every one of them tall, athletic, blond-haired and blue-eyed. And evil incarnate. It was why he hadn't suspected redheaded Mara's true identity. But little did he realize, she had used magic to change her looks from statuesque blonde to voluptuous redhead. He had been a fool.

Falon continued to shake her head as she crooned to the bundle in her arms.

Perplexed, Lucien looked to Rafael. How could they smell Corbet but Falon could not? Her senses were as sharp as theirs.

As they cautiously approached Falon, hyperaware and ever vigilante of a Corbet, they looked down at the child she held cradled in her arms. Lucien scowled. It was a dark-haired girl not more than three or four years old, and from the look of her fragile bones outlined against her pale skin, undernourished. He sniffed, and raised his surprised eyes to Falon.

"Lycan," she whispered.

She slid the dirty shirt up from the child's back, exposing old, yellowed bruises peppered with more recent purple ones.

Lucien's outraged growls reverberated in the heavy air.

Falon moved to the open side door of the van and gently lay the child down on the bench seat. Or tried to. The kid wailed like a banshee, loud enough to raise the damn dead.

"Jesus, Falon," Rafe hissed. "Quiet her."

"Hush, hush, sweetheart, I won't let you go." Falon picked her back up and she immediately stopped crying. Snuggling up to Falon's chest the girl put her thumb in her mouth and drifted off to exhausted sleep.

Despite the anxiety of the moment, warmth filled Lucien as he watched Falon cradle and soothe the child. Instinctively he had known she would be a wonderful loving mother like his own, but seeing it, knowing she carried his child, he felt blessed.

"I can't leave her," Falon said to them both. "She's terrified. Those monsters were going to use her as a sacrifice."

Lucien swiped his hand across his chin going back to drive mode, and said, "Falon, our window is closing quickly. We need you with us to get that sword."

"I won't leave her," she said adamantly.

"Can't we give her something to make her sleep?" Rafe offered, smoothing away the girl's damp tangled hair from her dirty cheek.

"You don't drug babies, Rafa, so you can go hunt."

"I didn't mean that, I meant—"

"Even if I were guaranteed she was going to sleep, I couldn't leave her alone." Falon looked down at the angelic child, then to Lucien and Rafe. "But you're right; I need to go with you."

"She's Lycan, Falon, even at this age she will sense we're her kind," Lucien said. "And in that she will instinctively know that when there is a hunt in progress her job is to remain silent."

"What if like me she doesn't know she is Lycan?"

"Then we're just going to have to deal with it." Because like Falon, there was no way Lucien was going to leave that little bit of a Lycan to fend for herself if a Slayer or one of those damn witches came calling.

Lucien emptied the pack on his back of clothing. With his sword, he quickly cut two holes big enough for the child's spindly legs to fit through. He slipped it back over his shoulders so that it hung flat on his back like a papoose sack. "I'll carry the child so you're free to use your power." He looked to Rafe, and said, "You okay with this?"

Rafe nodded. As if he had a choice. They both knew that when Falon had her mind made up it was a foolish male who tried to argue her out of it.

Falon slipped the sleeping child gently into the backpack and let out a relieved sigh when she didn't wake screaming her head off.

"Ready?" Rafe asked, extending his hand to Falon.

"I'm ready," Falon answered, taking each of their hands.

Like shadows they stuck to the outside of the buildings as they worked their way to the northern-most building of the village. It was an old converted abbey that served as town meeting place and rendezvous point. It was aglow with candles and witches and sorcerers. Some who played at it, and some—from the dark magic that swirled around them—who lived it.

"To the roof," Rafe said.

Hands clasped, they leapt upward and landed noiselessly on the roof. It was simple, slipping down the bell tower shaft to the center of the abbey. The revelers in the front portion away from where they were headed were oblivious to their presence.

Rafe led the way to the triple-bolted wooden door at the very end of a long narrow corridor.

This leads to the dungeons below, which leads to the tunnels that run the length of the village. At the very center is the Cross, Rafe said. *We need to stick close together and be on alert at all times. There's going to be a bunch of shit down there.*

Rafe unbolted each bolt, slid back the heavy wooden slats, and then hauled back the heavy door.

If the Cross is so coveted, why aren't the bolts locked? Falon asked.

Because no one but us has the balls or the power to face what's on the other side, Lucien answered.

The second the door cracked open, iridescent furies screeched toward them, darting and nipping at them. Falon shoved her hands, palms open, at them. They screamed hideously and flew back against the stone walls, liquefying on the spot.

The child stirred on Lucien's back and he found himself making little bouncy moves to keep her quiet.

Nice job, love, Rafe said and continued down the dark passageway. They didn't need flashlights. Not only was their nocturnal vision sharp, but it also had infrared properties. They could pick up on body heat. So when the rats and mice went scurrying underfoot they recognized them for what they were and kept moving.

As Rafe opened another door, the stench that wafted to them made them gag.

My God, what is that? Falon gasped.

Years of blood and torture gore, Rafe said.

As they entered the dungeon, Falon gasped again, and stood perfectly still, staring as if she were seeing a ghost.

What is it, Falon? Lucien asked, squeezing her hand.

She reached out, and he watched her face drain of color. As if an invisible hand grabbed her she was pulled away from them. Rafe grabbed her shoulders and pulled her back. "What is it, Falon?" he demanded.

"Ghost walkers," she whispered. "They want me to go with them."

Her body was pulled again, this time with more insistence. Lucien tightened his grip on Falon's hand. "Tell them not now. Tell them to come to you on the eve of the rising."

Intently, Lucien watched as one emotion after another flickered across Falon's face. He was relieved to see she wasn't afraid. There was a calm intensity to her features that was reassuring.

Her body relaxed. She blinked and looked up at Rafe then to Lucien with a lucid look that told them that wherever she had just gone, she was back. Her brows crowded together in confusion. "When I told them I'd call for them on the eve of the rising, they nodded, but said to make sure I didn't get myself killed before then, because only I could raise them."

"But Corbet said—" Rafa started.

"I told you he lied," Falon reminded him.

"Where did those ghost walkers come from, Falon? This dungeon?" Lucien asked, looking around the dreadful place. They stood in the center of a wheel of cells. The old stones were dark, stained from years of bloodbaths. Rusted manacles and twisted bars hung from the low ceiling. In the center of the circle was an open fire pit with a smoke-smudged shaft above it. Human-sized grates still covered it.

"It sickens me," Lucien said. "What cruelty man is capable of, not only to his fellow man but to creatures as well." His eyes scanned the torture devices left behind.

"I suspect hundreds, if not thousands, of lives have been mercilessly tortured here, and for what? Believing in a different god? Having a different color skin, or for something as simple as disagreeing with the powers that be?" He shook his head in disgust. He had been persecuted all his life by assholes that hated because they were taught to hate. "I'm sick of the hatred bred between Slayer and Lycan. I'm sick of living every second of every day looking over my shoulder."

"A month from now, Brother, that will no longer be an issue," Rafe said. "Every Corbet on this planet will cease to exist. Only then can we rebuild a nation born with the freedom of not being persecuted."

Falon's hand trembled in Lucien's. "What's wrong, angel face?"

She had paled and her blue eyes looked huge against her face.

"Are they back? The ghost walkers?"

"No," she hoarsely said, avoiding his gaze. "It's just that this place exudes misery and I don't like it."

"Tell me more about the ghost walkers. Do they normally appear like they just did?"

"No—I don't know. Usually, when they appear to me, I'm unconscious and they're not specific. But these were. I got the feeling they were trapped here."

"They would have had to die here, and that's not possible," Rafe said as he moved them forward through the circle of cells to another passageway. "Lycan could not have died here by a Slayer hand."

"Why not?" she asked.

"Until the first rising three hundred years ago," Rafe explained, "there was no such thing as a Lycan. Since we were created, no Lycan would be suicidal enough to come back here to England where no wolves have lived for over four centuries. We're still reviled here. But more than that, like wolves, Lycan are social creatures; we need to be part of a pack. A pack here in England no matter how savvy, would not survive long."

"I think they follow you, Falon," Lucien said thoughtfully. "They recognize you as their conduit back to the life that was taken from them."

Falon's hand iced in his big warm one. "When we leave here we're going directly to Sharia to find out how the hell this works." He squeezed her hand. "I would give anything to see my mother's smile again." Emotion swelled in his chest. For so long guilt and anger shrouded his feeling of loss. He quelled the spark of hope in his heart that one day he might see her again. Alive.

"I would give anything to hear Father reprimand us again for our unalpha hijinks," Rafe said wistfully.

Lucien smiled. Their sire had been a taskmaster but a loving one. It would be a day of all days to clasp hands with him again. He had loved their mother as fiercely as Lucien and Rafe loved Falon. He'd held Falon in his arms twice when she was at death's door. He could not imagine a life without her in it. The heartache would be unbearable; he would be reduced to nothing more than a shell of a man. Worthless.

Lucien shoved the feelings away refusing to think about loss when they were in the position of so much to gain.

As they came to another bolted door, the hair on Lucien's neck stood up. *There's something on the other side waiting for us,* he cautioned.

I'll go through first, Rafe said as he struck the locks with his sword. They rattled to the floor. With his sword tip he slowly pushed open the door.

The squeaking sound of scurrying rats disrupted the tense silence. As they moved through the door, the beady red eyes of hundreds of rodents flickered along the high walls and ceiling. But something else more sinister lurked.

Slowly they moved down the musty stone and timber passageway until they came to another door. This one was wrought iron and through it, Lucien could see moonlight streaming through a low window highlighting the cluttered room beyond its threshold. The child on his back stirred and cried in her sleep. Foreboding traced icy fingers down his spine. They had no choice but to go forward. Fenrir's death was paramount to triumph over the Slayers. They had to go through the door.

Once again, Rafe used his sword to demolish the locks. As he pulled the rusty chains wound around the door to the wall, they turned to a jumble of hissing rising cobras.

Falon screamed out in warning, pulling Rafe back just as Lucien grabbed his shoulder, but not before something struck Rafe's right sword hand.

Eighteen

WITHOUT THINKING TWICE, Falon tore the snake off Rafa's hand, and immediately covered the bite with her mouth even as she drew him away from the swarm of vipers. In her peripheral vision, she saw Luca hack the snakes to fish-bait size. She sucked the venom from Rafa as quickly and as deeply as she could, vehemently spitting the venom out each time she drew it into her mouth.

"I can't breathe," Rafa's voice choked out before he went down.

Falon's blood pressure shot sky-high.

"Lucien! Rafe's down," she screamed. She followed him down to the damp stone floor. His big body began to spasm and shake. "Rafa," she cried, taking his face between her hands. "Look at me! Stay with me, baby." When his body continued to convulse, she grabbed his bitten hand and continued to draw the poison from him. His body stilled some but his tan skin paled to an ashen shade of gray.

"Lucien!" she cried. "Help me!"

The little girl's cries added tension to the situation. When Falon looked up at Lucien, she saw three of him. Reaching out to him, her unsteady hand shook.

"Falon," Lucien said, dropping to his knees. "What's wrong with you?"

"I think—I ingested some of the poison," she said, swaying on her knees. "I'm okay." She turned back to Rafe, and caught her breath. He had turned a deeper shade of gray. "He can't breathe!"

Lucien gently set her aside, and opened his brother's mouth and breathed into him. Frantically, Falon pressed her healing hands to the bite on Rafa's hand, calling upon all of her power to rid his body of the poison.

The little girl strapped to Lucien's back cried louder, struggling to free herself.

"No, baby girl, you have to stay there," Falon tried to soothe as she attempted to heal Rafa.

But the little girl shrieked louder and for one so small and undernourished, she tore herself out of the papoose pack in quick fashion and crawled down Lucien's back to Falon.

She grabbed the child to her chest to keep her immobile and when she did, the baby put her hands on the one Falon used to grasp Rafe's bitten hand. Heat surged from the little girl into Falon, and then into Rafa. Like an electrical infusion the four of them hummed with power.

Falon's eyes widened in shock. Luca wore the same astounded expression.

What the hell?

The girl lay down against Rafael's chest as if she were snuggling up to sleep. Dismayed by the behavior but not questioning it, Falon and Lucien watched in awe as Rafa's body stopped spasming and a twinge of his color returned.

Rafa, Falon said, bending over his lips and kissing him. *Open your eyes.*

He didn't.

"Rafe," Lucien said harshly, "open your eyes damn it. We need to get the hell out of here. We don't have much time left."

He was unresponsive.

"He won't wake up without the antidote," a deep unwelcome voice said from the threshold of the wrought-iron door.

Falon's blood stilled in her veins as she looked up to see the last person on earth she expected to see.

Thomas Corbet.

"If you have it, give it to me." She stood, her stance slightly unsteady but strode toward him despite her weakness.

Lucien grabbed her wrist and pulled her back. "Don't go near him, Falon, he's vicious. He'll kill you."

Shaking off Lucien's hand, she strode closer. "He doesn't have the balls to kill me." She raised her hands. And with the force of the energy that she was able to summon and control, as well as the energy that was as much a part of her as her eyes and lips, the energy that she never questioned, Falon shoved him so hard into the stone wall across the room that his head hit with a sickening thud. It only served to daze him. Falon continued her mad stride toward him. She shoved him again, this time pinning him to the wall. She raised her hands and his body rose with them.

"Give me the goddamn antidote, or I'm going to tear you apart one piece at a time."

His blue eyes blazed in fury but, she thought ironically, there was paternal pride lurking behind the anger. A smile twisted his full lips that, she realized, were the twin to hers. God, with the exception of her coloring, she was a carbon copy of this man. Did Lucien see it?

She inhaled sharply and knew she would do anything; even reveal her secret, if it would save Rafael.

"I'll trade you," Corbet offered.

"I don't trust you to honor a trade." With her left hand raised she kept him pinned to the wall and with her right hand she unsheathed her poison sword. She pressed the tip to his throat. "There's poison on the tip of this blade. One prick by it and you become immobile, much like my Rafa is. In such an incapacitated state, all I need to do is cut off your head and you die the true death."

"But if you do that, you lose your precious alpha. I ask only a simple life-for-a-life trade."

"Give me the antidote!" she screamed. "Give it to me now, damn you!"

"Give me the child."

Falon gasped. "So that you can sacrifice her? Never!"

"I give you my word she will not be harmed."

"Then why do you want her?" Lucien demanded.

"She is my daughter," Corbet said simply.

Falon gasped. *She had a sister?*

"That's impossible!" Lucien bellowed.

Corbet sneered. "Improbable but not impossible. There are others like her. But she is mine. She was taken from me over a month ago by a group of ignorant Slayers who mistook her for full Lycan. I want her back."

Falon's brow wrinkled in confusion. Why did he want this half Lycan daughter but not her at the same age?

"What Lycan would lay with you, Corbet the most despised of all Slayers?" Lucien demanded.

Falon's skin frosted as she took a good hard look at the child. *Oh, my God!* It was—her *full* sister. How could her mother bear Corbet a second child? She had lied to Falon! About everything.

"Give me the child, and I will give you the antidote to break the spell."

"Wh-what is her name?"

"Alana."

Falon turned to Lucien, who stood furiously rigid behind her. She could see the bloodlust in his eyes. He wanted to destroy Corbet as much as she wanted to save Rafa. And because Corbet was Rafa's only lifeline, Lucien would not strike him down. And neither, she realized, did he have any designs on harming the child.

It became inexplicably warm in the room when only moments before it had been cool.

Falon's raised arms began to quiver and her knees shook. She blinked at the two Corbets.

"I—" The sword slipped from her hand as her knees buckled.

Lucien caught her, as she crumbled helplessly to the ground.

Corbet dropped to the floor from where she had pinned him to the wall and pointed to her belly. "The toxins are spreading in your body. While you will survive, the child will die inside you if you do not take the antidote soon." He looked past her to Rafa, whose breathing had shallowed. "Even the Eye of Fenrir cannot help him once the poison settles in."

Falon swallowed hard and nodded. For all things Corbet was, she knew in her heart he would not harm his daughter. And because she knew him for who he was, she allowed Lucien to take the sleeping child from Rafa's chest and hand her over to her father, Master Slayer Thomas Corbet.

He didn't look at the girl, but the way he made sure she was secure and comfortable in his arms spoke volumes. A twinge of longing for the father she never had was fleeting, but she felt it. It was what it was, and she was glad he had not raised her even if he had loved her enough to stick around. Thomas Corbet was the scourge of the earth and, father or not, she would kill him the first opportunity she got.

He reached into his tunic and withdrew a small leather pouch and tossed it to her. "Just a pinch for yourself, and several for your wolf. It works quickly." He strode past them and turned before he completely exited. "Where did you find Alana?"

"The witches . . ."

His blue eyes turned onyx. He nodded and disappeared down the corridor with her sleeping sister in his arms. An emptiness Falon could not identify, momentarily struck her numb.

"Here, angel face," Lucien said, having already opened the pouch. He pinched a small bit of the pale powder between his thumb and forefinger and, just as he was about to put it in her mouth, he hesitated. "What if it's poison?"

For the third time in the last ten minutes, Falon's blood pressure shot sky-high. What if it *were* poison? Did her father hate her that much to trick her into killing herself? Her gut told her no, and her brain told her even if he had lied about the antidote, she was going to lose her baby and Rafe if she didn't take it, so she might as well try.

"It's not," she said, wrapping her fingers around his hand. As his fingertips brushed against her lips Falon closed her eyes for the briefest of seconds as she tasted the bitter powder. Once it dissolved, she pushed Luca's hand away and said, "Tend Rafa, there's nothing more you can do for me."

Luca moved quickly to his brother. With tears in her eyes, she watched as Lucien tenderly lifted Rafa's head, opened his mouth, and then gently put several pinches of the powder onto his tongue, closing his lips and telling him to swallow.

"Damn it, Rafe," Lucien cursed, shaking his brother by the shoulders. "Swallow it!"

Falon rolled over and tried to stand but her legs were still too weak so she crawled to Rafa. Grasping his ring hand with one hand, with her other she grabbed Lucien's hand to her chest. She crawled over to lay her head on Rafa's chest, pressing her lips to his heart. Silent tears rolled down her cheeks.

"Rafa," she softly begged. "Don't leave me. Not when we have found each other again." She rubbed her wet eyes on his neck. "I love you, Luca loves you. *Please*, come back to us."

Lucien sat down, his back to the wall, and pulled Falon into the crook of his left arm and Rafa into the crook of his right arm. That was how they woke hours later when the village clock signaled the approaching midnight hour.

Nineteen

BEFORE RAFAEL OPENED his eyes he knew something had changed within him. Or maybe something hadn't changed but had become enhanced. His senses were as honed as ever. Instinctively, he knew Lucien and Falon were beside him. In addition, he could smell the lingering scent of the girl and—his blood boiled—Corbet! Then he remembered being bitten by a snake, but that was all.

His hearing, however, was crystal clear. Wherever he was, the scampering of rodents down the hall and the crisp wind as it rustled leaves outside was as distinct as if those things were under his nose. He opened his eyes and smiled. Fissures of energy snapped and crackled around him, showing him portals to smaller more intricate forms of energy. If he didn't know any better, he would say he was tripping. Had the venom done this?

He raised his head from Lucien's shoulder and looked across his chest to Falon's beautiful face. His blood warmed at the sight of her and his cock— Jesus, even half dead and nearly delirious, he couldn't control his primal reaction to her. She was so damn gorgeous. He loved her spunk and sarcasm and the way she surrendered everything to him as if he were the only man in the world she would ever love.

He scowled when he thought of the third person in their relationship. Unwanted jealousy snuck up on him. He wanted Falon all to himself. He didn't want to share her on any level with anyone. Not even Lucien who he loved second only to Falon.

He frowned thinking he had gotten past the jealousy. His frown deepened when he thought about everything they had been through, how could he deny his brother the right to love the woman Lucien loved above all others? How could he deny Lucien the same thing Rafe wanted, *needed* more than the air he breathed?

The answer was simple. He couldn't—certainly not after suffering the loss of Falon once before. It had nearly destroyed him. It would do the same thing to Luca. He couldn't stomach it. Wouldn't.

Hell, he still couldn't believe what he had agreed to!

It was unorthodox at the very least, and it would not go over well with the packs but at this stage of the game, when the three of them had gone through so much together and he and Lucien had since they were born, it was time to stop the infighting. Falon was right when she said they were beyond teenage jealousy. They were three powerful alphas, and damn if they weren't omnipotent united.

The clock struck again. It was almost midnight. "Falon," he whispered, kissing her forehead. "We don't have much time."

Lucien roused himself at Rafe's voice. When they locked gazes, a shit-eating grin split his brother's face. Lucien laughed, and slapped Rafe hard on the back. "I knew you'd pull through!"

"Rafa?" Falon asked, running her fingers over his face, and checking for herself that he was living, breathing, and warm.

Slowly, Rafe stood, drawing her up with him. "What happened?" he asked her.

"The chains. They turned into cobras. One bit you."

"I remember that. And I remember going down. Now I feel energized, and kind of trippy."

When Falon glanced at Lucien and his brother nodded, Rafe's suspicions were piqued.

"What happened?" he asked again, and realized as he asked the question that the little girl they had rescued was missing. "The little girl, where is she?"

"She, um—" Falon swallowed, and looked to Lucien for help.

"You were dying, Rafe, and the poison Falon sucked out of you affected her, too," Lucien explained. He exhaled and shoved his fingers through his hair, and continued, "That prick Corbet showed up and proceeded to inform us that the spell could only be broken with an antidote he conveniently was in possession of."

Like a nest of angry hornets, Rafe's rage swarmed his body. "And out of the goodness of his heart he gave it to you to save me and the baby?"

"He wanted the girl in trade," Falon injected.

"And you gave her to him?" he asked incredulous.

"Turns out that little girl is his daughter. He wanted her back," Lucien explained.

Rafe's jaw dropped. "That's impossible, she's Lycan."

"That's what I said. But if Corbet of all the Slayers in the world hooked up with a Lycan then I believe others could have, too. Corbet even said there were other hybrids out there."

Rafe jammed his fingers through his short hair unable to comprehend what Lucien was saying. "I don't believe it. Slayers revile Lycan, and Corbet most of all. I don't believe for one minute he would lay with a Lycan . . . or more precisely, that a Lycan would lay with him."

"Why is that so hard to believe, Rafa?" Falon said, her voice shaking. "Love has a way of transcending the most bitter hatred."

He looked down at her impassioned face. She believed this crock of crap?

"No! No Lycan would lay with a Slayer. It's forbidden!"

"Unless she was raped," Lucien said. "Which would not surprise me in the least with Corbet, but I can't see him touching a Lycan for any reason except to inflict pain."

"Rape isn't painful?" Falon challenged.

Lucien shook his head and gently smoothed his knuckles across her cheek. "I didn't mean that, angel face. I can only imagine it must be the most horrific pain a woman could experience. I meant to torture and kill."

"I don't believe it. I've seen the hatred and the unmitigated pleasure that bastard gets from killing Lycan," Rafe defended. "He's never discriminated male, female, or children for that matter."

"I believed him, Rafa," Falon said. "And I believed him when he gave his word she would not be harmed."

It was too much for Rafe to process: Corbet lying with a Lycan. *Never!*

"Maybe he used black magic like Mara did to hide who he really was," Lucien said.

"I don't believe that for a minute. Corbet *detests* Lycan." Rafe looked pointedly at Falon. "He hates with *every* part of his being. He will kill the child," he simply stated. But he saw the doubt in Falon's and his brother's eyes.

"Do you wish her dead, Rafa?" Falon asked horrified. "Because she is half Corbet, half Lycan?"

"No, I don't wish death on any child, not even a Slayer." He took Falon gently but firmly by the arms and defended his position. "Even so, my brother and I gave our blood vow the day our parents were killed that we would eradicate the world of every last drop of Corbet blood. Nothing has changed that."

"Then you *would* kill her?"

"I would keep my blood vow to my parents."

He watched the color drain from Falon's face. When her knees buckled he caught her in his arms. She hung limp as if she had no power left in her.

"Put your arms around me, baby, and hold on tight," he said softly.

He was surprised to see the tears swell in her big beautiful eyes then slowly track down her cheeks. His brows furrowed in confusion. He was completely at a loss. "I'm sorry my answer wasn't what you wanted to hear, love, but you've known from the beginning how I feel about Slayers in general and Thomas Corbet specifically. He killed my parents—in the most horrific way imaginable. For that, he and his entire bloodline will pay."

He gathered her closer, and kissed her nose. "If any Corbet survives the rising, they will continue to perpetuate the hatred that has propelled our senseless slaughter for nearly a thousand years. If one Corbet lives, we will continue to be persecuted. The remedy is simple: destroy the blood, destroy the threat."

She nodded and tightened her arms around his neck. "I understand the concept, Rafa. I just don't understand taking the life of an innocent child who bears me no ill will."

"She will learn to. They all do sooner or later."

He kissed her then looked over at Lucien as the last bell chimed, signaling the bewitching hour of midnight. "We need to shift now and get the sword. We're out of time."

In less time than it took to blink, they strapped on their sheathed swords and backpacks, and then shifted. Rafe took point with Falon flanking his right and Lucien his left. They passed through the wrought-iron door that had caused them so much trouble, and moved deeper under the bowels of the medieval village.

With Rafe's enhanced vision, he was able to see beyond the infrared of life forces. He saw their auras, was able to gauge their strength and instinctively know where to strike to end the threat.

Do you feel any different, Falon? he asked her as they moved through another wrought-iron door, this one open as if in welcome. Rafael paid extreme attention to their surroundings and the energy forces around them.

I feel lighter, more perceptive.

Me, too.

As they were halfway between the previous door and the next door, a pale yellow light illuminated the thick wooden portal. Each thick plank was strapped with large rusty hinges with decade's worth of dust-encrusted cobwebs cloaking most of the wood. The tiny incandescent sparks of energy that were the spiders that inhabited the webs flickered like fireflies on a warm summer night.

Do you see that? Rafe asked Falon.

She squinted, and said, *Little flickering lights, like fireflies.*

Rafe smiled and nodded. *Spiders.*

Careful the glow behind the door is nothing good, Lucien said.

A spell? Falon asked.

Rafe nodded. *Draw your swords and be ready for anything.*

With their powerful jaws, in unison, they drew their swords from the leather sheaths on their backs, and then side to side to side they closed ranks so that their bodies touched as they moved as one unit toward the door. The power of three.

There were no locks, no chains, no dead bolts. Just an old cobweb-encrusted tarnished handle. Rafe jumped up on his hind legs and pushed it with his front paws. It squeaked and groaned but slowly swung open as if there was a hand on the other side, pulling it open in welcome.

Every sense Rafe possessed was on high alert. His nose twitched detecting only the musty scents of age. As the door opened wider the glow intensified forcing them to squint against its brightness. Still connected they moved through the threshold.

It felt like sunshine on her face. The radiance drew Falon in with the promise of Elysian Fields. She felt light, effervescent, like a bubble as she drifted to the light.

Stop! Lucien commanded as they stepped into a pile of rubble. Falon blinked, and looked down. They were standing in the middle of a bone yard. From the looks of them human though some looked— half human and half wolf?

What is this? she asked.

What's left of the ones before us who tried to retrieve that. Falon looked straight ahead and there, suspended in the air not more than fifteen feet in front of them, was the Cross of Caus. It was beautiful. A classic broadsword with a golden pommel and a sapphire-, ruby-, and emerald-encrusted mount. The hilt was gold and the full length of the blade, polished silver with what looked like Latin inscriptions.

It's magnificent, Falon breathed as she was drawn to it. Rafael growled a warning.

Do you see the curtain? Lucien said.

Falon blinked and refocused. Ah, there it was, translucent, golden, and shimmering as if it were alive, a protective sheath surrounded the sword. Why had she not initially seen it?

You were too beguiled by the sword, Luca answered her thought. *Part of the lure to draw you in.* He picked up a bone in his jaw and tossed it at the shroud. On contact the bone sparked and sizzled on contact before it dropped in a film of dust to the floor. *So that it can destroy you.*

What do we do?

It begins at the floor and goes to the rafters, Rafe said. *We can't jump into it.* He moved slightly forward, then said, *Shift so that we can move more freely and stay connected.*

As they shifted they grasped hands. Falon in the middle, Rafa to her right and Luca to her left. Carefully they moved around the sword, taking care not to get too close to the iridescent shroud. Its beauty and power beguiled. The force of it hard to resist. But resist it they did. As they came around to a full rotation, the shimmering cadence faltered.

Did you see that? Rafe said. *It flickered as if something affected it.*

We just made a full circle, Lucien said.

Let's go around again.

This time the flicker was more obvious as if their energy force was disturbing the electrical field holding the spell intact.

Take my hand, Luca, Rafe directed. When he did the curtain blanched as if something had struck it.

The curtain that had been cast to protect the sword continued to shimmy and shake, and within its protective circle, the Cross of Caus began to bob back and forth as if it was about to lose balance and crash to the floor.

Rafael lifted his hands in the air, bringing Falon's and Luca's hands up with his. He stared straight at the curtain and commanded, "Release the sword!" As if mocking Rafe's command, the curtain moved in slow sensuous waves.

Still holding hands, Falon opened her hands extending her palms toward the curtain. "Come to me sword!" she commanded. Her voice greatly disturbed the sword within, almost as if it desired release to her.

The shroud responded violently. Vibrating it tightened. Falon called upon the power within her, launching it at the shroud. Fissures tore through the magic, disturbing it so thoroughly that for the briefest second there was an opening to grab the sword but it came and went before any one of them realized what it was.

Call upon the ring, Rafe, Lucien said. *And then as one we'll throw everything we have at this bitch. The one closest to an opening grabs the sword.*

Tightly clasping hands, they stared directly at the glittering hilt of the Cross and one by one they commanded the curtain to fall, and then in one powerful voice commanded it to drop. The Eye of Fenrir flared furiously as if it had its own vendetta against the sword.

Falon's energy bursts pummeled the curtain as she called the Cross to her. With a will of its own the captive sword struck the shroud from the inside causing it to shake violently.

The sword struck again. This time the curtain tore directly in front of Lucien. Lightning quick, he grabbed the hilt. As he pulled the Cross from the protective curtain, it flared molten as the metal came in contact with regular air.

Lucien hissed in pain. But he raised his hand triumphantly in the air howling his victory.

"Let's get the hell out of here," he said, then tossed the sword into the air. He shifted, catching it in his powerful jaws as it came down.

Instead of retracing their steps, Rafe directed them up through the back stairways to the rooftop, where they ran along the rooftops all the way back to the building where they had rescued little Alana.

It was the only thing that could hinder Falon's happy step. She had a sister. A baby sister! She was part of a family. A completely broken, dysfunctional pathetic excuse for a family but she had one—a mother, a father, and a sister. Were there other siblings? Half or full?

She wanted to know and she didn't want to count any of them out like Rafe did. Falon didn't hate because she was half Lycan, she hated because of the horrible things her father's side of the family had done and continued to do to her mother's side. And though tainted Corbet blood ran through her veins, and the bouts of darkness terrified her, Falon would fight that darkness in her to her death before she allowed herself or any other Slayer to destroy the two men she loved above life itself.

Twenty

MANY HOURS LATER, flying high in the clouds back to their world, Falon stretched out between Rafael and Lucien as worry clouded her heart and mind. She felt like a liar, a cheat, a charlatan. The information she withheld from the two men who loved her was a game changer. She had hoped for some kind of sign from either one of them that they would be willing to accept her situation but Rafe had been crystal clear, and her disappointment was shattering. Exhaling loudly, she looked over at Lucien who stared broodingly at her. Her cheeks warmed and so damn it, despite her dark thoughts, did other body parts.

And with that, her heart constricted painfully at the thought of losing his love and respect. She now understood completely why, after Luca discovered Mara was not only still alive but a Slayer, he had kept those facts from her and Rafe. For the simple fear of losing her. What he had done was wrong but she understood the reason behind it. What she was doing now was worse.

But she could not tell them! Not now. It would be devastating, and the nation needed the powerful alphas completely focused. Maybe she would tell them after the rising, if they survived it. If she had the courage . . .

Instinctively her hand dropped to her belly. What of her child? Would they allow her to live long enough for him to be born? And then kill him, too? *No!* She would fight for her child's life even at the expense of her own and his father's. She would tell them nothing. Just simply slip away one night, have her baby, and look over her shoulder for the rest of her life.

And what a miserable lonely existence that would be.

"Angel face," Lucien said softly, leaning into her. He smiled and pressed his hand over the one on her belly. "You look like you have the weight of the world on your shoulders."

She smiled a sad smile, forcing back tears. Tracing her fingertips across his full bottom lip she said, "Promise me, no matter what happens, you will never stop loving me."

He grasped her hand, and nipped her fingertip. "You own every part of me. There is nothing that will ever change that."

Fisting his hair in her hand, Falon drew his lips to hers and deeply kissed him. His strong arms slipped around her waist pulling her into him. Inwardly she sighed, feeling safe in his strong arms.

Lucien was slow and deliberate in his kiss, drawing her away from what plagued her thoughts. Her skin flickered warmly as his tongue languidly swirled along her lips then against hers. She loved kissing him, her wicked, wicked Lycan.

When he broke the kiss several minutes later she was breathing heavily and not thinking about anything except his hands and mouth on her.

His beautiful golden eyes glowed with passion and—a mischievous smile tugged at the corner of his full lips. "I love you, angel face," he said softly. "I vow to you I will never forsake you." He kissed her nose, and smiled. "Never doubt me."

She knew Lucien believed what he said, but he was making his commitment not knowing the truth. As such, it didn't count. She clasped him tightly to her.

Would Luca truly stand by her? Could he when faced with the truth?

Both alphas had the same demons but carried them differently.

While Luca dragged around the guilt of not doing what he had wanted to do the day Clan Corbet viciously slew his parents, it was Rafa who bore the responsibility by barring Lucien from going to their mother's aide. It would be Rafe who could not, *would* not, allow himself to set down the guilt, even after he destroyed Corbet and his entire line. It was a no-win situation for Rafa and his guilt because he held himself solely responsible because of his inaction.

Never mind he was only ten years old at the time and would have been as hideously tortured and killed as his parents and so many others that day had he not honored the promise he made to his mother. Thank the gods for that.

But even with the truth of what would have happened had he tried to save his parents, if Rafa knew the truth about her, he would never be able to look at her again without seeing his parents' blood on her hands. She would always pay the price for her father's sins.

She opened her eyes to find Rafa's equally brooding eyes watching her. Fear prickled along her spine. Did he know? Suspect? To diffuse the uncomfortable feeling she said, "Why are you looking at me like that?"

He slowly shook his head, not breaking his stare. "What aren't you telling us, Falon?"

Her throat tightened, and her hands shook. "Why do you say that?" she nervously asked, pushing out of Lucien's embrace.

"Don't answer a question with a question, Falon," he said quietly.

She opened her mouth to deny what he asked but decided that would add to the thickening tension. Instead she gave him a different truth. "I'm worried. I'm afraid, and I feel helpless."

Rafe nodded. "I'm worried, too, and afraid something is going to pop up we're not prepared to handle. And because of it, we'll lose the final battle."

Falon gasped. "Like what?" She was afraid to ask.

"Like more witches or an attack by demons or goblins we have no clue exist. Or that Fenrir is going to pull some magic wand out of his ass we can't overcome."

Falon's heart thundered inside her rib cage, choking her breath from her lungs. "We have the sword," she breathed, her voice shaky. Fenrir knew her secret and she knew in her heart if Corbet didn't reveal it, Fenrir would. Her father had given her two weeks. Fenrir would not be so indulging.

"Where are we going now?"

"North to the battleground."

"Where is that?"

"The tribes call it Naparyarmiut, but on the map it's Hooper's Bay. It's on the west coast of Alaska on the Bering Sea," Lucien said.

"The packs have been moving north for weeks, many of them will be there when we arrive with the balance to follow over the next week."

"What will happen? How will the battle commence?"

"As it did three hundred years ago, face-to-face, hand to hand, sword to sword."

Falon shivered as the image of the gruesome battle to come played out in slow motion in her head. Fenrir leading legions of powerful Slayers against them but in her vision, Rafe and Lucien were not with her, but together. Where was she? Had they learned her truth and—

"We must call out Fenrir before the rising," she said hoarsely. "With his death the Slayers have nothing."

Rafe withdrew the Cross of Caus from the scabbard on the floor beside him. His eyes shone brightly as he held it up and she noticed the ring on his finger glowed warmly. "With the sword, the ring and the power of the three, we can defeat him. We *will* defeat him." His eyes flared and he caught her gaze. "And then we will annihilate every Slayer and hybrid on the planet."

Falon lowered her gaze unable to look Rafe in the eye when she hid such a terrible lie. But it was exactly that shame and the fear of discovery that planted the seed of an idea in her brain.

"What will you tell the packs—about us?" Falon asked.

Lucien gathered her back into his arms and kissed the top of her head. "That we are united and anyone who has a problem with it is free join another pack."

Falon glanced at Rafe who nodded. "I am the eldest, and when I speak to the council, I will speak on behalf of Vulkasin and Mondragon when both packs arrive. If any human or Lycan challenges me, I will accept the challenge, and win."

"What if the packs as a whole reject us as a trio?"

"They won't," Rafe assured her.

Lucien squeezed her. "If I had any doubt that what we were doing would be detrimental in any way to either pack, Falon, I would not have agreed to this unusual relationship." He looked past her to Rafe. "I love my brother. I regret the years we spent separated. I regret the heartache our packs have endured. I would not put them through anything like that again." He sighed heavily. "I would step down as alpha first."

"You would do that, for me?"

He nodded. "For us."

Emotion caught in her throat. "Oh, Luca, I love you more for saying that, but alpha is as much a part of you as your golden eyes. You would be miserable with anything less."

He took her chin in his hand and raised it so that their eyes locked. "I would be more miserable without you."

He kissed her and in that brief moment, Falon believed if Lucien knew the truth he would not cast her aside. He pulled her into his lap and she curled up in his protective arms and as her eyes fluttered closed the last image she saw was Rafe's intense scowl.

Her dreams were fraught with despair. Of running from who she was, straight into the jaws of Fenrir. Those aimless gray souls, the ghost walkers howled mournfully around her, fearful she would not release them from their endless purgatory.

In them she looked for Rafael and Lucien's parents. *Tamaska! Arnou! Are you there?* She sobbed. *I love your sons! I hate my lie but I'm so afraid to lose them. Tell me what to do!* she pleaded. *Tell me what to do!*

Deafening silence answered. An omen. There was no answer therefore there would be no life for her with her alphas after the rising.

On every side of this feud there was heartache and pain. Slayers lost loved ones, Lycan, too, and even Fenrir, that disgusting excuse for a wolf had feelings. Imagine that? He wasn't just driven by his rejection. Deep down inside that wolf had a heart and wanted the same thing everyone wanted: to be loved. Unconditionally. How odd that her parents of all people loved each other enough to stay together all these years and even bring another child into the world. How difficult it must have been and still be.

Would Rafe or Lucien give it all up for her like her father did her mother? She would not ask them to, and she would never in a thousand years lay as her mother had with the man who destroyed so many people she loved. Anger swept away any compassion she had for her mother, father, or Fenrir. Her mother was weak, a traitor to her people and to her children. Thomas and Fenrir perpetuated an eight-hundred-year-old hatred. She would end it.

Her plan took root. When they arrived in Alaska, she would take the Cross of Caus and set out on her own odyssey to destroy her father and the wicked wolf Fenrir, thus ending the curse upon both peoples.

"ANGEL FACE," LUCIEN said softly. "Wake up, we're here."

Falon slowly roused, unsure of where *here* was.

"The hunting grounds. C'mon."

Before she could move, Lucien hoisted her up into his arms, and carried her out of the plane into the cold night air. The crisp artic air felt good in her lungs. The fresh scents of nature welcomed her. As Lucien set her down she saw Rafe loading a black SUV. He glanced up, and caught her stare before turning back to the loading.

Foreboding haunted her. Did Rafe suspect? Gently she tried to probe his thoughts but he had closed himself off to her. Even more cause for alarm.

"C'mon, let's get you warm," Lucien said, steering her toward the SUV. He settled her in the backseat, then climbed up front in the passenger seat as Rafe took the driver's seat. Without conversation they drove off the tarmac of the small airfield and into the blackness of night.

As they drove, Falon watched the blackness speed by, and her mood settled more uncomfortably within her. She kept telling herself there was no way out except with the deaths of the two beings who knew about her but who perpetuated the hatred. It was a twofer since both her father and Fenrir were in all Lycan's crosshairs. Layla she wasn't worried about. Her mother would keep her secret for fear of punishment for them both. At least in that her mother had some loyalty. And her sister! Alana.

That sweet little girl.

They had shared a kindred heart the minute Falon held her in her arms and told her she would protect her. The girl had instantly quieted and settled into Falon's arms. The emotion that had exploded in her chest was what she surmised a mother must feel for her child. And now, that poor kid would grow up hating Falon for killing her father. But did she have a choice?

She glanced up at the rearview mirror and caught Rafe's penetrating stare. "What is it, Rafa?"

He glanced at the road then back at her. "You tell me."

Once again that feeling that he suspected the worse overcame her.

"You've been quiet the entire trip back, Rafe, what's up?" Lucien asked.

Long minutes passed before he answered. "Corbet's claim that the child was his daughter is eating at me."

"It's been on my mind as well. Unless a Lycan was forced, I can't see how he could have sired a child."

"What if that Lycan, like me, didn't know she was Lycan until it was too late?" Falon offered hoping to steer the conversation away from connecting any dots. It made her feel guiltier. It was one thing to not know the truth but to know it now as she did and to propagate the lie to protect herself . . .

"I suppose that's possible, but improbable." Rafe looked up at the rearview mirror again and asked, "Did Layla ever tell you why she deserted you?"

Falon's chest squeezed so tightly she had to suck hard for a breath.

"Being out of the protection of her pack, she feared that so long as we were together, Slayers could sniff her out and thereby sniff me out."

"So for your protection, she abandoned you?"

It was a bitter pill to swallow but— "Yes."

"Why didn't she return to the pack?" Lucien asked, turning to face her.

"All she would tell me was that she had survivor's guilt. That she could not bear to relive what had happened, and being among her pack she would relive it constantly."

"Sounds like a cop-out," Rafe said.

Falon nodded, understanding why he would say that but knowing the truth, she understood completely, even though she would never have abandoned not only one but two children.

"Did she ever speak of her time with Corbet?" Rafe pushed.

Falon's belly dropped to her feet. "She—she refused to speak of it." And in hindsight Falon understood perfectly by what her mother hadn't said exactly what had happened. She fell in love with him. He stayed away from his clan to be with her mother and raise her. He battled his demons, but in the end, blood trumped love and child. Thomas Corbet's destiny would not be denied. It was as tragic as any Shakespearean play and for the first time, knowing the truth, Falon felt compassion for her mother and her father. Though she could not understand how on earth Layla could fall in love with the Master Slayer who had viciously destroyed her family, she understood the depths of love.

And the heartbreak of having it ripped from your arms.

"Did she speak of your father?" Rafe asked.

This time the blood leeched from her cheeks. "Only that he loved me."

"Is he still alive?"

"My mother said at the time she didn't know."

"Does she now?"

"I don't know," Falon whispered, wanting to jump out of the car and run.

Rafe slowed and made a wide banking right and turn and continued to drive in complete darkness. Just when she could stand the silence no more a soft rosy glow rose on the horizon.

"The Amorak have arrived," Lucien said excitedly.

"And with them answers," Rafe replied, catching Falon's eyes in the rearview mirror.

Twenty-one

FALON WATCHED IN awe as the amazing sight unfurled before her eyes. Scores of what she could only describe as teepee-style lodges dotted the glow amidst the darkness. Fires roared within them, illuminating the animal skin covers and intricate designs and scenes carved into the pelts that appeared to come alive with the flickering of the hearth fires.

"This is just the beginning, Falon," Rafe said. "In a week's time this entire valley will be full of similar structures. Hundreds of them."

"How will they be sustained?" she asked, thinking of the provisions it would take to feed and fortify the entire Lycan nation.

"Everyone pitches in and contributes. In the harbor there's a ship with enough food and sundries to last the nation two months. There will also be daily hunting parties to go out for fresh meat."

"Are we vulnerable here? Will the Slayers attack before the rising?"

"Slayers play by no rules. We must always be vigilant."

Rafe drove down what appeared to be a main thoroughfare and

seemed to know where he was going. At the edge of the encampment he stopped in front of a lodge that was easily twice as large as any of the others.

He put the vehicle in park, and turned off the ignition. He came around as Lucien was opening her door, and nudged him out of the way. Lucien took exception to it, and for the first time since they had shared intimacy as three, the tension rose between the two men.

Falon was glad for it, but only because it took the spotlight off her. She pushed between them breaking them apart, and looked up at the dark structure. Rafe moved to the large flap, held it back, and extended his arm. "Home for the next month."

"This is Vulkasin," Lucien said roughly. "My camp is farther down."

Rafe looked patiently at his brother, and said, "Move it next to this one."

"Falon comes with me," Lucien said, extending his hand.

Rafe stepped between her and his brother's outstretched hand. "She was mine first."

Lucien snarled and stepped closer.

"I'm not a bone!" Falon shouted. "I won't be treated like one." Once again she held the brothers apart. "Which place is bigger?"

Rafe scowled. "They should be the same size as Lucien and I are equally ranked alphas."

"Fine, then this one will do, *for the three of us.*" As she made the statement, a thrilling excitement mixed with harsh trepidation tangled in her belly. Excitement because for the next month she would be spending intimate time with both of her men here in this beautiful setting, and trepidation that she was wrong withholding the truth from them.

"I'm not so sure that would be the best situation," Lucien said.

"Why not? Because I'm not going to have you two coming in and out in shifts! And I sure as hell am not going to be skulking between two camps! How do you think that would make me look?" They both stared blankly at her. "Like I'm servicing the two of you, that's how!" She crossed her arms over her chest, and said, "Either the both of you stay here with me or neither of you do." She cocked her head sideways and raised a brow. "It's your decision."

Rafael looked at a scowling Lucien. They made to snarl at each other but didn't. Falon had to force her lips from quirking. God she loved these two with all her heart. Emotion jacked up her throat. And she would do anything to keep them.

"Well?" she asked, tapping her foot. "All or nothing."

Rafe threw his hands up in the air. "Fine, Falon, but don't expect me to be happy about the arrangement."

She stuck her tongue out at his retreating back just as Lucien caught her up in the circle of his arms. His wicked smile could disarm a stone. He kissed her soundly on the lips, then smacked her butt before he practically skipped away to help his brother. Falon laughed at him. In so many ways, though only separated by minutes, Lucien acted the younger brother. He got away with hijinks and naughtiness, while Rafe was the one expected to be serious and dutiful at all times. She was sensitive to that about him and tried to understand what drove him.

Falon turned back to the lodge, and pulled back the flap. Darkness.

"Here," Rafe said roughly, handing her a flashlight to show her the way. The light shone brightly into the large, airy space. Thick colorful woven rugs covered the floor, but central to the space was a self-contained adobe-style fireplace complete with a tall, narrow chimney that ran up through the middle of the structure. Several low, soft leather sofas surrounded it. In the corner behind the fireplace was a stack of fur pelts as tall as she was high and a large rough wood dresser. A table with four chairs was pushed to the right side along with stacked coolers and a washbasin. On the opposite side was a large claw-foot tub, and what she surmised was a portable commode. A chest-high folded screen rested against the wall closest to the tub.

The entire space felt open and she could see flap cutouts shoulder-high lining the skins and several higher up for ventilation.

"You like?" Lucien asked, coming in behind her.

She shivered from the cold, anxious to warm up the space. "I love it."

He dropped several boxes next to the table. "Good, because I'm tired and I'm hungry, woman. Fix me something to eat."

Falon laughed at his caveman talk. "If I refuse, are you going to drag me by my hair to the pelts?"

He donned that grin she loved so much, and swaggered toward her. "Oh, yeah, and while I'm dragging you by the hair I'm going to be ripping your clothes off and ravaging that sweet body of yours with my tongue."

Falon threw her arms around his neck, and said, "Then I refuse."

He nipped at her chin, and slapped her butt again. "Hungry!" he bellowed as he ducked out of the teepee.

While the guys were out doing whatever it was they were doing, Falon focused on feeding them. Her stomach rumbled. She was hungry, too. The last thing she had eaten was a sandwich hours ago somewhere over the Pacific Ocean. She needed to eat for herself and the baby.

Moments later she stood looking at the limited food items she had to work with. All of it meat. Typical. Men didn't do side dishes. She picked out two large cuts of beef and a smaller one, and seasoned them with the spices available. Lucien had lit the fireplace and showed her how the top portion slid back exposing a grill. Perfect.

While the steaks cooked she dug out a bottle of wine because she knew Rafe liked a nice cab. She had never been much on wine, mostly because with her nonexistent budget she couldn't afford it, and the stuff she had tasted, tasted like swill. Tonight she'd give it a shot. She uncorked the bottle and searched for glasses. She found plastic ones and decided to grab a couple of beers from the cooler for Lucien.

She checked on the steaks, then turned her attention on the pelts and making a bed. A warm wave of excitement washed through her when she thought of sleeping with both of her men in the same bed. The sexual anticipation aside, she was looking forward to snuggling between them and falling asleep in their arms. It was the one place she didn't think of anything but being in the moment.

And just like that her moment was shattered when her predicament intruded on her warm, sexy thoughts. It was an impossible situation. They were all under such an incredible amount of pressure. Their very lives hung in the balance, and she suddenly felt selfish wanting two men, and only on her terms. Suddenly she just wanted to tell them both the truth when they returned, and let the chips fall where they may, with the profound hope that they would be able to move beyond the issue of her paternal bloodline.

Gah! If it were so easy! It was anything but. She was screwed if they found out.

Lucien's and Rafael's deep voices drifted to her as she set the table. Her hand shook as she placed a knife on it. Inhaling deeply she focused on her chore and not the sound of them entering their temporary domicile.

Then there was silence—the kind that exploded. Falon's hands shook as she continued to set the table. When she was done, she slowly turned and caught her breath.

They stood rooted to the ground, wearing fresh clothes and looking like two predators, their hair damp as if they just stepped out of the shower. Rafe looked the epitome of *GQ* in his sleek black jeans and his fitted gold-pinstriped black shirt. His short golden-blond hair framed his classic features. She raised her eyes to his, and her heart stuttered in her chest. They were smoky and intense, full of promise. She swallowed hard as her eyes dropped to his full parted lips, then to the hollow at his throat where she could see the vigorous throb of his pulse. The urge to press her lips to it was overwhelming. She allowed her gaze to continue its carnal perusal to his wide chest, then to his hips and the thick rise in his jeans. She about melted on the floor when she saw he was barefoot.

Rafael Vulkasin was the epitome of alpha. And he belonged to her.

Dragging her eyes from Rafa, she indulged them in his brother. And like his brother, Luca was barefoot. Lucien's worn jeans hung sexily off his lean hips and the tight black T-shirt he wore hugged his rippling muscles like a second skin. She longed to run her hands up his chest as he circled her with his strong arms. His long dark hair was damp and curled around his face, shadowing his sinful lips and bedroom eyes. Everything about Lucien Mondragon screamed sizzling sensuality. And like his brother, he belonged to her.

Falon didn't know what she had done to win the hot-guy lottery twice but she was not going to question it. Ever.

"Hi," she said shyly.

Both of them smiled. Sensing her shyness, neither one moved toward her. For that she was grateful, she wasn't sure at that moment if she could handle both of them at the same time. Her hands shook nervously. "I— Your steaks are done. Come sit."

As they moved in, she quickly set the bottle of wine on the table, the two plastic cups, and Lucien's beer.

Hands still shaking, she set their plates in front of where they stood at the table and hers between them. Rafe and Lucien reached for her chair at the same time and pulled it out together. Hurriedly she sat before her legs gave way. When they sat down on either side of her, Falon's stomach did several slow rolls.

"I've never cooked steak before, I hope you like it."

"I'm sure it's perfect," Lucien said. "Thank you."

"You're welcome."

Feeling self-conscious as they watched her cut her meat, she took a bite nearly gagging on it. It tasted terrible! It was overspiced and overcooked. Not a hint of pink. And her men liked their meat rare. She forced herself to swallow it and looked up to see Rafe and Lucien exchange grimaces.

"I'm sorry! I don't know how to cook."

"It's fine, love," Rafael said. To prove it he took another bite, and chewed it as if he enjoyed it.

Lucien chased his with half his beer.

Mortified, Falon pushed her plate away from her.

"Falon," Rafe said, pouring her a full cup of wine, "you need to eat." He pushed the cup into her hand. "This will help it go down."

"Oh!" she cried. "You really do hate it!"

"No, it's fine, really." He took another bite and, like Lucien had, Rafe chased it with a deep sip of his wine.

She took a sip of the wine, and was surprised she enjoyed the cherry and oak taste of it.

"Angel face," Luca said as he wrestled with the piece of meat in his mouth. "The cooking is a beta's job." He took a long pull of his beer to wash the beef jerky down. "As alpha, your job is to lead beside your mate . . . er, mates . . . and"—his eyes twinkled mischievously—"to make mad passionate love to them."

Heat rose in her cheeks.

Lucien took her hand and kissed her fingertips.

"What is your role?" she shyly asked.

He lifted blazing golden eyes to her and slowly smiled. "To make mad passionate love to my woman and make her forget everything except me exists."

"Oh," she breathed.

Lucien sat back in his chair and pushed his plate away. He had more guts than she did; his steak was half eaten, Rafa's, too. Her heart warmed, knowing they'd choked down the food so she wouldn't feel like a complete failure.

Rafe scooted toward her and trailed a finger along her arm. "We showered and changed down at the community center." He drew her up, and circled her waist with his arms. "It would be my pleasure to draw you a bath."

"Ohh-kay," she breathed.

He moved her over to one of the sofas then proceeded to draw her bath. She had hoped the water would be warm and when she saw the steam rise, she smiled.

"It's hooked up to a water heater outside," Rafe said, catching her happy look. When the bubbles rose to the edge of the tub, Rafe turned to her, and extended his hand.

Heat washed over her in sudden shyness. "I'll get undressed behind the screen."

"Oh, Falon, that's not very nice," he complained. She smiled, and moved around him and pulled the screen out from between the tub and wall. As she set it up, obscuring their view of her, she secretly smiled.

When she settled into the velvety warm bubbles, she moaned in pleasure.

"Stop it, angel face, or you're going to have company," Luca threatened.

"You're welcome to join me anytime."

She giggled when he shoved the screen aside, and stared down at her, the lust plain on his face. "I'll settle for the view." He smiled again and pulled a short stool up, then sat down beside her. "For now."

Falon lay back against the back of the tub, and her breasts popped above the water, the soft white bubbles sluicing over them.

"Christ, Falon," Rafe groaned from where he stood by the warmth of the fireplace. "You're killing me."

She grinned, and moved deeper beneath the water. "It isn't like you haven't seen me before."

"Yeah, I get that but it's not like I see you like this every day." He threw back his wine, and poured another cup. His eyes caught and held hers. "You have exceptional tits."

"Thank you."

Lucien leaned over her, and kissed her. "And luscious lips."

Her hand snaked around his neck. "Yours aren't so bad, either."

When Rafe's tall form shadowed Lucien's, the heat in Falon's veins accelerated. She felt like a fat fluffy bunny being stalked by two big bad wolves. Absolutely thrilling.

"How much longer are you going to be in there?" Rafa impatiently asked.

"Why?" she asked coyly.

His eyes narrowed. "You know damn well why." Placing his hands on either side of the tub, he lowered his face to hers. "If you don't get out of there in two minutes, I'm coming in after you."

She slid deeper under the soapy water. "Like I just told your brother, be my guest."

Rafe reached in and grabbed her by the wrists and hoisted her dripping-wet body out of the tub and into his arms. Falon shrieked as she tried to squirm her way out of his grip. "Rafael! I wasn't done."

He strode across the small space to the bed of pelts she had made and tossed her onto it. "I haven't started," he growled, following her onto the luxurious fur. They felt wanton and sensuous against her damp skin.

Rafa dug his fingers into her hair. Lowering his lips to her ear he said softly, "I want you so bad right now it hurts." She closed her eyes and moaned, as he trailed his nose down her neck to the place where it met her shoulder. He kissed her then, nipping her skin and softening the sting with his tongue. Falon's body caught fire. She opened her eyes to see Lucien standing behind his brother pulling his T-shirt over his wide shoulders. When their eyes met she could not breathe. His flared like wildfire.

Falon closed her eyes, parted her lips, and then surrendered everything to them both.

Twenty-two

"LET YOUR HAIR down slow, baby," Rafa said as he helped pull the clips she had used to pile her long hair on her head when she took her bath. He spread it out around her like a shroud. Gently raking his fingers through it, he brought it to his nose and inhaled, then rubbed it across his face. "So soft." He smoothed it away from her face, trailing his nose across the high swell of her breast. "So sweet," he rasped as he licked a deep swath across her nipple.

Falon moaned, arching into him. When Luca slipped naked into the bed behind her and pulled her up against his hard warmth, the slow fire that had burned inside her since they'd arrived violently exploded.

"Perfect," Rafa purred as he spread her thighs and crawled between them. His lips trailed down her belly to nibble on the cradle of her hip before kissing a hot trail to her mons. Lucien wrapped her arms around his neck, causing her back to arch and her breasts to thrust into the cool air. Her nipples hardened not from the coolness in the air but because of Lucien's wanton fingers plucking them. His hot lips kissed behind her right ear, his tongue languidly circling the shell. Lucien's insistent erection jabbed her in the back, and each time she moved, he groaned in unrequited pleasure. Though they had her pinned to the furry bed, she had never felt more in control. She did this to them. She brought these two powerful men to their knees. There was no gloating, just a surge of empowerment and desire so palpable it filled her to bursting.

Never in her wildest dreams would she have thought the proud golden leader of Vulkasin, and the dark and deadly leader of Mondragon, would take her to the same bed at the same time and so unselfishly make love to her. Emotion painfully filled her chest, tightening her throat. It bore witness to their profound love for her. And she felt so undeserving in light of what she had learned about her father.

But— She closed her eyes and moaned when Rafa pushed her thighs farther apart and licked her wet seam open. When he gently drew her stiff clitoris into his mouth, she melted like butter in a heat wave. "Ah," she moaned, straining against Lucien's expert hands and wanton lips. As Rafa licked deep inside of her, he drove her to the brink of madness. Every thought fled from her mind. All she did was feel.

Rafa stilled her writhing hips with one hand. Splaying his long fingers across her belly with the other hand, he slid a thick finger inside her.

"Oh, Rafa," she moaned deeply. Her hips rose against his palm and lips. "That feels so good," she said before Lucien grasped her chin and turned her head toward him and kissed her with a voracity that left her breathless.

His tongue swirled and lapped the inside of her mouth in the same deep cadence that Rafa's finger slid in and out of her. She was drawn tight to begin with, and didn't need much to push her over the edge, and what these two men did for her, *to* her, was beyond any fantasy she could ever imagine.

Rafe caught her clitoris between his teeth and nibbled, flicking it with his tongue as Luca licked her nipple. Hot and wet, her body bucked into them, as that lovely familiar tingle intensified, racing for the finish line and then shattered in waves, each one cresting higher than the one before it.

She strained against Luca's mouth, crying out as she dug her fingers into his hair, fisting it as Rafa impaled her with his finger and tongue. As she thrashed and strained, Rafa slid a finger into her anus. It startled her, but because she was so wet and so loose it didn't hurt. Indeed, he moved his fingers together to the same beat and, oh god, that felt good. Her spasming body ratcheted up another level before coming completely undone.

Panting hard, her body twitched and jerked as it absorbed her orgasm, even in the aftermath. She was grateful they slowed and allowed her a moment to catch her breath.

But not for long. Rafe shed his clothes and settled back on the bed, trailing his finger down her thigh as his lips traced a path all the way down her leg to her foot. Slowly, he massaged her feet then, one by one, her toes.

"That feels so good . . ." When Luca dug his strong fingers into her hair and began to massage her scalp, she thought she had died and gone to heaven. If this was the reward for lousy cooking, she was going to burn every meal.

"Have I ever told you how fucking hot you are when you come?" Luca asked, leaning over her, his lips hovering above hers as his laconic eyes caught and held hers.

She licked her dry lips, her eyes rolling back into her head when he dug deeper into her scalp. Warm tingles crackled and flared on her head, neck, and shoulders, spreading all the way down her spine to her womb. Her nipples stiffened painfully, begging for succor.

He nipped at her lips, just as Rafe sucked a toe deep into his mouth, rolling his tongue around it. She was a live conduit of sensation. Her head and her toes were the envy of her middle. Her body wept for more. Falon arched nipping Luca's chest.

He hissed when her teeth scraped his skin. "No, angel face," he crooned. "This is all about you tonight."

"I want to taste you," she pleaded.

Rafe licked her instep, and followed through with a gentle bite. Shivers zinged crazily through her body. She moaned again, louder, then licked her dry lips.

"I so want to fill those pouty lips of yours," Luca whispered against her ear.

"Please," she begged.

Luca smiled the most wicked smile on record. It jarred her to her core. "Please, what?" he softly demanded.

"Please, fill me."

"When you ask like that, I can deny you nothing."

Falon turned in his arms. As she faced Luca on all fours, Rafe skimmed his hands up her bottom to her hips. He moved in behind her and spread her cheeks. He kissed the small of her back, taking his good sweet time about it.

Falon slid her hands up Luca's rigid erection. He groaned, thrusting his hips into her fingers as they circled his width. His cock was glorious and giving. She lowered her lips to the wide dewy head as Rafa slid a finger into her from behind.

Her breath caught in her throat as she sucked Luca deeply into her mouth. He groaned and laid back digging his fingers into her damp hair. "God, angel, that feels so damn good," he said roughly.

As she slowly set her cadence, Rafa slid his cock into her. She closed her eyes as her pussy fisted his thickness. He didn't move once he filled her balls deep. Instead, holding her steady by the cradle of her hips, he ground his hips in a slow sensuous circle into her. Falon squeezed her eyes tighter, overcome with sensation.

"Falon," Rafa breathed. "Don't move."

She exhaled around Luca's granite-hard cock, not knowing if she could obey. Slowly he dragged his length out of her. Her needy body trembled. Luca thrust into her mouth as Rafe withdrew. Rafa slid back into her as Luca withdrew. *Oh, that was amazing.*

With supreme control they moved in and out of her, and with even more control, Falon remained corpse still as the firestorm building inside her threatened to burn her alive. Luca's skin flushed hot with a film of sweat. His hands clasped her face, keeping her head steady. Rafa's hoarse breathing singed her back.

She wanted them to come with her. She was so close, right there, on the edge. Not being able to move heightened her pleasure. Luca's cock thrust deeper into her mouth, as Rafa's tempo picked up rhythm. No longer was it a slow grind. Now they were precision twin pistons, slamming into her, driving her mad with desire.

Then—

She snapped.

Her body braced for the impact but nothing prepared her for the intensity of what hit her. Her scream was drowned out as Luca came in her mouth and Rafa exploded inside her. She was impaled at both ends, and her body jerked and shook like a fish fighting a hook.

Wild waves of heat swept through her body and as their climaxes reached a crescendo, power surged through them as if a switch had been thrown. Lit up, Falon grasped Luca's hip, absorbing the pounding Rafa gave her at the same time she sucked Luca's pulsating cock deeper into her mouth as he came wildly. And then, after they were spent, she collapsed into them in a crazy, vibrating mass of raw sexual satisfaction.

For long minutes Falon lay gasping for breath. Rafa's harsh breaths behind her, and Luca's in front of her, made her smile. Lucien grinned and reached over to smooth her damp hair from her cheeks. He kissed her and said, "I love how much you love sex." He shook his head, his smile widening. "The look on your face when you come, Falon, is poetic it's so damn beautiful. It will stay with me always."

Rafa slid his hand up her back to her neck where he gently massaged her. "That was amazing," he said, and kissed her backside.

And that was how she fell asleep, sprawled out on luxurious furs nestled between two great alphas. She could not wait to wake up and explore more options.

Later, however, she woke to a cold empty bed. And to a foreboding that sat on her chest like a two-ton weight. Something was going on outside, and instinctively she knew it had everything to do with her. Quickly she jumped from the bed and used the meager bathroom facilities. After she had washed and brushed her teeth, she slipped on black thong panties and matching bra. Then pulled on a pair of black jeans, a pair of doeskin moccasins and a thin, white fleece, long-sleeved T-shirt.

As she exited the tent, she blinked back early morning sunshine. The air was crisp, the smell so clean and unaffected she inhaled it deeply into her lungs, the chill of it invigorating. She pulled her hair back and began to braid it as she followed Lucien's and Rafe's scent toward the middle of the growing encampment.

It bustled with activity. More tents had popped up since they had arrived last night. As she strode down the main drag she sensed how each person stopped what they were doing and boldly stared as she walked by.

It would have unnerved her two months ago, but the blood of the two most powerful alphas on the planet ran through her veins and their desire for her infused her with vital empowerment. She was on top of the world and nothing could knock her down this morning.

She smiled as the cool morning breeze caressed her cheeks. Call it earned arrogance, but the bounce in her step came directly from the power of three.

Halfway down the main thoroughfare Falon realized she was being followed. She didn't play coy; she stopped and turned around to face, Sasha, Anja's infuriated sire along with his entire pack, who appeared just as angry.

She waited for them to fully approach, and when they came within ten feet of her with no intention of stopping, Falon held up her hand. "Say what you have to say from there."

Without hesitation, Sasha continued toward her. Fisting her right hand, Falon brought it to her chest, and then as if she were tossing high-powered dice, she flung it at the impassioned alpha.

The velocity of the air she hurled hit him hard in the chest, knocking the wind out of him but not hard enough to force him to the ground. When he stumbled backward, his pack supported him. Falon held her ground as energy whipped around her with such force it unfettered her hair, rising madly around her as if it had a life of its own.

"Take another step, sir, and you'll end up in the Bering Sea."

"How dare you speak to me!" he shouted, his crystal-clear eyes so much like his daughter's. She understood his anger; she would be angry, too, but she begrudged him his indignation given the circumstances.

"As your equal, I dare to speak to you and more," Falon said, stepping closer to him. "In an unfortunate sequence of events, you have been dealt a terrible blow. For that I am sorry, but your anger and embarrassment will mean nothing if we fall during the rising." She took another step toward him. "Your daughter is beautiful and intelligent. Worthy of any alpha, including mine, but that will never be." Only feet from him, Falon finished. "Consider it taking one for team Lycan. I am vital to Rafa in a way your daughter never could be. Rafa is vital to all of our existences. Take your petty hurt feelings away from here before you poison the entire well."

Falon watched his face go from furious afraid, to angry indignation, to vengeful.

"You are a fool, Sasha. We need a united nation. Your selfish heart will tear down everything we have fought for."

"Watch your back, bitch," he sneered.

Falon cocked a brow, and said, "Indeed, watch yours, sir." She turned and stopped abruptly when she saw Lucien and Rafe standing forty feet downwind of her. Their eyes blazed in fury. Not at her but past her to Sasha and his pack. Falon glanced over her shoulder and saw a hint of fear flicker in the old alpha's eyes. But not enough to show respect. It would be his last mistake.

Falon turned and when she caught her men's gazes, she smiled and hurried her step toward them as they hurried their steps toward her.

Twenty-three

"I'D ASK IF you were okay," Lucien said, "but all I have to do is look at Sasha to know you've set him straight."

"He's understandably upset."

She reached for his hand, entwining her fingers through his. When she looked up at him with those big blue eyes so full of love and trust, Lucien wanted to drop to his knee and beg for forgiveness. He had been a prick when she was with Rafe. And he hadn't made it easy for her in many ways since then.

"I'm sorry, angel face," he said softly.

She slowly smiled, not taking her eyes from his. "For what?"

"For all the times I hurt you. For all the times I doubted you. For all the times I was a colossal ass."

Her smile widened, and she laughed. "No need to apologize, Luca. I fell in love with that colossal ass." She grinned, and scorched him with a lustful look. "And the other colossal thing."

His brows shot straight into his hairline but he grinned.

That colossal thing had wanted to say good morning in a very special way before he rolled out of bed at dawn. Falon was something to behold in the low glow of the fire. Long, soft, creamy limbs, sprawled out all fuck happy on the pelts. She had a sweet ass and the dimples just above it begged to be kissed. He'd told himself that all he had to do was kiss her there, and she'd roll over and—sweet Jesus he was hard. "I love fucking you," Lucien said.

"I'd say get a room," Rafe curtly broke in, "but we have to address the council."

Falon pouted.

"I want to suck on that lip so bad," Lucien said.

Falon giggled, and squeezed his hand. "You two left me in bed. Alone."

Rafe cocked a brow. "You were snoring like a sailor. You needed the sleep."

"I don't snore!"

Lucien laughed, and said, "You kind of do, but it's cute."

"I do not snore!"

"I'll record it next time," Rafe said, trying hard to remain the serious one.

And Lucien let him be the serious one. It suited Rafael. It was who he was, how he operated. One thing Lucien had always taken for granted about Rafa was his level head. He trusted his brother explicitly to do the right thing. And though Lucien had a healthy ego it wasn't the kind that would argue a good idea just because it wasn't his. Rafe possessed every quality an alpha needed. He understood that to lead he did not have to terrorize. He was intelligent, he was a master tactician and ruthless when necessary.

From the day they were born their father had groomed Rafe as the heir apparent. Lucien was groomed to second him in every way and step up if Rafe fell. While Rafe measured every move he made with methodical precision, Lucien was more impulsive. Both methods worked, some better at times, but they worked.

They were both worthy of leading a pack in their own right.

Lucien's chest hurt a little bit when he thought how his hatred and jealousy had consumed his every waking moment as well as his dreams. So much wasted time. He had to have known that the Rafe he knew would never have slain his chosen one because he wanted full alpha rights. That wasn't Rafael's style. Lucien squeezed Falon's hand. She'd seen right through him and called him out. It was what he needed, and he would forever be in Falon's debt for reuniting him with his brother.

"When will Vulkasin and Mondragon arrive?" Falon asked.

"With all that had to be managed, they're getting a later start, but I expect both packs will be here this time tomorrow," Rafe answered.

"Do they know—about us?" she hesitantly asked.

"Joachim and Anton have been apprised of the situation," Rafe said in a clipped, formal voice.

Falon grabbed his hand and pulled back to slow his forceful stride. "You say that like it's a bad thing."

He stopped and looked at her. Lucien understood his frustration. By the Blood Law she belonged to Rafe. Lucien had absolutely no claim on her whatsoever, yet he loved her. And Falon loved him enough to ask Rafe to share her.

"I am the eldest. I marked you first. You exchanged the mark. You are mine, Falon. In every Lycan's eye you belong to me." He looked from Falon to Lucien who wanted to remain objective but it was hard when Rafe could simply refuse to continue this setup. And they would have a serious problem.

Rafe exhaled slowly, then looked back at Falon. Her cheeks had pinkened—from anger or embarrassment, he wasn't sure. "Vulkasin opened their hearts to you and you embraced them as they embraced you." He shoved his fingers through his hair. "They never accepted losing you. They never accepted Anja. In their hearts you were their only alpha. As for them being separated so long from Mondragon— it's going to take some time for the packs to reunite and reestablish trust."

"Like Vulkasin, angel face, Mondragon threw their arms around you, embracing you as theirs. You carry my child. Seeing you with Rafe is going to be hard. And—" He inhaled deeply, and held his breath.

"And what?" she asked.

He expelled the air in his lungs and answered, "Rafe and I have a reputation, a persona if you will, and I'm afraid it's being severely compromised by our arrangement."

Her eyes widened. But why was she surprised? "They think you're both pussy-whipped, don't they?"

Lucien nodded with his brother. It didn't bother him, not in terms of his ego, but what bothered him was the chance that he could lose the respect or confidence of even one Lycan. He and Rafe were the alphas that would lead the battle and the nation would look to them for direction.

"But that's not true. This is about more than sex. Even though that is amazing," Falon said.

"We know that. For them to know it, it's imperative we stand united at all times on all fronts no matter how difficult it may be at times," Rafe said.

"Of course we will," Falon agreed.

"The council is flexing their muscles right now by summoning us before I got to them first, and I'm not sure what to expect from them on a few matters but I ask you to trust me to handle it," he said to Falon.

"Of course," she said.

"No emotional outbursts," Lucien warned.

"Seriously?" she asked indignantly.

"Very," Rafe said.

"I'll have you know I can control myself quite well when I have to."

"Make sure you do. If things go south in there, the last thing I want is you going ballistic on the council," Rafe said.

Falon shook her head, and looked away from him. Lucien grinned. He knew her as well as Rafe did, and if she thought for one minute that either one of them was in jeopardy she would come unglued.

"I don't think it would be a bad thing to showcase the power of the three of us if the opportunity presents itself," Lucien said.

"Agreed," Rafe said.

Falon nodded as they continued down the two-mile road that cut the camp in half. The council's large round lodge sat in the middle of the growing community.

Pulling the wide flaps back, Rafe stepped through, and held out his hand to Falon, who took it. Still holding hands with Lucien, they walked united and proud into the large dome-shaped center past the hundreds of gathered Lycan to the wide dais where the elders awaited them. Voices tittered and smirked as they walked past. Some of the gathered Lycan were there genuinely concerned about the effect the threesome would have on the nation, especially so close to the rising. It was an honest concern, one Lucien would have if he was on the outside looking in, and so he didn't begrudge any Lycan their genuine worry. He didn't even begrudge the ones that were there to get a look at Falon and decide for themselves if she was worthy of two great alphas. Their opinion didn't matter to Lucien.

Regardless of why any of them were there, Lucien would do what he had to do: answer any question posed positively and honestly to show the nation that this was a good thing, not a detriment. And if they still had a problem with it? It was their problem.

Despite his fortitude, tension gurgled in his stomach much like it did the day over a month ago when he last stood before the council. But that day he had been torn up inside. He hadn't wanted to slay Falon if she was given to him to do so. He couldn't have known, even in his wildest dreams that he was going to be gifted with her and, more important, that she would become devoted to him.

He squeezed her hand. *You're amazing, angel face. Don't let them pick on you.*

If they pick on either one of you, I'm going to kick some Amorak ass.

I would expect nothing less of you, Falon, Rafe chuckled.

WITH FALON BETWEEN them, Rafe to her right and Lucien to her left, they stood united before the council and the pack leaders who had assembled. Sharia's old eyes sparkled with mischief. Rafe wondered at her motives. When he'd thought she was on his side, she had turned on him. She spoke in riddles, never answering a pointed question.

"It has come to the council's attention that the decision regarding the Blood Law's eye for an eye was made without all of the facts presented." Sharia's ancient voice crackled above the din of the structure.

Rafe nodded, and chose his words carefully. "It had always been my contention that I slew a Slayer on the day in question. However, now that the facts have come to light, I realize I did not kill a Slayer that day."

Gasps and titters rushed through the dome. "You did not kill a Slayer, or the Slayer you thought you killed survived?" she asked.

"The latter," Rafe said.

"Based on that fact alone, the council hereby rescinds the order to give Lucien Mondragon your chosen one to accept as his own," Maleek, a senior council elder, said. The elder looked pointedly at Lucien. "You no longer have rights to Falon Vulkasin. Do you accept the council's decision, Lucien Mondragon?"

"I do," Lucien firmly answered.

Rafe held his breath, waiting for the other shoe to fall.

"Lucien Mondragon, is it true that the one you chose to mark, a woman by the name of Mara, was in fact a Slayer?"

"Yes," Lucien said, unwavering.

Shocked gasps tittered among the gathered.

"You understand the penalty for lying with a Slayer is death?" Maleek said with a little too much triumph in his tone.

Rafael scowled, wondering at the elder's intent.

"I do," Lucien clearly acknowledged.

Sharia raised her shaking hand, halting Maleek from continuing. She stood with assistance. "Lucien, did you know when you laid with her, she was Slayer?"

"No. Had I, I would have slain her on the spot. She used black magic to change her appearance and hide her stench. Her true identity was not revealed to me until several weeks ago when she showed herself to me in her true Slayer form."

"What did you do?"

"What I should have done sixteen years ago—I killed her. She died a truth death."

"That does not negate the penalty!" a voice shouted from the crowd.

Rafe swore, Lucien growled, and Falon hissed. It was Sasha Ivanov, and he was loaded for bear. *Stay cool*, Rafe said levelly. *Let him speak his piece. Let them all speak, then I will speak.*

I want to tear him apart, Falon seethed.

Steady, angel face, we don't need you getting into trouble.

The three of us are walking out of here together! she said.

Sasha strode angrily up the aisle past them stopping at the base of the dais. "Lucien Mondragon laid with a Slayer! He was going to mark her as his chosen one! She would have bred her Slayers into the packs and destroyed us from the inside out!"

"That is not being debated, Sasha," Sharia said firmly. "Is there any new information you have to share?"

"His life is the punishment!" he cried, turning and pointing to Lucien who stood rigid before his accuser.

"Lucien," Sharia said, her voice noticeably warmer. "Do you have anything to say in your defense?"

"You expect me to debate the truth?" he asked in surprise.

"No, of course not," the ancient said, suddenly sounding frail.

Maleek stood and looked at Sharia, then at Lucien. "Then it is the council's decision that you die the true death before sunset today."

"No!" Falon shrieked, breaking her connection with Rafe and Lucien.

Falon! Rafe warned.

"He will not die!" She shoved her hands harshly at Sasha, sending him flying into the dais, shattering the front steps to kindling. "Not today! Not tomorrow!" she shrieked, shoving her hands above the heads of the council, tearing a huge hole through the pelts comprising the large back wall of the dome. "Or any day because *you* said so!"

"Falon!" Rafe shouted. "Stop now!" he commanded her.

Tears tracked down her cheeks. He resisted the urge to take her in his arms and soothe her fears away. "Don't let them hurt him," she cried.

"No one is touching him," he assured her.

"Are you king of the nation now, Vulkasin?" Sasha sneered, dragging himself up from the dais.

"It has been expected for years despite the blood feud between me and my brother that together we would lead the nation against the Slayers on the night of the rising. I cannot do that with Lucien dead." His voice lowered dangerously. "The power of the three has been foretold." He reached a hand to Falon, drawing her to his side, and she turned to Lucien who took her other hand and stood to her left. "*We* are the power of the three. As such we have united in heart, body, and soul. We will lead the nation against Thomas Corbet and Fenrir. If one part of the whole is missing, we all die."

The ring on his finger flared angrily. Sasha's eyes fixated on it. Furious that the council was so obtuse to see they fucked with the truth, Rafe looked past the indignant Sasha to Sharia and the elders who flanked her. "How could any of you with so much to lose condemn even one Lycan to death much less one as powerful and revered as Mondragon?" His voice rose with his anger. "You condemn my brother, you condemn me, and I will fight for his life to my last breath," he promised. He turned and faced the gathered packs. Half of the nation filled the dome or crowded outside of it.

"The morning after the rising, when we stand together, triumphant and free of the scourge that has persecuted us for nearly millennia, many of the old laws will be obsolete. We will create a new covenant based on our new nation." He glared at Sasha. "There will be no punishment by death for lying with a Slayer after the rising, because they will be extinct."

Rafe looked up at the council who stood rigid and pale. "With all due respect, Lucien's fate is no longer in your hands but mine. He lives because *I* say he lives."

Sharia's old brown eyes glittered with youthful excitement. She nodded and once again stood with assistance to rise from the elders sitting on either side of her. "It has been foretold that the power of three is the only power to defeat Fenrir. For that to be, all three must be." She smiled and fist pumped the air as much as an ancient could. "The fate of the Lycan nation sits squarely on your shoulders. Do not let us down."

Rafe nodded respectfully. He wanted the hell out of there before anyone else could voice opposition. As they turned to leave, screams from outside the lodge filtered in to them. Lycan scrambled to move out of the way as the shocking sight of Anja, naked and disheveled, stumbled toward them. Her bright pale eyes fixed on Rafael.

"My god," Rafe whispered, taking a step toward her.

A nasty smile twisted her lips as she teetered before him. Fenrir's musky scent swirled off her body accosting anyone who stood too close. "You were not worthy of *me!*" she spat. "But I found one who is!"

"Anja!" Sasha cried, running toward his daughter as she collapsed in his arms.

He turned with her limp body so that all could see the deep bloody mark on her chest.

"Fenrir's mark," Falon whispered. Her fingers tightened around Rafe's.

Turning with his naked, bleeding daughter in his arms, Sasha held her out to Rafael. "You did this Vulkasin!" Ivanov shrieked. "You did this, and for it you will pay with the life of your bitch!"

He strode from the dome, his pack falling in behind him.

Guilt, anger, frustration, and finally compassion collided inside Rafael.

It's not your fault, Rafa, Falon said from beside him. *It's mine. Had I not hurt her, she would have made it to her pack.*

You gave her the opportunity to return to the cabin to recuperate, Rafa, Lucien added. *She refused.*

The repercussions of what this meant hit Rafael in stunning clarity. *Anja had been fertile when she left that day,* Rafa said.

Falon gasped beside him, and Lucien groaned.

If she carries that beast's spawn she must die.

Oh, Rafa! Falon cried. *It can't be true! He's so grotesque! She would have had to accept him. How could she do such a terrible thing?*

To get back at me.

Then she is a fool! Falon said.

I must know if the mark was consummated. He looked down at Falon's worried eyes, then to his brother's equally trouble eyes. *I have no choice in the matter.*

As always, Brother, you will do what is right.

And as it oftentimes was, the right thing was the hardest thing to do.

"Come," Rafe said, thinking not of this tragedy but of another tragedy avoided. "The world is not complete doom and gloom. The nation has accepted our arrangement and Lucien's hide is safe from persecution. We have much to be thankful for and much that needs our attention."

Twenty-four

FALON'S HEART WAS still fibrillating as the three walked hand in hand through the gathered packs that parted for them like the Red Sea had for Moses. Not because of the tragedy that befell Anja. While she had compassion for the she-wolf, and accepted her part in her plight, Falon's lingering heart palpitations stemmed from the threat against Lucien's life.

She had never been more terrified than at the moment the council handed down Lucien's death sentence. Her entire body went numb in disbelief. Had she eaten breakfast she would have vomited. But that quickly passed. Because there was no way in hell she was going to allow anyone to hurt one hair on Lucien's precious head. Not while she was alive.

But Rafael had come to the rescue.

He had been amazing. His command presence before the council and the convened alphas left no question who was in control. Falon's heart fluttered like a nervous schoolgirl's. He had been her first knight in shining armor. He would always be her hero. She squeezed his hand and when he looked down at her with those gorgeous aqua-colored eyes, so full of love, she melted. She did every time.

Heat flushed her cheeks.

His lips quirked. "What?" he asked.

"Every time you look at me that way, I melt."

Despite the shock and grave repercussions of what happened to Anja, it could not spoil what they shared. Rafa's lips slid into a warm easy smile. He had dazzling white teeth and, she sighed, beautiful lips that were more familiar with her body than hers were with his. She wanted to remedy that. Soon.

"Keep looking at me like that, sweetheart, and I'm going to give the nation a show they won't soon forget."

Falon opened her mouth to respond but couldn't. Emotion choked her throat. She loved him so much. She swallowed. What he had done for Lucien. Standing up for him against the council and the packs was suicide, but he risked it all for his brother.

"I am in awe of you Rafa," she said softly. "I feel so much right now, I don't have words to describe it."

"No words are necessary, love. We did what needed to be done."

"*You* did it."

"You called that, Rafe," Lucien said excitedly.

"Called what?" Falon asked, still trying to get her overflowing emotions under control.

She hadn't been prepared for any of what had just happened. She thought they were just going to discuss the *arrangement* between she and her alphas, not Lucien's trespass with Mara, and certainly no one expected Anja's shocking appearance.

"While you languished in bed this morning, the three of us were summoned by the council to appear before them for a hearing of sorts. Rafe and I hashed and rehashed every possible scenario of what could happen before we got there."

Falon socked him in the arm. "I was not languishing!"

"Don't forget the snoring," Rafe said.

Falon shook her head as Rafe opened the flap to their lodge for her. As she passed in front of him he smacked her on the ass. She turned around in a huff.

He was grinning like a teenager. "I've wanted to do that all morning."

Falon giggled, and moved into the space. It was kind of a mess. She was a lousy beta.

"You could have at least let me know what you anticipated instead of just telling me to keep my cool no matter what."

"I wasn't sure what would happen, and didn't want to worry you needlessly," Rafe said as he slung his double scabbards onto one of the low sofas.

The gem-encrusted mount of the Cross caught the morning sunlight that filtered through the open vents. Her belly did a slow uneven roll. Its presence reminded her of what she must do with it.

"I don't know if I should thank you for that or not. It would have been nice to know your plans in advance."

"But your reaction was the perfect segue for what I had to do," Rafe said, moving toward her.

Falon softly gasped as the energy dramatically shifted.

Suddenly nervous, she moved over to the little kitchenette and stared, not seeing the mess from dinner last night.

"I was proud of you, angel face." Lucien's deep voice sunk like warm honey into her bones. Slowly she turned and faced both alphas that stood hungrily staring at her. She blushed.

"I—ah— Are you hungry?" she asked, backing up into the stacked coolers. They both took a step toward her.

"Very," Rafa crooned.

Her chest rose and fell in short harsh rasps as moisture seeped between her thighs.

Lucien's nostrils flared, and that wicked smile that disarmed her every time he flashed it took what little breath was left in her lungs.

"You made every alpha and beta in that dome cream themselves when you stood up for me the way you did," Luca said.

Falon's eyes widened.

"Yeah, they'll be talking about you for the next century, angel face," Lucien said, extending his hand to her. She took it and he wrapped her in his arms and passionately kissed her. As she always did when he touched her, she melted. What he did next astounded her. Gently he pushed her out of his embrace, placed her hand in Rafa's, winked at them both and without a word, left them alone.

Stunned she looked up into Rafa's equally surprised eyes. "Are you okay with this?" he asked tentatively.

Astonished that he would even question it, she rose on her toes and slipped her arms around his neck. "Do you even have to ask?" She kissed him hard on the lips proving how she felt about being left alone with him.

He picked her up into his arms and strode over to the bed and sunk to his knees, still holding her. Their kiss deepened and Falon sighed.

I have missed our time like this.

He broke free of her lips and stared at her. "Are you having second thoughts about the arrangement?"

"No," she said, caressing his cheek. "I have no regrets, but I like this, too. Just you and me."

He smiled and pulled her shirt over her head tossing it to the floor. Cupping her breasts, he nipped at an impudent nipple through her bra. "So do I," he agreed. Pulling down the lacy cups of her bra,

Rafael squeezed her breasts together. Then sucked a taut nipple deeply into his mouth.

"Rafa," she moaned, writhing beneath his big body. "That feels so good."

Tearing his lips from her nipple, he rose, sliding his hands deep into her thick hair. His eyes blazed with brilliant passion holding her gaze. "Do you have any idea how damn much I love you?"

She swallowed, suddenly afraid of his fervor. Rafael was calm, cool, controlled. Rarely did he display such visceral emotion.

"What I would do to any man or woman who tried to hurt you?"

"Rafa—"

He snarled tightening his fingers around her scalp. "I'd tear them apart, Falon. I'd tear them into so many pieces they would be unrecognizable."

His lips swooped down on hers as his body swelled against her. Gasping for air, his ardor taking her by surprise, Falon turned slightly away from him so that she could catch her breath. "No," he said roughly against her lips. "Never refuse me this, Falon." An edge of desperation clung to his words. Did he think she could ever refuse him? Not as long as she breathed. Pulling her hair, bending her head back, he deepened his raging kiss.

In her heart she knew Rafa was not going to hurt her but his explosive passion alarmed her. What had come over him? Was this thing between the three of them too much? Did he fear she would favor Lucien over him? Or had Anja's desperate act provoked some deep-seated fear in him?

Tearing her lips from his, she gasped for air. "Rafa—"

His lips slid from her lips down her jaw to her neck, his teeth scraping along her jugular. "I'll kill them," he said fiercely, peeling his clothes off, and then roughly undressing her.

Naked Falon sat up on her knees hoping to slow him down just a little bit. The intensity of his stare told her he had no such plans to pull back. He dropped to his knees before her.

His eyes blazed with a preternatural glint she had never seen before. "Rafa—you're scaring me."

Nodding, he crawled on all fours to her. "You should be afraid, Falon." He moved over her pushing her into the soft, furry pelts, nudging her thighs apart with his knee. With his left hand he pulled her right leg up and around his hip. "Because I am going to fuck you like you've never been fucked before." He slid his right hand around her neck and lifted her head to his lips. Nipping her bottom lip, she flinched when the scent of her blood wafted between them.

Despite Rafa's dominance, she was soaking wet. He smiled wickedly catching her wanton scent. "You should see your face. Your eyes are dark with desire. Your creamy skin is flushed red with excitement, your nostrils flaring for more air." His gaze dropped to her parted lips. "I love your lips. The way they pout." He slid his tongue along her bottom one. "The way they look locked around my cock."

Her skin flushed warm and sultry just as her breath hitched so high in her chest, her lungs could not accommodate their increased need for air.

His full lips slid into a sly smile. "And after I fuck you?" He thrust deeply into her hot, wet pussy, and all bets were off. She loved the feel of him inside her. God he felt good. Once with Rafa was never enough. "I'm going to fuck you again." He thrust deeper into her. So deep he hit the tip of her womb.

"Rafa—" She gasped, rising against his lips hungry for his mouth on hers. "Kiss me like it's the last time."

His chest rumbled with emotion. Tears stung her eyes when she saw his glistening with his own tears. "There will never be a last time."

Gathering her tightly against him, Rafa kissed her. Slowly, deeply, with maddening passion, he kissed her. Deep within her, Falon's orgasm built. With each deep thrust, with each rise of her hips meeting Rafa's, as his tongue tangled with hers, and their soft erotic sounds as their bodies connected, floated around them, it built. What had begun as a slow burn, ignited into a firestorm.

She had all of him but wanted more. Sensing her need, because it was his, too, Rafa's body spiraled out of control pushing hers past the brink of coherency. In a wild, blinding emotional rush, their bodies hung suspended in time, then crashed in a cacophony of explosions as their orgasms tore through them with epic intensity.

They fell apart, their bodies no longer theirs to control. In a sweaty, heaving tangle of limbs, they held on to each other as wave after wave of aftershocks rocked through them.

Barely able to draw a deep breath, Falon licked her dry lips and closed her eyes, leaving the support of her body to Rafa. She was completely depleted. Emotionally, physically, sexually. If her life depended on her moving one more muscle, she would die where she lay.

Rafa groaned and rolled over onto his back bringing her limp body against his, settling her head against his chest.

"I can't move," she said slowly, speaking the words an effort in her state.

Rafael tightened his arm around her, and kissed the top of her head. "I've got you, baby," he said softly.

Hot tears stung her eyes. Her love for Rafael had never been more profound than it was at that moment. He did have her. He loved her with everything he had, and she never wanted to hurt him. Not for anything or anyone.

She refused to think of their future and his reaction if he learned of her relationship to Thomas Corbet. Closing her eyes, Falon cleared her mind, allowing only her love to shine through.

She woke to the strong steady cadence of Rafael's heartbeat beneath her hand. Feeling safe, and well loved, Falon traced her fingers along the hard swell of Rafa's pectorals then down his washboard abs. "Keep going in that direction, sweetheart, and you'll never get out of this bed."

She smiled against his neck where she had tucked her head. "I could stay in this bed with you forever." She pulled slightly away and looked up into his hooded gaze. He looked as well sexed as she felt. "That was amazing, Rafa."

He grinned, and it made her grin. "Epic would be a better word."

Her grin widened. Nodding, she said, "Yes, epic." And kissed his lips before settling back against his chest.

"Do you have any regrets?" she asked, wanting to know exactly how he felt about the arrangement. She knew it wasn't easy for either of them. But she didn't know how any one of them could be completely happy if it were less.

"Yes, no, maybe."

She rose up on her elbows and looked at him. He looked so sexy with his messy hair and kissed-swollen lips. "Tell me."

He smiled and closed his eyes and ran his fingers along her shoulder. "Yes, because I'm selfish and want you all to myself. Yes, because sharing you feels wrong to me on every level. Yes, because it could damage my relationship with my pack. And yes, because it's hard and confusing and I don't know how to do this."

He opened his eyes and held her soft gaze. "I understand all of that, Rafa. And if it's any consolation, I'm confused and unsure how to proceed as well. I just listen to my instincts and go with them."

He nodded. "That's the part of me that has no regrets. My gut tells me this is right for the three of us." He clamped his hand over his eyes and sighed. "I love my brother. I didn't know how much until I watched his heart break when you were at death's door from

Ian Corbet's poison blood. He loved you so much he allowed me to sit by your side. I watched him watch you. I felt his sorrow. His regrets. His love. I could not bear to see him hurt like I hurt."

Rafa slid his hand from his eyes and cupped the back of her head. "I have always watched out for Luca. *Always*. Even when we were feuding, there were times when he was headed for disaster and I intervened. It cut me to the marrow that he thought I would kill Mara out of selfishness. I had always held out the hope that we would reconcile. It took our mutual love for you to bring us together."

He kissed her nose, and said softly, "But I didn't agree to this for Luca or even for myself, Falon. I agreed for you. I could not bear to see you pine for him when you laid in my arms like you are now."

"Oh, Rafa," she sighed. "I feel so selfish for wanting you both when it hurts you."

"It doesn't hurt, Falon. Not like it did." He rolled her over onto her back and searched her face with his eyes. "There is one concession I will not make however."

She swallowed hard. "What is that?"

Sliding his hand down to her belly, he said, "If this child is Luca's, the next one will be mine."

Tears welled in her eyes. "Oh, Rafa, you are so brave and giving. I don't know what I ever did to deserve you, but I am so grateful you are in my life." She pressed her hand to his. "Of course we will have children together. I swear it to you."

She felt him rise against her hip. Her eyes widened.

"I told you I was going to fuck you again," Rafa said as his lips dropped to hers. "And you know I never lie."

AN HOUR LATER, feeling as if she had been in the saddle for a week, Falon stood staring at the coolers unsure what to prepare. She was famished, and after last night's disaster in the kitchen she didn't have much hope of success. Rafa had left with Lucien an hour ago to inquire about Anja's condition. Had she, or hadn't she? That was the big question. Falon didn't want to contemplate what would happen to the lovely Lycan if Fenrir's seed had struck home. Sasha would refuse to hand her over to the council, as any loving parent would. Falon could not blame him for any of his anger and resentment. Had it happened to her child she would feel the same. It was as if the entire world had gone crazy, and the only thing any of them could predict was that the next minute would be as unpredictable as the one preceeding it.

Their lives had become so fluid with change and upheaval that even the Blood Law seemed to have become obsolete. It was a terrifying time for them all.

"Falon!" Lucien bellowed from outside.

Shit! She had told them she'd have something for them to eat when they returned and she had nothing! She sucked it up, and strode to the tent flap. She'd admit her failure and hope they could go into Hooper's Bay for dinner. She could practically smell the succulent scents of spicy roast meat.

When she strode outside she gasped, bringing her hands to her mouth. "Oh—" She didn't know what to say. Rafael and Lucien stood grinning from ear to ear and behind them smiling as broadly were at least two dozen beta females. Each of them holding a platter of meat or a side dish. Men hurried to set up long trestle tables and in the blink of an eye they were all seated and eating.

Not wanting to disrupt the merry mood but needing to know, Falon asked, *What of Anja?*

Scowling, Rafa set down his sparerib. *The marks were consummated.*

My, God! How? Fenrir is so—big.

We didn't ask about the logistics, Luca said. *Anja confirmed the act, now we wait to see if that wolf's seed bears fruit.*

If it does?

Then Anja has a choice to make, Luca said.

Falon swallowed hard not wishing any such choice on any woman. *What if she refuses?*

Then for the sake of the nation, it will be made for her, Rafa said staunchly.

Oh, was all she could say. as she prayed to the gods Fenrir struck out.

Let's not dwell on what may not be, Luca said. *Let's enjoy the food and our company while we can.*

The conversation ran from raunchy bantering to serious battle strategies back to raunchy bantering. Falon half listened, concentrating on the delicious food in front of her. It beat anything she could remotely come up with. Ravenously she ate until she could not eat another morsel.

As she sat back, sated and feeling like an overindulged cat, Falon glanced at Luca and Rafa on either side of her as they enjoyed the savory dishes. If only she could satisfy them that way, she'd be the perfect mate.

Lucien grinned as he chewed a piece of roast venison. "I want you for dessert."

Warmth infused her. "I might be able to arrange that," she said, batting her eyes.

He leaned into her, and said, "I'm going to lick every inch of you like an ice-cream cone."

Falon was about to tell him he could lick her anytime, anywhere, when she caught the scent of her mother. Her nostrils twitched and she looked past the revelry to see Layla standing some fifty yards away on the edge of the encampment.

Anger swept through her. Abruptly she stood. "Excuse me, I need to speak with my mother."

She barely noticed that everyone at the table rose out of respect. Her focus was only on one thing. Wringing the truth out of the woman who gave birth to her.

She sensed Layla's fear as she quickly approached. She was smart to be afraid. Without a word Falon grabbed her by the elbow and steered her two hundred yards away from the camp stopping at the swell of a rolling foothill.

"How dare you lie to me?" Falon hissed. "About my father, about Alana!" She wrenched Layla hard, garnering a cry of pain from her. "If you think you're in pain now, continue to lie to me and you'll feel pain like you've never felt pain in your life."

"Falon, please," Layla cried. "Your father is here, he wishes to speak with you."

Twenty-five

"WHAT DO YOU mean he's here?" Falon demanded, looking quickly around. Thomas Corbet here among five hundred armed Lycan? He'd have to be mad to do such a thing. She didn't care that his life would be in danger—good riddance. What she feared was being exposed as his daughter before she had the chance to permanently silence him.

She narrowed her eyes. "Where is he?" she demanded.

"I will only take you to him if you promise not to harm him," Layla replied.

Falon snarled. "Are you serious?" She got down in her mother's face. "He destroyed Lucien and Rafael's parents in the ugliest, most hideous way possible! For that alone I want to tear him apart!"

But Layla refused to back down. Falon shook her head and strode away from her, unable to stomach it. But she whirled around and strode back to her. "You've been with him all this time, haven't you?" When Layla did not answer, Falon screamed. *"Haven't you?"*

Layla nodded.

"How could you?" Falon was sick to her stomach.

She ripped her father's amulet off her neck and flung it at her mother. "Tell him the only thing I want from him is his beating heart in my hand."

She turned on her heels, and strode angrily from the woman who'd given birth to her.

"Your sister asks for you, Falon."

Abruptly, Falon stopped in her tracks. It took every ounce of control she possessed not to turn around. Alana was an innocent, clueless to what she had been born into, and Falon's only sibling.

"That's low even for you, Mother," she spat.

"Thank you," Layla said from behind her. "For saving her life."

Falon closed her eyes and fought back tears. She had a sister she would never know. Slowly, she turned and faced her mother. "If you despised me so much, why did you show up at Mondragon and save me?"

"Oh, baby, I don't despise you! I love you with all my heart."

"You tossed me into the trash and walked out of my life when I was six years old."

"I didn't lie about why, Falon. Thomas was becoming unstable. He wrestled with vicious demons." Tears welled in her eyes. "He still does."

"Then why did you have another child with him?"

"Because I love him. Because he got better." She grasped Falon's hand, and brought it to her heart. "Because I desperately missed the daughter I had lost."

Falon pulled her hand away. Emotions crashed violently in her heart. "How could you love such a man?"

"I don't know, it just—happened. I love him as much as you love Luca and Rafe. I would do anything for him."

Falon's eyes narrowed. "Including fight me?"

Layla hung her head. "Even that."

Falon's resolve galvanized in her heart. "That's good to know. Once again, Mother, you pick him over me." She scoffed at the new tears tracking down her mother's cheeks. "Why did you even bother to come to Mondragon and save me? Did you not know of my power? Or was it because of my power you saved me in hopes you could sway me to my father's side?"

"When Thomas came to me and told me Ian had poisoned you, he was the one who brought me to you. I bit him and took his blood, Falon, because he knew it was the only blood that could save you!"

Horrified, Falon backed away from her mother. It wasn't her mother's blood, and Luca's and Rafa's blood, that saved her? It was her father's Corbet blood? Dear God!

"It saved you and fortified your powers, Falon. You are more powerful because of him, not because you are Lycan."

"That is not true! I have inherent Lycan power."

"Yes, but it would not be what it is without your father's blood. You have the power of both races and that combination has somehow manifested into something greater than the two entities combined." She grasped Falon's hands. "He was there with you in spirit just as Rafael, Lucien, and I were present in heart and body, praying you recovered."

"Oh, such a caring man," Falon snarled. "If he cared about me he would end this accursed thousand-year wolf hunt."

"He can't."

"He won't," Falon stated, flinging her mother's hands from hers. "And that's okay, but you give dear old Dad a message for me. Tell him if he really cares about me, he'll keep his mouth shut about his relationship to me and meet me the night of the rising, Slayer to Lycan, and accept the outcome."

Falon turned away from her mother for the last time and went back to her alphas. With each step she took toward them, the turmoil in her heart raged more furiously. She was so torn up with guilt about not telling them of her parentage she didn't know what to do. Tell Rafael and Lucien her identity and she lost them. And the nation lost the power of the three.

Hot tears stung her eyes. How could this be? *Why?* Why, when all she wanted was peace and to live her life simply and honestly with the two men she loved? The baby she carried was part Slayer. The grandchild of the most terrible of all Slayers. Rafe or Lucien would never accept that their blood comingled with Corbet blood.

Falon exhaled. Would she, after the rising, have to go off and have her child in secret to protect him from his father? From every Lycan? Or did she keep her secret? Could she live with herself? Or would she become like her mother, miserable and living the lie with her child?

Abruptly she found herself at the edge of camp. She stopped, not wanting Rafe or Lucien to see her like this. Today was a day of celebration for them. Her mood would bring them down. She turned back toward the low rolling hills and when she was far enough out of eyesight, she stripped and set her clothes aside, then shifted.

She ran hard. She ran from her life, her past, and what waited in her future. As much as she dreaded the rising, she looked forward to it more. Everything came down to that one night. The night that the Blood Moon would rise over the battleground just over the swell of the foothills.

The fresh scents of the north invigorated her turbulent heart. The salt of the sea and the rich earth mingled creating a euphoric perfume. She loved the raw beauty of the area and the untainted scents. She continued to run west to the sea where, if she were braver, she would jump in and let it take her away. Away from the inevitable heartbreak, she would cause the men she loved.

And there was the real issue. She could deal with it because of the child she carried, but Rafael and Lucien would be left with nothing but contempt to warm them each night for the rest of their lives.

She could not bear to see their shock followed by disgust, then ultimately their bloodlust to destroy her. Oh, when had it become so complicated? Why could they not see that despite the hatred, the two factions could be bridged by love? Her gut summersaulted when she thought of her parents. How could Layla fall in love with such a man and bear him two daughters? How could Thomas Corbet, the villain of every Lycan nightmare, fall in love with a Lycan? Love her enough to forsake his clan for all these years? But not enough to refrain from destroying her people?

Abruptly, Falon reached the edge of a steep embankment. To go any farther she would be swimming in the cold gray Bering Sea below. It would be easy to fling herself into the freezing water. But her baby would die, Rafael and Lucien would mourn her for the rest of their lives and in the end, the nation would fall to the Slayers.

In a finite snapshot of clarity, Falon understood her destiny. Her destiny had been to reunite the brothers, walk with them into the valley of death, and emerge victorious on the other side. What happened after was inconsequential because her purpose would have been served.

The rising was to pit one faction against the other and the strongest would survive. There would be no room in the new world of either Lycan or Slayer for a hybrid. There could be only one pure race. Which one it would be would be determined in less than a month. And what would she do after?

She stood on the edge of the cliff. A precipice. The cold sea air tore through her fur, a reminder of what was to come. How long she stood there gazing across the moody sea she did not know. But the biting wind felt good against her face.

Falon! Rafael called. *Return to me!*

She shook her head at Mister I'm-in-Charge-of-Everyone. *I'll return shortly.*

Where are you? Lucien demanded.

I'm safe.

She ignored their continuing calls. She was in no danger and despite the turmoil in her heart, she felt better.

Slowly she backed away from the edge and turned toward the place she would always call home. That place where Rafael and Lucien were. The wind shifted, and her hackles rose. Turning, she saw them. A large pack of genuine wolves. And behind them, pack Ivanov led by the great silver alpha Sasha. Falon didn't panic. She didn't show fear. At the very least, she could easily outrun them, but that would be the cowardly thing to do.

In well-rehearsed formation, the wolves moved around her, the big gray male snarling as he trotted toward her, his head and ears down.

I am not your enemy, she said to him.

He shook his head. His mate, a charcoal gray female just slightly smaller than the alpha, moved in beside him. Her golden eyes reminded her so much of her Luca. *Take your mate away now or he will die today*, Falon warned her.

Heeding Falon's warning, the she-wolf snarled and nipped at her mate's flank. Snarling, he shook his head. The she-wolf nipped him harder. He turned on her in a vicious display of power. She yelped when his fangs caught her muzzle, drawing blood. She backed away with her head down, showing her submission.

Falon's rancor rose that he would show such disrespect to his mate. She snarled and moved straight toward him. At once, the pack swarmed. But Falon kept her eye on the prize. The alpha. When he went down, the pack would be confused and she would give the she-wolf the opportunity to move out of harm's way.

The gray alpha was no match for Falon. She leapt onto his back, sunk her fangs into his furry neck, and flung him like a sack of flour into his oncoming pack. Like a bowling ball, he slammed into them and took most of them out.

Tell them to stand down, Falon said to the she-wolf. *Or they all die here.*

The she-wolf snarled and nipped at the pack as they regrouped. The big alpha stood up on shaky legs and growled at Falon, but he didn't make another offensive move. She stalked toward them as they backed into Ivanov. Sasha shifted to human form but his pack remained wolf.

"You, who are not even full Lycan, have divided the nation," he charged. "The council has commanded me to exterminate you."

His words hit her with the velocity of a Mack truck. It was a lie!

Falon shifted into her human form, not caring when she stood naked before a pack of horny Lycan. "A lie!" she challenged.

Sasha's crystal eyes glittered in the afternoon sun as they raked her from head to toe. His men moved anxiously behind him. Their testosterone levels were high, and she suspected many of them had hopes of finding a mate here amongst the entire nation. She knew from her own constant arousal around Rafe and Lucien, Lycan were highly primal. It was the cause of much infighting.

"You have the body of a whore and the heart of witch!" He sneered. "You have disrespected my name and my daughter's chance of greatness!" He shook with uncontrolled rage. "Your presence is a blight to the great Lycan nation."

He stepped toward her, allowing his pack to form a half circle around him. "Before you die the true death, whore, you will experience the terror my daughter experienced at the hands of that deformed wolf Fenrir."

"Why not get a piece of me first, Sasha," she cajoled. Falon lifted her chin a notch and held his glittering stare. When he refused to take the bait, she tossed out more. "Or aren't you alpha enough?"

He snarled taking a step toward her then another. "I am more than alpha enough to make you scream," he boasted. The instant he reached for her, Falon brought her knee up, and viciously caught him under the chin straightening him. She shoved him so hard with her hands, he bowled back into his pack. They scattered like bowling pins as she shifted and leapt into the bulk of them, ripping and shredding skin, crushing bones, and drawing blood. Leaving a swath of shredded Lycan, Falon leapt from the fray, not stopping to admire her handiwork, and ran for home.

As she looked over her shoulder to see if they gave pursuit, she stumbled and fell. There, standing on the rise of the foothill, was her father. Would he have come to her aide had she been overcome?

She doubted it. He raised his sword as if saluting her job well done. Shaking her head, she slowly rose, not wanting to feel anything for him except contempt. When he would not break his stare, Falon turned and ran.

Halfway back to the camp she was met by Lucien and Rafael and—her heart swelled. *Angor?* And behind him, more of the three-hundred-pound Berserkers! Rafael's mutant superwolves. Had her packs arrived?

Did they know about the *arrangement?* Would they embrace the power of the three or reject it?

Falon shifted to human just before Rafe and Lucien did, but it was Angor, the protective Berserker who'd tried to kill her the first time they met who she threw her arms around and hugged.

But her joy was short-lived.

Lucien grabbed her by the arm and spun her around. "You smell like wolf," he said dangerously.

Twenty-six

"I CAME ACROSS a pack while I was out running," Falon hurried to assure him. She reached down and grabbed her clothes from where she had left them and hurried to dress, hoping that would mask some of the scents. She didn't want to involve either of her alphas in something she considered handled.

Lucien was having none of it. He grabbed her hand and held it up. "Where did the blood come from?" He sniffed it and snarled. "Fucking Ivanov!"

"What happened?" Rafael asked, softly but deadly.

Falon yanked her hand from Lucien and dressed. She didn't want to make an issue out of what happened. Not because she was afraid for Rafe or Lucien, but because she knew what they would do to the alpha and they needed every Lycan if they were going to survive the rising. Besides, she'd handled him.

"It's nothing."

Rafael's eyes narrowed. "Don't lie to me, Falon."

She avoided both of their angry stares as she pulled on her boots. "I'm not lying." It was nothing. And now it was over.

Lucien shoved his hands through his hair, and turned toward the direction she had just come from. His nostrils flared as he picked up more scents. "I'm going to fucking tear him apart." He shifted and took off.

"Lucien! No!" she screamed as the wind caught her plea, carrying it away.

"Stay here, Falon," Rafael said furiously, then shifted and went after his brother.

As if she were going to let them go without her. She shucked her clothes and looked to Angor. "Come, my friend, let's make sure they don't get into trouble."

With the mighty Berserker at her heels and the rest of his pack closely following, they took off after Rafe and Lucien.

But it was over when she arrived. Sasha Ivanov lay torn in pieces at Lucien's feet. His remaining pack circled anxiously, whining and sniffing at their dead alpha. As Lycan do when their alpha has died a true death, the others revert to their human form. One by one, the pack shifted to human and each one lowered their head and haunches in submission to Lucien.

He was magnificent, like a gladiator of yore. Tall, muscular, naked, and proud. Falon caught her breath when he turned those blazing golden eyes on her. She stopped in her tracks, unable to tear her eyes away from him. He threw his head back and howled triumphantly. Her body flared with heat as his beast called to her. He stepped over Sasha's body, and strode toward her. Her breath hitched high in her throat as she stared at his blood-smeared body glistening in the afternoon sun.

His eyes never once wavered from hers. Not even when he caught her up in his arms and yanked her hard against his chest and kissed her. Her head swirled and her body shook with emotion.

He was claiming her for the world to see, and God help any one of them if they disrespected her. They would end up like the Siberian alpha.

Caught up in the primal moment, Falon dug her nails into Lucien's back, pulling him harder against her. Her beast snarled for release, wanting to mate, to mark and reestablish that this man belonged to her and she to him.

"Ivanov!" Rafe's voice thundered behind them. "Your alpha has paid the ultimate price for his transgression against my chosen one! You now belong to Vulkasin!"

Falon turned in Lucien's arms as Rafael and the Berserkers herded pack Ivanov past them back to the camp.

When they had passed she looked up into Lucien's blazing eyes. His beast lurked just behind the flames. "Lucien—" she breathed.

"Don't ever lie to me or Rafe again," he snarled, then pushed her to the ground. She fell on all fours. He was behind her, grasping her hips and plunging deeply into her before she realized his intent.

Breath locked in her lungs as energy blasted through her. Falon threw her head back as Lucien withdrew, then slammed into her again. She cried out in unadulterated pleasure, wanting him harder, faster, deeper. He did this to her. Made her crazy for more. Her wild, wicked, out of control, Lucien.

The raging beast within him broke free.

Her beast snarled in response. Her sweltering cunt fisted his cock, and in the most primal way a man could take a woman, they fucked.

And when it was over, their bodies refused to unlock.

* * *

ON HIS KNEES, balls buried deep inside of Falon, Lucien fought to control his enraged beast. He wanted to hurt Falon for lying, for scaring the shit out of him, for having the power to wreck him heart, body, and soul.

Her sweaty body twitched and contorted beneath his as waves of energy continued to spark after their climax. But it wasn't enough. He wanted her again, then again after that. He wanted to get so deep inside of her she would fall apart from too much cock, too much sensation, too much fear, pain and the same gut-wrenching ache he experienced each time he touched her.

He moved against her. She moaned. He threw his head back as his cock swelled inside of her. God she was hot, tight, and so wet.

"I'm sorry, Luca," she sobbed. "I didn't want to cause a problem."

Slowly, he withdrew, mindful of her cries for him to stay. He smiled triumphantly. For all that she loved his brother, Lucien knew when it came to fucking, he was the one who made her weep. He slammed back into her. He was the one who obliterated her mind. He withdrew.

"Luca!" she screamed.

He slammed back into her, pulling her hips so hard against him she cried out in pain. *He* was the one she screamed for.

"Do you like that?" he demanded, withdrawing.

"Yesss," she hissed.

He thrust into her. "Does that feel good?"

Her body constricted around him. "God, yes."

He bent over her back and bit her shoulder drawing blood. "More, Luca," she begged. "More."

He pulled completely out of her and rolled her over onto her back and stood. Her dazed blue eyes flickered as she licked her dry lips. A smug smile twisted her lips.

"You like it when I'm rough with you?" he hoarsely asked.

Arching her back, she spread her legs just enough to give him a peek of her glistening pussy lips. His mouth watered, he wanted to devour her.

"I love the way we fuck." She undulated, spreading her thighs a little more. "I love the way you take control of my body." She slid her hand slowly down her belly to her soaked pussy and slid a finger into herself. She bit her bottom lip and closed her eyes. "I love when you're inside me, and Rafa is watching."

His cock throbbed painfully.

Her eyes fluttered open. "I love it when you watch Rafe fuck me."

He dropped to his knees. She had him. She knew it, he knew it, the entire Lycan nation knew it. "There is nothing I would not do for you," he whispered.

Moving her hand way from her pussy he licked a long slow swath of her creamy honey. She moaned loudly. "This is mine," he said, nipping the inside of her thigh. "And this," he slid deeply into her. "Is yours."

And she took him there. To that place he had dreamed about the first time he laid eyes on her. The place he never thought he would go with her. The place only she could take him. There was no other for him. In this world or the next.

She quite simply completed him.

Later, when Lucien and Falon strolled hand in hand back into camp, they walked into mayhem. Word had spread about Sasha. Along with the news that Anja had run. Tension was so thick in the air you could cut it with a sword.

Along with pack Ivanov's tragedies of the day, packs Vulkasin and Mondragon had arrived and were setting up their camp while many of the Ivanov pack sat sullenly at the trestle tables in front of their lodge. One of the council members was just walking away when Falon and Lucien came around to the front of their dwelling.

Lucien scowled and looked beyond the elder's retreating back to at least one hundred other Lycan who mulled along the sidelines hoping to catch some good action.

"Looks like all hell has broken loose," Lucien said casually, not wanting to worry Falon. But he'd suspected by the time they returned the entire encampment would be in an uproar. And he was right.

"You slew an alpha, Lucien, and they want to know why," Falon said, acknowledging the white elephant in the room.

He squeezed her hand. "Rafe has spoken with the council, but I'll explain myself."

"Luca," Falon started. "I forgot something Sasha said before I attacked him. He said he had been secretly ordered by the council to kill me."

Lucien stopped, shocked by her words, and looked down at her, his eyes searching her clear blue ones. "He said that?"

"Yes. I didn't believe him, but what if he was telling the truth?"

He nodded, not wanting to believe Sharia would agree to such a thing. "Let's inform Rafe of this and then decide what to do."

Moments later in the privacy of their lodge, the three of them discussed exactly what had happened between Falon and Sasha, what followed when Lucien went after him and where they stood now.

Rafael nodded and said quietly, "Two things are happening outside. Ivanov wants to pick an alpha from within and not join with Vulkasin, and the council is insisting on trying Lucien for killing Sasha."

"What if Ivanov lies about what really happened?" Falon asked, suddenly afraid for Lucien.

Rafe's face tightened. "I spoke with Yuri, the sergeant at arms, on our way back. He told me exactly what happened, and it was just as you said, but he never mentioned the council taking out a hit on you."

"Did he say why Sasha came after me?"

"Vengeance pure and simple."

"What of Anja?"

"She's gone. Back to Fenrir no doubt."

Lucien shook his head not understanding that at all. "That monster will kill her."

Rafael looked hard at his brother. "I hate to say it, but her death would save us future grief."

"If she gave birth?" Falon asked.

"If she gives birth to that miscreant's child, then our children will have to live with what that brings," Lucien said. "Those who sacrifice their lives at the rising will have sacrificed them for naught if Fenrir lives on through his child."

He walked over to one of the coolers and grabbed two beers. He tossed one to Rafe, then grabbed a water bottle, took the lid off, and handed it to Falon.

"Thank you," she said, and drank.

After downing half his beer, Lucien asked his brother, "Has Yuri spoken with the council?"

"He was leaving to, right before you came back."

"I don't like it. Yuri has had time to think about what he wants out of this deal." Lucien shook his head. "I don't trust Yuri to tell the truth now, not if he can become alpha by lying."

"But Luca," Falon said, her voice trembling. "The Blood Law is clear: to kill an alpha is to kill yourself."

Lucien shoved his fingers through his hair and looked at Rafe then Falon. "I'm getting to the point of no return with the Blood Law! Sasha deliberately went hunting for you, Falon! To *kill* you, *an alpha*! He got his due. It's that simple and if the council has a problem with that, fuck them."

"I want to know if the council gave Ivanov the kill order," Rafael said. "If they're no longer looking out for the greater good of the nation then they are obsolete and need to be banished."

Lucien downed the rest of his beer and tossed it in the nearby trash can. "Let's get this bullshit over with."

For the second time that day, united as one, they walked to the council dome. This time all of Vulkasin and Mondragon followed with Rafael's Berserkers pulling up the rear.

Twenty-seven

IF THE DOME had been crowded before, now it was wall-to-wall, shoulder-to-shoulder Lycan. Most of the packs had arrived in preparation of the rising. Rafael and Lucien with Falon between them pushed and shoved their way to the dais. Immediately Rafe saw that one seat was vacant. Maleek's, the council spokesman. Rafe glanced at Lucien.

I smell a rat.

"Where is Maleek?" Lucien shouted above the din of the crowd. Sharia raised her shaking arms for silence. Slowly the din subsided.

"He was summoned but has not appeared," she said, her voice frail.

"Did someone go look for him?" Rafe asked, trying to keep the sarcasm out of his voice.

Sharia nodded but said, "The convened council has agreed to proceed without his presence."

"Maybe I haven't," Rafael said, stepping on the first step of the repaired dais.

"It is not you who deem what makes a quorum, Rafael," Sharia said angrily.

"In this case, since I have an accusation to make against the council it's only fitting that the entire council be present to hear it. It is only fitting that when I make the charge, I can see the reaction of every one of your faces and smell the truth or lies as you say your piece."

"The council is above reproach!" she shrieked. "How dare you insinuate otherwise."

"I dare because my chosen one was attacked today by an alpha claiming he was secretly sent by the council to destroy her!" Rafe growled, stepping toward her. Several Amorak moved out from behind the dais as if they could stop him.

"Do you think your goon squad is any match for me?" Rafael sneered.

Sharia's old brown eyes widened in fear. He lowered his voice, not wanting to scare her because in his heart Rafe knew if there was backhanded dealing among the council the stoic elder was not part of it. "I would never harm you, Sharia. You are the only one here I trust."

Her brown eyes softened as tears moistened them.

He took a step back and faced the gathered packs. "In three weeks our very existence will be challenged. Only one of us will survive, Lycan or Slayer!" Growls reverberated in the crowded space.

"Our old enemy Thomas Corbet has risen from the dead. The traitorous wolf Fenrir runs free, has marked one of our own and even now cavorts with her! He has only one goal: to aid the Slayers in destroying every Lycan on the planet so that he can begin his own dynasty."

More growls, louder this time.

"It has been foretold that the power of three is essential to our victory!" Rafael reached down and took Falon by the hand, and brought her up to stand beside him. He motioned to Lucien to take her other hand and step up. As one they faced the crowd. "We!" Rafael said triumphantly. "Are the power of three!" He raised his hand, and the cheers were deafening.

He saw some doubtful eyes and to prove his point he turned to Sharia. "Are we not the power of three as it was foretold?" he shouted over the noise.

Sharia struggled to rise but shooed off any attempt to help her. She made her way slowly to Rafael, and placed her hands on his shoulders. The cheering died down. "Vulkasin, Mondragon, and their chosen one Falon are the power of the three! Combined with the power of the Eye of Fenrir, they are our only hope for survival." The crowd kept silent, as her voice was weak.

"Even the power of the three cannot defeat Fenrir!" a voice shouted.

Rafael drew the Cross of Caus from the scabbard across his back, and held it up for all to see. "I possess the Cross of Caus, the sword of the original Slayer, Peter the Wolf Corbet, the only weapon capable of cutting that wretched wolf's heart out." He sheathed the sword and turned to Sharia, and taking her hand he motioned for one of the elders to bring a chair to him. When it was produced, he carefully set her down in it.

"Sharia, tell us the secret of the ghost walkers."

The dome went graveyard silent. She glanced at Falon whose hand trembled in his. Her big blue eyes shone full of fear. *You have nothing to fear, my love.*

She didn't answer. He turned back to Sharia. "Tell us."

"'Tis said that for the souls of the Lycan slain since the first rising to rise again, they must be called by one who possesses the sight."

Rafe looked at the crowd. "Falon possesses the sight."

A collective gasp washed through the dome.

"What else?" Rafe directed.

"'Tis also said that the one who possesses the sight must also be of the two bloods: the blood of the slayer and the blood of the slain."

Rafe's eyes narrowed. Not Mondragon and Vulkasin as he thought? Confused he looked at Falon, then back to Sharia. "What are you saying?"

"Slayer blood and Lycan blood, the two bloods."

Rafe looked at Falon who had blanched white. "I don't understand," Rafe protested. "Falon is Lycan and human. My Vulkasin and Lucien's Mondragon blood courses through her veins."

"And Corbet," Sharia whispered.

Gasps raised the roof.

"It's true!" Lucien shouted. "Fenrir used Balor Corbet's blood to save her life! It was the only way!"

Rafe nearly died of relief. He had forgotten that very important fact. Falon's knees buckled, and he caught her before she fell.

"Falon," he said worriedly. "What's wrong?"

He watched her struggle for composure. "I— It's been a long day." Gently he handed her to Lucien, and turned back to Sharia.

"What must she do to raise the ghost walkers?"

Sharia was focused on Falon and he saw something akin to shock dawn in her old brown eyes. It terrified him, but he pushed forward. "Tell us!"

"On the night the Blood Moon rises she must fortify herself with the Eye of Fenrir, and with the Cross of Caus shed her own blood on the very earth that holds sacred the blood of the first dead. With the power of the ring she must call upon the gods to restore the lives." Sharia paused and glanced at Falon then continued. "If she is pure of heart and truly of the two bloods, they will restore the lives. If she is not, there will be no rising of souls."

"What do you mean pure of heart?" Rafael asked, confused. Her love was pure, was there something else?

Sharia looked at Falon again, and said shakily, "She can have no secrets."

Falon fainted in Lucien's arms. The crowd surged forward.

"Falon!" Lucien and Rafe said at the same time. Sharia rose and touched Falon's brow. "She is fine, just overwrought. Let her have this time. She will need it."

Confused Rafe looked to his brother for explanation. Lucien shook his head as much at a loss as Rafe. If she was not in harm's way . . . He looked at Sharia, who held Falon's limp hand between her old ones. "Finish what you have come to say, Rafa," she whispered. "Then take her from here, and keep her under guard until she is better."

Rafe nodded, and turned back to face the restless crowd. He raised his hands to quiet them. "My purpose here today is many fold. To discuss the obvious, the rising. To inform those of you who were unaware that Thomas Corbet and Fenrir are more powerful than ever, and chomping at the bit to destroy every Lycan on the planet. But also to give you hope by revealing the power of the three." He held his right hand up to show them the ring. It flared crimson. "It contains untold power. It heeds my commands. It will lead the way. It will raise the souls, but most of all, it is at its most powerful when the power of the three are physically connected."

He inhaled then exhaled slowly. "Earlier this morning, the council rightfully rescinded its death warrant on Lucien. Sasha Ivanov had a problem with that. He had other issues with me and my chosen one. Several hours ago he attacked Falon, she fought him off, and when my brother and I learned of it, we handled it. Sasha Ivanov is no more."

Growls of indignant approval rippled through the dome along

with many disgruntled ones. "We are all aware of the penalty for killing an alpha, but Sasha was hell-bent on killing an alpha himself. He claimed he had the blessing of the council to do it in the form of a secret assassination request made by the council."

Roars of anger nearly brought down the dome.

"We did not endorse such a command," Sharia defended the council.

"Maleek is gone," Rafe said, looking at the crowd. "He is kin of Ivanov, and I suspect Maleek took the law into his own hands and approached Sasha with the lie. But I am not sure of anything until Maleek is found. And now that same council whose integrity has been compromised is calling Lucien out for killing an alpha when all he was doing was protecting his chosen one, also an alpha, against a murderer." He let his words sink in, then finished with, "The only transgression I see here is Sasha's and until we can prove otherwise, Maleek's."

Hundreds of heads nodded in agreement. "In light of what we are up against, and the simple fact that we need our numbers to remain strong, I hereby call upon the council to set aside any trial or acts currently in motion so that we use these next three weeks as a time to hone our skills and strategize against the Slayers and Fenrir and not fight amongst ourselves. I ask what Lucien did to Sasha be accepted as an eye for an eye in that it was Sasha's intent to kill Falon whether at the council's behest or acting alone."

Sharia looked over her shoulder to the elders who had stepped behind her. There was no need for any of them to confer; Rafael owned the floor, and nothing short of agreeing with him would fly.

"There will be no charges," Sharia said.

Once again as they departed the dome the crowds parted like the Red Sea had for Moses. When they cleared the crowds halfway home, Rafe said to Lucien, who carried Falon's limp body in his arms, "Do me a favor, Lucien. Don't fuck any Slayers, don't kill any alphas, and try really hard not to stir up shit between any of the other packs. I'm not sure I could convince our saint of a mother, much less the entire nation, to let you walk again."

Lucien grinned. "I can't make you any promises, Rafe, but I'll try."

Moments later they were met by their pack healer, Talia who ushered them into their lodge, pointing to the bed of pelts. "I want you two out of here. One of you is enough to handle but the both of you? Poor Falon probably needs a year's vacation."

Rafael watched from the foot of the bed as Talia gently tended to Falon. She looked pale and innocent. Vulnerable and suddenly frail. His heart swelled painfully with love. He looked at Lucien who had the same intense look on his face as Rafe felt.

We have been selfish with her, Rafe said.

Lucien squatted down beside her and smoothed her hair from her cheeks. *I forget sometimes because she is so powerful that she is a woman first with all the same vulnerabilities.*

And pregnant, Luca. She carries an heir.

"Get out of here both of you!" Talia hissed.

As they lifted the flap to exit, they nearly knocked Layla over. Rafe stopped short, sniffing her muted scent as if she were trying to cover it up.

"Is she all right?" Layla asked worriedly, trying to look past both alphas' shoulders.

"She's exhausted," Lucien said. Rafe heard the regret in his voice. He felt the same way.

At the same time, they moved aside, and Rafe held the flap up and said, "Go to your daughter, Layla, we'll be close but we don't want to stress her out with our hovering presence until she's stronger."

Layla nodded and moved past them.

As they stood side by side, they were met with loud cheers and warm welcomes from their packs.

Rafael grinned. "Well, I guess that's one thing we're not going to have to worry about," he said to Lucien as he slapped him hard on the shoulder.

"Looks like the arrangement stands."

Twenty-eight

DAYS DRAGGED BY and Falon had not come out of her exhausted state. Lucien paced outside the tent most hours of the day, many times bumping into his brother who was just as vigilant. When it became apparent that Falon became more restless when either one of them was near her, they spent more time out of the abode and took to sleeping in cots outside the front flaps.

Layla and Talia tended her day and night and on the fourth day, Sharia made an appearance in a litter.

Lucien shooed the Amorak assisting Sharia away after the litter settled on the ground before his lodge. He swept her from the seat into his arms. The old woman smiled and held on while Lucien set her gently down on the ground.

"Greetings, Sharia," Lucien said, grinning.

"You always were the cheeky one, Lucien."

"Some things never change."

Her brown eyes grew serious. "I'm concerned your chosen one has not come around."

Lucien nodded. "Talia says she doesn't want to. I don't know why. We did what she wanted. Rafael and I haven't been fighting over her, in fact, we've been damn civil about this *arrangement*."

"I know it must be hard for you both."

"It is hard but easier than I thought. Hell, I can't believe it's working as well as it is."

She had to stand on her toes to touch his cheek. "You and Rafa share a love only twins share. Growing up, you two shared everything. It does not surprise me you found a way to share the woman you both love."

"Apparently we shared too much of her between us. Physically wearing her out combined with the stress of the coming rising, I think Falon literally feels the weight of the world on her shoulders."

The old woman nodded gravely. "She is right to feel that way because it is."

It was not in Lucien's nature to feel helpless, but with Falon refusing to surface because of all that awaited her, he felt beyond helpless to pull her back. She needed to be here working side by side with him and Rafa, showing their solidarity, her strength, her poise, and her confidence. The nation needed to witness through all that was her that they could win the fight.

"Where do the packs stand with yours and Rafa's arrangement?"

"They have reunited. Rafe and I share alpha responsibilities."

Her eyes smiled as she nodded. "That is wonderful news, Lucien. I am proud of you both. Your parents would be proud of you, too."

Lucien's excitement spiked. "I would give anything to see them again."

She grasped his hand and squeezed it. "You may yet if we can get your chosen one to open her eyes. She is key to everything, Luca.

Without her standing with you and your twin, there is no chance of surviving the rising."

"I know." He extended his hand to the open tent flap. "Have you come to see her?"

"Actually, I came to speak with Layla. Is she inside?"

"She has not left Falon's side."

"Good. Then if you don't mind, I will have my talk with her."

THEY ENTERED THE tent, and Sharia immediately caught Layla's guarded stare. Sharia smiled, and looked past her to Talia who stood as she realized who walked into the room. As an afterthought Layla rose and nodded respectfully.

"Sharia," Talia said warmly, clasping her hands and guiding her to a chair near Falon's bedside. "I'm so happy to see you."

Sharia smiled. She'd always loved and admired the beautiful Lycan healer. Talia came from an old line of powerful spirit healers. She was loyal to both brothers and Sharia never once believed she had been held against her will by Lucien.

"You please these old eyes, Talia. You look more like your mother every day. She would be proud of you."

Tears glittered in the girl's amethyst-colored eyes. Wiping her cheeks, Talia smiled through her tears. "Can I get you something?"

"No, no. But if you would not mind, Talia, I'd like a word in private with Layla."

Talia cast Layla an odd look but nodded and exited, closing the flap behind her and Lucien.

Sharia looked across Falon who had lost noticeable weight. Her cheeks had hollowed and dark smudges circled her eyes. When she looked up at Layla, the Lycan glared at her.

"Why so hostile, Layla?"

"I don't need your hocus-pocus. I can take care of my daughter just fine."

Sharia looked at Falon, then back to Layla. "And a fine job you're doing. She's wasting away to nothing."

"I feed her soup, it sustains her until she wakens."

"Does she know?" Sharia asked pointedly.

"Does she know what?"

"About her father?"

Layla gasped. "What do you mean?"

"Does she refuse to face her reality because of the nightmare that is her heritage?"

"Speak simply, Sharia."

"Does she know Thomas is her sire?"

"That's a lie!" she said, looking away.

"You are the only one with lies."

Clasping her shaking hands together, Layla hung her head and slowly shook it.

"I often wondered if he had killed you. But when I saw Falon for the first time, and I saw her eyes, I suspected. When her power was revealed, I suspected more. But it wasn't until the day she fainted that I knew the truth. She was terrified her secret would be revealed. She is the one of two bloods, Corbet and Vulkasin. With the exception of her hair and skin tone, she is all Corbet. I'm amazed no one else has recognized it."

Layla raised tired weepy eyes to her. "When you are in love you see only what you want to see."

Sharia nodded. "As you did with Thomas."

"And as do Rafael and Lucien. They love her with every fiber of their being. It will destroy them when they learn the truth."

"But for her to raise the ghost walkers she must have a clear heart."

"We do not need the ghost walkers to win the day."

"We? Do you stand with your people or your lover?"

"He is my husband!"

"You did not answer the question."

"I cannot live in his world. They will slaughter me and my children."

"Children?"

"I have another daughter." Layla gasped, as if just now realizing something. "She is also of the two bloods and pure of heart!"

"That may be, but she is not of Vulkasin blood. Falon carries either Rafael or Lucien's child, either way it is the Vulkasin blood of her child and Vulkasin blood given to her by both brothers when she lay at death's door."

"Thomas has given her an ultimatum. She has just a few days left to tell Rafe and Lucien or he will."

"He thinks he can force her to his side?"

"He wants a chance to be her father."

"That time has long passed."

"I cannot make him see that. He wants his daughter with him. Willing or not, he will force her hand."

"And she will kill him."

"No!"

"What Falon does not understand is that even with her father's death, her secret must be told if there is any hope of raising the ghost walkers." Sharia moved closer to Falon and put her hand on her cool brow. "It is time to wake, Falon. More hearts will break than Rafa and Luca's if you do not."

Falon moaned, shaking her head.

"Wake up, girl, and face your destiny."

HOURS LATER, FALON opened her eyes. The first person she saw was her mother.

"Leave me," she said, quietly but firmly. When Layla blanched, Falon struggled to sit up in the bed and pointed to the door with a shaky finger. "Now!"

"Falon, please," Layla begged.

"Get out."

Tearfully, Layla stood and ran from the tent.

"Falon?" Talia said as she entered the tent followed closely by Lucien and Rafe.

She struggled for composure. As she did, the reality of her life came crashing down around her. Heartache mushroomed in her chest, pushing painfully against her lungs and rib cage. She sobbed and fell back against the soft fur pelts.

"Angel face," Lucien cooed as if she were a baby. He knelt down on her left side and took her cold hand into his big warm one. Rafael knelt on her right and took her other hand and brought it his lips.

"My love," Rafa whispered. "You've scared twenty years off my life."

She tried to smile, but her throat constricted as tears slid down her cheeks. It broke her heart as they tried to soothe her. Together, one at a time, then together again. Finally, when her crying became hysterical, they stood back and looked to Talia for help.

"Go," she said. "Bring all of her favorite foods. I'm going to clean her up."

And like she was a baby, Talia shampooed her hair and bathed her. Wrapping her in a warmed sheet, she helped Falon to one of the sofas, changed the sheets on the bed and threw fresh pelts on it.

Never once did Talia ask her to speak. Never once did she question her, and for that Falon was eternally grateful. She was afraid if she was questioned all of her fears and anxieties would come pouring out of her. Finally, as Talia added logs to the fireplace, Falon reached out and caught her hands and started to cry all over again. Talia took her into her arms and soothed her, rocking her gently.

"Falon, whatever it is, you need to get it out. Holding it in like this will kill you."

"It would be better if I were dead."

"No! Rafa and Luca would die if you died. I have never seen one man much less two love as powerfully as they love you."

"I'm not who they think I am, Tal. I'm a fake."

She laughed at that. "Oh, Falon, there isn't a fake bone in your body."

"I am not worthy of one of them much less both of them."

"Shush, only *you* are worthy of them." She rocked her and hummed, and Falon felt better but dreaded what she must do.

"You need to eat, something more than the soup your mother has been feeding you." Falon stiffened. Talia pulled back and looked at Falon. "She has not left your side this entire time."

"How long have I been asleep?"

"Four days."

Shocked, she cried, "Four days?"

She only had a week to hunt down her father and do what should have been done ages ago. And then after that? Would she have the courage to tell her alphas she had killed her father? For them?"

"Yes. Now," she said, getting up, "you're going to eat until you want to throw up. You've lost weight and—"

"The baby!" Falon cried, pressing her hand to her flat belly.

"The baby is fine. But he needs to eat like you do."

"Is it safe to come in?" Rafe called from outside.

"Yes," Falon answered. She smiled when they both came in bearing containers of aromatic food.

Her stomach did a little roll, but she swallowed it down. But when the food was plated and put under her nose, the smells were too much for her. She covered her mouth, ran to the sink and threw up what little there was in it. As she hung over the sink dry-heaving, her knees shook. She was so weak. Body and heart.

Strong arms steadied her. She felt so sick to her stomach yet she was famished. She rested her head back on Lucien's shoulder. He pressed a cool cloth to her brow. "Feel better now?"

"Yes."

He scooped her up into his arms, and set her down on the freshly made bed. Rafe propped pillows behind her so she could sit up. His concerned eyes caught and held hers.

"Tell us what's wrong with you."

"She's pregnant, and feels like the weight of the entire nation rests on her shoulders. I think that's enough to make any girl sick," Talia said as she set a bowl of broth and some crackers on the stand beside the bed.

Carefully, Rafe sat down on the edge of the bed and took her cold hands into his. "Falon, I can't help you with the pregnancy issues but you need to understand, you are part of the solution. Lucien, me, the Eye of Fenrir, the Cross, the packs, and the Berserkers, we're seasoned warriors who are well armed with poison swords. The odds are strongly in our favor to survive the rising." He kissed her forehead. "We need you strong and healthy that is true, more than we should admit, but stay with me, baby, and I promise you we will live to be very old and very happy."

She nodded wanting to believe every word he said. Yet she knew the truth. And if he did, too, he would never look at her again with the love in his eyes the way he did now.

Twenty-nine

OVER THE NEXT few hours, Falon managed to keep the broth and crackers down, and her tears at bay. Lucien and Rafael updated her on what she had missed the past four days, and Falon slowly began to relax.

"So the packs have united?" she asked, shocked that it appeared to happen so seamlessly.

"Without one grumble," Rafa said.

"They were beyond excited," Lucien added. "It was amazing to watch them reunite the way they did. It was like a long-lost family reunion. Laughter, tears, hugs, ribbing. It was all there."

"I wish I had seen it."

"You will see the aftermath as soon as you're able to move around. They're anxious to visit with you. The women have been driving us crazy. Once you conceived, they all conceived, every one of them," Rafe said, smiling.

"Lots of babies next year," Lucien said with a bit of strained smile.

Falon felt the familiar sting of tears. She forced them back. Everything was perfect, except—

"And don't even think about arguing with any of them. They will bite your head off," Lucien added, making a sour face.

Falon smiled at that. "It's good that they are so fierce with the rising so close. They will fight all the more for the lives of their children." As she said the words, Falon realized she had been so focused on her parental dilemma, she had forgotten how important the child in her was to her and his father. If her son was to have any chance at a normal happy life, she had some fighting of her own to do. She swallowed hard. And that fight, she realized when she woke up, began with telling his father and his uncle that his grandfather was master Slayer Thomas Corbet.

"You have no idea how feral a pregnant Lycan can be," Rafe said, tucking the blanket around her lap.

"I'm learning." She blushed, and asked the question she had been dying to ask but was too embarrassed to ask. But since they had not volunteered the information Falon blurted it out. "How do they feel about our *arrangement*?"

Rafael and Lucien grinned like boys who had stolen candy from the candy jar. Heat rose in her cheeks. "I'll take it by your leers that they don't have a problem with it?"

They shook their heads no.

"I'm glad. Everything is falling into place."

"We've been blessed with time. Fenrir's howls over the last week are closer and fiercer but he hasn't struck. Our scouts have reported that the Slayers are gathering outside of Nome."

"What of Anja?" Falon asked, afraid the news would not be good.

"It's as if she vanished into thin air."

"Fenrir's magic is strong; he can easily mask her scent as he did mine. I bet she is close by."

"She may be. Perhaps that's why he has not struck."

"Why do you think he has laid low?" Falon asked confused. "I would think he'd be terrorizing the packs as they arrive."

"I would have thought so, too, but he's arrogant enough to think he can take on the entire nation and win."

"Has there—" She swallowed hard. "Has there been any sign of Corbet?"

"No, but he's out there. I smell the bastard. I can feel him watching us," Lucien said softly. "Waiting."

Falon shivered hard, suddenly very cold. The emotional fatigue she had been battling returned, slamming into her.

"Angel face," Lucien said, squatting in front of her. "I give you my solemn vow that we will survive the rising."

Hot tears stung her eyes. When she nodded, they plopped onto his hands.

"C'mon, baby, have more faith in Rafe and me. In yourself." He nudged her chin up so that she looked him in the eye. "We can do this. The power of three."

Bravely she smiled through her tears, wanting to believe him but she knew the truth. They would not survive it if she didn't tell them and if she did the power of the three would die because they could not bear to touch her ever again.

Rafe rose and signaled Lucien to do the same. "We're going to go now and let you sleep," Rafe said, looking like that was the last thing he wanted to do. And it was, she realized, the last thing she wanted, as well. She may have only a few nights left with them and she wanted them near.

"I want you both here in bed with me."

"No—Talia said you need to rest," Lucien stammered, looking longingly at her and the bed.

She moved to the center of the big mattress and patted both sides. "No Olympics, just us three in each other's arms."

When neither one of them made a move either way, she pouted and said, "Pretty please?"

They didn't need a third invitation. They shucked their clothes and slid in beside her and that was how she fell asleep, snuggled between the two men she loved.

THE MORNING SICKNESS didn't help her appetite, but Falon managed over the next several days to eat enough to regain most of her strength. When she had first caught sight of herself in the mirror she'd cringed. She looked like a zombie. When Layla came by the morning after she awoke, Falon refused to see her. Each consecutive day she came by until on the fourth day Falon quietly but fiercely confronted her, forbidding her to return to the pack unless she came back to fight for them.

She didn't expect to see her again.

On what was to be the eve of the two-week deadline Corbet gave her, Falon lay in bed wide awake waiting for the moment she would sneak from the lodge with the Cross of Caus in hand, and track Corbet down. She knew he was close and she knew he was arrogant enough to make himself available to her.

Rafael's and Lucien's heavy breathing on either side of her signaled their slumber. She smiled. They had been more than chaste these last few days, holding back from touching her; even when she begged for just a kiss they refused. Their diligence for her good health was admirable if not frustrating for all of them. But tonight both had come to bed with erections they could not hide. Oh, how she wanted them. Badly. And still, they refused to do more than hold her until she was one hundred percent stronger. They were treating her like she was a fragile piece of china that would break with too much pressure. She wasn't but she could not convince either one of them of that. When she stroked Rafael's erection, he had grabbed her hand, and she knew it took every ounce of self-control he had to peel her fingers off him. When she rolled over and snuggled with Lucien, she kissed his neck as her hand slid down his belly. He groaned and gently pushed her away. Then they both threatened to leave the bed completely if she touched them again.

Which in hindsight would have worked to her advantage except Rafe would have taken the Cross with him and camped out in front of the lodge.

Stealth as the she-wolf she was, Falon slid from the bed and grabbed the backpack she had filled earlier with her clothes and hidden beneath one of the sofas. Sliding it over her shoulder, just as carefully she picked up Rafe's leather scabbard that sheathed the Cross and slid it over her other shoulder.

She shifted and, like a shadow, she slipped from the tent and moved quietly into the darkness.

Falon headed straight for the last place she'd seen Thomas Corbet, on the rise overlooking the place where she had her confrontation with Ivanov. Idly she wondered where the wolf pack was and if they held any ill will toward her. She had gone easy on them. For that they should be grateful. As she loped westward, she picked up Corbet's scent. As she came over the rise she saw his tall form standing bigger than life in front of a roaring fire warming his hands.

The wind whipped his long mantle around his wide shoulders. He looked up and saw her. His full lips so much like her own, turned up into a smile. Her heart fluttered. It was a proud fatherly smile, not the murderous smile of a Slayer.

Falon hesitated, not because she second-guessed what she had come to do but because she had to rethink her strategy. She had wanted to come upon him as a wolf with the sword in her jaws and in one clean sweep decapitate him, but that was impossible now.

"Come, Falon, let's talk before you attempt to separate my head from my shoulders," he invited.

Falon shifted and quickly dressed, then slid the scabbard over her shoulder.

"We have nothing to discuss."

"Hear what I have to say, then decide."

"No."

She drew the sword and pointed it at him. "*En garde,* Father. Come see what your daughter is made of."

LUCIEN ROLLED OVER in the big bed, craving Falon's warm silky skin. What he got was a hard muscular chest. "What the—?" He opened his eyes and stared at his brother's surprised eyes. The space between them was empty.

"Falon?" he called, thinking she was near, but the sheets were cold. He rolled out of bed and tossing his hair back, he raked it with his fingers. Aside from him and Rafe the tent was empty.

"She's gone, Rafe," Lucien said angrily.

They quickly dressed and grabbed their swords. "The Cross is gone!" Rafe said, furious.

Worry nagged Lucien hard. "Why would she take the Cross?"

"You don't think she went after Fenrir?"

"Holy shit! She's been so emotional, she damn well might have!"

Lucien tossed his brother a spare poison sword, and they took off into the night. Her scent was easy to pick up. They stripped, shoved their clothing into their backpacks and took off after her.

When they picked up Thomas Corbet's scent, they ran faster.

As they came into the clearing where Lucien killed Sasha, they came to a grinding halt.

What the hell? Rafe said.

There, on the rise in the shadow of fire, was Thomas Corbet. And he was getting his ass kicked by Falon.

Her furious voice cut through the still night.

"Fight me like a man!"

Corbet blocked her jab with his sword. He cross-blocked the next jab, and the next as Falon furiously tried to get in close enough for a kill shot.

Corbet was fighting defensively, wearing Falon down. But he didn't seem to want to hurt her. Why not? Did he think to take her hostage? Rafe and Lucien shifted, then dressed and moved up the hill.

"I will not fight you," Corbet said, as he blocked a sweeping upper cut.

"You are a coward then!"

"Listen to what I have to say. Afterward, if you want to fight to the death, I will fight you." He caught Falon's sword at the hilt with his blade and, in a sharp upper cut, pulled it from her grasp. He jumped into the air just as she did and grabbed it. Falon snarled and slammed into him, but he pointed both blades at her. "Hear me out!" he roared.

What the hell is going on? Rafe cursed.

Lucien drew one of his two swords and with deadly accuracy flung it, catching Corbet in the shoulder pinning him to the ground. Falon grabbed the Cross from the ground where it had fallen, and went in for her kill shot.

Corbet kicked the sword out of her hand as he yanked Lucien's sword out of his shoulder and flung it away from him.

"That will do you no good, Corbet," Lucien said, striding toward him. "You're done."

Rafael grabbed Falon, protectively moving her behind him.

Lucien yanked the Cross from the ground and tossed it to Rafe, then picked up the poison sword Corbet had pulled from his shoulder.

"The sword is poison. In less than a minute, you won't be able to move a muscle," Lucien taunted.

Lucien smiled, enjoying this moment as much as he dreamed he would. Pressing the sharp tip of his sword blade into Corbet's flickering jugular he nicked his vital vein before pressing the tip into the wound. "I have waited for this moment all my life." Lucien sneered. He pushed the point deeper. Blood bubbled around the steel, dripping thickly down the Slayer's neck.

Corbet's eyes glittered furiously as he grabbed the sword blade, slicing his hands before he shoved it away from his throat. Fresh blood seeped from the deep cuts on his hands down his arms to the ground.

Rafael stepped up beside his brother and pressed the tip of the Cross to Corbet's compromised vital vein. "You don't deserve to die so easily."

A knowing smile Lucien didn't trust twisted the Slayer's lips. "What do I deserve Vulkasin?" Corbet taunted.

"You deserve to die the same way my parents died."

Corbet actually laughed! His blue eyes morphed to onyx as they narrowed. "I'm about to cut you and your righteous brother so deeply you will never recover," Corbet predicted.

"No!" Falon whispered behind them. "Please, don't do it."

Lucien glanced over his shoulder and froze. As Falon raised hard onyx eyes to him, his heart stopped beating.

"Falon?" he whispered, unwilling to admit what he saw. *Slayer* eyes?

Corbet laughed. "The true mark of a Slayer will always rise to the challenge!" Corbet boasted. "Come, Daughter, now that your secret is out, come save your father, and let us unite!"

"Falon?" Rafael said, stunned, turning from Corbet, who could not move now that the poison had set in. "My God!" he shouted, grabbing her. "What have you done?" He shook her violently, and she took it. "*What have you done?*" he roared.

The pain in Rafael's voice echoed the unbearable pain in Lucien's heart. This could not be! His beloved a Slayer? How could she be Slayer when he knew she was Lycan? How could she be Slayer when he *loved* her? If his guts had been ripped out of him, Lucien would have been in less pain.

Too stunned by the revelation, he could only stare speechless at Falon.

But even as he did, it all made sense to him now. It was there; it always had been there. Her power, the Corbet resemblance, *her fucking last name!*

Holy hell! She was a Slayer! And not just any Slayer. She was the daughter of his mortal enemy, Thomas Corbet! And despite the shock and horror of this revelation any rage he felt paled in comparison to the agony of his heart being pounded into nothing but dust particles.

FALON'S BODY SNAPPED sharply to attention. The truth was out and as she expected and dreaded, the men she loved were beyond horrified. There was nothing she could do or say at this moment to assuage their horror but there was something she could do to the man that gave her life. The time was now to do what needed to be done. Grabbing the Cross from Rafe, she shoved him aside when he made to take it back. Spearing Lucien with her Slayer eyes, she dared him to move.

With both hands grasping the hilt, she raised the sword over her head, striding toward her father who lay immobile on the ground. Towering over Corbet she called for the strength to do what needed to be done. But she made the mistake of looking at him. His blue eyes so much like hers held hers captive. Her arms trembled and in that moment Falon wavered.

"Don't," she said, squeezing her eyes shut. "Don't look at me like that!"

"Falon," he said. "Come home with me."

Her eyes flew open. "How can you ask such a thing when you have destroyed countless Lycan!" she shouted. "You kidnapped my mother and forced yourself into her heart!"

She struck the sword into the ground next to his left ear. "You abandoned me!" she shrieked. "And all these years later you come back and expect me to love you? To go home with you? After what you have done?" She grabbed the sword from where it stuck in the ground, digging it into his leather tunic.

"I despise you. I despise everything about you!" She pushed it into the hide. His eyes never wavered from hers during her tirade but when the steel slid through the leather and into his heart, his eyes momentarily flickered. Her hands shook. "By the detestable fact that you are my father, you have destroyed any chance of happiness I could have had with the two men I love more than my own life."

She turned her tear-streaked face up to Lucien and Rafe who were too stunned to move from where they stood. "I didn't know," she cried. "I didn't know until Fenrir told me."

Unsteadily, Falon turned back to her father, raising the sword above her head, the razor-sharp tip pointed at his heart, this time determined to take her kill shot.

Her father's pleading eyes begged her to spare his life. "If you live, all those I love will die," she sobbed as tears streamed down her face.

"I can't bear that." She raised the sword higher. "Perhaps in the after-life, we can truly be father and daughter, but not in this one." She brought the sword down, but in the end, she could not do it. Sinking to the ground beside him she cried.

"I have no such weakness for you, Corbet," Lucien snarled, grabbing the sword from Falon's hands just as her father leapt from where he laid in the dirt. Shocked that he was not affected by the poison, and that he tricked them, Falon scurried back into Rafe who pulled her out of the way as he hurried to his brother's defense.

"My magic is stronger than any Lycan poison, Vulkasin." Corbet sneered from where he hovered twenty feet above them. With a flick of his hands, he conjured two swords, and hurled them like lightning bolts at Lucien and Rafael, skewering them both where they stood.

They stood impaled through the chest to the ground.

"No!" Falon screamed, jumping to her feet as her father drew them to him with an invisible string. "Free them!" she demanded. She moved beneath them, their blood dripping on her face and shoulders. With her own power, Falon sent her father reeling backward into the hill. But Rafe and Lucien who hung limp and bleeding but alive from the swords followed.

Rage, black and terrible infused her. Power snapped and sparked around her as her vision narrowed with bloody intent. If it cost her her own life, she would see Rafa and Luca free and her father dead.

Corbet's equal, Falon rose up before him. "If you love me half as much as you say you do, let them go!"

Corbet smiled indulgently. "If I let them go I will not survive the rising," he calmly explained.

"If you don't let them go now, you won't live to see the rising!"

"Falon!" he bellowed. "Do not threaten me!"

"Let. Them. Go. Now."

Vehemently he shook his head. "Their release is conditional, daughter. If you come with me now, I release them. Otherwise . . ." Corbet rattled the swords. Rafe and Lucien grimaced as their bodies rose and fell along the sharp blade, slicing deeper with the movement. Swollen streams of blood poured from their chests. But neither uttered a word, much less begged for their lives.

Rafa, Luca, I will get you out of this. I swear it! When there was no reaction from either one of them, Falon knew they could not hear her and there was only one way that could be: They had purposely shut down that portal.

They had already shut her out! Hopelessness shrouded her heart. Nothing would ever be the same again. The rage swirling inside of her mushroomed. Her eyes narrowed to slits when she looked up at her father. His dark magic hummed angrily around the swords impaling her alphas, keeping them immobile.

"Go with him, Falon," Rafa grit out. "We will meet again at the rising."

Her heart shattered at his implication. "No, Rafa!" she cried, reaching out to him. "I belong with you and Luca."

"You are Slayer!" her father bellowed again. "You belong with me!"

"No!" she roared furiously. "I am Lycan!" She hurled her sword at him catching him in the gut. But for one as powerful as he, it was nothing more than a scratch. Falon had overestimated her power but underestimated his.

"I will kill myself before I go with you!" she shrieked, feeling her control slipping. Desperate panic had ahold of her now. She couldn't lose Rafa and Luca. She wouldn't allow them to toss her away like yesterday's news because of something she had no control over.

"You would destroy my grandchild?" Corbet demanded.

Rafe and Lucien hissed in shock as if just realizing their child would be a branch on the infamous Corbet family tree.

Anguished realization hit Falon with stunning clarity. It didn't matter what her father did to her, to them, to anyone: Rafe and Lucien would never take her back. And there would be no love for the child she carried, either. Hanging her head, knowing anything she said or did would only make her more desperate, Falon gave up.

"Release them, and I will go with you." She raised her gaze to her father's triumphant one and gave him a stipulation of her own. "But I will not take up arms against them or any Lycan."

Corbet nodded, lowering himself as well as Rafe and Lucien to the ground and released the sword hilts.

"Why, Falon? Why give everything up for them?"

Tears blinded her. "Because I love them."

He pointed to them both. "Now that they know your truth they cannot bear to look at you! That is not love!"

Falon nodded, refusing to look at either alpha. "I can only speak of what is in my heart, Father."

"Neither alpha is worthy of your love." For several long minutes Thomas Corbet stared at his eldest daughter before he reached up around his neck, and withdrew the gold chain he wore. Taking Falon's hand he dropped the chain and amulet she had thrown at her mother into her palm. It belonged to her father.

"Take this, Falon; wear it always as it will always remind you of the true sacrifice of love."

As she accepted it, he pulled the swords one at a time from Rafe then Lucien. With a wave of his hand the bleeding stopped and they straightened upright and pain-free.

Solemnly, her father reversed his sword in his hand, and then presented it hilt first to Falon. Raising her gaze to his in question she found him warmly regarding her. What was he up to this time?

"There was a time, daughter, when my love for you and your mother was all that I possessed in this life. It was all I needed, all I wanted. There was nothing that could take me from either one of you. Except the darkness that has pervaded my soul since the day I was born. I had always run from the things I loved in hopes of running away from the darkness." He pounded his fist against his chest. "But it's always there. It never leaves. As your Lycan beast, it's always there on the prowl ready to erupt. But mine is born of hatred, while your beast is born of survival."

Cupping her face in his big hands, he smiled and leaned over her, kissing her forehead. "The blackness in my soul can only quiet with my death. If I live, all that I love will die." He knelt down before her. "If I die, all that I love has the chance to flourish."

He looked past her to Rafe and Lucien, then back to her again. Her hands trembled violently, the sword shaking against her leg. "There is no geater love than that of a parent for their child. No sacrifice too great. Take my sword, Falon, and do the deed before the darkness overrides the love in my heart."

"I cannot," she sobbed. "I cannot kill you in cold blood."

Without looking up at her he said, "Then allow your alphas the honor."

I cannot.

Do it, daughter, it is your only chance to survive the rising.

With a sob she turned to find that Rafael and Lucien had moved within steps of her. With trembling hands she offered her father's bloody sword, hilt first to Rafe and Lucien.

She choked back tears, and released the sword to Rafe who took it. "I'm so sorry," she sobbed. "So, so sorry."

She turned, and stumbled into the darkness, leaving Lucien and Rafael dazed and heartbroken.

"Rafe?" Lucien said hoarsely, emotion clogging his words and tears blurring his vision. "Let's do this together."

Rafe raised blank eyes to his brother and together they grasped the sword hilt and in a furious blow, they brought it down ending the Corbet legacy.

Thirty

HIGH UP ON the edge of the foothill, pulled tightly into a ball with her knees tucked under her chin, Falon numbly stared at Rafael and Lucien, who had not moved since they ended her father's life. It was as if they had turned to stone. It was how she felt. Cold and immobile.

The trauma of losing them—and she'd known the moment her father revealed her secret that she'd lost them—was too much for her heart to process. The sacrifice her father made—she could not fathom it. It had yet to completely process in her brain. Though she had never known him, didn't want to know him when given the chance, she felt his loss more than she should. That he was a cruel man, who would have eventually killed more Lycan, didn't play to her heart. That he loved her, her sister, and mother enough to die for them did. With that one selfless act, he redeemed himself in her heart. It was how she chose to remember him. A father who loved his family, not the destroyer of Rafa's and Luca's.

The little girl in her mourned for him the most. That six-year-old girl who cried for days when he left her. She mourned what never was and what would never be. The realization only cast the spotlight brighter on her true loss. An unconditional love that had turned out to be conditional after all. It hurt more, understanding it so completely. Of hating that part of herself that Rafe and Lucien despised so much they could never look at her with love again. Only contempt. Disgust and hatred. Hard shuddering sobs tore through her raw chest. Her throat burned, her eyes so swollen from tears she could barely see.

In the distance, two long, mournful howls filled the night as the twin alphas returned to their pack. Without her. "Oh, Rafa," she wept. "Luca . . ." She could not bear their pain or hers. Her heart ached so badly she could not breathe. Her stomach lurched and pitched as agony slammed through her wave after never-ending wave. She retched. The adrenaline pumping through her was too much for her system to take. On all fours, she retched up her guts as her heart and soul disintegrated into thousands of tiny pieces. Finally, when there was nothing left, she collapsed and lay unmoving on the hillside, staring blankly at the darkness.

Even when the cold arctic air seeped into her skin, and her teeth chattered and her limbs trembled, she didn't care enough to seek shelter. Instead, she shifted, curling into a tight ball and prayed for the gods to ease her pain.

But when she woke to the morning sun, the pain in the light of day was unbearable. She closed her eyes again and prayed for blissful unconscious sleep. Sleep found her but the bliss she desperately craved did not. Nightmares raged in her head. Of Lucien and Rafael furious and vengeful, cutting her baby from her belly, and destroying him before they did the same to her.

They turned the nation against her, refusing her help, denouncing the power of three.

Those aimless gray souls, the ghost walkers, screamed furiously, threatening her, knowing now there was no chance for their resurrection. Her mother and Talia, eaten alive by the maniacal Fenrir— that terrible beast the only being on the planet that would have her.

Horrified, she watched as swarms of Slayers overran the nation, cutting them in half before striking the final deathblow. And all she could do was helplessly watch until only Rafael and Lucien were left to face Fenrir's wrath and they, too, succumbed to the triumphant wolf's vicious jaws.

"No!" she screamed, coming awake. Wildly she looked around not knowing where she was or how many days had passed. She was naked, in human form. Dirty and hungry. She looked at her shaking hands, her broken nails, the fresh blood on her thighs and the pain in her womb.

"Oh, no!" she cried. "No, no, no . . ." *Not the baby, please, God, don't take him from me, too!*

"Shhh," a soothing voice crooned as a cool hand touched her brow. "The baby lives."

Relief for that one precious miracle was the last straw that broke her emotional back. She cried slow grateful tears. Her baby lived. He would grow strong like his father and one day he would know the truth. That, she swore to herself, she would never keep from him.

The days and nights blurred one into the other, and finally the tension in her body eased even if the heartache did not. The heartache would always be there, a dark miserable cloud preventing the sun to shine on her life. It would always be, and she had no will to fight it. There would never be another for her. Rafael and Lucien were her true loves. Her chosen ones, her true mates.

Blinking her swollen stinging eyes, Falon focused on her surroundings. She was still on the foothill, enclosed in a small glade of trees. Raising her nose in the air the salty scents of the Bering Sea teased her senses. Lifting up on an elbow she caught her breath as she came face-to-face with the gray she-wolf she'd encountered the day of Sasha's death. The genuine wolf whined and lifted her head and trotted toward Falon.

She licked her face, and whined again as if to say, "Welcome back."

Tears filled Falon's eyes and trailed down her cheeks unchecked. "Thank you," Falon whispered, rubbing her face in the wolf's silky fur. She whined but allowed Falon the time to collect herself. When she did, she sat back and looked for her backpack. Instead she found a blanket beside her she must have thrown off. Bringing it to her nose she inhaled Rafe's and Luca's scents. It was from their bed. Beside it was a small basket with food and water, and behind it, a fresh set of clothing. She remembered a soothing voice when she thought she had lost her baby.

Who? Layla? No, she would not dare return to camp. Sharia was too old. Perhaps Talia? Would she bear the wrath of her alphas to aide their mortal enemy? Did it matter? Falon swallowed against her raw throat and grabbed one of the water bottles from the basket. As she slowly drank she looked across the wide-open field. The tall grass blew gently in tune with the wind. A herd of caribou grazed peacefully one hundred yards off. The beauty of the place was lost on her. Would she ever look at the world in wonder again?

The she-wolf moved beside her and lay down like a sphinx gazing upon the valley below with Falon. Absently she stroked her as she thought of the first time they met when her pack had paired with pack Ivanov. Falon's thoughts went beyond what happened to Lucien's taking of her just down the way. Her body shivered in remembered desire even as her chest tightened painfully.

"Ah, Luca," she whispered. "You told me you would do anything for me. I beg you, take me back. Forgive me my parentage."

The wind kicked up defiantly scoffing at such an outrageous request. "Rafe, you promised me you would never stop loving me!" She choked back another sob. "You promised!" she screamed. "You promised!"

The wolf looked at Falon with sadness in her eyes. It was too much for Falon. She stood. On shaky legs, she made her way down to her father's place of death. Most of his gray ashes had scattered with the wind. Though the imprint of his body was still visible. She squatted next to where his face had been, and shook her head. "Why, if you loved my mother, could you not embrace all Lycan?"

She pressed her palm to where his heart would have been, and her tears dropped into the ashes. A thin tendril of smoke rose from the point of contact. It smelled of earth and rain and evergreen. Her father's scent. At least in his death, they had connected. As she stood, a tiny flash of metal caught the sunlight. She reached down in the ash and withdrew his amulet necklace. The one he had returned to her. She must have dropped it. The stone warmed in her hand a reminder of the sacrifice that went with it. Falon clasped it around her neck, and felt stronger already.

She looked beyond the ashes to the grass and saw the hilt of a sword sticking out. It was her father's. Reaching down, she grasped it and felt the souls of the hundreds of Lycan it had slain. She threw it back into the grass, not wanting their blood on her hands.

As she moved past the remaining ashes, Falon stopped. Though he was not the man she would have chosen to sire her, he'd been her father and she would lay him to rest. She grabbed a flat rock from the cold campfire and began to dig a small hole. After she scooped what was left of her father's ashes into the hole, she covered it with earth and then rocks from the campfire. As a last tribute, she struck his sword, blade first into the earth, his tombstone.

Returning to her hillside camp, Falon washed with the water

and dried herself with the blanket, then dressed in her jeans and—she smiled bittersweetly—the moccasins Lucien had made for her. She was warm enough in a long-sleeve pullover fleece. She finished the jerky and fruit, forcing down the food for the baby, even though her stomach protested and she had no appetite.

As the moon began to rise she noted it was waxing gibbous. One week. One week until the rising. One week since she lay in Rafa and Luca's arms. A wracking sob shuddered through her. One week and they had not come for her.

And they would not. She was Slayer, her father the master of all Slayers. Once she had been the love of their lives, now she was their mortal enemy. If she did not carry Lucien's or Rafe's child she would walk right through the camp and let them tear her apart. It would be easier than living the anguish that was now her existence.

For hours Falon sat quiet in the little camp with the she-wolf for company. Every thought returned to her broken heart and her yearning to know where her alphas were, what they were doing. She missed them. She missed Talia, her pack. Even, Falon thought shockingly, her mother. They were her people; did none of them see that?

The sun sank far on the western horizon. The sound of the sea wafted across the valley, eerie and soothing at once.

The wind shifted, and coming up from the east, Lycan scents swirled around her and—her heart thundered. Strong and powerful the two scents she would never forget swirled in the air around her. Rafa's and Luca's.

She stood, and hurried closer to the edge of her little camp. Had they come for her? She watched as a hunting party cleared the ridge. Rafe and Lucien at point, Joachim, Anton, and several others following close behind. They were in full-fighting wolf, and on the trail of the caribou herd that grazed there that morning.

Fascinated, though her heart ached to join them, she watched as

Lucien caught sight of a big buck two hundred yards straight ahead. He and Rafael split and the pack formed a gauntlet.

In perfect symmetry, born of power and cunning, Rafe and Lucien took down the huge male. His bleating reduced to a gurgle as the two alphas viciously killed him.

As the rest of the pack came around they shifted and expertly and efficiently cut up the carcass, stored it in their backpacks and headed back to camp.

Not realizing it, Falon had moved down to the ridge where her father had made his last stand. The wind shifted and she knew the second Rafael and Lucien caught her scent. Their bodies tightened, their nostrils flared, and they could not help but look her way.

Falon stood straight and proud as the wind whipped her hair around her body. She would not be ashamed of who she was. She was a combination of two bloods and, for better or for worse, she was who she was. A powerful, ferocious, and loving alpha.

For the first time in more than a week, anger sparked in her belly. She was not to blame for who she was! She had no choice in the matter. And yet she was punished for the blood that gave her life? The life two great alphas had thought enough of to save on several occasions? Was she truly less because of who her father was, or was she made less because of an age-old feud that had nothing to do with her?

Righteous indignation grabbed ahold of her. She had just as much right to life as any being! Good Lord, she was proof that the two bloods could blend and create something beautiful not ugly as each of the two parts were. And Lycan *were* ugly. They hated as the Slayers hated, they killed as the Slayers killed, justifiably so, but they still hated, still killed. Would they really change if the nation survived the rising? Would they all of a sudden, with Slayers gone, live happily ever after?

She doubted it. Lycan had their own issues just like any other culture. If they were to prosper, they would need her. If she was to thrive, she needed them.

Defiantly, she held their stares refusing to look away. Never again. She was who she was, and she was proud.

Cowards!

The pack caught up to their alphas, and followed their stare. She felt the tumultuous emotion roll through them. It rolled through her, too. There was yearning, fear, and regret, but beneath it, hope flared in each one of them. But not in their two stubborn, vengeful alphas. Those two had closed their hearts and their minds to her.

Cowards, she said again.

Falon nodded ever so slightly, and her heart leapt when Joachim and Anton nodded back. The movement was barely perceptible to her, and unseen by Rafael and Lucien who stood in front of them. Then the rest of the pack moved on, leaving the twin brothers standing alone, frozen in their stubborn refusal to once again do what was right out of pride.

The she-wolf she called Petra stood vigilantly beside her, her constant companion. Falon turned, leaving Rafael and Lucien staring after her. She had made up her mind. In the morning she would bathe in the creek below, dress, and with her father's sword strapped to her back and with Petra at her side, return to her people. If their alphas would not take her back, she would fight for a place among the pack, stand with them come the rising, and fight for their lives.

She smiled smugly, picturing cutting herself with the Cross and spreading her blood on the battleground. She would raise her arms to the gods and demand they raise the ghost walkers. Her heart pounded. At least she would be able to return to her stubborn beloved alphas what her father so viciously took from them. Maybe then, they would not look at her with such hatred.

Thirty-one

RAFAEL SAT MOROSELY staring at the bonfire, a warm beer in his hand, and his heart at his feet. He had lost his best friend, his lover, his life mate, and the one person who could make him forget the horrors he had endured. That person had turned out to be not just the daughter of his greatest enemy, but a direct descendant of the first Slayer, Peter Corbet. The one who had started it all!

He stood and hurled his beer into the fire. Those around him started but didn't dare ask what was wrong. They knew. The entire nation knew! He couldn't even deny that his chosen one, the woman who may this very moment carry his child, was a Corbet!

He rammed his fingers through his hair, and began pacing. Since he'd learned the ugly truth he had not stepped foot in the tent he'd shared with Falon. He'd had all of her belongings removed and burned. He couldn't stand the scent of her. His chest tightened. Smelling her, seeing her things, brought back too many memories.

Swallowing hard, he looked for something to throw again or, even better, something to tear apart and annihilate just as his heart had been annihilated. He grabbed the bench he had been sitting on and smashed it over his knee. He roared furiously as he hurled the pieces into the darkness.

How had he been so blind? How had he *not* seen her for what she was? A *fucking Slayer!*

Raising his fists to the heavens he roared his frustration, heartbreak, and fury. "Is this some kind of test?" he yelled. "Because if it is, fuck you Singarti! *Fuck you!*"

The beast within him snarled and snapped, clawing for release. Never, not once, had Rafael lost control, but tonight, after seeing Falon standing there on the ridge, looking so proud and defiant? He was not sure he could contain the beast. His impulse had been to rush to her and take her in his arms. A lifetime of hatred for her father stayed him even though he smelled her sorrow and felt her pain, clinging to her like a shroud despite her proud demeanor. God, he didn't want her to feel this pain. He knew it was not her fault, her father. She was an innocent, but she *was still* a Corbet.

"Argh!" he screamed, dropping to his knees. The pain in his heart was unbearable. He could not breathe when his very breath, the woman he loved, had been snatched from him by fate.

He was incomplete without her. She was his heart. His soul. Without either he was not whole. And the gaping hole in his heart would not stop bleeding.

He wanted her. In his bed and in his life. Even now.

But he knew each time he would look at her eyes, he would see her father and all that he had destroyed. His parents, most of all.

Slowly, Rafael rose. There was only one thing he could do. What he should have done the instant he learned the truth. Giving up, he released the beast.

*   *   *

LUCIEN WATCHED HIS brother from across the camp. Rafe's agony mirrored his own. Lucien's life mission had been to destroy the entire Corbet bloodline. To fulfill his vendetta meant destroying Falon. How could he destroy the one thing he loved above all others? The one thing he would still, even knowing what she was, sacrifice his own life for?

How could he embrace a child of his knowing the vilest of Slayer blood flowed through his veins? How could he be sure the child would not turn out like his grandsire? How could he be sure that Falon would not one day turn those onyx eyes on him? He could not be sure of any of those things. All he was sure of was how he hurt. How the pain had not eased with the passage of time, but intensified.

His gut shuddered at the thought of Falon turning on him but, if he were honest with himself, he knew Falon would never hurt him, not on purpose. Much of the anger that Rafael still wrestled with had left Lucien. He realized it when he saw her. His anger was at fate, and that had driven him this last week. Not anger at Falon. Fate switching up the game just before the final inning pissed him off.

What he felt from the instant he learned the truth about Falon was such a profound sense of loss his heart and brain at first would not accept the information. They had compartmentalized it, knowing it would be impossible to cope with.

The day he'd watched powerless as his parents were massacred, he'd experienced fear so soul shattering it paralyzed him. He hadn't left his bed for months, hadn't spoken a word for a year. He could not process what he had witnessed. It was the same with learning Falon's truth.

But when he saw her standing on that bluff so rigid and proud, his walls crumbled. This time, his will to survive triumphed over his anguish. He refused to accept that Falon was lost to him forever.

How could he? She was alive! His baby lived in her belly! He had learned from his years separated from Rafael that love can and does conquer all. *If* you are brave enough to put your heart on the line. Falon had taught him that lesson well. He could not, *would* not live without her if he had a choice.

He told her not long ago that there was nothing he would not do for her. And he'd meant it. She was his and he was hers, and as much as he despised Thomas Corbet with every fiber of his being, he loved Falon more.

Lucien shucked his clothes and stuffed them into his backpack then slid his sword across his shoulder. He shifted, his mission to bring his chosen one home, where she belonged. With her family.

FALON WOKE WITH a start. Petra growled beside her. Grabbing her sword, Falon stood, ready to face her attacker. Her heart pounded wildly in her chest. Was it Fenrir? Or a rogue pack?

When her eyes focused, she gasped. Standing twenty feet from her was Rafael's golden wolf. He snarled viciously and took a step toward her. Her skin shivered when she realized the beast was loose and that he had come for one thing: to end this, permanently.

Falon dropped the sword and then extended her hand. "I will not raise a hand against you, Rafa," she whispered.

He snarled, shaking his great golden head. Taking several steps closer, he snarled louder, his head low, his ears pinned back.

Petra growled beside her, and Falon was touched that the wolf would stand beside her in the presence of such a great and powerful alpha.

"Speak to me, Rafa, before you destroy me."

He shook his great head.

"After all that we shared? You cannot find it in your heart to speak to me man to woman before you kill me?" Her voice hitched in her throat. "Do you despise me so much?" The tears she could not control. They flowed down her cheeks in streams.

Rafa's beast snarled so loudly she jumped back a step. To her great relief, he shifted and stood before her, her glorious golden alpha.

"Rafa," she breathed, reaching out to him. But he stood rigid, and unwavering.

"What do you have to say?" His voice was barely controlled fury. His fists shook at his sides.

"Why are you angry at me?"

He grit his jaw.

When he refused to answer, she continued, "I'm not to blame. And after having this time to think, I don't feel ashamed. I am who I am, proof that the two bloods can create something good."

His eyes glittered like molten gold.

"I am proof that hatred isn't inbred. It's learned." She took a step toward him. "*You*, Rafa, taught me to hate Slayers. For *you* I killed them. For *you* I bought into the whole terrible tragedy. But—" She took another step toward him. "It could have gone the other way." It took every ounce of self-control she had not to touch him. Oh, how she wanted to soothe the angry lines on his face, kiss his stern lips, take him in her arms and promise him all was right in their world if only he would set aside his hatred for her father.

"My father, the Master Slayer, loved my mother, a Lycan healer. I was born of that love. The child in England, my sister, was also born of that love." She was glad to see the spark of surprise in his golden eyes. "Thomas abandoned me and my mother when I was younger because he could not control the demons inside of him that had been pounded into him from the day he was born. But there was a man inside who wanted to live like you, and I want to live. Freely, with no hatred, no bigotry, no dutiful assassinations. Not constantly looking over our shoulders. And for a while he did. For twenty-four years Thomas Corbet let the world think he was dead. But duty called him back to his roots, and he surfaced and he did what he was bred to do, kill Lycan."

She pressed her open palm against his chest and felt the lurch of his heart against it. "I want to freely live with you and Luca like my father wanted to live with my mother. Free of hatred, bigotry, and bias. It's possible if you will look past your hatred, Rafa. It can happen if you open your heart back up to me."

She moved in closer so that only inches separated them. "I love you for who you are, not because of the blood that runs through your veins. Please afford me the same courtesy."

"Every time I look at your eyes, I see your father. Every time I think of the child in your belly, I see him with blond hair and onyx eyes!" Rafael said tightly. "But worst of all, every time I look at your hands, I see the blood of my parents staining them." He grabbed her shoulders and shook her. "I can't forget what he did! I cannot forgive him. *Ever!*"

"I'm not asking you to forgive him, Rafael! I'm asking that *you don't blame me!*"

"I—"

"It's not fair! The sins of the father are not for the child to bear!" She grabbed his shoulders, and shook him. "Don't you see that? I am my own person. He had no hand in my life! Except providing one single sperm to my mother's egg. Are you going to throw away a lifetime of happiness because of something neither one of us had control of? Are you so selfish?" She shook him hard like he had her. "Is your hatred and pride going to prevent you from happiness, Rafe?

Because it is *you* who is making this choice not me, not the packs, not even the damn council!"

He stood unmoving, defiant. The spark of hope that had flared died. "Is your hatred for my father greater than your love for me?"

He swallowed and for the first time, she saw doubt in his eyes. "I don't know," he whispered hoarsely. "I don't know."

"Oh, Rafa, let it go. Just set it down and walk away from it. Please. If you don't it will eat you alive, and that I cannot bear to watch.

"There is one wrong of my father's I vow to you I will set right, Rafa," she said softly, touching his hand. "The night of the rising, I will spill as much of my blood on the battleground as it takes and demand the gods raise the ghost walkers. In that perhaps when you think of me you will not think of what my father took from you."

His hand trembled. Falon moved in closer to him and, because he would not, she wrapped his arm around her waist. Holding his arm there, she slid her free arm around him hugging him to her. "I would give my life so that your heavy heart was lightened even a little bit. I love you that much."

His arm tightened slightly around her. His heart beat wildly against her cheek, pressed to his chest. "I don't know if my heart can handle any more, Falon," he whispered against her hair. "I have suffered enough for ten lifetimes."

She pulled back and looked up into his eyes. "I know you have. Lucien, too. Both of you amaze me because you are so brave. It's one of the things I love about you most. And while I can't promise you a rose garden, Rafa, I can promise you no matter what this crazy fucked up world throws at us, with each other we have a much better chance of catching it, then getting hit by it."

Clasping his face in her hands, she rose up on her toes and kissed him. His arms tightened around her. "I give you my vow, I will never betray you, stop loving you or fighting for you. I will give it to you in blood. I will give it to you in tears. I will give you everything, but please promise me you will not abandon me like my father and mother did. I need you, Rafael Vulkasin, I need you much more than you need me."

He pressed his forehead to hers and exhaled.

It was a start. She smiled, and nearly fell over from emotion overload.

"Thank you." She didn't kiss him or stroke him, or suggest they get intimate. Rafael still had to emotionally process what just happened but while he did—

"Where is Luca? I need to see him."

"I'm right here, angel face."

Thirty-two

FALON SMILED AND nearly fainted with relief at Lucien's voice and his telling endearment. He had come back for her.

He caught her up in his arms, his eyes serious. "I told you there was nothing I would not do for you, and that included not holding you responsible for your father's deeds."

"Oh, Luca, thank you!" She threw her arms around his neck and kissed him with all the love in her heart. She kissed his chin, his cheeks, his nose, his neck.

Happiness filled her so fully that tears streamed down her face. She couldn't stop smiling through the tears and then, when Rafael touched her shoulder and whispered, "I'm sorry," she lost all control, and crumbled into a pile of emotional mush.

Lucien caught her up in his arms. "We're going home, baby."

When they came down to the bottom of the hill, Falon had collected herself enough to slide out of Lucien's arms. She shifted and, with the wind in her face and her alphas flanking her, she ran happily around them, nipping playfully. Lucien licked her face, while Rafael, still struggling with his emotions, kept his distance. Falon pounced on him, licking his face, encouraging him to let completely go. When he finally did, he raised his head to the moon and howled triumphantly. Lucien joined in and then so did she. Their howls reverberated off the hills across the valley to the sea. They were together again. The power of three.

They took off running for home, each wanting the same thing, each impatient for it.

But when they arrived, Falon stopped at the threshold of their lodge and shifted. "What of the packs?"

She didn't care what the council thought; she cared what her family thought.

"I can't speak for them at the moment except to say they were upset," Lucien said, devouring her with his eyes.

"Okay, fair enough." She smiled, putting her hands out in the stop position when they made to follow her in and said, "I need a bath first."

Their hungry eyes blazed but they did not follow her in. Only Petra joined her.

Not much later, clean and comfortable, Falon slid naked into the large bed, luxuriating in the soft furs.

I'm ready, she called softly.

They nearly knocked over the lodge in their zeal to get to her. Naked and aroused they fell onto the bed on either side of her, and showed her just how much they'd missed her.

Her need to be loved by them was surpassed only by her body's craving to have them both inside of her at once. To have their hands and lips and tongues touch every part of her. Lucien took her from behind as Rafa slid into her from the front. They filled her to overflowing and in a slow, erotic cadence they gave and took, gentle and passionate, rough and slow, until it was too much, and in a wild manic firestorm of energy crashed together, the velocity of their combined orgasms taking them to a place they would never recover from.

And just like that, still connected, they fell asleep. It was how they awoke, and switching places, Rafa and Luca took her there again. And again, until exhaustion finally shut them down.

Even when they awoke late in the afternoon, the thought of separating, of losing their connection, was difficult. Because now, there were no secrets. Now, they understood that even under the most duress, their love was unshakable, their commitment to each other undeniable, and their power unstoppable. They were united in heart, body, and soul and together there was nothing they could not face and defeat.

The energy that connected them continued to thrum between them when they reluctantly left the bed. It stayed with them as they dressed and exited the tent to face not only their united pack, known again as Vulkasin, but the entire nation that waited outside, wanting to know where the alphas stood with the half Slayer Lycan.

When they emerged, they were met with complete silence. Even the birds that regularly serenaded the area stopping singing. The constant breeze had stilled. The sound of the sea quieted.

Nervous, Falon raised her chin, and raised her hands clasped tightly with Rafael and Lucien's. Petra stood in front of her, alert and vigilant, her constant companion.

"My loyalty is and has always been to Vulkasin and Mondragon!" she shouted. "Now, I belong to you, the entire nation." She inhaled. "I will fight beside you during the rising. I will spill my blood on the battleground and with my power return your loved ones to you!"

Cheers pierced the quiet. "I promise you, if the gods refuse to give us victory, I will die with you." Louder cheers reverberated around them. Emotion choked her throat. Those silly tears welled up in her eyes spilling over. "I carry the heir to Vulkasin." She caught eyes with the females who stood silent and strong. "As you would for yours, I will fight to the death for my child. But I will not, even for his life, betray any of you."

If the cheers had been loud before, now they were deafening. Falon nodded unable to speak she was so caught up in the emotion.

"The Slayers are close," Rafael said. "Fenrir has united with them and schemes of ways to bypass the rising. From this moment forward, never be without your armor or your sword. Be ever vigilant, leave nothing to chance. They will pick us off one by one if they can and they will be hell-bent on getting to Falon, myself, and Lucien. There will be no more privacy. All that we see, all that we do from now until the rising will be seen by all."

He nodded when there was no rebuttal, not that he expected any. "We move camp to the sea side of the battleground now."

Several moments later, as they were breaking camp, Falon sought out Talia. She touched her on the shoulder. Startled, the petite beauty turned quickly, and relaxed when she saw Falon. Talia's purple eyes smiled, and she hugged her friend. "I'm so glad those two asses came around."

"Thank you, Tal, for looking after me."

"You're welcome. I knew it was just a matter of time before those lunkheads realized you're not responsible for your father, and that they loved you despite your heritage."

"I didn't think they would be able to move past it. It's why I kept the secret."

"It worked out; that's all that matters."

"How is it that the packs don't have an issue with my Slayer heritage, but Lucien and Rafe did?'

"Oh, trust me, when they returned and told us what happened, the packs were beside themselves with all the emotions. And Lucien and Rafael? Oh, gods! You couldn't get near either one of them without getting your head bitten off. It was terrible, Falon. I wasn't sure they, Rafe especially, could move on. We were terrified that without you we wouldn't stand a chance against the Slayers." Talia smiled. "But when one of the European pack alphas made a snide comment about you the other night, Rafael unraveled. I knew then we had a chance. And because the packs trust Rafael and Lucien, when they returned with you, it signaled they were okay with it, because of that trust, the packs didn't question their judgment."

"That's amazing that they are so blindly trusting."

"Not blindly. Rafael has never let his pack or any other pack down, and though Lucien's methods of operation are um, less traditional, he, too, has never let one Lycan down. Then there is you, Falon. You're an enigma to so many of the nation and your powers have become legendary. They know what you are capable of and pray that the power of the three trumps the rising. You have given Rafe and Lucien hope, and through them the entire nation hopes. I told you when we first met it was your destiny, I wasn't kidding."

Humbled by her words, Falon had none in response.

"It's why when this camp went to hell in a handbasket, I came to you and made sure you were taken care of."

"I will never forget your kindness, Talia."

"I'm here for you always, Falon. Now we have to get packed."

"I can't find my clothing."

"Um—yeah, Rafe kind of sorta burned all your clothes. He refused to go back into the tent. Lucien, too. It was really bad."

"If that was the only casualty, I guess I'm lucky."

"I have clothing for you. It's not the chic stuff the guys bought you but it'll do for now, and you have your moccasins."

Falon smiled, and looked down at the handmade moccasins Lucien made for her. They were one of her prized possessions.

"I'll bring you the clothes in a minute."

HOURS LATER, THE entire camp had broken down and moved across the wide valley that was the first battleground backing up to the sea. The only way the Slayers could come at them was head-on from the valley, and if they were pushed to the edge, they would shift and dive into the water and swim down to a predetermined rendezvous point.

No sooner had they settled in for the night, did Fenrir's terrible howl echo from their old camp. Armored and armed, the nation rose as one turning east. The howl echoed again, closer.

Rafael and Lucien moved to the edge of the camp facing east. With their swords in their right hands, they thumped the blade against the steel breastplate of their leather-and-metal armor. The sound rang out and, in the same battle-drum cadence, the entire nation thumped their swords to their armor.

Fenrir's howls intensified furiously. The battle cadence picked up rhythm and volume, drowning out Fenrir's howl. Long minutes later when the Lycan swords quieted, only silence filled the air around them.

Over the course of the next three nights the moon waxed, darkening from pink to red. Each night, Fenrir's howls came closer growing in velocity. And each night the nation took to their battle cadence, always the last to retreat.

On the morning of the rising, dark foreboding clouds rolled in over the sea. Lightning and thunder raged overhead. On the eastern rise Fenrir howled and rose to show his terrible self. With the exception of Falon, Lucien, Rafe, and a handful of their pack, no Lycan eyes had ever set on the mystical wolf. They knew what to expect but the nation did not. And when they beheld the giant wolf, terror struck their hearts.

Lucien leapt up to the top of a van and turned to his people. "He is beatable!" he shouted. He extended his hand to Rafe who tossed him the Cross. Lucien raised it high above his head. "I hold the Cross of Caus! The sword of Peter the Wolf Corbet, the original Slayer! It is the only sword that can kill Fenrir! By night's end, it will see that wolf slain, and it will set us free!"

The wind whipped up and tugged at the sword, as thunder crashed above them. Jagged bolts of lightning zigzagged in the dark sky. The nation moved anxiously, unsettled and worried even with the proof of the sword.

Lucien hopped down from the van and strode to where Falon stood with Rafael. "It's nearly time, Falon. The sun will set in forty minutes, and the Blood Moon will be full on its rise."

They had already discussed timing, she would venture out onto the battlefield surrounded by her pack, and do what she had to do to raise the ghost walkers, and pray she had enough time to do it properly before the Slayers or Fenrir got near her.

But Lucien and Rafael had not been idle their monthlong stay in Alaska. They had a few tricks up their sleeves to keep the Slayer hordes at bay.

As the sky darkened, Rafe, Falon, and Lucien hopped back on top of the van. "This is it, do or die," Rafael began. "We survive this, we live in freedom, we succumb and the Slayers will not rest until every wolf is dead. For our survival we must stand toe to toe, and fight to our last breath until every Slayer has died the true death.

"Though the swords are deadly, never take it for granted that all you have to do is cut them. Go for the kill shot every time, don't give them any quarter." Rafael raised his sword, as did Falon and Lucien.

When the three tips met, they sparked with energy. The nation raised their poisoned swords and cheered.

"Power, power, power!"

Rafael nodded and thumped his sword blade on his breastplate. The chanting continued as the nation thumped their breastplates and as the power of three leapt off the van, arms locked, they turned to the battleground and marched fearlessly toward their destiny.

Falon, Rafe, and Lucien shifted, as did pack Vulkasin. Surrounding the three, they ran for the center of the battleground. On the eastern side, the Slayers spilled into the valley.

The wind kicked and swirled, parting the dark clouds just enough to reveal the blood-colored moon. Rafael gave the command to fire, and thousands of arrows flew through the air, darkening it to black. As the arrows struck home, Lucien gave the signal for the spiked walls to be drawn. They flew up without flaw, stabbing anything in front of it with poisoned wooden spikes.

It was an awe-inspiring but terrifying sight.

Hurry! Rafe called. *That will slow them only so long!*

Falon turned back and shifted. Rafael took her right hand and slid the Eye of Fenrir from his hand. He held her gaze, and she saw the trust in his eyes. He slid the ring onto her right ring finger. It's potent power sluiced hotly through her. "I won't let you down, Rafa."

Naked as the day she was born, she took her father's sword and cut her forearm. She winced at the pain. Blood dripped in a steady stream to the ground. She took Lucien's sword and did the same. It burned intensely.

The ground thundered beneath her as she looked up to see one thousand Slayers race toward her. Rafe handed her the Cross and she cut her wrist the deepest with that one. Pain seared her arm, but the three cuts blended into one thick stream. She held up the Cross and Lucien's sword, the sword of his mother's people. "Great Spirit Mother, Singarti, I, Falon Corbet Vulkasin, am of the two bloods! I reach out to you with a pure heart, the blood of my father, the blood of my mother, and the blood of Vulkasin. I demand you—"

Fenrir's furious roar tore through her chant, the percussion of it knocking her over. Rafe and Lucien quickly righted her.

"I demand," she shouted above the howling wind as she raised the swords again, "that the Lycan souls that have fallen beneath a Slayer sword be restored to life!"

Lightning struck the Cross, sending a lightning bolt of electricity straight into Falon. Heat so intense it did not register shot through her. She screamed and watched the horrified looks on Rafael's and Lucien's faces and behind them to the vicious deformed one of Fenrir as he dove through the pack for Lucien and Rafael whose backs were to him.

In slow motion she watched in horror as Fenrir's fangs sunk into Rafael's back.

"Noooo!" she screamed, and hurled the electrified Cross at him. It sliced into his right eye. Clawing at his head, Fenrir furiously roared. Lucien jumped at Fenrir, reaching for the sword as the wolf flung Rafael away and yanked the blade from his blind eye.

Howling mightily, Fenrir raised the sword triumphantly over his head. "Your power has failed to raise the ghost walkers!" he roared. "You cannot win!" The awesome power of the wolf did not intimidate Falon.

It was his words that terrified her. She had *failed* to raise the ghost walkers! The entire nation had looked to her to raise their loved ones, and with them fight the final battle. She had failed them all.

"We have just begun!" Lucien shouted, jumping high into the air behind the raging wolf. "Focus, Falon!"

Despite her doubt, Falon's power churned within her. Building with the velocity of a hurricane. Concentrating on it, she manipulated the energy stirring it into a tight vortex, and then launched a ball of fire at him, slamming into Fenrir's sword hand. The beast snarled angrily when the Cross dropped from his burning fingers and more when Lucien caught the sword. He tossed it up to Falon as she leapt over the wolf, and drew him away from Rafael, who lay wounded on the ground behind her.

In an explosion of battle calls and the sound of steel on steel, fighting broke out around them. After three hundred years of waiting, the battle was on. Fenrir grabbed a sword from the ground, and turned on Falon who faced him with the Cross. "You are no match for me alone," he taunted.

"She's not alone," Rafael said from behind her, moving to her right.

Thank God.

"You're going to lose this one, wolf," Lucien said, taking his place on Falon's left.

Fenrir laughed. "Your chosen one's power is not so powerful after all! Even your great spirit mother is staying out of this one because she knows her powers are overrated."

He laughed grotesquely. "Where are your precious ghost walkers?" he taunted, sweeping his long arm outward. "Gone forever, because you are a weak nation! And the Cross?" he pointed at it. "You have only one. And with it, one chance." Fenrir's red eyes blazed with hatred as they focused on Falon. "You will regret the day you were born when I am done here!"

Leaping into the air, Fenrir somersaulted over them, landing in the middle of dozens of Lycan. In seconds they lay in pieces on the blood-soaked ground.

"Coward!" Falon cried, leaping after him. But Fenrir was too fast.

Even as he shred a bloody swath of Lycan in a matter of minutes, she was not fast enough to catch up to him. Zigzagging through the battlefield, he decimated one pack after another even taking out Slayers in his furious rampage.

With nothing left to destroy, having worked himself to the cliff's edge overlooking the churning sea, the beast turned and faced Falon.

Triumph burned bright in his red eyes even as the blood of hundreds of Lycan dripped in rivulets down his grotesque body, pooling around his feet. Holding out his deformed hand to her, he said, "Come with me now, and the killing will end. Forever. My word is my oath."

Falon stopped yards away from him as Rafe and Lucien moved in on either side of her. Clasping hands, the power surged between them. Their combined auras flared golden with power. "The killing *will* stop, Fenrir. Not because you deem it so on your terms but because I do on mine."

Do not fail me now when I need you most, she prayed to the gods. Raising their hands, Falon called upon the power of three, the power of the ring, and finally, the greatest power of all, her love for the two men beside her.

The wind kicked up around them, the sea rose ominous and black before them, as waves crashed violently into the cliff's edge. "I command you, Fenrir, return to the ring!"

"I will never return!" he roared, backing up to the very edge of the cliff. "You do not possess the power to force me!"

"I command you, return to the ring!"

The Eye of Fenrir flared bloodred on Falon's hand. Waves of power emanated from the eye, reaching out like a hand to the traitorous wolf.

"No!" he roared, the percussion of his roars blowing them back several yards. Fenrir snarled, raising his arms to the sky. Lightning struck his fingertips, emblazoning him with dark power. It was a weird and awesome spectacle. His body glowed, and shook as power shot through him.

Like Frankenstein after the electrical storm, new life surged through the wolf. His eyes narrowed. "You have awoken the beast," he said menacingly, and threw his hands at the three of them, sending lightning bolts straight at them. They separated to dodge them and when they did Fenrir jumped into the air and focused solely on Falon, lighting her up with one jagged bolt after another. One struck her in the shoulder and, as if she had been hooked, Fenrir continued to rise into the black of night, reeling her in to him.

Rafael jumped up, and grabbed her right arm, Lucien her left, and pulled her toward them, but Fenrir's power was too much. He continued to rise, pulling her with him, drawing her deeper into the turbulent sky.

"Release me!" she commanded. Wild wind tore at her hair; ripping her father's amulet from her neck. Her hands clamped numbly to Rafe's and Lucien's, but she felt them slipping away. Rafe grabbed her leg, Lucien her waist, refusing to let go, but even the power of the three was not enough to stop Fenrir from dragging her skyward.

"Return to the ring!" Falon commanded again but her words were swept from her mouth by the wind before they were heard.

Rafe! Lucien!

Falon, Rafe said, grasping her waist with his left arm. *Take the Cross and give it your best shot.*

As she grabbed it from him, Fenrir struck it from her hand with another lightning bolt.

He laughed, and pulled her higher, faster. Her eyes teared, blinding her.

Fenrir roared furiously at the same time her body stopped its ascent as if she had been anchored to earth. His tyrannical hold on her loosened.

"My God," Lucien and Rafe said at the same time.

Forcing her eyes open, and willing them to focus, Falon looked down and her heart literally stopped. From the ground, like a ladder, holding on to Lucien and Rafael were hundreds if not thousands of Lycan.

My God. Ghost walkers. Those that had been slain had risen.

Emotion mushroomed in her chest. The enormity of what she had done stunned her. She could not speak or breathe or even hear or feel, she was so overcome with awe.

An ethereally beautiful woman with Lucien's smile and golden eyes handed her the Cross. "Destroy him, daughter, so that we may live."

Falon choked back a sob, unable to process what was happening, but her instincts guided her. She nodded, and took the sword. With her alphas and the ghost walkers anchoring her, omnipotent power emblazoned through her. This moment in time churned to the speed of a slow-motion reel. It was why she had been created. What she lived for. Her destiny. She would see it done!

Rising above Fenrir, Falon lunged, plunging the sword deep into his heart. "You lose!"

He howled in furious pain. His enormous body writhed and jerked against the steel, shaking Falon like a rag doll. But she held on, digging the blade to the hilt into his black heart. She came face-to-face with him, eye to eye; his dank, hot breath singed her cheeks.

"You lose all," she sneered as his heartbeat shuddered against the blade. "And now . . ." She reached into his chest with her left hand, and pulled out his beating black heart. "You don't even have a heart."

Holding it up, Falon shouted, "Come, take his heart, Witch! Take it and never return!"

Gilda's gleeful cackles swirled around them as the wind shifted. The specter of the druid witch appeared. Hands outstretched, she snatched the black heart from Falon's hand.

"The price is paid!" Gilda cried as she whirled away to a place Falon could not fathom. And did not want to.

It was time to finish what fate had set into motion. With both hands she withdrew the sword from Fenrir's chest. Raising it high above him, in a wide two-handed swipe, she separated Fenrir's head from his body and watched it fall to the ground, turning to dust before it landed.

It was over.

For long exhausted moments, Falon stared at the ground and the dust that once was the terrible wolf Fenrir.

It was over, she told herself again.

Her brain could not process that information. For so long the fear of the rising affected everything she did. Everything she felt. Knowing in the back of her mind that no matter what she did, it would not matter because she and the ones she loved would not survive.

But they had survived! She laughed. *They had survived!*

"We won!" she cried, looking at her beloved alphas. Throwing her arms around them both she cried, "We won! We're alive!" Emotion overwhelmed her, and with it the tears started. "We're alive," she sobbed, unable to keep it all in.

"Yes, angel face," Lucien said, hugging her tightly. "Thanks to you, we're all alive."

"Brave, brave, Falon," Rafa said, kissing her forehead. "You are amazing."

"Let's go home," Luca said.

"Home," she breathed. "Yes, home."

When they settled back to the ground, the battle of evermore was over. Slayer dust and abandoned swords littered the field. Blood saturated the ground. In wonder, Falon saw that not one Lycan life had been lost.

How could that be? She witnessed Fenrir's slaughter of hundreds. Had they risen with the others? Did it matter? What mattered was—they had all survived.

Falon stood back as she watched the emotional reunion between Rafa, Luca, and their parents. They cried like little boys, hugging and kissing them. It was heartwarming and heartbreaking to watch. Her hand slid to her belly. It was what she wanted for her child. A loving solid family. Something she'd never known and something her alphas had longed to have returned. Tears, those damn tears, stung her eyes again. It was beautiful to watch them interact, touching, caressing, kissing, and hugging. Tamaska could not keep her hands off her sons, and Arnou, so much like Rafael, could not stop smiling and wiping at his eyes.

Like Rafael and Lucien, the packs swarmed around their long-lost relatives. Petra nudged Falon's bloody hand, and leaned into her as if to say, "I haven't forgotten you."

Rubbing her behind her ears, Falon was grateful for the friend.

"Falon!" Rafe and Lucien called, pushing through the crowd. She smiled and ran to them, caught up in their embrace.

"C'mon, angel face," Luca said, kissing her nose. "Rafe and I have some very special people we want you to meet."

"It would be my pleasure," she said, smiling so wide her face hurt.

"They already love you," Rafa said, a lilt in his voice she had never heard before.

As they approached, Falon slowed her pace. Naked was not how she envisioned meeting her alphas' parents for the first time. Tamaska felt her discomfort and took the soft doeskin tunic from her shoulders and slid it over Falon's head.

"Is that better, Daughter?" she asked warmly.

It was the second time she'd called Falon that, and the second time emotion tightened hard in her chest.

The great alpha Arnou extended his hand. She took it. It was big and warm like his sons'. Then he pulled her gently into the fold of his arms and hugged her. "Our prayers have been answered," he said with a smile in his voice. "Our family is complete now that we have a daughter."

Overcome with emotion, she didn't know what to say so she simply nodded her head. Her prayers, too, had been answered. She had a father she could respect and a loving mother who would sacrifice her own life for her children's. She was part of a family that would never cast her aside.

She had found her place in the world, and for the first time since she was born, Falon knew who she was and where she belonged.

It was good to be home.

Epilogue

Eight months later, Vulkasin compound

IF FALON WASN'T in so much pain, she'd laugh at the way the three alphas, Arnou, Rafa, and Luca paced nervously at the foot of the bed she shared with the two of them.

Tamaska's eyes, so much like Lucien's, twinkled. If any of the pack witnessed the fear in any of their alphas' eyes, they would be shocked.

"What is taking so long?" Lucien demanded of his mother. "It's been two days!"

Rafael stopped his pacing long enough to swipe his hand through his golden hair. "How long does it take, Mother?"

"Tami?" Arnou quietly asked.

Falon looked at the serene beauty. She was the calm in the craziness that ensued after the rising. It was as if no time had passed. Arnou had been alpha when he was killed; he resumed the role without one stumble or grumble from the pack. Respectfully both his sons stepped aside. But Arnou was not about to take the pack responsibility solely on his shoulders. Rafael stood to his right, while Lucien stood on his left. Falon and Tamaska together before them. They were as united in heart and spirit as a pack could be. Never once had Falon doubted that Arnou or Tamaska would not lay down their lives for their sons or their sons' chosen one.

If she had felt a sense of belonging to Vulkasin when she was with Rafael and Mondragon, when she was with Lucien, she had no true understanding of what a real family was until the packs reunited under Arnou and Tamaska.

There had been joyous celebrations for a month. And as Falon was two weeks past her due date, so, too, were the pack females. They waited only for the Vulkasin heir to be born so that their babies could be born, too.

A sharp pain shot across Falon's belly. She cried out in surprised pain. It was not a contraction. Tamaska's knowing eyes caught and held Falon's. "Take deep cleansing breaths, Falon, and slowly exhale."

Falon nodded, the pressure of the baby's head making her want to push him from her. "It's time to start pushing," Tamaska said, just as Talia came in with more clean linens.

Rafa and Luca scrambled on either side of Falon, nervously wanting to touch her but afraid to. "Each one of you put your hands beneath her knees. Talia, support Falon's back. When I say, push, you lift her knees and press them to Falon when she pushes."

The brothers looked at each other, then at Falon, and exhaled. "Ready, baby?" Rafa asked.

Before she could reply, her womb constricted painfully.

"Push, daughter!" Tamaska urged.

Talia's steady hands supported her back as she rose; gritting her teeth, Falon pushed. As the contraction waned, Falon lay back in the bed. Luca slid the sheet back across her naked body and leaned into her, taking her hand into his. "What can I do for you, angel face?"

"Nothing," she gasped as another contraction quickly built.

"Push," Tamaska said, and once again, with Talia to support her back and her two alphas supporting her legs, Falon pushed.

She pushed for hours. Her tired, naked body was sweat-soaked. When either Luca or Rafa tried to soothe her with cool compresses or words of encouragement, she pushed them away. She didn't want to be touched or cajoled; she wanted the baby out!

"The head is crowning, Falon," Tamaska said. "Give me three more big pushes."

Exhausted, Falon tried. This time, Talia took a knee, while Rafe supported her back. As a team they pushed. Falon strained, bearing her teeth, and screamed as the baby's head pushed out of her. Panting heavily, the next contraction came slamming through her almost before the last one ended. She screamed again as she pushed.

"The head is out," Tamaska said evenly. "Two more pushes."

"I can't," Falon gasped, falling back into Rafa's arms. "Too tired."

"You can do it, Falon," Rafa said, gathering her up.

"You killed Fenrir, you can push a baby out of you," Luca chided.

The contraction seized her belly. Rafe lifted her as Luca and Talia pushed her knees up and toward her. "The shoulders are out," Tamaska cried. A second later she happily announced, "We have a granddaughter, Arnou!" The baby's lusty cry startled them all. "A beautiful, blond granddaughter."

"Let me see her," Falon whispered, anxious to meet her daughter. Her body continued to contract.

Falon caught the disappointment in Luca's eyes. He had hoped she would bear him a son, but it was Rafa's seed that struck home that night in the pond. And while she was sad for Luca, her heart was overcome with happiness.

A grinning Rafa took the baby from his mother. He kissed the little mite on the forehead, and with tears in his eyes he looked down at Falon as he laid the warm baby on her chest. "We have a daughter,

Falon." As he leaned over to kiss her, warm tears dropped on her cheeks. "Thank you, my love, I will treasure her always."

As their lips met, another painful contraction gripped her. Falon cried out, holding her daughter to her breast. "I feel like I'm still in labor," she said, fighting the urge to push.

"The afterbirth must be delivered. I need you to push one more time," Tamaska said.

Taking the baby from her, Rafa handed his daughter off to his father as he took Luca's place at Falon's knee as Luca moved to her back.

Luca's concerned golden eyes caught and held Falon's.

You would tell me if something is wrong? she asked him, feeling as if something were wrong.

I would never lie to you, angel face.

"Push!" Tamaska commanded.

Falon pushed with the little bit of strength she had left in her. But when she heard another baby's cry, and not that of her daughter, adrenaline spiked through her. She pushed to sit up.

"We have a black-haired grandson, Arnou!" Tamaska announced, holding the lusty baby boy up for all to see.

"My son?" Luca asked in disbelief.

"Two babies?" Falon asked in more disbelief.

Tamaska smiled and quickly tended to the baby, before she placed him on Falon's chest where his sister had laid just minutes before.

"Two babies, Falon," Talia said happily. "I have a niece and a nephew!"

The only emotion that overrode Falon's shock was her joy.

Twins! A Vulkasin daughter and a Mondragon son. Lord help them all!

Helping Falon to sit up, Rafa gently took his daughter from his father and set her in the crook of Falon's right arm while Luca set his squalling son in her left. Tamaska continued to do what midwives did, while Falon smiled through the happy tears streaming down her cheeks.

"I love you both so much," she sobbed, barely able to speak. She gazed in wonder at her perfect daughter, and then at her perfect son, and wondered what she had done to be so blessed.

Luca leaned in, and kissed her. "Thank you, my love, for such an extraordinary gift. I promise we will not allow him to be the butt head that his father is notoriously known for."

Falon smiled. "I would have him no other way."

"I suspect his older sister will keep him jumping through hoops," Rafa laughed. "She may be blond but I'll bet anything she'll be as demanding as her mother."

"I'm not demanding!" Falon defended.

"Had you not been so demanding, my love, we would not all be here today, together as a family," Rafa said. "There are no words, Falon, to express to you how grateful I am that you decided to steal a sandwich that fateful night one year ago."

She smiled as she thought back to the night she met Rafa, the night her life changed forever.

"Nor can I."

And with the birth of the Vulkasin twins, a rash of other births followed. All told, sixty-three babies were born within a week of the twins to pack Vulkasin, the most powerful Lycan pack in the world.

And while they were enjoying their peace and prosperity, another Lycan gave birth at the same time the Vulkasin twins entered the world. This one knew no comfort of family or warmth of shelter. Alone, she gave birth on a cliff overlooking the churning Bering Sea.

When the once regal Lycan laid eyes on the half wolf, half

human creature that emerged from her womb, she howled mournfully at the full moon. Damning every Vulkasin, she swore eternal vengeance on them.

The babe mewled, the sad, sickly sound stirring the maternal part of her that wanted nothing to do with the abomination. The babe continued its sad little cry and she could ignore it no longer. Taking it into her arms, she brought it to her breast, and he latched on to a nipple, suckling greedily.

From the ashes around her, a terrible specter rose hovering above her. Protectively, she tightened her arms around the babe and looked up.

"He is mine!" she hissed at the familiar but unwelcome form.

"Only because I gave you my seed," the specter countered.

"Leave us!" she commanded.

"Return to your pack, Anja. Give him what I never had."

"They will shun him! I will raise him here, away from the pitiful stares and mocking laughs."

The specter rose higher. "Then he shall know my pain and it will be his legacy!"

About the Author

Karin Tabke is a full-time writer who draws on a lifetime of stories and backdrops that few outside of the law enforcement community ever see, let alone hear about. Controlled chaos now reigns supreme through the pages she writes, where hot heroes serve, protect, and pleasure from page one to the end. Visit her at www.KarinTabke.com.